T0285571

# DEATH
# TAKES THE
# LEAD

Books by Rosemary Simpson

WHAT THE DEAD LEAVE BEHIND

LIES THAT COMFORT AND BETRAY

LET THE DEAD KEEP THEIR SECRETS

DEATH BRINGS A SHADOW

DEATH, DIAMONDS, AND DECEPTION

THE DEAD CRY JUSTICE

DEATH AT THE FALLS

MURDER WEARS A HIDDEN FACE

DEATH TAKES THE LEAD

Published by Kensington Publishing Corp.

# DEATH
# TAKES THE
# LEAD

ROSEMARY
SIMPSON

KENSINGTON
PUBLISHING CORP.

www.kensingtonbooks.com

KENSINGTON BOOKS are published by

Kensington Publishing Corp.
900 Third Avenue
New York, NY 10022

All Kensington titles, imprints, and distributed lines are available at special quantity discounts for bulk purchases for sales promotion, premiums, fund-raising, educational, or institutional use. Special book excerpts or customized printings can also be created to fit specific needs. For details, write or phone the office of the Kensington Special Sales Manager: Kensington Publishing Corp., 900 Third Avenue, New York, NY 10022. Attn. Special Sales Department. Phone: 1-800-221-2647.

The K with book logo Reg. US Pat. & TM Off.

Library of Congress Card Catalogue Number: 2024940676

ISBN: 978-1-4967-4107-3
First Kensington Hardcover Edition: December 2024

ISBN: 978-1-4967-4110-3 (ebook)

10 9 8 7 6 5 4 3 2 1

Printed in the United States of America

"All the world's a stage,
And all the men and women merely players;
They have their exits and their entrances,
And one man in his time plays many parts."

—from *As You Like It*, by William Shakespeare

# CHAPTER 1

Fifth Avenue was changing more rapidly than any of its current householders would have predicted.

As Prudence MacKenzie's carriage made its way along Fifth toward Broadway, it passed the gleaming white marble Stewart Mansion. Built directly across Thirty-fourth Street from Caroline Astor's brownstone, and once labeled the most beautiful private home in the city, it had sat empty for two years after its former owner's death. Now it was leased to the exclusive Manhattan Club.

Rumor had it that Mrs. Astor was planning a move closer to Central Park where the Vanderbilts had already established themselves in what had been dubbed the Triple Palace. Three connected brownstones, their only drawback was the proximity to the Roman Catholic St. Patrick's Cathedral, especially on a Sunday morning.

More than one acquaintance had hinted that the late Judge MacKenzie's daughter might consider following Mrs. Astor's lead. The banker who administered Prudence's financial affairs had recently taken to reminding her that the MacKenzie mansion, occupying two lots on Twelfth Street, was among the rapidly dwindling number of spacious single-family prewar homes on Lower Fifth. Commercial interests, hotels, and the newly popular apartment houses were steadily encroaching. Time to consider selling?

It was a topic Prudence avoided discussing whenever it was broached.

Just as Fifth Avenue was reconfiguring itself, so were the social mores of the elite New Yorkers who lived there. Even Prudence's destination on this April midday of 1891 would have been unthinkable in her mother's generation. An unaccompanied lady venturing out of the privacy of her home to lunch in a public restaurant? Not only scandalous, but impossible. Decent establishments didn't serve unescorted females. No exceptions.

Not until very recently had restaurants such as Delmonico's opened private dining rooms for ladies' luncheons, many of them with separate entrances for their female guests. Tearooms catering to this new clientele had increased in popularity, though none matched the opulence of Maillard's Confectionery, housed in the lavishly appointed Fifth Avenue Hotel that occupied the entire block between 23rd and 24th Streets.

But Maillard's wasn't where Prudence had agreed to meet Lydia Truitt for what her friend's note had described as a long overdue visit and afternoon's amusement. A table had been reserved at the Bristol Bakery and Gardens on Broadway, in the midst of what was increasingly being recognized as the hub of the city's theatre district.

James Kincaid's frown had told her all she needed to know about the location; like other older staff in the MacKenzie household, the coachman had been hired years ago by her father. She knew without having to be told that he considered monitoring her safety and good name to be as important as the care and currying of the horses he drove. It amused her no end that despite a successful venture into private inquiry work with an ex-Pinkerton named Geoffrey Hunter and admission to the New York State Bar, her devoted and occasionally overbearing servants could not reconcile themselves to what she suspected they considered an unladylike quest for independence. *Tant pis,* as one of her French governesses would have said.

The facade of the Bristol Bakery and Gardens had a respectable air to it, despite its location and Kincaid's wrinkled forehead. Trust Lydia not to venture too far from conventionality.

"What time will you be expecting me?" Kincaid asked, holding open the carriage door while a street urchin clung to the harness of the team of restive bays.

"No need to come back for me," Prudence answered, ignoring the twitch of disapproval at the corner of the coachman's mouth. "I'll get a hansom cab when I'm ready."

"Shall I let Danny know you'll be needing him?"

Danny Dennis drove a hansom pulled by the largest and whitest horse in New York City, Mr. Washington, so named because of his enormous yellowish teeth. Hunter and MacKenzie, Investigative Law, kept Danny on retainer, as much for the gossip he picked up as for his encyclopedic knowledge of the city's streets and alleyways.

"I shouldn't bother." Prudence enjoyed being vaguely mysterious when she didn't feel like answering questions. It might not be strictly proper to be off on her own, even for a single afternoon, but there was nothing dangerous or indecorous about sharing tea and crustless sandwiches with an acquaintance she hadn't seen in well over a year.

She breathed a sigh of relief when the carriage rolled off, and smiled delightedly as she threaded her way through the tearoom's crowded dining salon. Lydia Truitt beamed back at her from a small table bedecked with white linen, gleaming silverware, and a crystal vase of spring flowers.

Lydia hadn't changed a bit, despite being of what the French called *d'un certain âge.* Widowed at nineteen during the last year of the war, she'd been spared the physical and emotional exhaustion that ravaged too many women whose lives were shortened by yearly childbearing. Lydia was still slender, energetic, devoted to the blind father who had trained her in the sometimes-dangerous career of cryptographic analysis. Benjamin Truitt was the brains of the operation, Lydia its legs. Like the ex-Pinks Geoffrey Hunter employed for particularly difficult cases, she was also adept at disguises and shadowing a suspect.

Today she blended in with the elegantly clad ladies enjoying the sense of freedom that came from frequenting a females-only tearoom. Her flower-bedecked hat was modishly raked on upswept dark red curls, the wasp waist of the gown that was a very good copy of its far more expensive Worth original testified to a tightly laced corset, and the bustle with which every woman struggled was the reduced size Paris had decreed for this spring's season. It was another of Lydia's disguises, of course. Prudence knew for a fact that her friend often dispensed with a corset in the privacy of the home she shared with her father, and while she hadn't seen Lydia indulge in public, she'd once caught a glimpse of a box of cigarillos in her reticule. Benjamin Truitt didn't smoke; his lungs had suffered nearly as badly as his eyes from the artillery explosion that took his sight.

They ordered tea, an assortment of sandwiches and cakes, a silver dish of exquisitely decorated chocolates, and sherry to be tipped discreetly into their bone china cups. All around them rose softly modulated voices, the occasional click of cup against saucer, the whisper of white linen napkins across silk-skirted laps. Discretion was every woman's armor. Though it would have been easy to eavesdrop on another table, very few of the bakery's patrons did. They were too busy with their own conversations to listen in, and they all knew that nothing important or outrageously titillating would be mentioned in public, no matter how private the setting seemed to be.

"Is Clyde Allen still with you?" Prudence asked, when they'd caught up on nearly everything else.

"Almost two and a half years now," Lydia said. "He comes and goes without any warning, stays away for days at a time but always reappears. Watches my father like a hawk, and never without that wickedly sharp whittling knife in his hand. I've gotten used to him and the wood chips he leaves all over the house. Clyde's presence in our spare room is the only thing that makes it possible to leave Father alone without worrying about him."

"I guessed as much. That's why I asked."

Benjamin Truitt and Clyde Allen had met during the war, Prudence remembered. Something about being in the same hospital ward, one of them losing his eyesight, the other half his face to scar tissue.

"I've given up trying to question either of them," Lydia said. "All I get is a wall of silence. Clyde is protecting Father against something or someone only the two of them know about. He was either a deserter or a spy who changed his coat. I wouldn't want to get on his bad side. He and Father rub along the way a lot of the veterans do. Not saying much but understanding without words just about everything that matters."

"We're a couple of odd birds ourselves," Prudence said, dividing the last of the sherry between her cup and Lydia's.

"How so?"

"Society girl who becomes an inquiry agent? Respectable war widow privy to encrypted information the government and competitive businesses wouldn't hesitate to kill to keep secret?"

"I seldom think of it that way," Lydia said.

"It's definitely more challenging than paying social calls all afternoon." Prudence's impatience with the acceptable activities allowed women of her class was something she rarely bothered to hide. Hints about the idiosyncratic behavior of a young lady bearing a distinguished name often appeared in the city's gossip columns.

"Finish up." Lydia softened the command with a quicksilver smile. "We have to be somewhere in twenty minutes."

"I wondered when you'd get around to it," Prudence said. "I brought my derringer." She patted the drawstring reticule that was barely large enough to hold the gun Geoffrey insisted she take with her whenever she left her house or the office. Despite its notorious inaccuracy, she'd practiced enough to ensure that as long as the distance was minimal, the two bullets it discharged would find their target.

"We're going to the theatre." Lydia paid the bill and put on her gloves. "Actors aren't dangerous."

"I wouldn't be so sure about that," Prudence said. "Remember John Wilkes Booth."

"Speaking of the Booths," Lydia grimaced. "I saw his older brother Edwin playing Hamlet last week at the Brooklyn Academy of Music. The *Times* review the next day called it his farewell performance. I hope so. He isn't the fiery declaimer he once was. You could hardly hear him beyond the first few rows, and many of the most famous monologues were shortened or omitted, as if his memory was failing him. It was embarrassing, Prudence. I never want to see an actor fail like that again. Booth is fifty-seven years old but gives the impression of being worn-out, ill, and ancient."

They'd reached the sidewalk and begun walking up Broadway. Arm in arm, slowly, savoring the bright afternoon and the lingering warmth of the sherry.

A horse-drawn streetcar slowed to allow passengers to disembark, leaving behind a steaming pile of manure, so much a part of New York City life that nearby pedestrians hardly noticed. There weren't as many street sweepers on this stretch of Broadway as along Fifth Avenue and the Ladies' Mile shopping district. The droppings would remain where they were until some enterprising urchins descended on the area's theatres this evening to brush them away for tips.

"I didn't realize you were such a theatre lover," Prudence said, turning her attention from the busy street to her friend, suddenly aware that she knew surprisingly little about Lydia's private life. They'd worked together on a case involving an opera singer and her murdered sister, but Lydia hadn't displayed any special love for theatrics.

"My mother was from a family of players," Lydia said quietly. The words and tone of voice had the quality of a confession rather than a boast. "Every one of them in vaudeville, except her. She was the only one who hated being trained to dance and sing and memorize the lines of their skits. The Fabulous Fanchams, they were called. A life in the theatre was the last thing she wanted, so she said yes when she met my father and he asked her to marry him." Lydia sighed. "I don't mean they didn't love each other, because they did. Only that I don't remember ever seeing her smile or hearing her sing. My father once said that if she'd had the bad luck to be born Catholic, she would have made a good nun. I'm not sure exactly what he meant and I've never wanted to ask."

"I love stories like that," Prudence said, squeezing Lydia's arm. "They always remind me how different people are beneath the masks they wear."

"So, as I said, I'm taking you to the theatre this afternoon," Lydia confirmed. "But not to any show to which you can buy tickets. Not yet at least. We're going to a rehearsal."

"I've never seen a play before it opened." In truth, Prudence had been to very few of the city's theatrical productions. The theatre didn't have the cachet of the opera; socialites among

Mrs. Astor's Four Hundred claimed to be scandalized by the raunchy burlesque shows and wildly sexual musical comedies that entertained the working and lower middle classes. Shakespeare was acceptable, and almost anything exported from the Old Vic could be counted on to respect the proprieties, but one had to be careful.

Not many American playwrights were writing serious drama; catering to the lowest popular taste was seemingly the only way to make enough money to pay a company of performers and keep a theatre open. Any female who trod the boards shed her good reputation as soon as the curtain rose. No wonder that in all of their conversations over the years Lydia had never spoken of her family's profession. It made Prudence wonder about Benjamin Truitt's background. All she knew about her friend's father was the fact of his blindness and the undeniable brilliance of a mind that unscrambled supposedly unbreakable ciphers as easily as a sighted person read his morning newspaper. Yet he'd been drawn to the misfit daughter of a troupe of vaudevillians.

"My father's family was even more eccentric," Lydia said, reading Prudence's thoughts as she had done so often in the past. "But we haven't time to go into that now. We're here. This is the theatre where *Waif of the Highlands* is rehearsing."

"That's a terrible title," Prudence said.

"That's not all that's dubious about the play. You'll see."

The doorman who ushered them into the theatre greeted Lydia with a hushed warning. "Mr. Hughes is in a rare mood today. I'd sit in one of the back rows if I were you, Miss Truitt. It might be a good idea if he doesn't find out you've brought someone with you." He nodded at Prudence but didn't seem to expect an introduction.

"It's a closed rehearsal," Lydia explained. "They don't want anything about the play leaking out until just before it opens. Stealing the best scenes of someone else's show is bread and butter in this business."

"Is that Barrett Hughes he was talking about?" Prudence asked. The name was nearly as familiar on both sides of the Atlantic as that of Edwin Booth or Henry Irving.

"Writer, producer, director, and star of the production," Lydia confirmed. "It's also his troupe."

"Mr. Ward asked me to tell you he probably wouldn't be immediately available after the rehearsal," the doorman whispered as he led them toward seats where they had the best chance of being unnoticed. "He said it wouldn't be more than half an hour or so, but he'd like you to wait, if you can. Something's up, but I don't have any idea what. It's always drama with actors."

"That's what the audience comes to see." Lydia waited until the doorman had disappeared down the aisle toward the empty stage before continuing. "Septimus Ward is my cousin. His mother and mine were sisters."

"He's why we're here?"

"It's a little more complicated than that," Lydia hedged. "But yes, Septimus plays the second lead. Star-crossed lover in this case, but the best role he's ever gotten. A chance to make the shift out of vaudeville and into legitimate theatre. He's good, Prudence. Very good."

Actors drifted onto the stage with scripts in their hands as stagehands lit the gas footlights and positioned props. A pianist ran scales in the pit while a violinist tuned his strings. The cacophony barely resembled music.

"It won't be a full ensemble until the last few rehearsals," Lydia murmured. She'd settled into her seat as if everything Prudence found new and needing explanation was comfortably familiar.

"Here's the great man himself," she said as a tall male figure strode across the stage and down the side steps to the house, scattering actors and stagehands in his wake.

Something in Lydia's voice made Prudence lean forward,

straining to make out the features of Barrett Hughes's face in the semidarkness.

The air of authority was unmistakable.

As was the current of anticipatory fear rippling through the company of performers.

# Chapter 2

The footlights weren't usually dimmed during a rehearsal, but it didn't matter. The magic began the moment Septimus Ward stepped onto the stage.

Tall, slender, broad-shouldered, with regular, slightly craggy features whose contours caught the glow of the flickering gaslight, he wore a full sleeved white shirt open at the throat and black trousers almost too tight to be decent. Dark blond hair gleamed golden in the shadowy theatre. Deep, sapphire-blue eyes flashed across the pit and into the farthest recesses of the house as he positioned himself to deliver his opening lines.

Prudence drew in a breath. She couldn't help it. You didn't often see a man as dangerously handsome as this one.

"I should have warned you," Lydia whispered, the lilt of a conspiratorial smile in her voice.

"Yes, but can he act?" Prudence murmured. Male beauty could be striking, even seductive—Geoffrey Hunter was the first example that came to mind—but in her experience it was seldom combined with the warmth and intelligence she demanded of the opposite sex.

"Wait." Lydia lightly tapped a gloved finger on Prudence's

arm. A fond parent showing off a talented child couldn't have been more confident.

The deep baritone voice, pitched to reach effortlessly to the last row of orchestra seats and the uppermost balcony, was as mesmerizing as the eyes. Prudence felt Septimus Ward draw her into another world as surely as though she'd stepped through the proscenium arch into a dream. If the play itself was as appealing as the young romantic lead, audiences would flock to buy tickets. *Waif of the Highlands* could become the season's newest hit.

It didn't hold up. As scene followed scene, it became obvious that the storyline was pure melodrama. Trite, Prudence realized. A poor servant girl captures the heart of an equally poor but handsome young man, yet cannot spurn the advances of a wealthy and much older suitor. Her indigent family depends on her to rescue them from illness and near starvation. Definitely not Shakespeare, Prudence decided. Not even close.

Barrett Hughes played the part of the rich admirer. Smooth, in perfect control, he delivered every syllable in the practiced tones of an actor who'd been famous since before Prudence had been born. At least twice Septimus's age, but so skilled at disappearing into the character he was playing that the years didn't matter. He could and had portrayed heroes far younger than he and villains far older. His most celebrated role was that of Ebenezer Scrooge, in the stage adaptation of the novella *A Christmas Carol* that Charles Dickens had published in 1843. If Edwin Booth could be said to personify a tortured Hamlet, then Barrett Hughes was the world's most infamous miser brought to life. His Scrooge interpretation was a tour de force, but it was whispered among theatre folk that Hughes despised being forever branded as an elderly, crooked-back skinflint.

All this Lydia whispered in bits and pieces as the drama onstage unfolded. Like many famous actors of his generation, she told Prudence, Barrett Hughes owned and managed his own troupe. He wrote, produced, and directed many of the plays in which he starred, *Highlands* being the most recent among them. He had a reputation for merciless criticism that sometimes reduced his performers to tears—male and female alike.

Despite frequent interruptions, the lack of costumes and abbreviated sets, and some of the actors not being off book yet, Prudence was easily persuaded that *Waif of the Highlands'* histrionic style and its exaggerated rags-to-riches storyline were likely to guarantee good box office. The critics were almost certain to pan it, but as long as Hughes and his company played to a full house every night, they could claim the columnists were tasteless boors not worthy of more than a moment's attention.

When Flora Campbell took center stage to sing, Prudence exchanged a quick glance with Lydia. They'd come to see Septimus Ward perform, but it was the equally blond and bewitching Flora who would enthrall theatregoers and steal the show from everyone else, Septimus and Barrett Hughes included.

As Prudence watched and listened, she realized that Flora personified the waiflike qualities the play's title promised. Thin as insubstantial smoke, the bright silvery gold of her hair and the pale blue of her eyes captured every beam of light on the stage. As the lyrics poured from her throat, her fellow actors and even the stagehands stood motionless, momentarily lifted out of themselves, transfixed by the look of the girl and the liquid syllables floating in the air. It wasn't an operatic voice, nor one that would fill every inch of breathable air like that of the queen of Broadway theatre, Lillian Russell. Flora's gift was a sweet sound that spoke of home, hearth, and the innocence of youth.

Flora's character would break every theatregoer's heart, Prudence decided, and Flora herself was destined to become New York City's next theatrical sensation. She was Eleanora Duse at her most emotionally natural, Sarah Bernhardt languishing in love and death in *La Dame aux Camélias*. Septimus and Flora's scenes together created moments of enchanting sadness and

doomed love. Time stood still as the star-crossed lovers agonized their way to tragedy and loss.

And this was only a rehearsal.

*Waif of the Highlands* was so different from anything Prudence had ever seen or read about in the theatre column of the
*Times* that she wondered what the critics would label it. Cate-
gorizing new work was the first job of every pundit. Once a tag
had been affixed to a play or a book, it was almost impossible
to escape it. *Highlands* was a melodrama by plot and dialogue,
but surprisingly well written, eschewing many of the clichés of
the genre. Flora sang, and so did Septimus, but no one else did
and there wasn't a chorus lurking in the background. So it
clearly wasn't a musical. Something entirely new, deserving of a
special designation. Bound to spawn imitators if successful.

"Do you mind waiting, Prudence?" Lydia asked as the last
of the director's notes were given to the actors assembled onstage near the gas footlights. "I'd like you to meet Septimus."

"Not at all. I told Kincaid I'd find my own way home, so no
one is expecting me."

"Geoffrey?"

"He's taken some rare time off. Declared yesterday that the
office would be closed today and sent Josiah home early. I
think he's had news from North Carolina that needs privacy
and uninterrupted time to digest."

"His father?"

"Possibly. Colonel Hunter wasn't wounded in the war, but
he hasn't been what Geoffrey calls a whole man since the surrender. Bitter, angry, so estranged from his son that they
haven't corresponded for years."

"His is not the only family to have broken apart because of
the fighting."

"Slavery, you mean."

Women weren't encouraged to discuss intellectually weighty
topics, but neither Prudence nor Lydia had much patience for
the rhetoric of retired generals and politicians. Lydia lived and

worked with a man who'd given his eyes and the best years of his life to his country. Prudence was the child of a judge who'd taught his daughter that America had gone to war with itself over whether dark-skinned men and women could or should be bought and sold by paler-skinned owners. Slavery and its soul-destroying ramifications was a topic neither of them chose to avoid. Today, however, they were interrupted.

"Mr. Ward is in with Mr. Hughes." The theatre's doorman had approached quickly and quietly as a stagehand extinguished all the gas footlights except one. The stage stood dim and empty, lonely looking, the only sounds a shuffle of departing footsteps and far-off conversations as the actors filed out into the alleyway through the stage door. "I don't think he'll be long, Miss Truitt." He sketched a quick bow in Prudence's direction.

"Bobby knew Septimus's mother. And mine, too," Lydia explained. "Septimus anticipated half an hour. Isn't that what you said?"

"I did. But from what I could hear outside Mr. Hughes's office, he'll be out in two shakes of a lamb's tail."

"They're arguing?"

"Going at it hammer and tongs."

"Do you have any idea what it's about?"

"I don't like to say. None of us knows for sure, but there's been bad blood between them from the beginning."

"It can't be easy to work in an atmosphere like that," Lydia said.

"You know I've been around theatre folk all my life," the doorman said. "Thought about becoming an actor myself, once upon a time. Players aren't like other people. They don't live inside their skins like the rest of us do."

"What does that mean?" Prudence asked, fascinated by discovering another world she hadn't dreamed existed.

"They're touchy and twitchy. Looking around all the time to see if anyone's watching them. Performing a role even when they're not onstage. They might hide some of their feelings, but never for long. Actors are volcanoes, like those Italian places that are always erupting. Vesuvius and that Etna one." Bobby shook his head as though they were a lost cause. Actors.

"Hughes or my cousin?" Lydia asked.

"Both of them, I'd say. Whatever they're fighting about, one's as bad as the other."

"I wonder if that's why he asked me to wait. He said there was something he wanted to talk about."

"I think I heard a door slam," Prudence said.

"I'll be on my way then." The doorman faded toward the lobby.

Barrett Hughes charged across the stage like an angry bull. He shouted something that neither Prudence nor Lydia could make out, then stopped in midstride to stare into the wings he'd just exited. When no one answered or appeared out of the darkness to confront him, he flung one arm above his head in a gesture worthy of Scrooge at his "Bah! Humbug!" best, and disappeared, banging the heavy metal stage door behind him.

Moments later Septimus Ward came striding up the aisle in their direction, his handsome face grim. Features stony and bleak.

"That was quite a performance Hughes just gave us," Lydia greeted him.

"I wish that's all it was, but he won't budge an inch, the bastard. He thinks I'll cave, but he's wrong. I want what rightfully belongs to me and I'll do whatever I have to in order to get it. No papers were signed. It's his word against mine."

"This is Prudence MacKenzie," Lydia said, gesturing toward the silent woman beside her. "She's the one I told you about. We've worked together on some of her private inquiry cases. She's an attorney now, too."

"Miss MacKenzie, I apologize for my language." The actor in Septimus switched into a more self-controlled persona. "I'm sorry you had to see and hear that."

"Perhaps it would help if you told us what the quarrel is about," Prudence said.

"We could go somewhere for tea," Lydia suggested. "I think we're about to be asked to leave, anyway."

A stagehand had appeared to turn off the last remaining footlight and make sure the ghost light was lit. He jingled the ring of keys he was carrying and gestured toward the back of the house. "I'm locking up, Mr. Ward," he called. "Bobby said he'd keep the lobby door open for a few more minutes."

Septimus waved his thanks. "I could use something stronger than tea," he said.

"There's a saloon around the corner that has a ladies' lounge. Walsh's Tavern," Lydia said. She caught the look of surprise on Prudence's face and smiled. "Don't be too shocked. It's mostly respectable lower middle-class working women. We'll stand out a bit, but the bartender knows Septimus. He won't turn us away."

By which, Prudence decided, she meant they wouldn't be mistaken for prostitutes trolling for business.

Walsh himself ushered Septimus and his two lady companions into the comfortable snug he called The Back Room. A tall, corpulent, red-nosed man with scant wisps of gray hair left atop his head, he cultivated the custom of the actors in the theatre district, allowing them to run up tabs when no one else trusted them to honor the debt. Eventually.

He'd once dreamed of declaiming Shakespeare in London's great theatres. But Walsh had been born a dirt-poor Irishman condemned to emigrate and work with his hands to keep from starving. He never forgot his love affair with the stage, so when he scraped together enough money to open a tavern, the second dream of his life, he located it where every seat at the bar and every square table on the floor would be peopled by theatre folk. "The best in the world," he was often heard to say.

"You'll have a double whiskey, I think," he told Septimus, whipping a rag across the table he'd selected for them in the otherwise empty lounge. "And the ladies will have my finest sherry."

He brought the generous-sized drinks, set them down, and studied Septimus for a moment. A good bartender was as adept as a priest at reading a man's face. "I'll maybe close the lounge for a while. So as to give ye a bit of privacy."

"I'd appreciate it," Septimus said. He held out a fisted hand.

"Don't even think of it," Walsh said. "Your money's no good here today."

"*Slàinte Mhath*," Septimus said, raising his glass as Walsh closed The Back Room door behind him and turned the sign on it from OPEN to CLOSED.

"Cheers," Lydia replied, sipping what was a very good sherry.

Prudence lifted her glass and nodded, guessing that what she'd heard Septimus say was a Scottish toast she'd never be able to pronounce.

"Barrett Hughes didn't write *Waif of the Highlands*," Septimus said. "I did."

# CHAPTER 3

"Start at the beginning," Prudence said.

"If she represents you," Lydia put in, "everything you tell her is confidential."

"I don't need a mouthpiece." Septimus followed half his double whiskey with a swallow of beer chaser. "No offense intended, Miss MacKenzie."

Lydia started to protest, but Prudence shook her head. He was a strange one, her friend's cousin. Classically handsome features, voice like black silk, a presence that commanded attention. But she sensed that he wasn't a formally educated man, and wondered if away from the exotic setting of the theatre he would be out of his element. The only other time she'd heard *mouthpiece* used to refer to a member of the legal profession was on the streets of Five Points near the Quaker mission where she sometimes volunteered. It might not be precisely gutter slang, but it was close.

"Flora and I were touring in the same vaudeville company," Septimus began, swirling the tumbler of whiskey in precise circles on the table. "Her family's like ours, Lydia. They're all players. Singers, dancers, jugglers, sketch artists, comedians. Flora was the only one of them who had a hunger for something bigger and more legitimate than vaudeville. She wants to be another Lillie Langtry."

"Why Lillie Langtry?"

"Langtry's tour came through Chicago while we were playing there. Flora couldn't talk about anything else for weeks." A trace of ancestral Scots crept into his voice as the whiskey and the beer chaser began to make themselves felt. "She wanted to try for a spot in Lillie's company, but she couldn't get an audition. The company manager turned her down flat."

"What do Flora and Lillie Langtry have to do with your writing *Waif of the Highlands*?" Lydia asked. A quick glance at Prudence confirmed that both women suspected what the answer would be, but they needed to hear Septimus say it.

"I was already creating most of the comedy sketches for our troupe, and I'd tried my hand at longer pieces, too. They weren't half-bad, some of them."

Another round of drinks had appeared on the table with nothing more than a click of the snug's door and a swish of Walsh's white apron to mark his brief presence.

"So you wrote a play to make Flora famous?" Lydia emptied one of the sherry glasses lined up in front of her as Septimus stared at his second double whiskey.

"She didn't ask me to," he said. "It wasn't like that."

"What *was* it like?" Prudence prodded softly. One foot below the table discreetly urged Lydia to say nothing else about Flora. Not yet.

"I'd had an idea for a long time, but I hadn't been able to put it into words," Septimus said. He seemed to be drifting away as he eased into the telling. "It was about two young Scots immigrants who fell in love but were forced apart by a wealthy man's obsession for the girl. She was beautiful and very poor. Her family—parents, younger brothers, and sisters—

would die of starvation if she didn't give herself to this man. So she did."

"And the songs?"

"I wrote them, too. Words and music both." He smiled and picked up the glass of whiskey. "Vaudevillians wear many hats, Miss MacKenzie. There's a wealth of unsuspected talent behind the soft shoe dancing and the slapstick."

"How did the play make it to Broadway?" Prudence's fingers itched for the pen and notebook in her reticule, but she was afraid Septimus would shut down if she took notes. She'd have to rely on her good memory and past experience questioning witnesses to remember what he said.

"It nearly didn't. By the time I finished the last scene, well over a year after I'd started, we'd completed one tour and moved on to another. I worked on *Highlands* every night after the show and well into the morning hours. There were times I couldn't have told you the name of the town or the theatre where we were playing, but I had to keep supplying new sketches and routines because that's what you do in vaudeville. If an audience doesn't laugh at something, the act gets pulled and replaced with something or someone else. The pace can be brutal, and there's no mercy shown to a performer who can't hold his own on stage."

"I had no idea," Prudence murmured.

"No outsider can imagine what it's like," Septimus said. "They put a star on the dressing room door when you've made it into the big time. That's every actor's dream, that star. He'll do just about anything to get it.

"About six months ago Flora and I got booked into Tony Pastor's Theatre on Fourteenth Street. It was a change from traveling like gypsies from town to town, and Flora thought it could be the break she'd been angling for. Her family was dead set against it because Tony didn't need the whole troupe. He had to replace a singer who was growing a belly, if you know what I mean."

*Pregnant.* There were polite euphemisms to avoid directly mentioning a condition never willingly acknowledged in public, but Prudence had learned to prefer directness of expression. At least in the privacy of her own mind.

"He needed a soprano and a tenor because that's what his audience expected. We were it."

"You never told me you were a song and dance man," Lydia said.

Septimus shrugged. "All we Scots are fierce dancers. You know that. I can't sing the leads in Gilbert and Sullivan comic operas like Durward Lely, but I'm not at all bad at ballads."

Two double whiskeys had taken the edge off his anger. Prudence thought he might be one of those men who waxed eloquent under the influence, much easier to deal with than the vicious street brawlers and wife beaters whose savage tempers were fueled by drink.

"So you left the troupe you'd been with and took your act to Tony Pastor's," she reminded him. She'd ask Lydia later who Durward Lely was. A tenor, presumably Scots. Did all theatre people measure themselves against other performers?

"Flora and I weren't married, so we had to take rooms in separate boardinghouses," Septimus explained. "Tony likes his players to keep up appearances."

"His theatre is in the same building where Tammany has its headquarters." Lydia was never sure how much Prudence knew about the lives of ordinary New Yorkers and the city in which they lived.

"Turns out Flora was right about getting a break there. Barrett Hughes was in the audience one night. He's a notorious womanizer and it's common gossip that the older he gets, the younger he likes his partners to be." A trace of bitterness crept back into Septimus's voice. "Keep them coming," he said to Walsh, who had stuck his head through the doorway to check on how they were doing.

"Don't you think you've had enough?" Lydia asked, reaching out to touch the hand that had curled itself around an empty glass.

"Not yet, I haven't. Not by a long shot." This time, when Walsh placed a full glass on the table, Septimus spilled a few drops as he raised it to his lips.

"He wined and dined her, but Flora was just the latest in a long line of casual conquests. Until she told him about *Waif of the Highlands.* Hughes was looking for a vehicle to add to this season's repertory, and he knew he needed to transition from Scrooge to handsome, cultivated, rich older man parts. He can't attempt young romantic leads anymore without risking being laughed off the stage and pilloried in the reviews. It's just a fact of the profession. The lighting's gotten better over the years since the switch from candles to gas, and audiences want believability."

"What happened?" Lydia asked.

"We struck a deal. He'd take writer's credit for *Highlands*, as well as producing and directing it. Play the starring role of the rich older suitor, of course, which I agreed to considerably beef up. Flora would play the young servant girl. He said it would make her a star overnight."

"Who suggested you play the young man she really loved?"

"I did. I insisted on its being part of the agreement. Or else I'd take the script to someone else. I didn't have anywhere to go, no contacts with other producers and directors, no favors I could call in, but Hughes didn't know that. He agreed. Said I'd be a star, too."

"Did you sign a contract?" Prudence asked.

"Nothing in writing. A handshake."

"So only the three of you know that Barrett Hughes isn't the author of *Waif of the Highlands*?" Prudence had to be sure she'd gotten it right, that Septimus hadn't left out anything essential to the telling of his story.

"And now you and Lydia." He drank down half the third double whiskey. Followed it with more of the beer chaser.

"What was the argument about?" Lydia asked. Septimus was as close to being drunk as she'd ever seen him. They had to get the rest of the story before he changed his mind or became incapable of telling it.

"I told Hughes I wanted my author's credit back. I could see he was right. *Highlands* may not be a piece of classical drama, but it'll be a big box office success. Melodrama with a song everyone will be humming as they walk out of the theatre. The scenes I'd written came alive during rehearsals. Hughes realized it, too. Long before I did."

"What was his reaction?" Prudence asked.

"He laughed. Said a deal was a deal, and I ought to know better than to try to change the terms we'd shaken hands on."

"Was that all?" From what the doorman had described, there had to have been more. *Going at it hammer and tongs.*

"He threatened I'd never work in the theatre or vaudeville again. Not for as long as I lived. Worse. He said if I didn't stick to the agreement we had, he'd close the show before it opened. He'd fix it so Flora never got another break. Ever. He'd see her selling herself on a street corner before anyone would allow her to set foot in a theatre again. He could do it, Miss MacKenzie. Barrett Hughes is a force to be reckoned with. His name is as well-known in the profession as Edwin Booth's."

"Aren't you exaggerating a little?" Lydia asked. "One man can't have that much power."

"You've never been a part of backstage," Septimus said. "Maybe you've heard the stories, but you haven't lived them. You haven't experienced what it's like."

"Does Flora know about the confrontation with Hughes?" Prudence was determined to stick to what she considered the pertinent facts of what could shape up to be an interesting case. If Septimus decided to hire her after all.

"She'd already left the theatre. And I didn't tell her what I planned to do."

"Why not?" Lydia asked. "It affects her as much as it does you. More perhaps."

Head down, staring into his empty whiskey glass, Septimus mumbled something incomprehensible. His cheeks stained red. The knuckles of his clenched fists paled.

"But Flora knows that you're the author of *Waif of the Highlands,*" Prudence insisted, her litigator's mind already picturing the delicate blond actress on the witness stand, tearfully assuring a jury under oath that Septimus Ward's work had been stolen from him. There wouldn't be a dry eye or disbelieving spectator in the courtroom.

"You wrote it for her," Lydia reminded him. "Presumably you shared what you were working on as you went along, shaping the play to her talents, perhaps even incorporating whatever suggestions she made."

"She saw the handwritten script," Septimus said. "Many times. We used to run lines with each other when a scene didn't want to play right."

"Would you call her a cowriter then?" Prudence asked. It was important to get the details clear from the beginning. Her father had always insisted that an attorney could never afford to be ambushed in midtrial.

"No. The writing was mine. Every word of it. Flora had ideas, but they were all about adding lines and business to the character she was going to portray. Nothing that had anything to do with the overall plot or structure of the play itself." Septimus looked up from his whiskey, caught Lydia's eye, and pushed away the empty glass. "Maybe I have had enough."

"What next?" Lydia asked.

"I'm not sure. I can't be the reason the play doesn't open. It wouldn't be fair to Flora."

Prudence and Lydia exchanged looks. *He's in love with her, poor fool.*

"Did Hughes leave open any possibility of negotiation?" Prudence knew that in the heat of anger it might not seem like it, but often there remained a thread of reconciliation that could be teased out of the worst disagreements. It was up to her to find it.

"It's my play. I wrote it," Septimus said.

"Yes, but would either you or Hughes consider billing yourselves as coauthors? Would that smooth things over enough for the production to continue? Perhaps open a door for future collaboration?" It was a long **shot,** but negotiation was made up of feints and starts, suggestions and potentialities. Prudence knew that threats and ultimatums seldom worked. "For Flora's sake?"

It might be slightly unfair to bring Flora's name into the mix, but if her career and entire future were at stake, Septimus might be willing to take a first step. In the end, it could turn out to be a good decision for him, too. How many times had Prudence read in the *Times* about a lucrative business deal concluded between two titans of industry whom she knew heartily despised one another? The operative condition was whether Hughes would agree to compromise. And that would depend on how strong he believed his upper hand to be.

"It's my play," Septimus repeated stubbornly.

"You may have to choose between seeing it produced, with you and Flora in leading roles, or consigning it to oblivion," Lydia said.

"Hughes won't compromise. He already has the best of the deal. Why should he give any of it up?"

"If that's what you believe, why challenge him in the first place?" Prudence asked.

"I could feel it slipping away from me, Miss MacKenzie. With every rehearsal, *Waif of the Highlands* receded farther into the distance. It was beginning to seem as though someone else really had written it. I couldn't let that happen. It may have been a crazy idea, but I had to try to get her back."

He wasn't talking so much about the play as he was Flora Campbell, the waif of the play's title. The young woman to whom he'd given his heart and for whom he'd created the role that would make the critics christen her a second Lillie Langtry. He was losing the love of his life. Flora was willfully walking into the arms of an intoxicatingly important man. And Septimus had set her on that path. He'd made it possible. Life was imitating art.

"Think it over before you do anything else, Septimus," Lydia pleaded as her cousin rose unsteadily to his feet.

He shrugged off the hand she touched briefly to the sleeve of his jacket. "I'm not making any promises." The words were slurred, pronounced with belligerent cockiness, as though the whiskey had suddenly surged to his brain. He grabbed his hat from the table and jammed it on his head. Just before he disappeared into the public room of Walsh's Tavern he straightened, set his shoulders, and said something neither of the women could make out. When he waved goodbye to the barkeeper, his gait was as steady as that of a judge. As the saying went. Septimus Ward was an actor who'd more than once played the role of sobriety.

"What just happened?" Lydia asked.

"Flora Campbell isn't in love with him," Prudence said. "But she is in love with the play that will catapult her into fame and fortune. And with the man who's going to make her dreams a reality."

"Barrett Hughes."

"I misspoke just now. Flora isn't in love with Hughes, either; she's just realistic enough to know he's the vehicle she has to ride. And she's willing to do it."

"My poor cousin. I'll let him sleep it off tonight, but I'll try talking to him again tomorrow."

"Do you want my help?"

"I think it's better if I tackle him alone first," Lydia said. "I don't know where he lives. I've only ever met him at whatever theatre he was playing. I'll have to show up at rehearsal again."

"Tomorrow's Sunday," Prudence reminded her.

"Monday then. That should give him time to think things through. And sober up."

Or dig in his heels even deeper.

# CHAPTER 4

"There's an article in today's paper about the company of German actors from Munich that's been playing at the Amberg." Josiah Gregory rattled his copy of the *New York Times* to make sure he wasn't being ignored. "Apparently their farewell performance on Saturday night was as uninspiring as everything else they presented. The reviewer isn't kind, except to write that the German language newspapers raved over the performances. Probably because the audiences were composed largely of German speakers with limited English."

He shook the paper again, then folded it into a neat rectangle and laid it on his desk. Miss Prudence had given only the briefest description of her outing with Lydia Truitt, falling unusually silent on the exciting subject of a play in production. Word had begun spreading among Josiah's theatre friends that Barrett Hughes would be opening in yet another hit, but that this time the famous actor wouldn't be wearing a false nose and padding on his back. Josiah had counted on being able to supply details of the drama with the intriguing title *Waif of the Highlands*, but Miss Prudence had disappointed him.

He sighed as she disappeared into Geoffrey Hunter's office,

closing the door behind her with a quiet click. He'd find out eventually what his employer at Hunter and MacKenzie, Investigative Law, was reluctant to discuss this morning. It was annoying to have to wait for a case to explode before becoming part of it, but Josiah had been the firm's secretary since its inception. And secretary to the attorney and United States senator who'd occupied these offices before that.

Josiah's nose was never wrong. Something was waiting in the wings.

"It's not that Josiah can't be trusted with information as confidential as this," Prudence explained to Geoffrey as she seated herself in one of the client chairs across the broad expanse of his desk.

"But he does have friends in that world," Geoffrey said. "And there's nothing theatre people do better than gossip about one another. Or so he himself says."

"Septimus Ward told a very convincing tale."

"Do you believe him?"

"I do."

"*In vino veritas*?"

"It was more than that, although he did consume a considerable amount of whiskey in a very short period of time." She frowned, then pleated a fold of her skirt and frowned again. "The thing is, I could very easily imagine him working away night after night to create the perfect vehicle to launch Flora Campbell's career. He's deeply in love with her."

"But she not so much."

"I haven't been introduced to her, so I shouldn't speculate."

"But you will anyway."

"From what I observed during the rehearsal, Flora Campbell is one of those rare stage presences who captivates an audience as soon as she steps into the gaslight. So is Septimus, for that matter. And Barrett Hughes's fame practically guarantees him an enthusiastic reception no matter what role he's playing. The three of them together could become theatrical legends. Hughes definitely, Septimus and Flora if *Waif of the Highlands* opens as planned."

"It's that good?"

"Not classically so, but the story will resonate with audiences, and the song Flora sings—all alone on a darkened stage—is one you can't get out of your head. I've only heard it once, but I haven't been able to forget it."

"A moneymaker then."

"Money and fame," Prudence agreed.

"There's a lot at stake here."

"More than I first thought. I counseled negotiation, but the more I've thought about it, the less approachable I believe Hughes will be. Septimus is a nobody, an upstart vaudevillian with not much more than good looks and a first-class voice to recommend him. But, Geoffrey, he's only one of many handsome young talents jostling to step onto the stage of a legitimate theatre. Hughes has probably had hungry second leads nipping at his heels throughout his entire career."

"Septimus needs to be able to present handwritten manuscript pages in court to prove authorship."

"According to what he told us, Flora is the only one who saw those pages while he was writing the play, the only one who could swear to when they were composed."

"And you don't think she'd be willing to testify to that?"

"Not if it meant financial backing would disappear, and the play would be consigned to a rubbish heap somewhere. Hughes is the known quantity behind the production. Without his name attached to it, I doubt *Highlands* stands much of a chance of opening."

"You don't represent Septimus Ward," Geoffrey reminded her gently.

"I will," Prudence replied. "If Lydia has any influence with her cousin."

"Still. Until then . . ."

"I know. It's not a case. Not yet. But this one has already gotten under my skin."

The office door burst open while the urchin who shot through it was still arguing with Josiah about whether he should be allowed entry. One of Danny Dennis's street Arabs, he was barefoot, dressed in ragged short pants and a frayed jacket. A shapeless cap hung down over his ears. But his eyes were bright, his voice loud, and his attitude determined.

"Miss Lydia says to come right away," he whooped, clinging to the doorknob Josiah was trying to wrest from his hand.

"It's all right, Josiah," Prudence said, rising from the client chair. "I know this boy. His name is Little Eddie."

"I followed you and Miss Lydia once," Little Eddie said. "You gave me the slip out the back door of that hat shop. Doesn't happen very often."

"I remember. Now what's this about Miss Lydia?"

"She's standing out on the sidewalk because the landlady won't let her any farther inside than the parlor and her cousin's room is up two flights of stairs. She says something's wrong, but she needs help finding out what it is. I've never seen Miss Lydia this mad before, Miss Prudence. You better come quick before the landlady calls a cop to arrest her."

"Is Danny downstairs?"

"Him and Mr. Washington both. Flower, too."

"I'll come right away. Geoffrey?"

"You'll have to man the fort alone, Josiah. I don't think we're expecting any clients this morning." Geoffrey flipped a coin at Little Eddie, who caught it one-handed, bit the silver, and slipped it into a securely hidden pocket not even one of his light-fingered friends could pilfer. "Run down and tell Danny we're on our way."

Prudence checked her reticule to be sure the two-shot derringer she always carried was fully loaded, then pinned on her hat. She nodded approval as Geoffrey picked up and swung the custom-made sword cane he was seldom without nowadays.

She didn't think it was her imagination—New York City's streets had become increasingly dangerous. The cases they agreed to investigate were bringing them into neighborhoods where safety wasn't something you could take for granted.

The red-gold dog named Flower sat as rigidly still as a Chinese statue atop Danny Dennis's hansom cab, a stray spring breeze ruffling the soft fur of her long ears. Possessed of an exceptionally sensitive nose and an intelligence beyond her years, she was not quite ten months old and took her training very seriously. Mr. Washington, the largest and whitest horse on New York City's busy, horse-filled streets, approved her grave earnestness and watched over her as she slept at his feet every night amid a tumble of street urchins. Between the two of them, Mr. Washington and Danny Dennis welcomed strays of every description to the clean, sweet-smelling stable where neither animals nor orphaned children were ever turned away.

"Do you know what this is about, Danny?" Geoffrey asked, running a hand down Mr. Washington's long nose as he waited for Prudence to join him at the curb. She'd gone back for the small black doctor's bag she'd lately packed with first-aid supplies and now kept beneath her desk. Dr. Charity Sloan at the Friends Refuge for the Sick Poor had supplied bandages, splints, tweezers, scissors, and an array of small, cork-stoppered brown bottles. "Just in case," Prudence had said when she'd brought the bag to the office. "Just in case."

"Little Eddie claims she was standing on the sidewalk about to have a fit," Danny said. "I don't see Miss Lydia that upset about anything, but that's what he reported."

"Had he been following her?" Sometimes Danny's boys shadowed people just for the experience of remaining undetected. Lydia acted as courier for many of Benjamin Truitt's cryptography cases, as adept at disguising herself in her treks around the city as Danny's striplings were at picking her out of a crowd. She always rewarded their diligence with a coin or two. It was a kind of game they played.

"I don't think so. Not this time."

Flower made a woofing sound but didn't turn her head as Prudence crossed the sidewalk and approached the cab. She was one of the dog's favorite people.

Trinity Church's steeple receded into the distance as Danny directed Mr. Washington up Fifth Avenue to where it intersected with Broadway and 23rd Street at Madison Square. The streets narrowed as the cab moved away from the prosperous shops of the Ladies' Mile and into what was becoming known as the uptown theatre district. Entertainment venues as well as private homes were moving toward Central Park and away from the Tammany Building on Fourteenth Street where Tony Pastor's Theatre still operated. Boardinghouses crowded the side streets, there were fewer trees, more trash, and bigger heaps of horse dung on the cobblestones.

"There she is." Danny gestured with the whip he seldom if ever used to urge Mr. Washington forward. A crack in the air above the horse's broad back was signal enough when there was too much traffic noise for a click of the tongue to be heard.

Lydia Truitt took a stride forward but thought better of stepping into the street.

"Thank goodness you've come," she said as Prudence and Geoffrey climbed down from the cab.

"I'll wait," Danny said, retrieving Mr. Washington's feed bag and Flower's water bowl from beneath his high seat perched at the rear of the hansom cab.

"Something's not right." Lydia clutched at Prudence's arm. "I can feel it. I learned long ago to sense when Father needed me. I'm never wrong about when trouble's brewing."

Prudence made her way gingerly up the boardinghouse steps, careful not to touch the railing with her clean gloves.

"Septimus didn't show up at rehearsal this morning," Lydia said, taking the arm Geoffrey held out to her. "I went to the theatre to talk to him. Like I told you I would. Barrett Hughes was furious. He'd had to put Septimus's understudy in his place, and apparently the man wasn't nearly as good."

"Was there any mention of Saturday's quarrel?" Prudence asked. She raised the brass knocker and noted with approval that it had been recently polished.

"Not a word," Lydia said. "Hughes wouldn't even speak to me other than to snarl that my cousin had better climb out of his bottle if he wanted to be onstage opening night. I got this address from Bobby, the doorman."

The landlady who answered Prudence's knock was nearly as broad as she was tall, a solid presence more than intimidating enough to deal with any actor who tried to sneak away without paying his week's rent. She took in at a glance Prudence's fashionable and very expensive walking suit, recognized Geoffrey's sword cane for the dangerous weapon it was, and shrugged her shoulders. "You'd better come in then," she said, opening the door wide and standing aside. "He's still not up," she told Lydia. "And there won't be a special breakfast laid out when he does come down."

"Cold porridge will do," Lydia answered, determined not to get too far on this woman's bad side. "And as much black coffee as the pot will hold."

The landlady sniffed. She'd had years of experience handling actors and their hangovers. There was something about the bottle that seemed as much a part of their lives as the grease-smeared scripts they carried with them everywhere.

"You'll want the door opened if he's still not answering," she said, reaching for the ring of keys dangling from her waist. "Though how anyone could sleep through the pounding I've already given it, I swear I don't know."

"But you didn't go in?" Geoffrey asked.

"They don't much like being burst in on," she said. "Actors only want to be seen at their best, and coming out of a drunken sleep isn't it." She had a soft spot for Septimus Ward, though she was loath to admit fondness for any of her boarders. Actors would break your heart. Every one of them. Tessa Carey's father, her husbands, and two of her brothers had all done their best to ruin her life and would have succeeded had she not been stronger and more stubborn than the five men put together. She'd had her time on the boards, too, but once the weight started coming on, she'd found herself increasingly uncastable. *Resting,* actors called it when they were out of work. Tessa had found running a boardinghouse to be a far more reliable way of earning a living than the theatre ever provided. "Come along then. It's a bit of a climb," she said to Geoffrey.

"Lead the way." He smiled at her and hung the cane over one arm.

Two flights of narrow steps, a turn on the top landing, the third door on the left. Each boarder's name had been inked onto a card and placed in a holder attached to his door. Not quite the dressing room star so few attained, but a nice touch just the same.

Mrs. Carey raised a practiced fist and beat a loud tattoo on Septimus's door. No answer. Not a sound from within. She nodded at Geoffrey, who cracked the head of his cane against the wood. Stood back. Hammered on it again. Waited. Shook his head.

"All right, then," the landlady said. "We're coming in, Mr. Ward," she announced in a voice that would have filled an empty theatre. The key she inserted into the lock clicked loudly in the silent hallway.

He was on the floor, one foot caught in the bedclothes trailing from a thin mattress sliding from the iron bedframe. His arms were outflung, one hand inches from a brown bottle that looked too small to have held whiskey. Septimus's eyes were half-open. His lips moved as he breathed. The smell of vomit and feces hung in the fetid air.

Lydia fell to her knees beside him as Prudence set down her black doctor's bag and opened the window. The landlady fetched a pitcher of water and a towel from the washstand while Geoffrey untangled the sheets from the actor's bed and slipped a pillow beneath his head. It wasn't unheard of for a drunk to choke to death on the spewed-up contents of his stomach, but it looked as though Lydia's cousin would be spared that indignity. This time, at least.

"I told you something was wrong," Lydia said. She dipped the towel in the pitcher of water and wiped last night's blood-streaked dinner from Septimus's lips. "Give me a hand with him, Geoffrey. We'll get him back in his bed."

"Wait," Prudence said, picking up the small brown bottle, examining the torn label, turning it toward the landlady. "Get a pail of milk up here. As quickly as you can."

"Cream works better," Tessa Carey said. "I've got a fresh bottle in the kitchen." She disappeared out the door and down the stairs.

"Don't move him," Prudence directed, snapping open her doctor's bag although she already knew it contained nothing that would help Septimus now. It was probably too late, and he'd already emptied his stomach, but milk had been known to turn the trick. Sometimes. Not always. But it was worth a try.

"This isn't whiskey," she said, setting the brown bottle on the floor again. "It's rat poison."

# Chapter 5

The spring air from the open window lessened the stench of vomit and emptied bowels, but Septimus's body shook with convulsive chills despite the warmth. Geoffrey draped a blanket over the actor's legs and torso, tucking it around him as tightly as he could. He left the three whiskey bottles and the smaller bottle of rat poison where they lay on the floor, only turning them so their labels faced upward.

Ants crawled over a chipped plate and tin spoon, busily cleaning away brown smears of what might have been stew from the table where Septimus had eaten his last meal.

Her partner looked in Prudence's direction, gestured toward the bottle of rat poison, then bent to pick it up.

"Be careful," she warned. "Don't take off your gloves. Arsenic can be absorbed through the skin."

Geoffrey nodded, smoothing out a fragment of the label where a portion of the cautionary skull and crossbones could be deciphered. "The question is how this got ripped. Was it accidental or deliberate?" He glanced down at where Lydia knelt beside her cousin, one hand smoothing wisps of blond hair from his forehead. Tears streamed down her cheeks.

Prudence shook her head. Even if they managed to get the landlady's milk into his stomach, she doubted Septimus had any real hope of recovery. His raspy breathing was fitful and uncertain.

"Don't leave me, Septimus," Lydia urged as Tessa Carey returned, carrying a bottle of thick, pale yellow cream.

"We'll have an easier time getting it down him with this." The landlady inserted a short piece of flexible tubing into a hole she'd cut in the bottle's cork. "I've fed many a drunk with baking soda and warm water when all he could do was suck like a baby." She put the tube into her own mouth and drew up the cream until it spilled out and over her fingers. "Here now, love," she instructed Lydia. "Hold this between his teeth and rub his throat until he swallows."

Prudence read a desperate hope on Lydia's face as she followed Mrs. Carey's directions. It looked for a moment as if Septimus would manage to keep down the cream his cousin forced on him, but when it bubbled out from his mouth again the liquid was tinged with bright red blood.

"Let's try again," Lydia urged. Septimus's head fell to one side and the tube slipped from his mouth. His lips moved and when he fastened his eyes on Lydia's face it was with a silent, desperate plea that she understood all too well. He was dying. He knew he was dying, and he had last words he wanted her to hear.

Geoffrey slipped one arm beneath the pillow on which Septimus lay, raising him so he could speak without choking. Prudence took the tubing and the bottle of cream from Lydia's fingers, handing her friend a clean handkerchief with which to wipe the actor's lips. Septimus's skin had paled to a faint gray tone that signaled a weakening circulation. He hadn't much time left. Minutes, seconds perhaps.

Lydia leaned over her cousin as close as she could get, one ear almost touching his mouth, whispering words Prudence could not make out. She fell silent, holding one of his hands in both of hers. They heard a mumble of something indecipherable, the exhalation of a name. *Flora.* The soft hiss of his last breath. Then he was gone.

Prudence held Lydia in her arms as Geoffrey lowered the body to the floor and closed Septimus's eyes with gentle fingers.

Tessa Carey pulled the tubing from the bottle of cream and inserted a fresh cork that she took from her apron pocket. "No sense letting it go to waste," she said. "He was a fine young man. A shame the whiskey took him." She looked around the room, taking stock of its furnishings and the few possessions Septimus had placed there. "Rent's paid through Saturday," she told Lydia. "That gives you five days, six counting today, to see to his things. Shall I notify the parish priest?"

"He wasn't Catholic." Lydia's lips felt numb, and she stumbled as Geoffrey helped her to her feet.

"I'll say a rosary for him anyway," Tessa said. "I do for every one of my actors when his time comes. It can't do any harm and it might do some good."

A scampering of bare feet on the stairs announced the arrival of Little Eddie before his skinny form barged through the doorway. He skidded to a stop when he saw the body on the floor and sketched a hasty cross in midair. "Copper on his way up," he announced. "Danny thought you'd want to know."

"How did that happen?" Prudence asked.

Little Eddie shrugged. "There's never any secrets in this neighborhood," he said.

"There'll be a morgue wagon from Bellevue next," Tessa Carey predicted. "They don't like the corpses to lie too long where they died. Something to do with the board of health."

"Now then, what's going on here, Tessa?" said the uniformed patrolman whose broad shape filled the doorway, blocking Little Eddie from slipping past him. "Wait just a minute, young man." A large, freckled hand came down on Little Eddie's shoulder, effectively pinning him in place.

"It's Septimus Ward, Jimmy," Mrs. Carey said. "He was drinking himself into a stupor with whiskey and picked up the rat poison by mistake." She pointed at the small brown bottle Geoffrey had carefully replaced where it had lain within easy reach of the actor's outstretched fingers.

"That did for him then." Still keeping hold of Little Eddie, Officer James Kilaren aimed his truncheon at Prudence and Geoffrey. "And who are these fine folks?"

Geoffrey handed the policeman one of his business cards.

"The lady is Septimus's cousin," Tessa Carey explained. "She's the one kept insisting something was wrong when he wouldn't answer his door. I don't allow female visitors to the rooms, as you well know, Jimmy, so it was myself as was knocking to beat the band."

"But he didn't answer, so you used your passkey?" Officer Kilaren settled Little Eddie against the wall, wagged a warning finger in his face against bolting, and turned his attention to the corpse. "He's gone then? You're sure and certain?"

"We were all here when he took his last breath." Tessa mimicked Septimus Ward's final moments, the retired actress in her still capable of playing a scene. "Will ye have a feel of him?"

"I'll leave that to the Bellevue boys."

Septimus's lips had turned a bloodless blue-gray.

Officer Kilaren took a small notebook from his pocket, licked a stub of a pencil, and made a few notes, stepping closer to where the dead man lay, the toe of one boot briefly nudging the bottles to roll a few inches across the splintery floor. "That's it, then. Rat poison. How old was he? Do you know?" he asked, pencil poised above the page where he'd made a quick sketch to illustrate the brief description he'd include in his report.

"Thirty-four," Lydia said. "Our mothers were sisters."

"Thirty-four?" Tessa Carey repeated. "Who would have guessed it? He had a much younger look about him." She slid a speculative finger over the thin layer of theatrical makeup she applied to her face every morning, wondering if her boarder had done the same. Too late now. She couldn't very well run a hand down his cheek to find out.

Then how old was Flora? Prudence wondered. Was she, too, older than she was passing herself off as being? It was a question she'd have to save for a private moment, for after the policeman had finished taking his notes and gone.

"Will you notify a detective at Mulberry Street Headquarters?" Geoffrey asked.

"They won't thank me for it," Officer Kilaren replied. "Another drunk mistaking rat poison for his whiskey won't interest the detectives at all. Someone will sign off on the report I'll write and that'll be the end of it."

"What about an autopsy?" Prudence asked, more to alert Lydia to what she should expect than because there was any doubt the Bellevue morgue would perform one.

"They're too busy to bother with an open-and-shut case like this one," Kilaren said, putting away his notebook and gesturing to Little Eddie to step away from the wall. "Now what brought ye here, lad? It's not your usual pitch. I'd know if it was."

"I was hitching a ride on the back of a hansom cab," Little Eddie lied. "So, when it stopped, I jumped off. I saw that lady there waving her arms around and calling out that there was trouble, so I stayed to find out what it was. Curious, like."

"Get away with ye then." Kilaren cuffed him lightly on the side of the head. Like many of the beat cops, he often went out of his way to say a kind word or slip a coin to the urchins who lived short, miserable lives on the city's streets and in its alleyways. *There but for the grace of God.* "There's a penny in it if ye flag down the morgue wagon when ye see it coming."

Little Eddie's feet pounded on the stairs. The outside door squeaked open, banged shut.

"I've got hot water for tea on the hob. Could ye do with a cup?" Tessa Carey asked.

"I could that," Kilaren said, looking around the small, dingy space one last time. He touched a forefinger to his helmet and followed the landlady from the room, leaving the door to the landing open.

"He must have sent for the morgue wagon as soon as he saw the crowd of neighbors outside." Geoffrey raised, then lowered the ragged lace curtain over the room's single window. "They're still there. They won't leave until the body's carried away."

"That wasn't much of an investigation," Prudence said quietly.

Lydia seated herself in the wooden chair at the table where Septimus had eaten and presumably worked on the final draft of *Waif of the Highlands*.

Geoffrey shook one of the thin pillows out of its case, stoppering the whiskey and rat poison bottles tightly before loading them into it. "There's more than a few drops of liquid in the bottom of at least one of them," he said, careful not to unintentionally sniff at the contents. "We can take them to someone I know on Blackwell's Island."

Tea mug in hand, Officer Kilaren led two Bellevue attendants into the room, not bothering with introductions or instructions. They knew what to do.

Septimus's body was hoisted onto a canvas sling and covered with a stained white sheet. Kilaren signed the form held out to him without bothering to read it, washing away the smell of death with the last of his milky, sugared tea. He nodded in Lydia's direction, mumbled something about condolences, then followed the Bellevue men out the door.

"We'll come back whenever you're ready." Prudence took one of Lydia's hands in her own, helping her to her feet. "Nothing more needs to be done today."

"My father will have to be told." Lydia straightened the bonnet that had been knocked askew when she knelt over her cousin. "Both our mothers are dead, and there's no one else I know of. Not anyone who was close to him."

"You can send word to the house or the office when you're ready to come back," Prudence offered. "Morning or afternoon, it doesn't matter."

"I'll make sure Mrs. Carey locks the door." Geoffrey didn't need to put into words the thievery that was bound to take place as soon as the other tenants learned that Septimus was dead. "And I'll pay Little Eddie and some of his friends to camp out in front of the door for the night. Flower, too."

"I don't think Septimus had much of value," Lydia said.

*Except perhaps early, handwritten pages of the play he'd regretted surrendering to Barrett Hughes.* But Geoffrey didn't say it aloud. This wasn't the moment for a search.

"Danny will see that you get home." Prudence guided Lydia out to the sidewalk where a curious crowd watched her climb into the hansom cab.

Little Eddie's face lit up as he held out his hand for the coins Geoffrey pulled from his pocket.

Flower's tail wagged with ferocious energy. There was nothing the young dog loved more than trailing along with Little Eddie and his gang. She cocked her head to one side as Danny gave her the instructions no one doubted she understood, then woofed a bark of warning to anyone who might think to follow them inside.

"We can walk up to Broadway and get a hansom there," Geoffrey said as Danny and Mr. Washington vanished down the street.

"Blackwell's Island?" Prudence asked.

"The faster we get Ambrose Deslar to look at these things, the better." Geoffrey had wrapped the pillowcase containing the whiskey and rat poison bottles in a dark sweater he'd found hanging from a peg in Septimus's room.

"Is he a chemist?" Prudence asked.

"Chemist, doctor, dabbler in the dark arts. It's a wonder he's able to keep his license to practice medicine. No hospital in the city will admit him to its wards or operating rooms except

Charity Hospital, and that's only because I suspect he's black-mailing somebody on the hospital board. He works out of a laboratory in the basement, but only the most desperate patients are brought to him. He's a genius, but something of a devil, too. You'll see what I mean."

They took a ferry to Blackwell's Island, the city's East River repository for criminals, workhouse inmates, incurables, and the insane. Nellie Bly had had herself committed to the women's asylum there to expose the unsanitary living conditions, starvation diet, physical abuse, and poor medical treatment to which the female mental patients were subjected. Just the name *Blackwell's Island* caused anyone who heard it to shudder in fear and revulsion.

The main entrance to Charity Hospital was up a double set of stairs that might have graced a European palace, but it was the only architecturally pleasing thing about the five-story building. Originally constructed as a penitentiary hospital, it had been rebuilt by the prison population of the island after a devastating fire some thirty years before.

Standing for a moment on the path they'd walked from the ferry landing, Prudence and Geoffrey took in the imposing structure with its rows of barred windows and only one visible door. Patients confined within its brick walls had no hope of escape.

"We'll go around to the back," Geoffrey said, taking Prudence's arm to steady her as the path grew narrower and more rock-strewn. "That's where deliveries are made, and there's a separate door leading directly into Deslar's basement laboratory."

"He has his own entrance?"

"You'll see why."

A pile of horse droppings had been swept to one side of a small, paved courtyard. The delivery door was secured by an impressive-looking lock, a handbell hanging against the wall.

"Ring the bell and someone slides open a panel in the door to check who you are," Geoffrey said. "No one gets in or out without scrutiny."

"I don't see another entrance," Prudence said. "Didn't you tell me that your doctor friend has private access to his laboratory?"

"Look to the far right," Geoffrey urged. "And down below ground level. It's been constructed so a casual visitor won't notice it. You have to know what you're looking for."

It wasn't until she was a few feet away from the narrow stone stairway leading downward that Prudence realized she'd found it.

"Careful," Geoffrey warned. The stairway was without a railing. If it rained, the steps would be too slippery to navigate.

"He's expecting us. I sent a telegram while we were waiting for the ferry."

The door had been left off the latch and a gas lamp lit in the otherwise dark hallway. Not a sound broke the stillness until a black cat welcomed them with head butts and a thunderous purr.

"His name is Erebus, after a dark god of the Greek underworld," Geoffrey said, allowing the cat to wind around his legs but not reaching down to pet it. "He bites."

"I already like your Dr. Deslar. He has a sense of humor."

"You may change your mind after you've met him."

The man who looked up from his test tubes when Geoffrey knocked on his open laboratory door was hairless and narrow shouldered, but with a belly so broad that the stool on which he sat had a specially built circular back to keep the rolls of fat from spilling over and unbalancing him. He stared at Prudence long enough to allow her to recover from the sight of him, then waved them in. Erebus darted between their legs and leaped up onto the table where foul-smelling liquids bubbled amid a tangle of tubing.

"Let's see what you've brought me." The voice was jarring, like the grating sound of sandpaper or the squawk of a crow. Years of exposure to toxic chemicals had ruined Deslar's throat and vocal cords. He was painful to listen to, difficult to understand.

"Will the lady be more comfortable waiting outside?" The skin above Deslar's eyes where eyebrows should have grown wrinkled upward.

"The lady will remain here, Doctor," Prudence said. She matched his croaking monotone with a flat reply of her own.

"Don't pass out on us." He gestured toward a stack of white cloth masks. "I advise you to put one on before I uncork the bottles you've got wrapped up so nicely there, Geoffrey."

"We're looking for evidence of a deliberate poisoning," Geoffrey said.

"If it's there, I'll find it."

No one in that laboratory doubted the doctor's assertion for a moment.

# CHAPTER 6

"This is rotgut whiskey." Deslar ignored his own advice to don a mask before uncorking the bottles arrayed before him like soldiers on parade. "I presume we're hypothesizing that it's all your victim could afford?"

"He was an actor," Geoffrey said. "But not a famous tragedian. No one you'd ever heard of."

"Living from hand to mouth then. Taking his empty bottles to be refilled from a saloon's cheapest casks whenever he had two coins to rub together. They don't call it rotgut whiskey for nothing, you know. Over time, it can eat through a dedicated drinker's stomach and intestines like they were made of paper. I advise against sampling the stuff, should you ever be so inclined."

"My late father was a whiskey drinker," Prudence said. "I remember sitting on his knee in the study when I was little and smelling the contents of his glass. Whiskey and cigars. They always remind me of him."

"I venture to say your father's drink was imported and very expensive." Deslar upended one of the bottles, waiting patiently for a single drop to roll out onto a glass slide.

"I'm sure it was," Prudence said.

The more she listened to Deslar speak, the easier it became to understand him. His teeth overcrowded his mouth so badly that saliva pooled on his tongue and lips, causing him to swipe exceptionally long, thin fingers across the lower portion of his face. A stained handkerchief protruded from the cuff of his shirt, but she had yet to see him use it. When he stood to reach for another slide, she saw that his arms and legs were also longer and thinner than she had expected. His body looked very much like that of a scarecrow with a thick roll of cotton batting around the stomach area.

"You'll find that many of us who devote our lives to medical research do so because we have a personal problem that requires solving," Deslar said as he felt Prudence's eyes follow his movements. "Some grave and as yet incurable malady afflicting a family member or perhaps a physical or mental defect that has plagued the scientist himself since birth. It's hardly ever idle curiosity, and there's not usually a great fortune to be made in a laboratory."

How to respond to so personal a confession? Prudence remained silent.

"Two of your bottles contain traces of rotgut whiskey, but nothing else." Deslar recorked them and set them aside. "This is Fowler's Solution," Deslar said, examining the smaller bottle. "The red-and-white label, what's left of it, is distinctive. One to five drops for an adult is the usual dose. Advertised for treating everything from skin rashes to blood diseases and syphilis. Your policeman probably believed the victim overdosed."

"I thought it was rat poison," Geoffrey said. "I believe that's what we all assumed from the skull and crossbones warning."

"Arsenic in granular form is the preferred way to kill rats," Deslar agreed. "But people with domestic pets sometimes dissolve the granules in a liquid like Fowler's and paint it on baseboards to kill the rodents without poisoning their cats. The line between arsenic as medicine and arsenic as deadly poison is a thin one, best not tinkered with."

He removed the cork, held the small brown bottle well away from his face, and tipped it upside down until several drops fell onto a glass slide. "Too thick to be unadulterated," Deslar murmured, handing the bottle to Geoffrey as he balanced the slide in one hand and with the other deposited another piece of glass atop the first. The dark liquid spread to the edges of the slides but no farther. "I've done this many times over," he said, catching a worried frown on Prudence's forehead. "I rarely drop or spill anything that's too dangerous, but that's what Erebus is for. Aren't you?" he asked the cat whose tail twitched across the tabletop in agreement. "He's immune to just about everything by now, as long as the dose isn't too high."

"What did you mean by 'too thick to be unadulterated'?" Prudence asked.

"I doubt a poor actor could afford to feed a cat in addition to himself," Deslar said. "He'd have no reason to add arsenic granules to his Fowler's to get rid of rats without poisoning a pet because he didn't have one. Your dead man bought this bottle of so-called tonic to treat himself. In addition to a list of maladies as long as your arm, including heart problems, Fowler's is also recommended for an embarrassing and unfortunately fatal condition contracted in a manner I prefer not to describe." It was as close to being explicit as Deslar could come in the presence of a lady. "Let's see what we find in that last bottle of rotgut."

He laid aside the slide, casting a quick glance at Geoffrey's fingers. "You've handled the bottle of Fowler's, so you'll need to wash your hands if you've gotten any of it on you," he warned.

"I didn't," Geoffrey said. But he put his clean white handkerchief next to the bottle in case he was asked to pick it up again.

"Now this is interesting." Deslar bent over the microscope

beneath whose lens he'd positioned a slide smeared with liquid from the bottle that held more than a few drops of whiskey. At least two good swallows had remained. "Some of the crystals haven't dissolved fully."

He stepped aside to allow Geoffrey to peer through the eye-piece, then grunted in surprise when the ex-Pinkerton gestured to Prudence to take his place.

"Arsenic is a mineral," Deslar reminded them. "That's why the crystals look the way they do."

"So, someone thickened the Fowler's Solution with the granules used for rat poison," Geoffrey said. "Then poured the result into one of Septimus's whiskey bottles."

"Easy to accomplish, guaranteed to kill, and likely to be un-detected. Men die of alcohol poisoning all the time, especially in the tenements."

"Murder?" Geoffrey asked. "As we suspected."

"Or suicide. Though by now you'd think people would real-ize that it's not an easy way to go."

"There's a novel by a Frenchman that gives a graphic de-scription of death by ingesting arsenic," Prudence commented. "*Madame Bovary* by Gustave Flaubert."

"And for anyone who doesn't read novels, the newspaper accounts and penny dreadfuls should be warning enough," Deslar said.

"Is it at all possible that this was accidental?" Geoffrey asked.

"Were the police at the scene?" Deslar wiped his fingers across Erebus's thick black fur.

"The report is probably already filed. Death by misadven-ture. Meaning that the deceased knew drinking rotgut was dan-gerous but chose to do so without regard for his own safety. It wraps things up very nicely. Case solved. No complications."

"Accidental only if your victim drank from the Fowler's bottle by mistake," Deslar said. "He didn't. He ingested the ar-senic that killed him when he upended a bottle of whiskey he had no reason to believe had been tampered with. Whoever did the meddling counted on the whiskey bottle being emptied before the body was found."

"But it wasn't," Prudence said.

"Your victim's last swallow didn't drain the final few mouthfuls. He dropped the bottle, but it rolled instead of tipping over."

"Someone had to have bought the whiskey for him. Added the arsenic before arriving at Septimus's boardinghouse, and maybe even purchased a bottle of Fowler's to leave at the scene," Prudence continued, picturing in her mind what she was describing.

"Is the autopsy being done at Bellevue?" Deslar asked.

"The policeman on the scene doubted there'd be a postmortem," Geoffrey said.

"Have the victim brought here," Deslar ordered. "I'll do it. Is there a next of kin to claim the body?"

"Lydia," Prudence said. "His cousin."

"The sooner you can get her to Bellevue, the better," Deslar directed.

"What does that mean?"

"Only that cadavers sometimes go missing, especially if the police aren't particularly interested in them and it doesn't look as though there's family to pay for a funeral."

"Body snatchers? I thought that was a thing of the past," Prudence exclaimed. Bodies of vagrants and criminals had been made available for medical dissection by a law passed almost forty years before. Intended to put an end to grave robbing, it had made cemeteries safer but not entirely secure places.

Deslar shrugged.

"You can buy a corpse from Bellevue if you know the right attendant," Geoffrey said.

"That's dreadful."

"Medical schools have a hard time keeping themselves supplied with legitimately obtained bodies. I understand they pay generously for fresh specimens. The more recent, the better."

"Is that what you meant by cadavers going missing, Dr. Deslar?" Prudence asked.

"I'll let you draw your own conclusions, Miss MacKenzie. But I'd advise your victim's cousin to identify and request his remains as soon as possible. Before nightfall would be my recommendation. The type of pickup and delivery we're talking about is best made under cover of darkness."

In the end, Danny Dennis had seen to the retrieval and removal of Septimus Ward's body from the Bellevue morgue.

Being a more than usually handsome corpse, it had been placed with other bodies in the glass-enclosed viewing window before which members of the public gathered to gawk, gossip about, and identify the dead. Naked beneath a thin towel covering only his private members—for decency's sake—the deceased actor had swiftly attracted an admiring crowd. Neck cushioned on a wooden block, the clothes he was wearing at the time of death hanging from a hook fastened to the wall behind him, Septimus looked for all the world like the personification of one of the grimmer illustrations in a book of European folk tales. A handsome prince fallen victim to an evil witch, perhaps.

There was a moan of disappointment from spectators when a sheet was spread over the dead man's body, his clothing taken down from its hook and draped over the sling in which he lay, and the remains carried from the viewing room. Seasoned observers knew the table wouldn't remain empty for long. Bellevue always had a surfeit of corpses to display.

With a street urchin sitting on either side of the body to keep it upright, and the canvas curtain lowered across the open passenger seat of the hansom cab, Danny drove through the city's busy streets to the dock where the ferries that crossed to and from Blackwell's Island were moored. He paid the captain of a small barge to convey him, his curtained cab, and enormous white horse across the East River to the cluster of forbidding, escape-proof buildings that housed some of New York's most wretched and hopeless inhabitants. The captain pocketed the substantial sum Danny handed him and asked no questions.

The autopsy was swiftly and professionally executed. Dead bodies were Dr. Deslar's gateway to the medical discoveries for which he had sacrificed a promising career to isolate himself in a damp hospital basement with only a black cat for daily company. So far, the revelation of what he hypothesized to be the single underlying cause of all human disease had eluded him. Like the philosopher's stone of the Middle Ages, it remained the object of a consuming quest. He never for a moment doubted its existence.

"There you are," he said, removing, weighing, and depositing Septimus's digestive organs in formaldehyde-filled glass jars. "I won't need all this tissue, of course, but I'll do the fine cutting later. For the moment, what you need to see are the effects of the arsenic he ingested. There's no doubt that's what killed him."

It wasn't the first time Geoffrey had witnessed the cutting open of a human body, but he'd never gotten used to the ease with which anatomists slid their scalpels through layers of skin, fat, and muscle to uncover the slippery biological structures they removed for examination. He'd heard of medical students vomiting into buckets kept beneath the tables on which their assigned cadavers lay, and he'd seen hardened police detectives turn pale and divert their eyes during the procedure. He hadn't known Septimus Ward in life; that made the evisceration marginally easier to bear.

He wouldn't describe in detail what he had witnessed to Prudence and Lydia. Nor would he dwell on the pungent scent of formaldehyde that seemed to penetrate his clothing and lodge in the pores of his skin. He would tell them enough to verify that Dr. Deslar agreed with their conclusion that Septimus had died from the effects of having ingested arsenic in both granular and liquid forms. Nothing more.

"I suppose it's possible that your actor committed suicide," Deslar mused, dipping his hands into the weak solution of carbolic acid that Joseph Lister had pioneered to reduce mortality in hospital wards. "Unless you have a witness or a confession, you can't prove who poured the poison into the whiskey bottle. Did you know that some suicides prepare their chosen potions days or even weeks in advance and pretend even to themselves that ingesting them is somehow an accident? Has to do with Christian teachings on the taking of one's life, I suppose. Even during the act, one seeks to deceive oneself. Pitiful, really."

Septimus's stitched and meticulously washed body lay white and empty on Deslar's operating table, the clothing in which it had been re-dressed before leaving Bellevue folded at its feet. Preparing a corpse for burial was women's work, but Deslar's presence on Blackwell's Island did not include access to Charity Hospital's staff. He swept and mopped his own floor, trimmed his own lamp wicks, laundered but didn't bother ironing his own shirts and undergarments.

With Deslar's help, Geoffrey slipped Septimus's stained shirt and trousers over flaccid limbs and flesh that felt heavier in death than in life. Danny's hansom cab would transport its burden—and the two street Arabs propping it up—to a funeral home whose owner, like the barge captain, asked no questions. There would be a viewing and a short service, followed by interment at Green-Wood Cemetery in Brooklyn.

Geoffrey folded and stowed in his jacket pocket the official New York City Health Department form that Deslar had filled out and signed but would not file. "I didn't ask how your own work is progressing," he said as Danny and his small helpers removed Septimus's body on a folding canvas stretcher.

Deslar flung out one long, skinny arm, taking in the clutter of books, papers, unwashed glassware, and saucers of desiccated cat food littering the floors and counters of his laboratory. "There was a surgeon named Criley who claimed to be on the verge of some great medical discovery based on operations and dissections he'd performed during the war. He refused to be precise about what his procedures entailed, which made it difficult to discern exactly what direction his research had taken, but I've read everything by and about him I could get my hands on. For a very brief while, I thought he might have been on to something, but he wasn't."

"He's dead?"

"Drank too much of one of his own concoctions, or so the story goes. His assistant destroyed anything that might have been valuable except what he could sell."

"Hair loss remedies are advertised in all the newspapers." It was no secret to Geoffrey that Ambrose Deslar's passion for scientific investigation was driven by his own peculiar maladies.

"They're mostly geared toward what happens naturally to a man as he ages," Deslar said. "The only surefire cure for that is a hairpiece. Nobody understands why some people lose hair in patchy clumps and there aren't many documented cases of the type of alopecia I suffer from. Not a hair anywhere on my body. Apparently, I was born this way, which is why my parents boarded me out to a farmer and his wife before I was old enough to walk. If they'd needed money, I've no doubt they would have sold me to P.T. Barnum."

"The *Times* gave a good account of his funeral," Geoffrey said.

"Saturday's paper. I read it. There'll never be another like him. Who else would have had the gumption to make a fortune from exploitation of freaks of nature? People flocked in the thousands to his shows and museum. I can't imagine what it must feel like to have to make your living by being stared at all day. I had my share of that a long time ago." Deslar nodded at the chaos of his underground laboratory. "I'm comfortable here. Safe. And who knows, Geoffrey? I might even discover why I can't grow hair and have to waddle through life with fifty extra pounds of fatty flesh encircling my belly like a blanket roll."

Erebus insinuated himself under Deslar's outstretched right hand, arching his back and purring as the doctor stroked him.

It was difficult to tell who was comforting whom.

# CHAPTER 7

"We have our own ways of doing things," Barrett Hughes informed Lydia, leading her across the stage where only the dim ghost light pushed back the darkness. "I'm surprised you don't remember that, given your mother was a Fancham."

"She died when I was a child. I don't have any real memories of her, just images created by what my father has told me."

"We were on the same bill together, the Fabulous Fanchams and I," Hughes reminisced. "Just once, a very long time ago. It was a tour of the mining camps. I was declaiming Shakespeare soliloquies, and they were doing acrobatics, swallowing fire, and cavorting around the stage in the skimpiest costumes the women could get away with. I don't have to tell you which act the miners preferred." He smiled the broad, genial grin that entranced audiences when he wasn't performing the villainous role that had made him famous.

"There's to be a viewing tomorrow and the opportunity for people to say a few words. Then a burial procession to Green-Wood Cemetery." Prudence had impressed on Lydia the necessity of getting as many cast members of *Waif of the Highlands* to attend the funeral service as possible. It was apparently a truism in the detecting business that guilty parties often or always showed up at the obsequies of their victims.

"I'm expecting the company to arrive at any minute," Hughes said. "You're welcome to stay and join us. As a Fancham."

The stage door creaked open, letting in fresh air and a steady stream of actors and behind-the-scenes members of the troupe. One by one they joined their director onstage as the gas footlights were lit and three rehearsal musicians tuned their instruments in the pit. Hats, coats, and gloves lay piled on set pieces. The head of the costume department passed among the players, handing each of them a small piece of their character's ensemble—a scarf, jacket, shawl, or item of jewelry.

And then Lydia remembered what Septimus had told her when they'd first talked about the family's profession. He'd been newly arrived in New York City, paying a duty call on his uncle by marriage. "Theatre folk are the most superstitious people in the world," he'd said over a piece of Lydia's excellent lemon cake. "Every time someone in the company died during a show, we had to appease his or her jealous spirit or face certain failure. It's like keeping the ghost light lit onstage because every theatre in the world is haunted. The rituals don't make sense to other people, but players are careful never to forget to perform them."

"I'll stay," Lydia said to Hughes, recalling some of what Septimus had described. She wasn't religious, but there had been times in her life when ritual had brought unexpected solace and comfort. There didn't seem to be any harm taking part in what Septimus would have wanted her to share. Lydia wasn't on the boards herself, but generations of Fancham talent ran in her blood. It was, she thought, what had made it so easy for her to don the disguises that allowed her to move unremarked between her father and the clients who demanded anonymity.

The custom was surprisingly simple and quickly completed. Cast and crew gathered in a wide circle around the ghost light, joined hands, and for a very few moments murmured private messages to the departed Septimus. It was like the buzz of a swarm of bees returning to its hive. The head of the costume department retrieved the bits and pieces she'd handed out, folding them carefully into a large wicker basket. Chatter rose from whispers to full-throated conversations. Actors cleared their throats and stretched their limbs, stagehands arranged furniture and positioned props, Barrett Hughes descended the side steps from stage to auditorium, standing in the middle of the third row of seats.

"Places, everyone," the stage manager called. "From the top. Act one, scene one."

And the rehearsal began.

"Barrett Hughes has offered me the position of dresser," Lydia reported when she met with Prudence and Geoffrey at their office later that afternoon, recounting in detail how the company had gathered around the ghost light and murmured individual invocations to their departed comrade. "Apparently the young woman who saw to Flora Campbell didn't show up at the theatre today. Didn't send any explanation, either. That's a cardinal sin in Hughes's rulebook, so she's out even if she does eventually make an appearance. I overheard him yelling at the wardrobe mistress. They're behind schedule already; being one person down throws everything into chaos."

"How did he happen to offer you the job? You don't have any experience in backstage work, do you?" With Lydia, Prudence knew it was always best not to assume anything.

"I'm a Fancham. That seems to be recommendation enough."

"But Septimus was a Fancham, and he and Hughes were at each other's throats, if what we were told and what we heard is to be believed," Prudence protested. This unexpected development wasn't logical and didn't make sense. "What does a dresser do anyway?"

"Dressers work for the wardrobe mistress, and they're usually assigned to specific cast members," Lydia said. "They make sure the right costumes are ready for each scene, help the actors and actresses get in and out of them, then clean and repair whatever is worn. A famous star will usually hire her own dresser, but *Highlands* isn't that big a production and Flora Campbell is still an unknown. I got the impression I'll work more as a seamstress than anything else."

"Did you take the job?"

"I told him I'd let him know when he came to Septimus's viewing," Lydia said.

"Very clever."

Lydia shrugged. "I can't get the sight of Septimus lying on the floor out of my mind. If Geoffrey's doctor friend is right, there's no doubt his death was murder. Premeditated. Arsenic is a terrible way to die."

"It is," Prudence agreed. She knew what Lydia would ask next.

"So does that mean you'll look into it for me?"

"There's never been any doubt about that," Geoffrey said gently. He gestured to Josiah to put down his stenographer's pad and pencil and refill Lydia's empty teacup. The cryptographer's daughter looked drawn and tired to the bone. Probably hadn't slept last night, certainly hadn't bothered to eat. His Southern reticence wouldn't allow him to claim Lydia as family, but he hoped she understood that she was as close to kin as it was possible to be without sharing a bloodline.

"Lydia, does a dresser ever get to suggest that a job might be too much for one person alone?" Prudence asked.

"Not usually. Dressers are low on the backstage hierarchy."

"But you said the costume department is behind schedule."

"That's what I heard Hughes complain about, but I don't know any of the details. My guess would be that he's underpaying as many people as he can for as long as he's able to get away with it. The dresser—or seamstress if that's what she really was—who didn't show up today isn't the first one to walk away from the production. Are you volunteering to fill in the gap?"

"He doesn't know who I am, does he?"

Lydia thought for a moment. "I introduced you to Septimus as a lawyer and inquiry agent, but he wouldn't have said anything to Hughes. Bobby the doorman would recognize you as having come to last Saturday's rehearsal with me, but he doesn't know your name. Can you sew, Prudence?"

"I can embroider."

"That's not sewing."

"It means I can thread a needle and I know what to do with it. My maid, Colleen, can teach me how to do a seam. How hard can it be?"

"You'll need to be able to iron."

"Colleen can take me down to the laundry room in the basement and show me what to do."

"I assume from this conversation that the two of you have decided it was one of the company who put the arsenic in Septimus's whiskey," Geoffrey said. He'd become accustomed to Prudence's runaway flights of fancy, but this one seemed especially ill-considered. "And that you're planning to disguise yourselves as dresser and seamstress in order to find the guilty party."

"Motive, means, and opportunity," Prudence said, leaning over Josiah's pad to watch him sketch and label a triangle in the center of which he wrote the word *crime*. "And if I recall some of the stories you've told about your Pinkerton years, pretending to be someone you're not is a time-honored part of detecting."

"Have you narrowed down your lists of suspects?" Geoffrey asked, choosing to ignore what he couldn't deny.

"Barrett Hughes," Lydia said. "He was cheating Septimus out of the recognition that should have rightfully been his."

"If Hughes didn't do it himself, he could have hired someone to commit the murder for him," Prudence added.

"He has to have financial backers," Lydia continued. "Mounting a play is an expensive proposition. Making a mistake about what will be popular with the public can lead to bankruptcy."

"As can scandal and a lawsuit about authorship of the play in question. Attorneys don't come cheap," Prudence said. She'd yet to plead her first case, and now that Septimus was dead, she'd lost a potential client. That didn't mean she'd given up on the career she'd dreamed of since she was old enough to understand what a lawyer did.

"So, Barrett Hughes and any of his financial backers. Who else?" Geoffrey asked.

Lydia shrugged. "I don't know. That's why Prudence and I have to become part of the company."

"We'll start digging into Septimus's life before he agreed to give Hughes credit for *Highlands*," Geoffrey said. "Did he owe money? Had he had affairs? Were there bad feelings, grudges, or vendettas hanging over his head? It's just possible that his death had nothing to do with the play he was rehearsing. Everyone has a past. Sometimes that past has a way of destroying a person's present."

Prudence and Lydia exchanged glances. Trust Geoffrey to toss complications into what looked like an open-and-shut case of jealousy and greed.

"Actors feed on gossip," Lydia ventured. "They thrive on spreading stories about one another. The more exaggerated and licentious, the better."

"Pass on to me what you learn," Geoffrey said. "I can send Amos Lang to run down the truth behind the fictions."

"Amos Lang is an ex-Pinkerton whose special skill is the ability to slip in and out of anywhere without being noticed. No one ever remembers having seen him," Josiah explained to Lydia.

"The Ferret," Lydia said. "My father and I have worked with Pinks and ex-Pinks. Even professionals who know him can't tell you what Amos looks like or where to find him, but they all know *of* him."

"We have to get through the viewing first," Prudence reminded them. "It's probably best if neither Geoffrey nor I attend."

"I've spoken to my father. He was fond of Septimus, so he's more than willing to listen for us, and Clyde Allen will be his eyes."

"I'm sorry you have to do this on your own," Geoffrey said. He knew Lydia was as strong and capable a woman as he'd ever met, but the Southern gentleman whose roots he could not entirely shake didn't like the idea of putting so heavy a burden on feminine shoulders.

"I'll be all right, but thank you for being concerned."

"What time does the viewing begin?" Prudence asked.

"It's scheduled for early in the afternoon, from one to two, followed by the trip to the cemetery. I've ordered a single carriage to hold the three of us and told the funeral director not to expect more than a handful of people at the viewing and only immediate family at the burial."

"It might be interesting to see Hughes's reaction if a woman in black shows up," Prudence said. She tapped a forefinger against her lips, a sure sign that she'd thought up something Geoffrey would attempt to veto.

"No," he said.

"Why not? You were the one who said we had to investigate Septimus's background and everyone he might have known. Suppose we introduce a mysterious woman in full mourning, thick veil hiding her face, lace gloves on her hands, draped so heavily in crape that no one will be able to tell whether she's fat or thin, old or young. She doesn't say anything to anyone, just stands for a few moments beside the open coffin, then leaves. We can station Danny Dennis outside—though not driving Mr. Washington—to whisk her away. And two or three of his street Arabs can hang around the entrance to the funeral home to spot anyone who might try to follow the hansom cab. What do you think?"

"I think you don't have enough to do to occupy your time," Geoffrey said.

"Brilliant!" Lydia exclaimed. "Absolutely brilliant."

"It's settled then," Prudence said. "I'll tell Colleen to get my mourning clothes out of mothballs."

# CHAPTER 8

"I've got all morning," Prudence told her maid, donning one of the aprons that covered female staff from bodice to hem. "Don't look at me like that, Colleen. I haven't come completely unhinged. It's just another role to play. I have to be able to sew and iron reasonably well or I'll never get away with it." She unearthed the basket of embroidery hoops and silks from the back of the armoire where she'd stowed it when the last of her governesses gave up on Prudence's ever mastering the ladylike art of fine needlework. "I don't know where the thimble has gotten to, so I'll borrow yours or do without."

"This may take longer than one morning, Miss Prudence." Colleen had spent dozens of hours of instruction at her mother's side before being deemed ready to enter service. Her thirteen-year-old fingers had bled from needle pricks and her shoulders had ached from wielding the heavy flatirons that had to be repeatedly warmed on hot cast-iron stoves. It had taken years to work her way out of the basement laundry and kitchen to parlor maid, upstairs maid, and finally—lady's maid. She didn't say it aloud, but she thought Miss Prudence was sadly mistaken if she believed she could learn in a single morning skills it had taken so long for Colleen to acquire.

"I assume I'll be repairing rips and tears before the wardrobe mistress trusts me with more important work. The wardrobe mistress is what they call the person who's in charge of the costumes the actors wear," Prudence instructed. She'd had Lydia write out a short list of terms and titles with which she'd be expected to be familiar.

"Yes, miss, I know."

"How do you know?"

"Well, I've gone to the theatre many a time on my day off. And I've been backstage at the vaudeville, too."

"How did that happen?" Vaudeville was considered too rowdy and suggestive for supposedly innocent young housemaids, though as soon as she asked the question, Prudence realized how ignorant it sounded.

"They like to hire Irish girls for spots in the chorus," Colleen explained. "We speak English, and the tall ones look good in gaslight. I've a cousin who was on the stage for a while. She's married now, with a baby on the way."

Though not necessarily in that order, Prudence supposed.

"And she took you backstage?"

"She did."

"Please tell me you weren't seeking a job as one of the dancers. I hear they show their legs to well above the knee."

"I wasn't, Miss Prudence. Me mither would have smacked me black and blue if I'd come home a showgirl." Colleen sounded as though she would have been glad to take the job if she could have figured out a way to avoid her mother's slaps.

"That's all to the good then." Not for the first time, Prudence was astounded at what a servant had to reveal about his or her life outside the MacKenzie household. She took a pair of scissors to a piece of cloth, then ripped it nearly in two. "Now show me how to repair this. We'll pretend an actor snagged his costume on a piece of scenery."

"You'll have to stretch out the tear in an embroidery hoop," Colleen instructed. "To hold it tight while you stitch." Fingers itching to take over, she watched her young mistress fumble through step-by-step directions, nearly give up two or three times, then flash a triumphant grin as she finally wrestled the torn material into submission. Her stitches were far from being small and regular, but they held the two sections of the tear together and gradually became more uniform as she continued to work.

"This isn't as difficult as I was afraid it might be," Prudence crowed. "I haven't forgotten everything Mademoiselle tried to teach me after all. Learning how to iron is bound to be easier, so I think we can assume success is right around the corner. You see before you the Hughes Company's newest dresser *par excellence*!"

Colleen decided it was going to be a very long morning.

By the time Prudence left the basement workrooms to dress for her appearance as a mysterious Woman in Black at Septimus Ward's viewing, her fingertips were pockmarked with tiny pinpricks, and she'd managed to char half the linen napkins on which she'd practiced the new skill of ironing. She'd also dropped one of the heavy irons, scorched her own skirt, and reddened the delicate skin on both hands. Colleen had rubbed goose grease into the sore spots, produced a pair of white cotton gloves housemaids used to polish silverware, and carried a tray of tea laced with restorative whiskey up to Prudence's sitting room.

"Not too much," Prudence cautioned as Colleen poured a generous dollop of whiskey into the teapot. "I've got to have my wits about me at the viewing."

"I've heard people talk about a Woman in Black," Colleen

said, "but I don't think I rightly understand what she's supposed to be."

"The Woman in Black may have been a ghost originally, perhaps in a novel or a newspaper account. Maybe a penny dreadful. I'm not sure. In this case, we want to insinuate that she's a love interest from Septimus Ward's past. She supposedly knows things about him that he never revealed to any of the actors he was rehearsing with. So, whoever killed Miss Truitt's cousin should wonder whether the lady—who doesn't speak to anyone or reveal her face—could be a danger to him. Or her. It's more to throw the members of the company into confusion than anything else. Encourage them to talk and speculate."

"A ghost? That's dangerous, Miss Prudence. What if there really is a ghost and it gets angry because you're pretending to be one but you're not?"

"I said the *idea* of a Woman in Black might have come from a ghost story, Colleen, not that anyone at Septimus Ward's viewing will believe that's what they're seeing." Prudence put down her teacup and gave her maid a reassuring pat on the arm. "Let's get me dressed now. Danny Dennis is sending a carriage."

"Not himself?"

"He thinks he's too recognizable. It'll be one of the younger drivers who's just taken up the trade and isn't known to too many others yet."

"He'll have your address though, miss."

"Danny vouches for him."

"He's Irish then."

"Just arrived."

"A step ahead of the rozzers, I've no doubt."

It wasn't a word Prudence had heard before, but she knew instinctively that it had to be a derogatory term for British law enforcement. Colleen's overly strong pull on her stays confirmed her guess.

"I'll need to breathe," Prudence said, rocking back and then forward as the whalebones tightened. "I won't be talking, but I would like to be able to get air into my lungs."

"Sorry, miss." Colleen's strong fingers loosened the strings she'd tugged with reflexive ferocity. "Will you wear the Worth gown or the Redfern?"

"I'd prefer the Redfern, but the Worth is more likely to be recognized for what it is. We want to give the impression that there is money and power behind our Woman in Black. She's not exactly a menacing figure but definitely one who intimidates."

Yards of crape descended over Prudence's upstretched arms to drape themselves gracefully to the floor. Colleen used a button hook to fasten the detachable bodice and a specially designed comb to smooth the jet beading. When the wide-brimmed hat, heavy veiling, and black gloves had been donned, Prudence MacKenzie had disappeared. In her place was the Woman in Black, unnamed, unknown, enigmatic, and inscrutable.

"The carriage is here," Colleen announced, peering into the street below.

"Wish me luck," Prudence said.

"Is your derringer loaded, miss?" She handed Prudence a small black reticule heavy with beading and more than a handkerchief.

"Over and under. Two shots."

"Then that's all the luck you'll need." But Colleen made a quick sign of the cross—just in case.

Bailey's Funeral Home and Mortuary was far from being one of the hushed, elegant establishments patronized by society families. It was a narrow, converted storefront squeezed between a tailor's shop and a general store with sparsely stocked shelves. A double-hung metal door in the sidewalk indicated where deliveries were made. Prudence kept her eyes averted as she climbed out of the closed carriage Danny Dennis had supplied.

"I'll go around the block a few times, miss," her driver said, his speech heavy with the brogue that made ordinary words sound like song lyrics. "Twenty minutes is Danny's orders, not a second more."

"That should be enough," Prudence said.

"Don't step outside unless you see me," the driver warned. "It's not a safe block for a lady on her own."

Prudence smiled behind her all-concealing veil. She was sure Danny had charged the young Irishman with seeing that no harm came to his passenger, but she was also certain that she could ward off any menace with a sharp word or the sight of her derringer. After all, she'd navigated the streets of Five Points, and there were no more dangerous sidewalks anywhere in the city.

The windowless parlor in which Septimus lay took up most of the storefront, leaving only a small office space and an even smaller withdrawing room where ladies could retreat into a modicum of privacy. Prudence spotted Lydia standing beside the coffin to greet mourners, Benjamin Truitt next to her, his blind eyes concealed by smoked glasses. A shadowy figure behind him had to be Clyde Allen, one hand resting lightly on the Bowie knife whose broad blade was reputed to measure nearly ten inches long. Branched candelabra had been lit at the foot and at the head of the coffin, though there were only two floral displays, one certainly from the family, the other presumably from Barrett Hughes and his company of actors. Lydia whispered something to her father, who nodded, but did not turn his head in Prudence's direction.

But others did. Barrett Hughes was the first to notice the Woman in Black standing motionless in the doorway. Scandalously unaccompanied. One by one the other dozen or so members of the theatrical troupe of which Septimus had been a member became aware that their director had shifted his attention away from their dead colleague. Heads nearly touched as they whispered questions, wondered about the woman's identity, gave birth to speculations as outlandish as anything they'd read in a script.

Prudence gave them just enough time to begin to stir before taking her first step in the direction of the open coffin where Septimus's body rested atop cushioned white satin. She looked neither to the left nor to the right as she moved into the narrow room, the only sound the rustle of her skirt against the strip of carpet that ran down the aisle separating two banks of wooden chairs. Colleen had assured her that nothing of her face could be seen behind the thick veiling, but she kept her features rigidly tight just in case. The Woman in Black, wherever she was reputed to show up, never displayed any emotion, never allowed a sob or an exhalation of sorrow to escape her.

She could feel Lydia's eyes on her as she approached the bier. Prudence thought she detected Clyde Allen's savvy gaze as well, but only for a moment. He'd moved closer to Benjamin Truitt, and a glint from the Bowie knife told her it was halfway out of its sheath. She forced herself to ignore the menace of Clyde's weapon, concentrating instead on the expressions she could read on the faces of the men and women staring at her.

Prudence assumed that the usual daily rehearsal had been called for that morning. From what she'd observed, it was a demanding business, made all the more exhausting by Barrett Hughes's insistence on perfection. He'd obviously canceled the afternoon practice, but since only about half the company was at the funeral home, attendance hadn't been mandatory. Which meant that each of the actors who'd come to the viewing had to have a personal reason for making the effort.

The heavyset actress with the head of springy gray curls played the heroine's mother, but in that role her hair had been unpinned to hang lankly on either side of her face and she'd moved with the hunched posture of an overworked scrubwoman. Prudence saw tears glittering in her eyes, spied a handkerchief clutched in one hand, and understood that for whatever reason, she'd nurtured a tender warmth for Septimus. According to the cast list Lydia had provided, her name was Gertrude Marrow. Like so many of her fellow actors, she'd been born into a theatre family, toddling onstage in her first role at barely three years of age. Prudence marked her down as an excellent source of information, and hoped she was one of those easygoing performers who loved a good gossip, especially when constrained to stand still while a seamstress from wardrobe pinned the hem of her costume.

Four or five young men who played minor roles as the heroine's brothers and the rich man's servants clustered together in the first row of seats. They'd filed by the coffin, cast quick, nervous glances at the corpse, then retreated from the reality of death. They weren't that much younger than the dead man and they all liked their whiskey. *It could have been me* hung in the air above their heads.

The handsome actor who was Septimus's understudy was conspicuous by his absence. The kindest interpretation for his nonattendance was that he was stunned by his good fortune and making the most of the free afternoon to bring a new interpretation to the lines he would be speaking on opening night. The role would have made a star of the deceased former vaudevillian. It could do the same for Morgan Sandling. Prudence mentally moved him up the list of suspects. *Cui bono?* Who profits? Lydia hadn't known much about him other than his name and that he'd appeared in one other play directed by Barrett Hughes, in so minor a role as to be unnoticeable.

Two teary young actresses who played the heroine's sisters sat together near the head of the coffin where they could see Septimus's face on the cushion that raised his upper torso for better viewing. Whoever had done the preparation of the body had had the sense to leave the skin lightly powdered, the lips closed but not stretched in a rubbery smile, and the hair combed casually and not stiffened with an overapplication of

Macassar oil. From time to time one of the actresses stretched out a hand, clutched futilely at empty air, and voiced a well-practiced sob.

One other important member of the cast was missing. Flora Campbell, who had been on tour with Septimus, had been the inspiration for the play he'd written, had stolen his heart and jeopardized his career. He'd given up everything for Flora except the role he would play as the lover her character abandoned. It would have earned him good reviews and an assured place in the ranks of young leading men, but he'd stripped himself of something far more rewarding—recognition as author of *Waif of the Highlands*. Lydia had told her that there was a belief among theatre people that almost any decent-looking fellow could be taught to say lines and manage a sword fight, but the creation of those lines and the imagination it took to craft a story was a much rarer gift. Who remembered the names of the actors who originated the roles Shakespeare wrote for them?

Yet Flora wasn't there.

As she paused at the coffin, laid a red rose atop Septimus's crossed hands, and then turned to walk with queenly dignity out of the viewing parlor, Prudence had to wonder whether the part she'd just played had done what it was intended to do.

Or not.

# CHAPTER 9

"Miss Prudence made an impressive entrance," Amos Lang said, shifting a plug of tobacco from the left to the right side of his jaw. He held an empty tin can in one hand, ready to receive the pungent expectorate already moist with saliva.

Geoffrey Hunter did not supply visitors to his Wall Street office with a spittoon.

"Who wasn't there?" Geoffrey asked, uncapping the Paul E. Wirt fountain pen he'd been unable to resist buying after reading Mark Twain's endorsement of it in *Harper's Magazine*. The pen was decorated with mother-of-pearl and abalone inlays, instantly recognizable to any connoisseur of the burgeoning market for expensive writing instruments. Geoffrey had very few compulsions, but one of them—infrequently indulged—was for intrinsically beautiful objects that also had a utilitarian function. Like the pen he now twirled between his fingers.

"That's interesting," Amos said, setting his can on the floor and pulling a small notebook from his jacket pocket. He'd lately taken to recording notes and impressions, something he'd never done before, not even during his Pinkerton years. He thought the laudanum he dosed himself with every night might have begun to dull the prodigious memory he'd enjoyed all his life, but it was too late to change his ways. Sleep wouldn't come without the contents of the ubiquitous brown bottles he and countless others depended on to get them through long, memory-haunted nights. "Flora Campbell didn't show up, and neither did Morgan Sandling. Septimus Ward's understudy," he explained for Josiah Gregory's benefit.

The secretary nodded, adding Sandling's name to the growing list of suspects.

"What about Barrett Hughes?" Geoffrey asked.

"Our chief suspect, you mean?" Amos paged through the notebook. "He was as much in charge of his company at the viewing as I imagine he is in the theatre and at rehearsals. A very commanding personality. Dignified, but I'd judge him capable of flying into a rage if he thinks he's being crossed."

"That's what Prudence and Lydia observed when Septimus confronted him about acknowledging authorship of *Highlands*," Geoffrey commented.

"He's like a pot simmering on the stove. Turn your back and it's capable of boiling over." Amos paused, gaze fastened on the pen sliding through Geoffrey's fingers. "Though I suppose you'd have to turn up the heat."

"Which Septimus did."

"I noticed that eyes followed Hughes whenever he moved around the viewing parlor. As if trying to anticipate what he would do next, what he might demand someone else do or say. No one is entirely at ease around him."

"The director as god," Josiah murmured, his pencil racing through the shorthand whorls and curved lines only he understood.

"As far as I could tell, that's an accurate description of how things operate in the theatre world. Disagree or fight your director's instructions and you're likely to find yourself out on the street. With a reputation for being difficult to get along with. I don't have detailed profiles of all the *Highlands* cast yet, so take everything I'm saying today with a grain of salt."

"Your early conclusions are usually borne out by fact," Geoffrey said.

Amos nodded. He was seldom wrong about someone, even at first meeting or initial observation. It was a kind of natural gift, this ability to see through a man's skin to what lay beneath, a talent Amos had honed through years of practice. "I'll need to find out exactly where Hughes was and what he was doing for at least the past week or so. The same for everyone in the company who might have had a reason to want Septimus Ward out of the picture."

"Morgan Sandling," Geoffrey said. "What can you tell us about him?"

"Precious little, at this point." Amos ran a finger down a notebook page. "Handsome, on the stage since he was old enough to walk and talk. Always in minor roles with only a few lines. At least one other play with Barrett Hughes. Never married and doesn't seem to have had affairs with any of the female cast members. Apparently got along well with our victim, stepped in every now and then during rehearsals to work on a scene. A few years younger than Septimus. That's about it for now."

"Flora Campbell?" Geoffrey asked.

"I overheard one of the younger actresses say that Flora had sent a note claiming to be prostrate with grief." Amos read from his notebook. "There's more to her relationship with the deceased than meets the eye, but it may take me a while to find someone willing to talk about it. Someone who knows what the connection actually was. I'm assuming for now that they were lovers."

"Prudence and Lydia should be able to confirm or disprove that. Lydia says the costume shop is rife with gossip. That's where she expects them to spend most of their time, at least until opening night." Geoffrey chuckled. "Miss Prudence took sewing and ironing lessons from her maid."

"Colleen?" Josiah asked.

"The very same."

"I know she's a lady's maid now, but Colleen started out in service in the scullery. Or was it the laundry room?"

"I think it best we don't ask too many questions," Geoffrey said.

"Miss Prudence is good at undercover work," Amos declared. "I remember Allan Pinkerton saying that women's talents at deception were often underrated."

"Will you stay in New York or try looking for answers out on the theatre circuit?" Geoffrey asked. He'd had his disagreements with Allan Pinkerton and his famed detective agency and often changed the subject whenever they were mentioned. He especially didn't like the idea of Prudence in a dangerous undercover assignment.

"I'll stay in the city until there's nothing more to discover here." Amos closed and put away his notebook. Picked up and spit into the tin tobacco can.

Josiah shuddered and Geoffrey averted his eyes.

Amos smiled.

The wardrobe room with its irons forever heating on a pot-bellied stove was warmer than anywhere else in the theatre, musty with the smells of costumes worn shiny and thin with sweat and streaks of greasepaint. If clothing from a previous play could be repurposed, it was. Racks of old and new costumes, each one sheathed in an off-white muslin bag, were positioned against each wall. The effect was of walking into the center of a plumped-up cocoon where the only sounds were the whirr of a sewing machine and the murmur of actors talking aloud to themselves and one another as they were being fitted.

"You're new at this, aren't you, dear?" Gertrude Marrow said to Prudence, who was hesitantly attempting to turn a sturdy brown skirt into the ragged dress worn by the character of the heroine's mother. Gertrude stood atop a wooden box nailed together by one of the stagehands out of lumber left over from set building.

Prudence, pins securely anchored in a cushion strapped to her wrist—she didn't dare put them in her mouth the way the costume mistress did—knelt on the floor at the actress's feet, cutting, ripping, and occasionally pinning the material she thought might be a cheap wool.

"I am," she confessed, reassured by Marrow's understanding tone of voice. "But I'll get it right, don't you worry about that."

"So you joined the company with Lydia Truitt, did you? Are you one of poor Septimus's cousins, too?"

"Second or third cousin, I think. I can never get the cousin thing straight."

"No matter. He was a lovely man. I'm going to miss his smile."

"I didn't know him very well. Hardly at all, in fact. His and Lydia's mother were sisters."

"I know the story," Gertrude said. "Pamela ran away from a show the family was playing in to marry that blind Benjamin. He still had his sight then, of course. Her father vowed he'd never speak her name again. The Fanchams weren't known for being forgiving if you crossed them."

"I never heard that." Prudence sat back on her heels to gauge the effect of what she'd been doing. The ragged skirt looked quite convincing.

"Anything you want to find out, you just talk to me, honey. I've been in this business since long before you were born."

It was on the tip of Prudence's tongue to ask how many years that was, but at the last moment she clamped her lips shut and shook out the tattered hemline appropriate to a starving slum dweller. She guessed that Gertrude Marrow had to be in her sixties, maybe seventy. She had the jutting bosom and protuberant belly many older women developed, skin so wrinkled the makeup settled into it like mud in a cracked riverbed, and a head of frizzy gray hair carefully arranged to cover the bald spots.

Despite her obvious age, Gertrude had the good humor and gusto of a much younger person, a zest for living that nothing quelled, and a caring personality that comforted and encouraged the younger members of the cast. More importantly—she knew everything there was to know about every player who had trodden an American stage. She might not be generally known to the theatre-going public, but Gertrude was a legend among her peers, her parlor floor a haven for struggling actors who couldn't scrape together the coins for a bed. All you had to do was mention her name and the stories flooded out.

"Lydia and I have been wondering . . ." Prudence began.

"Wonder no more, honey. You let Gertrude tell you all about it."

"What we were trying to figure out was whether Septimus and Flora were a couple. Offstage as well as on. We didn't either of us want to ask her, and Lydia said he was close-lipped about his personal life. Now that he's passed away . . ."

"I'd say they were very much what you'd call a yoked pair, but I wouldn't let Barrett Hughes hear you asking about the two of them together."

"Why not?"

"Everybody in the business knows that Hughes only hires leading ladies for his company if they're willing to share something more than a stage. If you get my meaning. Sooner or later, she has to give it up or she'll be out on her ear, contract or no contract. He's got ways of getting what he wants."

"So Flora had to . . ."

"Bestow her favors on the gentleman? I couldn't tell you the precise moment it happened, but yes indeed, Flora Campbell paid her dues. Just like everyone else."

"How did Septimus feel about that?"

"Now that's interesting," Gertrude said, taking Prudence's hand to step off the wooden box without stumbling.

"How do you mean?"

"There was something going on between Septimus and Hughes that might or might not have had anything to do with Flora." She paused for a moment, looking at Prudence as though she'd just realized something important. "I didn't see you at the viewing."

"I told her not to bother," Lydia said, breezing into the costume shop with a length of pale yellow velvet over one arm. "She and Septimus hadn't ever exchanged more than a few words, despite being cousins of some sort. You know how that is."

"What did you make of the Woman in Black?" It seemed to be Gertrude's turn to ask questions.

Lydia smoothed out the velvet on the cutting board. "I've heard that actors will go to any lengths to find a role to play."

"You're saying it might have been one of us? Some kind of macabre stunt?"

Lydia shrugged. "I happened to be looking at Mr. Hughes when she came in. Stood in the doorway, rather. I'd swear he blenched. Just for a moment, of course, but not something you'd mistake."

"He doesn't like practical jokes. Especially if he's the butt of them." Gertrude walked along the racks of costumes, occasionally pulling up a muslin cover. She gave a snort of satisfaction when a set of coal-black bombazine dresses appeared. "I didn't think the mourning costumes had been sold off. They're too expensive. And someone is always dying in a melodrama." She pulled out one of the gowns. "This might be a good fit for you, Prudence, if a crowd scene needs building out. You wouldn't even have to hem it."

*Meet a challenge with a counterchallenge.* It was a dictum Judge MacKenzie had drilled into his daughter. "It looks as though it were made for me," Prudence declared, holding the dress up against her body. "Or someone my size, at any rate."

"It was made for the actress playing Tiny Tim's mother, if I'm not mistaken," Gertrude said. She was never wrong. "In the scene where the ghost of Christmas Yet To Come takes Scrooge to Tiny Tim's funeral. But there's no beading on it. The Woman in Black who showed up at Septimus's viewing was covered in jet." She placed the mourning dress back on the rack, tugging down the muslin bag that protected it from dust and insects.

"What if she was real, not a hoax?" Lydia asked.

"Septimus was in love with Flora." Gertrude linked her two forefingers together and tugged on them. "Everyone knew it except Hughes. He can't conceive of a woman who won't respond to his advances. Arrogant, narcissistic prat!"

"Perhaps it was someone from his past," Lydia insisted. "A woman Septimus might have loved and then thrown over when he met Flora."

"There's only ever been Flora," Gertrude said. "If you'd made your way into the theatre like a true Fancham, you'd know that. Septimus and Flora were barely out of leading strings when they met. Vaudeville has always thrived on children, the smaller and cuter the better. When they aren't dancing or singing, they get thrown all over the stage like bowling pins, and they're always at the top of every acrobatic pyramid. Wondering if they'll fall and crack their skulls open is part of the thrill of the act."

"It doesn't sound like much of a life," Prudence muttered, then busied herself with her pincushion, hoping Gertrude hadn't heard her.

"Septimus was a private kind of person," Lydia said.

"No one in our profession is private," Gertrude snorted. "Can't afford to be if you want to make the papers. Publicity is as good as a rave review. I've been at it all my life and I know what I'm talking about."

"If it's Septimus you're gossiping over, you might as well give it up," the wardrobe mistress said from the open doorway. Cynthia Pierce carried a sheaf of sketches in one hand, a sewing basket in the other. "That looks good, Gertrude. At least from here it does. We'll see what Mr. Hughes has to say. Ready or not, he wants a costume parade tomorrow. What's that yellow velvet doing on the cutting table?"

"It's for Flora's gown when she marries the rich man," Lydia said. "I'm sure that's what you told me we'd be using, Miss Pierce."

"I did," the wardrobe mistress said. "But himself wants Flora all in white now. I told him it would bleach her out, but he's insisting he knows best. White is for angelic innocence, and that's what she personifies."

"She'll look like a skinny candle without a flame," Gertrude Marrow said. "Gaslight doesn't take well to white."

Cynthia Pierce set down her sketches and her sewing basket. She folded the pale yellow velvet and handed it to Prudence. "Here you go. Make yourself useful. You might as well learn where things are stored. This goes in the big trunk at the back of the second prop room." She detached a key from the ring at her belt. "We have to keep it locked or the better pieces would disappear. Do you know where the prop rooms are?"

She didn't, but she'd ask one of the stagehands.

The soft pile of expensive velvet felt like flower petals on her skin as Prudence threaded her way through the backstage jungle of coiled ropes, discarded pieces of scenery, and pails of sand stored there against fire. Backstage was never entirely empty; stagehands and members of the various crews were always moving sure-footedly in the semidarkness. Prudence walked slowly and carefully, keeping an eye out for obstacles both human and otherwise. She didn't dare sweat onto the precious velvet.

The trunk she'd been told to look for stood off by itself in a far corner of the prop room. Bands of dull brass gleamed against dark wood. It would easily take two men to lift and carry it. She dusted off the seat of a wicker chair with her apron, then laid the velvet down, checking to be sure there were no stray bits of wicker that might snarl it. So far so good.

The key she'd been given slid easily into the brass lock, turning without resistance. Too late, she realized she should have brought a lantern with her. Light from the gas lamps in the hallway was barely bright enough to outline the mountains of props in the storage room. She'd had no trouble locating the trunk, but she doubted she'd be able to see inside when she had to arrange the velvet without wrinkling it. Too bad. She'd do the best she could and perhaps come back later with a lantern to make sure all was well. She'd gotten off to a good start with the wardrobe mistress, but a single false step could see her out the door.

Prudence stood to one side, allowing the feeble yellow gaslight from the corridor to wash over the trunk as she raised the lid.

Dark eyes without a spark of life in them stared up at her. Female hands whose broken fingernails had been scraped bloody lay curled on a bosom that didn't move with the breath of life. The skin of the face was paler than milk, the mouth twisted into an agonized grimace. She lay in a nest of fabric of all colors of the rainbow, but she wore the black dress and apron of a working girl. She didn't look old enough to be called a woman.

And she was dead, locked inside the trunk where someone had made sure her cries would not be heard as she beat her hands frantically against the lid and gradually suffocated.

A scream rang out. Footsteps pounded through the backstage area.

When a stagehand burst through the open doorway, all Prudence could do was point.

# CHAPTER 10

This time there was no doubt. It was murder.

"She didn't climb in there and lock herself in." The patrolman, whose beat included the Argosy Theatre, peered into the trunk. "Anybody recognize her?"

"She was one of our dressers," Barrett Hughes told him. "Hazel Nugent. The wardrobe mistress can give you all her details."

"We can save the questioning until the detectives get here." Patrolman O'Rourke patted his jacket pocket for the notebook he'd left beside his plate of sausage and eggs that morning. "Nobody leaves the building." He was new to the job, bought for him by an uncle who realized it was the best position his nephew was likely to get. O'Rourke hadn't completed the training every officer was supposed to undergo, but his uniform fit well, he could twirl the nightstick until it sang, and he knew enough to keep potential witnesses from quitting the scene of a crime. "Who found her?"

"One of the women working in the costume shop came to put away some material." Hughes turned away from the open trunk and the disturbing sight of Hazel Nugent's contorted face.

"The detectives will want to talk to her."

"I'm here, Officer." With Lydia at her side, urging her every few moments to take another sip of the hot sugared tea Gertrude Marrow had brewed in her dressing room, Prudence had refused to return to the costume shop. She'd found the body and she wasn't leaving the prop room until a detective arrived to take charge.

In the meantime, Lydia had slipped a note to Bobby the doorman who passed it on to one of Danny Dennis's street urchins. If the boy ran fast enough or hooked a clandestine ride on the rear of a hansom cab, there was a decent chance Geoffrey Hunter would make it up Broadway before the detective from Mulberry Street Police Headquarters.

"Hazel was a deft hand with a needle," Gertrude said, sketching a quick sign of the cross even though she wasn't Catholic. "She was going to do for me and Flora both after we opened."

"Had you known her before this production?" Prudence asked, keeping her voice down to avoid drawing the patrolman's dubious attention.

"This was her first or second costume job. Cynthia usually likes to hire more experienced seamstresses, but Hazel was too good at what she did to pass up. She could look at you and even without taking a lot of measurements know exactly how to cut a pattern so whatever she was making fit like a glove. She never complained, even when Barrett Hughes yelled his loudest."

"How well did she know Septimus?"

"That's not a question I can answer." Gertrude took the empty teacup from Lydia. "And I don't think it's one you need to be asking. Not while she's lying dead right in front of you."

"Prudence," Lydia whispered as Gertrude turned away. "Doesn't Stephen Phelan work out of Mulberry Street?"

"All the detectives do. It's supposed to make their division more efficient." She whipped around to look at the open prop room door. "If Phelan's assigned to this case, he'll recognize me."

"Faint," Lydia said.

"What?"

"Faint! You don't have to go all the way down, just make a good try at it."

Prudence widened her eyes, took a few staggering steps forward, and flung out one arm as if to grab on to something to break her fall. She felt Lydia cushion her back and someone else hold her upright.

"She needs to lie down, Officer," Lydia said. "There's a fainting couch in the costume shop. We'll take her there."

Before Officer O'Rourke could object, Lydia had guided Prudence into the chaos of backstage and down a narrow hallway. Gertrude Marrow trailed along behind, ready to catch the newest dresser if she tripped. But it also hadn't escaped her notice that the fainting spell came on very quickly and too long after the discovery of Hazel Nugent's body to be directly related. Gertrude's reputation for knowing everything about everybody in the theatre world hadn't been earned without considerable effort to be always in the right place at the right time. Something else had unsettled the girl and Gertrude wanted to know what it was.

Cynthia Pierce spread a blanket over Prudence's legs and chafed her hands, which weren't as cold as she'd expected them to be. "We'll have you right as rain again in no time. You've had a bad shock, finding Hazel the way you did."

"The patrolman said she'd have to be questioned by a detective," Gertrude said. "On account of being the one who opened the trunk."

"She's already told her story once," Lydia protested.

"Officer O'Rourke didn't take notes," Gertrude said. "Did you notice how new his uniform looked? I'll wager he hasn't been on the job for more than a couple of weeks."

"You know I don't allow food or drink in here." The wardrobe mistress took the teacup from Gertrude's hand. "You need to take this back to your dressing room, or I'll put it outside the door."

"It's empty!"

"Makes no difference," Cynthia said. She was shorter than the actress she was confronting, but much broader, one of those women who settled into middle age by spreading out through the middle and adding jowls to her chin line.

"I'll get rid of it," Gertrude said. "It was a gift from an admirer."

"Cost a pretty penny, too, I've no doubt." Actors were notorious for knowing the dollar value of every item given them by admiring fans.

"I'm going back to the prop room," Cynthia said as Gertrude carried away her precious cup. "There's no telling how much damage the police could do to what's stored in that trunk if I'm not there to keep an eye on them." She laid a hand on Prudence's forehead. "You don't feel clammy so you're not likely to pass out again. Lydia can stay with you, just in case. Lock the door behind me if you don't want to be disturbed for a while."

"Where did Hazel keep her things?" Prudence asked, swinging her feet off the fainting couch as soon as she and Lydia were alone.

"You know as much about this place as I do." Lydia studied the racks of costumes, the sewing paraphernalia atop the tables, and the two treadle-powered Singer sewing machines. "Cynthia had us put our umbrellas and reticules in that wicker basket behind the door, so I'm guessing that's where Hazel's things will be also."

"Let's take a look."

"I told you we'd find them here," Lydia said triumphantly, holding aloft a black satin reticule embroidered with a purple pansy and bright green leaves. Hazel's umbrella was worn around the edges and difficult to unfurl, but no New York City lady went out without one in April. "She sewed her initials onto the reticule and the umbrella both. That's a bit odd, isn't it?"

"Not for a working woman who doesn't want her things stolen or claimed by someone else." Prudence rummaged through the remaining contents of the basket. "There's a pair of shoes on the bottom, and a corset."

"Maybe the fainting couch is used for something other than fainting."

"Cynthia doesn't look like the type to allow any carryings-on to happen in her workshop," Prudence said. "I don't see anything else Hazel might have brought with her when she came to work."

Lydia pulled open the reticule's drawstring and upended the bag, spilling its contents onto the cutting table. "Trolley fare, a handkerchief, a small vial of laudanum, a piece of paper with an address written on it, two extra hat pins, and a key. That's it. No, wait a minute. There's another piece of paper but this one's all balled up. It's heavy, Prudence. There's something inside." She peeled away the newsprint and held up a ring. "Looks like eighteen-carat gold, with a cluster of garnets. More than a seamstress could afford on her own. That may be why she wasn't wearing it."

"Stolen?" Prudence slipped the ring onto her finger and held it out for the stones to catch a glimmer from the flickering gaslight. "Look. It won't go over my knuckle, and I've got small hands. That's odd."

"What do you want to do with it?" Lydia asked.

"Are you wearing a pocket under your skirt?"

"I always do," Lydia said.

"Then that's where we'll put everything that was in the reticule, including the ring and the paper with the address on it." Prudence folded the paper into a small square, handing it and the reticule to Lydia. "I'm guessing that if Hazel moved recently, she might have written down the address of her new boardinghouse when she went to see the room."

"Then we need to search it before the police mess everything up," Lydia declared. "The problem is I've sent word to Geoffrey and he's probably already on his way. He'll expect us to be here."

"Can't be helped. Cynthia will tell the police detective that I was taken ill and had to lie down so when they find out that you're gone, too, they'll assume you took me home. Geoffrey will figure out that we were on to something. I only hope the detective who shows up isn't Stephen Phelan. He'll suspect something's fishy as soon as he sees Geoffrey, and when Hughes gives him your name and mine, he'll know we're on a case. Our career as dressers will be over before we've had half a chance to begin."

"Keep your fingers crossed it's not Phelan then. There have to be twenty or thirty detectives at Mulberry Street. I'd say the odds are in our favor."

"In our favor or not, we have to get out of here. Any ideas?"

"Bobby. The doorman. People are coming and going by the stage door in the alley, so if we can make it around to the front of the house and into the lobby, he'll let us out. And he won't give us away if I ask him not to."

"How can you be sure of him?"

"He was a stagehand once upon a time, and he remembers the Fabulous Fanchams. My grandfather did him a favor. Stagehands get injured. A lot. So, when Bobby broke a leg, my grandfather made sure he got a job as a doorman. Septimus told me the story."

"All right, then. Let's go."

They wound their way through the murkiest parts of the backstage area, down into the dimly lit corridor that ran beside the house and into the lobby. Nobody stopped them. Nobody seemed to notice they were passing by. The few members of the

company they saw were clustered together whispering about
what had been found in the prop room, who could have had it
in for Hazel, and what the murder would mean for the life of
the play. Would it open? Would the police shut it down?
Would Hughes pay a bribe to keep the production on track?
Would they get paid? Did anyone know of any casting calls?

"Let me check before you go out," Bobby urged, unlocking
the ornate main door. "What am I looking for?"

"Any sign of a police wagon," Lydia said. "Or a patrolman
who might be keeping an eye on the theatre. On who's coming
or going."

"Got it."

It took only a moment for Bobby to glance right and left.
"Coast is clear," he said, ushering Lydia and Prudence onto the
sidewalk, wishing them good luck as he turned the key in the
lock.

"Do you know where this address is?" Prudence asked.

"It's down this way," Lydia said. "We'll have to hurry. I
hope you've got good walking boots on."

Hazel Nugent's boardinghouse was two blocks east of
Broadway, in the middle of a tree-lined stretch that looked as if
its better days had been relatively recent.

"Now what do we do?" Lydia asked, comparing the numbers beside the front door to the address on the piece of paper
she'd taken from Hazel's reticule. "The landlady isn't going to
let us into her room."

"We have the key," Prudence said. "We look respectable.
And I have these." Two five-dollar gold pieces rested on the
palm of her hand. "Geoffrey says he's never seen them fail."

"The landlady will know she didn't come home last night
and the night before," Lydia said. "So, if we tell her Hazel was
injured at the theatre and had to be taken to a hospital, and that
we've come to fetch some clothes and other things she needs,
we just might be believed."

"Miss Nugent is a lovely young person," the landlady said, leading them up to Hazel's room on the second floor, Prudence's gold coins tucked into her apron pocket along with her conscience. "What did you say happened to her?"

"She had an accident with one of the sewing machines," Lydia said.

"Stitches?"

"I beg your pardon?"

"Did she run her finger under the needle? Did she have to be stitched up?" The landlady choked back a laugh. "Must have been serious if she had to stay in the hospital."

"The machine tipped over. I don't know all the details," Lydia said, taking up a position outside Hazel's room, back to the door, key in one hand, but plainly not about to use it until the landlady went downstairs. "Thank you for your help."

Prudence looked pointedly at the pocket in the landlady's apron.

"I'll put the kettle on in case you want a cup of tea before you go."

They watched her retreat down the stairs.

"I think I hear the clink of thirty pieces of silver," Prudence said.

"You'll have to tell Geoffrey he was right. Money works when nothing else will." Lydia slid the key into the lock and stepped inside Hazel's room, Prudence close behind her. "Best not to take chances," she said, locking the door from the inside. "We don't want the landlady interrupting us."

The room was small. *Cozy* would be the advertised description. A narrow bed, neatly made up with a white coverlet, basin and water pitcher atop a three-drawer commode, chamber pot in the open shelf, a battered armoire. A braided rug on the floor, mended lace curtains on the single window, one gas jet beside the door, a half-melted candle in a saucer resting on the seat of a chair placed beside the bed.

"Bare, I'd say, but neat. Tidy. The floor's been swept, and

the corners dusted." One by one, Prudence slid open the drawers of the commode. Neatly folded undergarments, a spare corset, tightly rolled stockings. A woolen scarf and mittens for winter weather, two plain nightgowns without embroidery on them, a stack of handkerchiefs bearing the initial *H*. A jewelry box containing a string of pearls, someone's wedding ring, and another bottle of laudanum.

"No family pictures anywhere," Lydia remarked, scanning the scantily furnished room's surfaces. "There's a change of skirt and shirtwaist in the armoire, a dress she probably wore to church or to somewhere special on her day off, a hat that's been refurbished with feathers and flowers salvaged from another bonnet, and what looks like a man's winter coat. That's it. I checked all of the pockets and gave everything a shake. She wasn't hiding anything in there."

"There's a suitcase up above." Prudence set the bedside candle on the floor and dragged the chair over to the armoire. "Shall you, or shall I?"

"I'm taller," Lydia said. "It's going to be a stretch." She climbed onto the chair, steadied herself against the armoire, reached up for the suitcase, and brought it down, narrowly missing Prudence's head.

"This better be worth it," Prudence muttered. "At least it's not locked."

"Empty." Lydia stared at the well-worn interior of the case. "Nothing in the lid or around the sides?"

"Nothing." Prudence ran her hand along the bottom of the case and into the liner compartments. "I'd feel it if she'd hidden something underneath the facing. I thought there might be letters inside, but there's nothing," she said, closing the lid and handing it up to Lydia, who'd climbed back onto the chair.

"It's dusty up here." Lydia ran her hand along the top edge of the armoire. "I used to hide my journal in a hollowed-out copy of *Little Women*. It sat on my bookshelf in plain sight for years. No one ever opened it."

"She doesn't have a bookshelf. No books, either."

"Not even a *Godey's Lady's Book*. That's odd for a seamstress."

"I get the feeling this wasn't intended to be more than a temporary lodging. There's been no effort to add anything personal."

"I wonder what brought her here."

"To the city? Or to this boardinghouse?" Prudence asked.

"Both, I suppose. We don't know anything about her background."

"The wardrobe mistress might know. Cynthia Pierce had to have asked questions and gotten satisfactory answers before hiring her."

"She doesn't strike me as someone who would employ just anyone," Lydia agreed. "There's something else to consider, too."

"What's that?"

"Dressers know more about the costumes of a show and the personalities of the actors than almost anyone else. They have to be trustworthy because the competition is always ready to pay for inside dope."

"Inside dope?"

"What the leading lady is wearing in the climactic scene. Which actor is showing up drunk at rehearsals. Costume ideas get stolen all the time and rumors that an actor can't hold his liquor can influence box office sales."

"I feel as though I've walked into a whole new world I never dreamed existed," Prudence said.

"You have," Lydia confirmed. "And now murder has been added to the mix."

# CHAPTER 11

They declined the landlady's offer of tea, gave only the vaguest of answers to her questions, and omitted entirely the fact of Hazel Nugent's death.

"She'll be able to give the police a good description of us," Lydia said as they stood in the foyer adjusting their hats and putting on gloves before opening the street door. "And we didn't carry anything out. She probably already suspects we lied to her about Hazel being in the hospital."

"Two more five-dollar gold pieces in exchange for not volunteering that information," Prudence said. "That's the last of them, but I think she'll stay quiet unless she thinks she's about to find herself in trouble. And that will depend on what kind of questions the detective on the case is smart enough to ask."

"He's bound to want to know if Miss Nugent had visitors," Lydia said. "Us, I mean."

"And the answer is that she didn't. We already knew she wasn't here, so technically we were paying a call on the room, not the person."

"Let's hope the landlady sees it that way."

"She will. I hinted that we'd be back. With more five-dollar gold pieces. She'll catch on quickly once the police tell her what happened. No landlady wants to be involved in a murder investigation. She'll choose to believe we're the friends we've claimed to be and that we came to make sure Hazel's small personal belongings didn't end up in a police locker instead of with her family."

They'd taken only a few steps to the sidewalk when a carriage pulled up. Driven by a coachman wearing an emerald-green plume in his hat, it was pulled by an enormous white horse with gigantic yellowed teeth. Danny Dennis and Mr. Washington.

"Ladies." Geoffrey Hunter stepped from the vehicle and executed a gentlemanly bow. "May I offer you the comfort of one of Danny's finest conveyances as you traipse around the city?"

"How did you know where we were?" Prudence asked, taking the arm he extended. She smiled at Geoffrey as he handed her into the carriage.

"Bobby the doorman and two of Danny's boys. You didn't think I'd leave the theatre unguarded, did you?"

"I really didn't give it a second thought. Did you, Lydia?"

"I should have realized there were eyes on us. But no, I rather naively thought we were on our own."

"You'll be glad to know that the detectives sent out from Mulberry Street aren't our old friends Steven Phelan and his partner," Geoffrey said, pulling the carriage door closed and tapping on the ceiling with his cane.

"You saw them?" Prudence sat far enough back on the tufted leather seat not to be visible from the street as Mr. Washington moved off at a slow, steady trot. "You talked to them?"

"I didn't have to. Bobby had all the information I needed, so I didn't go any farther than the lobby. He sends his best, by the way. Detectives Maurice Dority and Theodore Gormly are on the case. Dority has been around for a while, but Gormly is still wet behind the ears."

"That's a relief. We'd be out of our dresser jobs in a heartbeat if Barrett Hughes found out we were private inquiry agents," Prudence said.

"I appreciate the promotion," Lydia said. "Where are we going?"

"Septimus's boardinghouse. If you haven't already cleaned out his room?" Geoffrey asked.

"There hasn't been time. No, that's not being strictly honest. I haven't been able to bring myself to go back there. The landlady said the rent was paid through Saturday. I thought I'd wait as long as I could."

"We can't delay until Saturday." Geoffrey nodded at Prudence, who picked up one of Lydia's hands and held it in her own. "If someone at the theatre puts a bug in Dority's ear about a possible relationship between Hazel Nugent and Septimus and then just happens to mention that he committed accidental suicide by drinking rat poison . . . you can see where that could lead."

"How long do we have?" Prudence asked.

"They'll be interrogating the cast and crew for most of the rest of the morning. After that, it'll be Hazel's room in the early part of the afternoon and then on to Septimus's. If Dority is as good at his job as he should be, he'll send patrolmen to the two boardinghouses to make sure no one goes into the rooms until he and Gormly can get there. So not as much time as we'd like."

"What do we hope to find that we haven't already looked for?" Lydia asked.

"Anything that will prove Septimus was the real author of *Highlands*," Geoffrey said.

"Tessa Carey will know if he had any visitors in the days before his death," Prudence added. "She strikes me as the type of landlady who knows everything about her boarders."

"Is there any other kind?" asked Lydia.

"I haven't been able to get rid of them." Tessa Carey climbed the stairs to Septimus's room with the determination of a heavyset woman bent on not allowing her weight to interfere with her duties. "Nor the dog, either. They come and go at all hours, and I can't hardly tell one of those boys from another, bless their hearts."

"They haven't caused you any trouble, have they?" Geoffrey asked. Flower and two of Danny Dennis's street urchins had been on guard day and night outside Septimus's door since the discovery of the body. Geoffrey had seen to it that Mrs. Carey received a generous purse to sweeten the deal.

"I'm not a hard woman, Mr. Hunter. If they weren't sleeping in my hallway, they'd likely be out on the street or hiding in an alley. I know Danny lets some of them bed down in his stable, but he can't take them all in, can he?" She paused to catch her breath. "One of them brings me a free newspaper every day, and I swear to Holy Mary that dog smiles at me whenever I give her a stew bone."

"We won't be long," Lydia said when the door to Septimus's room had been unlocked and its guardians shooed on their way. "My cousin didn't have much."

"I don't know many actors who do," Tessa Carey said. "It's always been a hard life except for the handful of headliners. And it's not easy staying on top."

"I saw Edwin Booth's last Hamlet at the Brooklyn Academy of Music," Lydia said.

"I wouldn't have had the heart to go. Too sad when a great actor has lost his gift." Mrs. Carey handed over the key. "Lock up for me when you're finished. I'll keep the kettle going. You're going to need a strong cup of tea."

Prudence stood at the head of the stairs, stripping off her gloves and listening to the landlady's slow descent.

"I'll take the trunk." Geoffrey watched Prudence lock the door behind her. "Lydia, do you mind looking through his clothes? Checking the pockets? You're probably the best one of us to recognize something that shouldn't be there."

"I'll give you a hand with that," Prudence offered. She remembered how painful it had been to sort through her late father's wardrobe, separating the charity donations from what could be given to the male household staff.

They worked in silence, as though the room had assumed an otherworldly aura because of the death that had taken place there. Septimus was gone, but something of who he had been hovered over them as they touched the things he had used.

The trunk Geoffrey tackled was small enough to be hoisted onto a man's shoulder, which made it ideal for someone in a troupe of traveling performers. One of the first lessons learned on the road was to travel light. He lifted out and set aside a moth-eaten quilt that smelled of bad air and stale cooking. Suitable for a cold winter's night when nothing better could be found, he thought, remembering the many times during his Pinkerton career when he'd been glad enough of a horse blanket to keep from freezing.

A spare pair of boots in need of mending. Bits and pieces of what looked like costumes too ragged for even the costume shop to repair. Kept as souvenirs? Hoarded to put on in the privacy of his room to make the clothes he wore in public last longer? A couple of books that might have fallen off a pushcart and been picked up in the street for free. One a romance, the other a collection of home-brewed nostrums that sounded disgusting if not deadly. Finally, at the very bottom of the trunk, shoved so hard against its side that some of them had adhered to the damp wallpaper lining, a handful of pages bearing inked lines that were clearly written in play format.

"I've got it," he said, wiping clean the food-encrusted table. He laid the pages side by side, rearranging them until he judged them to be in order. "Will someone tell me whether these are scenes from *Waif of the Highlands*? Remember, I've never seen a rehearsal."

Lydia leaned over and ran a finger lightly over the dialogue lines, first whispering, then reciting them aloud. Prudence joined her. It was a scene between Caitrin, played by Flora

Campbell, and Duncan, to have been played by Septimus Ward. Begging her not to give herself to the rich gentleman played by Barrett Hughes, Duncan declares his love and pleads with her to marry him despite his poverty. Caitrin weeps and wrings her hands, but she reminds him that her family's only hope for survival is through the marriage she is determined to make. Only she can save them from starvation, consumption, and the disgrace of sending their female members out onto the street to earn a living. Lydia read Duncan's lines while Prudence gave voice to Caitrin.

"That's terrible," Geoffrey said. "Overblown, overwritten, and likely to make anyone with good taste gag."

"Except for a few minor word changes, it's exactly what's being rehearsed at the Argosy Theatre right now," Lydia said. "Believe me, if you saw the play in rehearsal and heard Flora Campbell sing her sad farewell song to her impoverished lover, you might still gag, but you'd realize that the general public will pay good money to languish in romantic misery for three hours."

"They will, Geoffrey," Prudence agreed. "I wouldn't have thought so myself if I hadn't sat through a rehearsal with tears running down my cheeks. It's an awful play, but it's going to be a raving success."

"This is Septimus's handwriting?" Geoffrey asked.

"I'd swear to it," Lydia confirmed. "We may still have two or three letters at home that he wrote to my father."

"If a handwriting expert confirms that these pages and the letters you have were written by the same person, there's no way Barrett Hughes could deny that Septimus wrote *Highlands*," Geoffrey said. "But . . ." He turned to Prudence.

"But there's no means of disproving that Septimus entered into an agreement to cede his author rights to Hughes. Which Septimus then repudiated. Legally speaking," she told Lydia. "Now that he's dead, I doubt there's even the shadow of a case."

"I don't care about the play," Lydia said. "I want to know who killed my cousin. I want to see the guilty person hanged for it. And if the same individual murdered Hazel Nugent, I want him tried and convicted for that crime, also."

"We'll take these with us." Geoffrey folded the papers carefully and tucked them into his jacket pocket. "We can pack the rest of his things in the trunk."

"What's the point?" Lydia asked. "The clothes won't fit either my father or his bodyguard, the bedclothes and towels are worn and stained, and I wouldn't trust anything that was left on the table." Her voice trembled. "I didn't realize he had so little."

"Actors always put a brave face on things," Geoffrey said.

"I wasn't aware you knew any theatre people." Just when Prudence thought she had learned everything important about Geoffrey's past, he revealed another facet to his character that she wouldn't have suspected. It was, she admitted to herself, part of his charm. Part of his attraction.

"They make good Pinkertons, though the ones I met only took it on when there wasn't anything else available to them."

"Amos Lang?"

"The Ferret? I've never asked, but I doubt it."

"It's kind of you to try to distract me by talking about Amos," Lydia said, folding Septimus's spare pants, extra shirt, and winter coat. "I'm not finding it as hard as I thought I would. What's this?" She fumbled in the coat pocket and withdrew a small, square jewelry box.

"That looks like it might contain a ring," Prudence said.

"Earrings," Lydia declared, showing them what lay on the satin-lined interior. She took one of the earrings from the box and rubbed it against a tooth. "These pearls are real. Septimus couldn't possibly have afforded them."

"Is there a jeweler's name?" Prudence asked.

"No name on the box at all. That's unusual."

"See if there's anything else in his pockets," Geoffrey instructed.

Lydia had already patted down her cousin's clothes, but now she went over them more carefully, even working her fingers along the seams. "Nothing," she said, putting the earrings into her reticule, handing the rest of Septimus's belongings to Geoffrey. "There's not even enough to fill up his trunk. I wonder if he pawned things to buy the pearls."

"If that were the case, he'd have the tickets," Prudence said. "We didn't find any."

"Would he have left them with the landlady? For safekeeping?" Lydia wondered.

"I'll take this down to the street so Danny can strap it onto the back of the carriage," Geoffrey said, hoisting the small trunk to his shoulder. "Why don't you see if Mrs. Carey has made that tea she promised us?"

"Pawn tickets?" Tessa Carey exclaimed, pouring strong dark tea into heavy china cups. "He had more when he took the room than your man carried out, that's for sure, but Septimus never gave me any tickets to hold for him."

"Do your other tenants ever do that?" Prudence asked.

"They do. From time to time. They know I won't lose them." She set a small pitcher of cream and a bowl of sugar cubes on the table where her boarders ate their meals. "And yes, I called him by his Christian name. Septimus. I was born into the theatre and so was he. That makes us family, you know. This young lady, too." She smiled at Lydia. "He told me about you. About your mother. He liked to talk, Septimus did. Liked his tea, too."

"Did he have any visitors to his room, Mrs. Carey?" Lydia asked.

"No visitors allowed anywhere but the parlor," Tessa Carey replied. "Not that I wouldn't put it past some of the boarders to smuggle a woman upstairs while I'm not here. But they all know what happens if I catch them. Thrown out onto the sidewalk with their possessions and no refund of their deposit." She sliced a raisin loaf cake and passed the plate around. "Baked it this morning, I did."

"Delicious." Geoffrey took a second piece. "Would you know anything about Septimus that could tell us why he died the way he did?"

"He wasn't that much of a drinker," Tessa Carey said. "So it's no wonder he mistook the rat poison for whiskey." She looked around the table at the set expressions on all their faces. "Here now. There's something you're not telling me."

"There's a possibility he didn't drink the rat poison from the bottle it came in," Geoffrey said.

"What does that mean?"

"Someone might have deliberately poured the poison into one of his whiskey bottles," Prudence said.

"Holy Mother of God, who would do such a thing?" Tessa Carey crossed herself.

"Someone who wanted him dead." Lydia touched the napkin to her eyes, then wiped her lips of milky tea.

Mrs. Carey got up from the table and left the dining room. They heard the key turn in the front door lock and a security bolt slide into place.

"We don't need to be interrupted." Tessa's bulk filled the doorway. "Jimmy Kilaren showed me the business card you gave him. The police officer who was here when Septimus was carried away?"

"I remember," Geoffrey said.

"So I know you're what's called an inquiry agent."

"We both are," Prudence said. "We're partners."

"I suppose a woman can do the job as well as any man," Mrs. Carey said. "And what about you?" she asked, looking in Lydia's direction. "Are you really his cousin like you said you were?"

"I am," Lydia said. "But I've worked with Mr. Hunter and Miss MacKenzie in the past, and they're helping me now."

"He was a lovely young man. Handsome as the devil. Talented. Never late with the rent. He promised me a free ticket to *Waif of the Highlands*." She walked to the cupboard where folded napkins and cutlery lay atop a stack of plates. "I was wondering what to do about this," she said, taking a large cardboard box tied closed with butcher's twine from one of the drawers. "He gave it to me for safekeeping. That's what he said. *Safekeeping*. Septimus didn't tell me what it was, and I didn't ask. But I think it should go to you now, miss." She handed the box to Lydia. "It's what he would have wanted."

"The police will probably pay you a visit this afternoon," Geoffrey said.

"One of the dressers at the Argosy Theatre was found dead this morning." Lydia slid the shawl from her shoulders and wrapped it around the box.

"Jesus, Mary, and Joseph." Another sign of the cross.

"We don't know if there's a connection," Prudence said. "But it's too much of a coincidence to ignore."

"You'd best be on your way then," Mrs. Carey said. "You wouldn't want Jimmy Kilaren to find you here."

"It'll be two detectives from Mulberry Street Headquarters," Geoffrey said.

"If I know Jimmy, he'll want to stick his nose in whatever's happening on his beat. What do you want me to tell them?"

"As little as possible." Lydia reached out a grateful hand to touch the landlady's arm.

"They won't learn anything from me," Mrs. Carey promised. "Not that there's anything much to tell that you don't already know. We'll just keep that box between us, I think."

"I might come back for another cup of tea and some more cake," Lydia said, moving toward the door.

"You do that, miss. You'll always be welcome." The landlady unlocked the front door, stepped out onto the stoop, looked both ways along the street. "There's no one coming yet."

Geoffrey dropped a handful of coins into her apron pocket as he passed.

She nodded, then closed the door behind them.

"It's got to be the manuscript for *Highlands*," Lydia said as soon as Mr. Washington had pulled away from the curb.

"We'll open it back at the office," Prudence decided. She had a vivid mental picture of papers spilling over their laps onto the carriage floor and flying out the windows.

Geoffrey glanced back as they turned the corner. A uniformed policeman was striding down the street, swinging his baton.

"Just in time."

# CHAPTER 12

Josiah cut the butcher's string with a sharp knife, lifted off the cardboard cover, and placed the manuscript box squarely in the center of the conference room table. He unloaded the tea tray he'd prepared, pouring a dark Louisiana chicory-flavored coffee Geoffrey liked and a pale English blend of Indian teas for himself and the ladies. Pastries from his favorite German bakery had been artfully arranged on a blue-and-white Meissen china serving plate, linen napkins and sterling silver teaspoons placed in front of each chair. "There we are," he said when he was sure everything had been set out to his satisfaction. "I've locked the outer office door and taken the telephone off the hook."

"It's not *Waif of the Highlands*." Prudence removed the topmost piece of paper, reading the title aloud before passing it to Lydia. "*The Hereditary Prince*. A play in three acts by Septimus Ward." The manuscript was handwritten, unbound. "What do you suppose this is?"

"I had no idea he was writing other plays." Lydia handed the title page to Geoffrey, who glanced at it, then passed it along to

Josiah. "I think I told you he'd always written skits for the vaudeville troupe he and Flora were with, but I didn't know he was interested in serious drama."

"What do you call *Waif of the Highlands*?" Josiah asked.

"Melodrama. At its literary worst and box office best," Lydia said.

"Every bit as overblown as most of them are," Prudence added.

"We won't know whether this is another piece of popular theatre or something better unless we read it." Geoffrey took a sip of the inky brew no one else could tolerate.

"Shall we?" asked Lydia, sliding the box forward, narrowly missing a half-eaten piece of *apfelstrudel*.

"Shall we what?" Prudence stirred a sugar cube into her tea.

"We can't read it aloud the way a cast does at its first rehearsal," Lydia continued. "But we can pass the pages to each other as we go."

"I'll take notes," Josiah offered. Hunter and MacKenzie's secretary was never without a sharpened pencil and the stenographer's notebook that was as much a part of him as the lavishly embroidered vests worn beneath a sober black suit.

"I'm willing," Geoffrey said.

They settled into a quiet broken only occasionally by the clink of cup against saucer, the brushing of a finger along a crumb-strewn napkin, and the soft whisper of paper passing from one hand to another. Josiah's pencil whisked along his stenographer's pad, jotting down notes in the shorthand only he could decipher. Every now and then one of them made a soft murmuring sound or glanced up to read the expression on someone else's face. As the box emptied and the pages piled up beside it, the quiet grew more intense. They read a bit faster, straining to reach the end of the play that had gripped their attention and taken hold of their imaginations almost from the opening line.

Lydia was the first to finish. She heard Prudence give a sigh as she passed the final page to Geoffrey, who nodded before handing it to Josiah.

The tea, coffee, and German pastries had been consumed. Somehow, without interrupting the reading, Josiah had removed plates, napkins, and cutlery, leaving not a speck of sugary frosting anywhere. Now he placed the last page atop the pile of facedown manuscript pages, turned it over so the title showed, straightened the edges, and carefully, almost reverently, returned it to the box from which they'd taken it.

"He was my cousin, so perhaps I'm biased," Lydia said. "But I don't think I've read or seen anything in the past few years that's touched me as deeply as this."

"It's hard to believe the same person could have written *Highlands*," Prudence said.

"I wonder if anyone else knows about it." Geoffrey tapped a forefinger against the tabletop, always a sign that he was thinking.

"It's handwritten," Lydia reminded him. "Septimus didn't own a typewriting machine, wouldn't have known how to use one if he had, and obviously couldn't afford to hire a printer. I'd say this is the only copy in existence."

"It's not a first draft," Prudence said. "He took the time to make a clean copy."

"And probably burned the original and whatever notes he'd made," Lydia agreed.

"He gave the box to Mrs. Carey for safekeeping," Prudence reminded them. "That says to me that he was afraid to keep it in his room."

"And perhaps that he intended to do something with it in the near future," Lydia said.

"If *Highlands* turned out to be a success, wouldn't that make its author sought after? And his work likely to sell at a high price?" Geoffrey asked.

"He'd have to find a producer," Lydia said.

"We're out of our depth now," Prudence added. "We need to bring in someone who knows the backstage and financial world of the theatre."

"A retired actor would know all the gossip. They always do," Lydia said.

"Not retired," Prudence said slowly. "But perhaps close to retiring, who knows everything about everybody—actors, directors, producers, backstage crews. Someone who's been in the theatre all her life. In vaudeville, touring companies, troupes in Chicago, Boston, New York City."

"With a soft spot for Septimus," added Lydia.

"Gertrude Marrow," Prudence confirmed. "Do you think she'd keep our secret?"

"It's intrigue. Mystery. As devious as the plot of a melodrama, but with more than a hint of danger. Two private inquiry agents working undercover as theatrical dressers to solve a murder. Two murders. I think she'd jump at the chance to be part of the plot."

"Gertrude plays the role of the heroine's mother in *Highlands*," Prudence explained to Geoffrey and Josiah. "I don't know what her real age is, but if I had to guess, I'd say she won't see sixty again. I gather from backstage gossip that she's known to be a soft touch for young actors and actresses down on their luck. More than a few of them have slept on the couch in her parlor until they found work."

Josiah had left the conference room with the tray of tea things. When he returned, he carried two small objects which he deposited beside the manuscript of *The Hereditary Prince*. Pearl earrings gleamed against the black satin lining of the jewelry box in which they rested. The cork stopper from the small brown bottle of rat poison showed traces of the arsenic granules that had been added to its contents before being tipped into one of Septimus Ward's whiskey bottles. Lydia took

Hazel Nugent's garnet ring from her reticule, placing it next to the earrings. Geoffrey added the pages he'd found adhered to the interior of Septimus's battered trunk.

It was all they had to go on at the moment.

"It's getting late," Lydia said as she and Prudence descended from Danny Dennis's hansom cab in front of a narrow brick building on a street of nearly identical row houses. "Suppertime for someone who's been rehearsing all day. Or answering questions during a police interrogation."

"We don't dare try to recruit her at the theatre," Prudence said. "There are always too many people around."

"I'll wait here for you, miss." Danny tied off Mr. Washington's reins and unhooked his feed bag from where it hung next to the whip he seldom used.

"I know Mr. Hunter had a private word with you," Prudence said. "But there's really no need to worry. The neighborhood looks safe, and we won't be long."

"I'll be out here when you're ready," he insisted, waiting until they'd rung the doorbell and the door opened before turning away to tend to New York's largest white horse.

"May we come in for a moment?" Lydia asked.

"Why am I not surprised to see the two of you on my doorstep, looking hale and hearty and one of you not at all distressed at having found a body curled up in a trunk?" Gertrude Marrow asked, stepping aside to usher them into her hallway. "You'd better follow me into the sitting room."

A fire burned in the room that was as well and opulently furnished as any of the parlors in Prudence's family mansion. Velvet cushioned chairs and settee, Oriental rug on a well-polished oak floor, tasseled lampshades on tabletops of inlaid marble, lace curtains flanked by heavy drapery across the bay window. A mantelpiece crowded with silver-framed photographs. None of the furniture looked worn; nothing needed to be mended or replaced.

"I'd a wealthy admirer once," Gertrude said before either of her visitors could remark on the unexpected luxury. "He's gone now, but he left me well taken care of. Every actress's dream, isn't it, Lydia? As a Fancham, you should know about things like that."

"I suppose I should, but my mother died when I was very young, and she seldom talked about her family."

"Your father would have told you what he knew. If you'd asked him. And then there was Septimus. Your cousin. Son of your mother's sister." Gertrude gestured them toward the cushioned armchairs arranged on either side of the fireplace. "I'm right about that, aren't I?"

"Did the police stay long?" Lydia asked, choosing not to answer the question. She wasn't sure yet how to react to what she was learning about the family she hadn't really known.

"About as long as you'd expect when nobody had anything to tell them. Coppers have never been among our favorite people. They all believe actresses are loose women, actors are light-fingered, and the stage crew is running from the law."

"Have arrangements been made yet?" Prudence asked.

"For Hazel's funeral?" Gertrude shook her head. "The police took her body to Bellevue. There's no telling when they'll release it."

"Does she have family?" Lydia held out her hands to the fire. April was an unpredictable month in New York, sunshine and daffodils one day, a cold rain the next.

"Nobody knows. We'll take up a collection, so she doesn't wind up in one of the common graves on Hart Island."

"Was Hazel Nugent her real name?" Prudence kept her voice low-pitched and matter-of-fact.

"That's a question I didn't see coming," Gertrude said. "I think you'd better tell me why you asked it. And why you think I should give you an answer."

Prudence took the garnet ring and a Hunter and MacKenzie business card from her reticule.

"Hunter and MacKenzie, Investigative Law," Gertrude read. "You didn't bother trying to hide *your* name, so I suppose that means you're the MacKenzie."

"I am," Prudence said. "Private inquiry agent and recently admitted to the bar in New York State."

"A lady lawyer? It's about time we got some decent representation in the courts. Are you Miss MacKenzie's client, Lydia?" Gertrude asked.

"You called me by my Christian name in the costume shop, so there's no need to get formal now." The garnet ring in the palm of Prudence's hand reflected the fire's red flames. "We wouldn't want you to slip up when any of the company might be near."

"All right then." Gertrude slipped the ring over the tip of her little finger, twisting the gold circlet and feeling the sharp edges of the garnets. "This must have cost a pretty penny. No nicks or scratches, no loose stones. I'd say someone gave it to her recently. But I never saw Hazel wear it."

"Septimus's death wasn't an accident," Lydia said. "I asked Prudence and her partner to find his killer for me."

"I thought the boy was too smart to mistake rat poison for whiskey." Gertrude twisted the ring from her finger, handing it back to Prudence. "He couldn't hold his drink as well as some of them because he wasn't a guzzler, but he wasn't careless. Septimus was ambitious and he was intelligent enough to know that whiskey and success don't mix. You'd better tell me all of it."

"We need your help, Gertrude," Lydia said. "Nobody knows as much about the theatre and its people as you do."

"That's true. I've been around a long time."

"You'll have to keep what we tell you under your hat," Prudence said. "And you can't let on to anyone what we're doing."

"I said it before, and I'll say it again. Septimus was handsome as the devil and polite as the pope toward an old lady actress like me. He would have gone far, maybe made as much of a name for himself as Joe Jefferson. Nobody ever played Rip Van

Winkle like he did." Gertrude seemed to drift off for a moment. "Sorry. I forget where I am sometimes. So many of the great ones are retired or dead now. But Septimus, that boy had talent. I'll do whatever you need me to do. A shame he got himself involved with a minx like Flora Campbell."

"What makes you say that?" Lydia asked.

"She's a pretty little thing, and she's got a decent enough voice, but her real talent is twisting men around her little finger. Septimus thought she hung the moon."

"What about Barrett Hughes?"

"Barrett knows for sure and certain that *he's* the one who hung the moon. There's no doubt in his mind. But every now and then he lets one of his women get under his skin for a while. Never for very long because he's too much in love with himself to tolerate competition from a female, but he has his moments of weakness. I'd say Flora's come closer to snagging him than anybody else in quite a while. He doesn't think she's intelligent enough to be worrisome, but he's wrong about that. She knows what she wants, and she knows how to get it."

"So you'll help us?" Lydia asked.

"Ask me anything you want. If I don't have the answer, I'll sure as hell know who does."

"Septimus wrote another play," Prudence began.

# CHAPTER 13

Two days later, on a Saturday when Hughes had not scheduled a rehearsal, Gertrude Marrow arrived at the Hunter and MacKenzie office to give her first report. There'd been some dickering back and forth over the remuneration she expected to receive—no one in the theatre worked for nothing—but in the end they'd settled on payment based on an hourly rate, the reckoning of which she would submit to Josiah.

"She shouldn't be given what you authorize for ex-Pinks," Josiah had stated firmly before negotiations ended. "She has no training and no experience in detecting."

"That's not what we'll be paying her for," Geoffrey said. There were times when he wanted to remind Josiah of the many instances of detecting in which *he'd* participated—without a scrap of formal instruction.

"I told the Bellevue morgue people I was Hazel's aunt," Gertrude said, handing a wrinkled form across the desk to Geoffrey. There were stains on it that were better left unexamined.

"And they released the body to you?" Geoffrey asked, smoothing out the form.

"They'll hold it for another twenty-four hours, then if I haven't arranged for transportation to a funeral home or cemetery, they'll ship it to Hart Island for burial in one of the mass graves."

"There's nothing here about autopsy results," Prudence said, leaning over Geoffrey's shoulder to read what Gertrude had brought them.

"They didn't do an autopsy. The attendant I talked to told me that. First thing. People don't like their relatives being cut open. He said the police decided it was an accidental death, so no need to do any dissecting."

"Accidental death? How on earth did they reach that conclusion?" Prudence straightened, her voice indignant and the expression on her face furious. "Hazel's a woman and she wasn't important. That's why they concluded there was no need for further investigation."

"There weren't any bruises on her body," Gertrude explained. "And it didn't look as though she'd fought off an attacker. So, the theory is that since she was short, she stood on a box to reach into the trunk and dig around in the contents. Somehow she lost her balance, fell in, and the lid slammed shut and locked. Nobody realized she was in the prop room, so if she screamed or banged on the trunk lid, nobody heard her. She suffocated. That's what I was told."

"I've never heard anything more ridiculous in my life," Prudence said, so angry now that the fingers she clasped together turned white around the knuckles.

"I'm going to give you a name and an address," Geoffrey said, taking a page from Josiah's stenography notebook. "I'll arrange for the body to be picked up and taken to its destination. All you have to do is give this information to the morgue attendant who keeps the register."

"Dr. Ambrose Deslar," Gertrude read aloud, "Charity Hospital, Blackwell's Island. This isn't a funeral home."

"An autopsy needs to be performed," Geoffrey said. "Dr.

Deslar is an acquaintance of mine. And very good at what he does."

"I'll accompany the body," Gertrude said, folding the paper and stowing it in her reticule along with the form releasing the corpse to her custody. "Hazel shouldn't be alone when a stranger cuts her open."

"Have you ever witnessed an autopsy?" Prudence asked gently. "It's not for the fainthearted. Especially if the body on the table is someone you've known in life."

"I've seen what was left of a stagehand about your age who fell headfirst from the flies," Gertrude said. "It wasn't pretty. What was left of him didn't look human. And when I toured the mining camps not a day went by that one of the fools didn't take a knife or a hatchet to a man poaching on his claim. So I don't think an autopsy will bother me all that much."

"It's not a good idea, Gertrude," Geoffrey said. "Deslar doesn't allow casual visitors to his lab. He's not your ordinary doctor."

"Do you want to know what I found out from David Belasco or don't you?"

"Who's David Belasco?" Prudence asked.

"The mining camps I mentioned? He toured them as a young performer, just like I did when times were tough, and you took any acting job you could get. We were in one of the smaller troupes together. He came to New York about ten or eleven years ago, managed a couple of theatres—the Madison Square and the Lyceum. But his dream was always to be a playwright and producer. Mark my words, he'll make a big name for himself. He's already being talked about. Everything he writes sells."

"What does that have to do with Hazel Nugent's autopsy?"

"You gave me a copy of the first act of Septimus's play."

"I did." Geoffrey had hired a professional typist to transform the handwritten manuscript into something resembling what a printer would create.

"I took that first act to David, plunked it down in front of him, and sat there while he read it. If you want to know what he thought, you'll have to let me witness the autopsy."

"That's blackmail," Josiah said.

Gertrude shrugged.

Geoffrey nodded.

"Three weeks ago, a play David cowrote with Henry De Mille played its two hundredth performance at Proctor's Twenty-Third Street Theatre. Audiences love it. *Men and Women* is the title."

Josiah waved his pencil in the air. "I read the reviews."

"If you intended to see it, you're too late," Gertrude said. "It's gone out on tour now—Cincinnati, St. Louis, Chicago, Salt Lake City, San Francisco, Los Angeles. Only the biggest markets. David Belasco has his finger on the pulse of what the future of American theatre will be. That's why I took Septimus's play to him. He read the first couple of pages for old times' sake, but he finished what I handed him because he couldn't put it down."

"He said that?" Prudence asked.

"David told me if the rest of it was as good as the first act, he'd think about producing it. I didn't tell him the playwright was dead. I said I'd be in touch." She took a business card out of her reticule and laid it on Geoffrey's desk. "David Belasco doesn't bother with anything that's marginal. If he says something is good, he means it'll play well, and he'll turn it into a hit. The genius is in the casting and the staging, but you have to have a high-quality script to begin with. Like building a house on a foundation of stone instead of sand."

Geoffrey handed Belasco's card to Josiah, who slipped it into the file labeled *Septimus Ward*.

"I'd say you've earned a trip to Blackwell's Island, Gertrude."

\*    \*    \*

It was late in the day when Hazel Nugent's body arrived on Blackwell's Island. Gertrude, Prudence, and Geoffrey, accompanying the coffined remains, had caught the last regular ferry. Danny Dennis had hired a skiff to transport them back to Manhattan after the autopsy. He and Mr. Washington would be waiting at the dock, no matter how behind time or dark it turned out to be. Money talked, but knowing the right contacts for the right job was even more important.

"Whoever examined her at Bellevue didn't bother removing her clothing," Ambrose Deslar said as he handed out canvas aprons to his visitors. Fully dressed, Hazel Nugent lay face up on his exam table.

"How can you tell?" Gertrude asked. She hadn't so much as looked sideways at Deslar's oddly shaped and hairless body. Theatre people got used to associating with what Barnum had advertised as oddities of nature and others called freaks. The further from the norm, the more valuable the exhibit. Gertrude figured that Geoffrey's doctor friend wasn't frightening or disgusting enough to be worth big billing. "You haven't taken them off, either."

"Clothes never look the same when you dress a corpse as if you put them on a living person," Deslar explained, pale fingers moving quickly along the length of Hazel's body. "If you've seen enough of them, you can tell at a glance whether the corpse in front of you dressed himself before he died, or a mortuary worker did it for him."

Silence fell as Deslar removed Hazel's garments one by one. It didn't seem dignified or respectful to continue talking as her nudity was revealed under the hissing gaslight beneath which she lay.

"I doubt this young lady had much knowledge of the opposite sex." Deslar palpated her breasts and abdomen. "Definitely not pregnant."

"Why did you say that about knowing the opposite sex?" Prudence asked.

Gertrude guffawed, then abruptly stopped the laugh with a hand to her mouth. "Just look at her. Now you tell me whether that's the body of a woman who's spent a lot of time in a man's bed. You can always tell. At least I can, and probably every other female who's been around the block a few times."

Prudence felt her ears turn red and knew the flush must be showing on her face, too.

Deslar swabbed Hazel's eyes, nose, mouth, and ears. Scraped under the fingernails that had been torn ragged as she beat and scratched against the lid of the trunk. Ran cotton in the creases of her skin. He hummed as he worked, some unrecognizable tune that he might have made up as he went along.

"Let's turn her over before I open her up," he said, nodding at Geoffrey, who stepped closer to the table. "She'll feel heavier than she really is, but that's the way of it. Slow and easy does it."

They all saw the purple bruise in the center of Hazel's back. The size of a small hand or a fist.

"That was made when she was alive," Deslar said.

"Someone pushed her into the trunk, then closed and locked the lid so she wouldn't be able to get out," Prudence said, seeing in her mind's eye how it had been done.

"*Shoved* is the word I'd use," Gertrude elaborated. "Hit her hard in the back then gave an almighty shove and slammed down the lid before the girl knew what was happening to her."

"What a horrible way to die," Prudence said softly. "Trapped in yards and yards of smothering material and not being able to breathe." She turned toward Deslar. "Did it take long?"

"Depends on how much air was in there. How much she used up shouting and fighting to get out." The doctor's sagging shoulders were more eloquent than anything he'd said.

Gertrude had tears in her eyes as she stroked Hazel's tangled hair. "We need to get her fixed up. She can't go into the ground looking like this."

"I'm not finished yet," Deslar said. He nodded at Geoffrey,

who helped him turn the body over once more. "You might want to move away or close your eyes or wait outside." He reached for one of the surgical scalpels lying on a nearby tray.

"We'll stay," Prudence said.

"I'm not leaving," Gertrude added.

Deslar was quick and professional. He made the Y-incision, then lifted out, weighed, and placed in individual containers the organs he would examine. Peeled the face back to reveal and remove parts of the brain.

Geoffrey passed around a small tin of camphorated petroleum jelly.

"Bread, fatty bacon, and an apple," Deslar said, poking through the contents of Hazel's stomach.

"A boardinghouse walkaway lunch," Gertrude declared. "Some of the landladies sell their boarders a nickel's worth of leftover breakfast bread and fried pig belly. She probably got the apple off a barrow."

Prudence shuddered.

"There's a new French restaurant near the theatre," Gertrude began, averting her eyes from the semi-digested lumps of Hazel's last meal. "I haven't been there myself—can't afford it on a regular basis—but I know Barrett Hughes is fond of the place. He likes to take his young ladies to obscure but intimately romantic dining rooms. He's good at what he does. I've told you that before. You could probably count on the fingers of one hand the young women who've managed to elude his wiles."

"So we can surmise from what Hazel ate that she wasn't being courted by him," Prudence said. "At least not recently. That's logical. I don't see someone like Hughes spending time and money on a seamstress."

"I did more than visit David Belasco yesterday," Gertrude continued.

"Meaning?" Prudence stepped back from the table and its

array of formaldehyde-filled jars. She'd seen other autopsies, but they were never easy on the stomach or the sensibilities.

"Hazel Nugent got the position as part of the company's costume department because she was a wonder with the needle. Cynthia Pierce, the wardrobe mistress, told me she could do marvels with a scrap of cloth and a spool of thread. But she didn't come from a theatre family. I made inquiries. No one I talked to had heard of her or any other Nugent working in any of the companies currently playing the city."

"What does that mean?" Geoffrey asked.

Gertrude shrugged. It was unlike her not to voice an immediate opinion.

"That's why we asked for your help," Prudence said. "Sometimes it takes an insider to learn what's really going on."

"Then I'd say our Hazel was a newcomer and an outsider, taking a chance that her sewing skills would find her work. Which they did. But why would she choose an iffy, backstage theatre job when she could have hired on in one of the fancy couturier shops? It doesn't make sense—unless she was using the costume shop as a first step to something better."

"Now I'm really lost," Prudence said.

"What if our Hazel had a secret ambition to be an actress?" Gertrude suggested. "That would horrify any decent family, so she can't reveal the plan she comes up with. Somewhere there could be a mother and father who believe their beloved daughter has found a respectable position as a governess. I'd lay odds on it. She never talked about them because she didn't want anyone to know what she'd done."

"Backstage to onstage?" Geoffrey sounded skeptical. "How often does that happen?"

"Almost never," Gertrude conceded. "But someone like Hazel wouldn't know that. She might have believed Hughes would eventually find her a minor acting role, something that could lead to larger, more important parts. He very possibly encouraged her to think that. I have no proof of it, but leopards don't change their spots."

"If you're right, that's two young women we know of being preyed on by Hughes. Flora and now Hazel," Geoffrey said.

"That still doesn't tell us why someone would have wanted her out of the way. Would have taken the chance of killing her in a theatre where rehearsals are going on." Prudence frowned and reached for more of the camphorated petroleum jelly.

"Septimus. He's the link," Geoffrey said. "She knew or suspected something about his death. It's the only logical explanation."

"Both deaths were cleverly conceived," Deslar said, handing Hazel's clothing to Gertrude. "Septimus's poisoning has been declared accidentally self-administered by our esteemed police department, and Hazel's suffocation is likewise considered an unfortunate but not criminal occurrence. Even the bruise on her back, if we were to draw it to the attention of the Bellevue morgue, could be explained away as being caused by something solid in the trunk on which she landed when she fell. A shoe, perhaps. You did say there were costumes stored inside it as well as folded lengths of material. I don't think the circumstances that have led to these conclusions were unpremeditated. They can't be laid entirely to luck, especially in Septimus's case. That has the aura of careful planning about it."

"And Hazel?" Geoffrey asked.

"Less directly so, perhaps," Deslar said. "More a situation where whoever killed her was prepared to act spontaneously. If he hadn't come up behind her as she leaned into the trunk, he might have engineered a fall backstage where there are coils of rope and buckets of sand ready to entrap the unwary. A gas leak in the costume shop. A loose step somewhere. Especially when it's darkened after a rehearsal or a performance, a theatre is rife with mishaps waiting to be blundered into."

"Lydia should be warned," Prudence said. She slipped Hazel's stockings on her thin legs as the men turned away respectfully.

A naked, dissected corpse was not the same as a female body being reclothed.

"Where is she?" Gertrude asked.

"Home, with her father and his caretaker, taking advantage of no rehearsals being called until Monday. Something about needing to spend time following a lead Clyde Allen had come up with at Septimus's viewing. She wouldn't say any more than that. You know how she is."

"She would have made an excellent Pinkerton," Geoffrey said. It was the highest praise he could offer.

# CHAPTER 14

"I wouldn't say anything if I didn't think your Lydia could be in danger." Clyde Allen whittled ferociously on a piece of white oak, chips flying, the figure of a man gradually emerging from the heart of the wood. "I don't like to stick my neck into someone else's business, but I can't turn my back on this, Ben."

"I heard the front door open. She's home now," Benjamin Truitt's scarred and sightless eyes were hidden by smoked glasses even within the confines of his own home, but the acute hearing the blind sometimes develop conveyed almost everything that went on around him. "You're going to have to tell her."

"I don't know that I can." Clyde set aside the oak and the knife. He picked up the sheet of newspaper that had caught most of the shavings, rolled it into the shape of a log, and fed it into the firebox of the J.B. Clute potbellied parlor stove in front of which he'd stretched out his legs. He was always cold. Had been ever since the war. "I don't have the words to describe what I think I saw. Not to a lady, anyway."

"You'll have to find them," Benjamin said. "I can't have my daughter going into that theatre every day when there's a man there who makes a habit of taking advantage of women. She may be mostly in the costume shop, but he's got the run of the place, and from what she's told us, every last one of the actors is scared silly of him."

"He could fire any of them in a heartbeat," Lydia said from the doorway where she stood taking the pins out of her hat. "I assume you were talking about Barrett Hughes, but I only caught the last few words." She crossed to the stove and held out her hands. "Shall I make tea for us?"

"Just what's needed," Benjamin said. He thought whiskey might be more in order, but refrained from saying so. He himself had no problem imbibing, but Clyde had an unhealthy attraction to the bottle and an idiosyncratic all or nothing way of dealing with it. With what Lydia had to be told, it was probably best that he stay religiously sober.

Benjamin heard his daughter leave the parlor for the kitchen, listened to the sound of the kettle being lifted off the stove, the clink of a spoon measuring out tea leaves, the stacking of cups and saucers, the splash of milk into a small pitcher. He hoped Clyde was coming up with the right words to tell her what could not be kept secret.

"There now, tea and something sweet to nibble on. What could be better on a cool spring day?" Lydia set down the tray she carried and handed each man a cup of the steaming brew. She offered round a plate of sliced apple cake.

"Where were you today?" Benjamin took a bite of the cake his daughter had baked. "I thought you told me the *Highlands* rehearsal had been canceled."

"It was," Lydia said. "Prudence and Gertrude went with Geoffrey to Hazel's autopsy, and I decided to catch a matinee of *Alabama*. It opened at the Madison Square Theatre at the beginning of the month and was praised in all the reviews as an entirely American play. Which would make it a rival of *Highlands*. I thought I'd better see it before our rehearsals pick up again in earnest on Monday." It could also be an indication of whether Septimus Ward had been looking toward the future when he wrote *The Hereditary Prince*, but Lydia hadn't told her father and Clyde about that discovery yet.

"*Alabama?*" Benjamin asked. "From the title I'd guess it's set in the South, probably around the time of the war."

"Old Southern colonel plantation owner and an estranged son who fought for the North," Lydia said. "It reminded me of Geoffrey's rupture with his family."

"Speaking of the war," Clyde began. He set down his teacup and saucer and brushed crumbs from his lap.

"It was a very pro-South, Lost Cause plot and point of view," Lydia continued. "Too melodramatic for my taste, but so is *Highlands*."

"Clyde has something he needs to talk to you about." Benjamin folded his hands and tilted his head to one side.

"Clyde?" Lydia took one last bite of apple cake and prepared to listen. Her father's caretaker was a notably silent man; she always found it difficult to nudge him into conversation.

"You were mentioning the war just now," Clyde said. "It was over a long time ago. Twenty-six years and nine days to be exact."

Lydia waited, knowing from past experience that Clyde could not be rushed.

"Three days ago I saw a man I hadn't laid eyes on in all that time."

"Three days ago was when we were at Septimus's viewing," Lydia said.

"That's where he was. That's where I saw him."

"Where is this going, Clyde?" Lydia's voice was soft but insistent.

"Mr. Barrett Hughes was in a troupe of actors who played the hospital I was in. Not the one where Benjamin and I were in the same ward, but one before that, when they weren't sure I'd make it out alive and my face was so bandaged up, only half of it ever saw the light of day."

"Traveling troupes of actors came to all the hospitals. I remember how much we looked forward to their visits. The nurses and attendants wheeled the patients outside or into the dining hall, the ones who weren't actually dying," Benjamin explained. "I couldn't see a damn thing, of course, but I could hear. It was like being transported back in time to listen to a scene from Shakespeare or a rowdy minstrel song. Except for the women who came to read to us, it was the only amusement we had."

"Tell me about Barrett Hughes," Lydia said. She knew Clyde wouldn't have brought up the actor's name unless he had something serious to impart. "Did he recognize you? Did you remind him of when you'd last seen him?"

"I never said a word to him. Not then. Not three days ago. He wouldn't have known who I was even if I'd told him where that infirmary was. Those troupes usually only did one show before moving on to the next hospital or campground." Clyde cleared his throat and reached for the whittling he'd set aside. "There was a night nurse, very pretty, very young. When we'd all had our laudanum and the lamps were extinguished, she was usually the only medical person on duty. Sometimes I woke up because the laudanum wasn't dulling the pain enough. I'd see her lamp at the end of the ward. She'd be sitting there reading or knitting. And when she sensed I wasn't sleeping she'd pick up the lantern and come down to my bed and give me another few drops. Once in a while I'd hear her humming to herself. It was like being a little boy again, listening to your mother's voice. We all loved her, all of us in that ward."

"What happened?"

"The actors gave their show that night, and I went along with the others, even though at first I hadn't wanted to. It was recitations. Poetry and speeches from Shakespeare. Kind of put us to sleep, but it was better than lying in bed wondering if we'd still be alive in the morning. Not caring, really. I already knew my face was ruined beyond anything a doctor could do for me."

Benjamin stirred in his seat.

"It was late, well after midnight. Everybody was sound asleep except me. Where my skin had been burned and scraped off itched and throbbed like the devil. I was about to sit up, so she'd see I needed her. Nurse Vivian Knowles. I've never forgotten her name." Clyde paused, pressed one finger against his upper lip. "Barrett Hughes was quiet as a mouse when he came into the ward. It was a tent; there were so many of us. So all he had to do was pull back the flap; there wasn't even a proper door. He stood there in the light from her lamp, not saying anything. Swaying. Staring at her. He had a bottle of whiskey dangling from one hand and while I watched, he raised it to his lips and drank."

"You could see all this from your bed?" Lydia asked.

"I had one good eye and the pain that kept me wide-awake." Clyde ran the whittling knife over the wooden doll he was carving, notching out legs and arms. "She stood up, and then she looked around the ward. Quickly, like she knew she should be afraid and needed to find help. I felt her eyes pass over me. I don't think she realized I wasn't asleep. There wasn't anything she could do except scream, and Hughes hadn't made a move in her direction yet. Sometimes, when a patient was on his feet and out of his mind with fear or pain, she could back him toward where he needed to go just by staying calm. I think she meant to move Hughes out of the tent without raising a fuss, without waking any of us up. Lord knows, if it hadn't been for the laudanum, some of us wouldn't ever have slept.

"She took a couple of steps in his direction, and then she stopped. I don't know what she read on his face, but it couldn't have been pretty."

"You're sure it was Barrett Hughes?"

"I may be a one-eyed jack, but I remember everything I see. I got a good look at his face when he was spouting out the

Shakespeare, and I guarantee you a five-dollar gold Half Eagle it was him standing inside our tent that night."

"I didn't mean to imply that you could be mistaken. I know you better than that, Clyde." Lydia was well aware that the man who left wood chips all over the house was as sharp-sighted with one eye as most men were with two.

"Let him tell you the rest, honey," Benjamin said.

"He grabbed her by the arm. She stumbled, and he took the lamp out of her hand and swung it up high, like he wanted her to know he could pour the kerosene on her head and set her on fire if she resisted him. She didn't, but it wasn't to save herself. I think she realized he was drunk enough to set the whole tent ablaze if she crossed him. None of us would get out alive. I didn't see what I know happened because he dragged her behind one of the white curtains they used to make private spaces for when someone was taking his last breath. There was one of those alcoves near where she'd been sitting, with a bed in it where she could lie down for a bit or where a patient could be moved who wasn't expected to make it through the night.

"I heard the noise of him having his way with her and I tried to get up to go pull him off, but I couldn't move. Not an inch. I was in bad shape, Miss Lydia, half in this world, half headed into the next. It wasn't just my face that had me in that ward. I was all over wounded. That and the laudanum kept me off my feet. I couldn't stand up without help, and I couldn't take more than a step or two without passing out. I had to lie there, knowing I was so much less than a man that I wished I could just go ahead and die right that minute. I couldn't even holler; they'd wired my jaw shut, what was left of it."

"You don't have to tell me everything," Lydia said. "Not if it brings back bad memories."

"I'm not leaving anything out. No matter what." Clyde held on to the whittling knife, but no more chips fell from the wooden figure he'd been carving. His hand shook as though a palsy had come over him. "Hughes came out from behind the curtains, picked up his whiskey bottle, and left. Disappeared out that tent flap as though nothing had happened. I waited. After a while—I don't know how long—Nurse Vivian came out, carrying the lantern again. She'd pulled her clothing straight and repinned her nurse's veil, but I could see the bruises on her neck and face. They'd be swollen and purple once daylight came. She'd have to make up some story to explain them."

"She said she'd tripped over something on the wooden sidewalk that ran between the tents so nurses and doctors didn't have to wade through the mud," Benjamin said.

"You've heard this story before?" Lydia asked her father.

He shrugged and resettled the smoked glasses that had slipped down his nose.

"Hughes and his whole troupe were gone before breakfast," Clyde said. A drop of blood appeared on the forefinger that pressed itself against the knife point. "We heard that Nurse Vivian Knowles went home to Vermont that same day. Something about a family member being in need of her care. She was a volunteer, you see, so she could leave anytime she wanted. A couple of Sisters of Charity took her place. Angels of mercy we called them. I thought about that night many a time, but there wasn't a thing in the world I could do except track down the actor who violated her and castrate him the way you do a bull who injures too many cows. But if I did that, somebody was bound to tie him to Miss Vivian, and I knew she wouldn't want her shame to be out in the open. She left the way she did to keep it quiet. So I let it go. All of us in that war let go a lot of what we saw. There wasn't any other way to live through it. I've always wondered whether someone else in that ward waked up long enough to witness what Hughes had done. And then decided to keep quiet, just like I did. You know what they say. A secret's only a secret when just one person knows about it."

"I know you're bound and determined to find out what happened to Septimus, Lydia," Benjamin said. "He was my own wife's nephew, so I feel an obligation, too. But whether this Barrett Hughes had anything to do with his passing or not, he's a man who can't be trusted around women."

"I've been inside a few theatres," Clyde said. "There's too many dark places where a man could accost a woman and no one else would be the wiser."

"You had to be warned, Lydia," her father said.

"Prudence carries a derringer in her reticule. I prefer keeping mine in a pocket." Lydia slid one hand through a concealed slit in the voluminous folds of her dress. The weapon she pulled out was a pearl-handled Remington Model 95. Over-under, double-barreled.

"That's a fine piece," Clyde said, when she'd handed it to him. He hefted it for weight and flipped it once to test the grip. "As long as you can get to it in time."

"I was caught once without a weapon," Lydia said, referring to a case she'd worked with Prudence before Clyde attached himself to the Truitt household. "It won't happen again." She took back the pistol and felt the rounded side of the teapot. "We need more hot water." As though the story Clyde had told and the gun she'd showed hadn't changed a thing.

"I can't leave you to keep an eye on her," Clyde said when she'd taken the teapot to the kitchen. "You're in too much danger. We both know that."

"She'll tell Prudence and Geoffrey and that odd secretary of theirs about Hughes. Hunter was one of the best Pinks ever to work for the agency. He'll have someone in that theatre by the time the next rehearsal starts."

"How?" Clyde asked.

"Never ask a Pink that question," Benjamin said. "Most of what some of them do is either against the law or skirting so close to the edge, it hardly makes a difference. My guess is that a new stagehand will appear in the shadows and the stage manager who hires him will be paid to keep silent about why and when. Prudence and Lydia will be as safe as they ever are in any of the cases the two of them get themselves into. Certainly in less danger than Lydia is every time she has to put on a disguise and deliver something to one of those clients I never meet but whose money I gladly take."

"What did Vivian Knowles look like?" Lydia asked, carrying a tray with more tea and another plate of sliced apple cake. "Do you remember, Clyde?"

"I'll never forget her face. She was the only reason I decided to go on living."

"Describe her for me," Lydia said softly.

"She had the palest, smoothest skin I've ever seen," Clyde began. "Dark hair that curled out from under the nurse's veil they all wore. And the prettiest little white teeth. When she smiled, it was like the sun coming out."

Lydia nodded reassuringly as Clyde closed his eyes and sank into his past.

# CHAPTER 15

The sun wasn't up yet, but the sky had lightened when Lydia crept down the staircase from the second floor, soundlessly unlocked and opened the front door, then sat on the porch to lace up her sturdy walking boots. She'd heard her father's light snores in the upper hallway and Clyde's snorts from the small bedroom just off the kitchen which the original builders of the house had intended for a live-in cook. Without the smell of early-morning coffee to rouse them, she thought the two men might sleep for another hour or so, enough time to allow her to cross the Brooklyn Bridge on the pedestrian walkway and locate a hansom cab to take her to the Argosy Theatre.

Sunday morning. A day of rest for most workers, when New York's streets and sidewalks were largely empty until it was time for church services. Even then, the crowds of worshippers couldn't begin to match the throngs of weekday laborers and office workers who earned their livelihoods in America's largest city. Sunday air was fresh and temporarily free of the stench of ripening manure. With the trees leafing out and April's first blossoming flowers studding parks and gardens, it was almost like a walk in the country, Lydia thought. Except for the hard pavement beneath her feet and the sight of barefoot, orphaned children huddled together for warmth in alleys and the below-ground areaways leading to a basement or kitchen door.

The bridge over the East River, opened only eight years before, hadn't yet acquired the sooty patina and thick speckled layer of bird dropping of older bridges. It still beckoned with a new promise of prosperity. Pedestrians seldom loitered; they marched briskly toward the hope of a new and better life. There was always a breeze and the briny, saltwater smell of the water far below their feet.

A row of hansom cabs stood waiting at the Manhattan shoreline. Lydia climbed into one of them, leaning back into the leather seat and congratulating herself on having escaped the fond but confining care of the two men who looked out for her as carefully as a pair of old and war injured veterans could. She knew they'd tiptoe around the house so as not to wake her until Clyde finally knocked on her bedroom door and opened it to find her gone. She hadn't left a note telling them her whereabouts, so there was no chance he'd reluctantly leave her blind father alone and set out after her. No one needed to know what she was planning. If she was unsuccessful, she'd never mention it.

"Argosy Theatre," she told the cab driver.

"Theatre's closed today, miss," he said.

"I'm with the company," Lydia told him. "Opening night's right around the corner. We'll be in there at all hours until the curtain goes up."

He nodded, raised his whip over the back of his patient horse, and set off for the theatre district. Actors and theatre folk were a funny bunch. He'd driven enough of them to know they weren't like ordinary people. He wondered if he should have asked for the fare in advance. You never knew whether they'd pay or try to wheedle their way out of it. Still, this young lady looked respectable. He felt the slight thud of a street urchin jumping on to the rear of the cab and shrugged.

Probably one of Danny Dennis's boys on an errand for the cabbie all of the city's drivers knew and respected.

He hummed under his breath to the rhythm of his horse's hooves on cobblestones and loosened the wool scarf around his neck. April could be unpredictable, but he thought this morning's sunlight foretold the warmth of true spring.

"It was Miss Lydia," Little Eddie told Danny. "I recognized her right away. She walked across the bridge, then took a cab to the Argosy Theatre and picked the lock to the stage door. I know 'cause I hitched a ride on the back of the cab and watched her break in from behind some trash bins in the alley."

"There's no rehearsal on a Sunday." Danny brushed Mr. Washington's gleaming white coat with sure, swooping strokes.

"Ain't nobody there 'cept the ghosts." Little Eddie shuddered.

"No such thing as ghosts," Danny said. He'd learned during his days in the Irish Republican Brotherhood that once a man was dead, he was really and truly gone. The stories and myths he'd grown up with had all been shattered long before he'd had to leave the country. He didn't believe in much of anything anymore, which is why he was kind to animals and orphans.

"Then why do they always leave a ghost light burning?" Little Eddie protested. "It's to keep the old actors from jinxing the new play." He wouldn't say the word *dead*, but he knew Danny understood what he meant. There wasn't a street dweller anywhere who didn't believe for sure and certain that the deceased were restless and vindictive.

Danny flipped him a coin. "Go tell Mr. Hunter what you saw. He's at the Fifth Avenue Hotel. If you can't find him, go to Miss MacKenzie's house and let her know. Take Flower with you. She needs the exercise."

The young dog was already standing at the stable door, thickly plumed tail waving back and forth as she waited for one of the humans to join her. Like her mother, Blossom, Flower possessed an exceptionally sensitive nose and a memory of city streets that was even sharper than Danny Dennis's. Unlike her mother, Flower had never had to scavenge trash bins for food and feel her red-gold coat thicken with the filth of the alleys in which she slept. She understood most of what the humans said and knew that the words *Hunter* and *MacKenzie* meant adventure. Mr. Washington's stable was a warm, safe refuge, but Flower had been born with a taste for danger. She wasn't fully grown yet, but Danny had already told her many times over what a special dog she was.

Boy and animal trotted out the stable door together, setting off for the Fifth Avenue Hotel at a steady lope that both of them could maintain for blocks at a stretch. You didn't survive very long in the city without stamina and the ability to outrun your enemies.

Mr. Washington chomped his immense yellow teeth together and shook his head.

"All right, boy, if you think we need to," Danny said. "We'll harness and hitch up in case we're called for, but I don't think there's anything to worry about in an empty theatre. Like I told Little Eddie, there's no such thing as ghosts."

Lydia dropped the package of lock picks back into her reticule and eased open the stage door. She stepped inside, closed and relocked the door, then stood in the heavy silence, listening, hearing nothing. Backstage was dark, with just the faint glow of the ghost light beyond the curtains in the wings. A stool always sat beneath the ghost light, just in case a supernatural visitor wanted to sit on the empty stage and stare out at the audiences he'd played to during his lifetime. Recite a monologue. Inspect the phantom sets that had once defined his world. Ghosts of long dead actors and actresses were known to haunt theatres the world over. No prudent member of the profession denied their existence. Everyone took care not to offend their sensibilities.

She walked across the stage, staying well behind the stool so as not to steal the scene being played out in the ether. The floorboards had been swept after the last rehearsal, props put away, the dust sprinkled with droplets of water to keep it from floating in the air and clogging up sensitive throats. Dressing rooms were on the far side, most of them down a spiral staircase that shook under the feet of performers anxious not to miss their cue. Barrett Hughes's private space was on the same level as the stage, down a dark corridor that also contained three other dressing rooms, one each for his female costar and two supporting players. If an actor didn't merit a private dressing room, the extra spaces stayed locked and empty. Not every theatre had four star dressing rooms, but Hughes prided himself on always being above the average. He'd spent enough nights in his early years crowded into poorly ventilated, dimly lit rooms shared with too many fellow actors not to know the value of solitude and quiet in which to prepare an entrance.

Hughes's door was locked but opened easily under Lydia's picks. She'd brought a small bull's-eye lantern with her, lit from the ghost light on the stage. It cast enough brightness to make out the interior of the dressing room, but not be seen beneath the door against which Lydia stuffed a makeup towel. Experience had taught her not to take chances, not to believe that everything would go exactly as planned. Because it seldom did.

She worked through the drawers along the length of the mirrored makeup counter, opening one after the other, fingers creeping carefully toward the back of each drawer where everyone, including her, shoved items they were trying to hide or no longer needed. Snaggle-toothed combs, half-used tubes of makeup, nearly empty jars of cold cream, sticks of eye and lip paint. The detritus of the profession. Small brown bottles containing dregs of laudanum, packets holding one crumpled cigarette or cigarillo, stained and smelly handkerchiefs. Dressing gown hanging in the armoire.

Barrett Hughes was a careful man. There wasn't a single item in his dressing room that didn't belong there. Which meant she'd have to break into the small office where the company records were kept, where Hughes often sat behind a huge, carved desk to play the roles of producer, director, and actor-manager of the company he'd named after himself. Where he summoned performers to warn them they were in danger of being replaced. It was, she remembered, where the confrontation with Septimus had taken place.

Lydia didn't hear the dressing room door open, didn't notice she was no longer alone until a shadow passed in front of the bull's-eye lantern.

"Lydia? What are you doing in here?" Flora Campbell asked.

She hadn't expected to have to explain her presence to anyone. The theatre was closed. It was a Sunday. No rehearsal called and the play hadn't opened yet. All of that rushed through Lydia's brain as her lips parted but her throat refused to function. Even if she managed to think of an excuse, she doubted she'd be able to voice it. She stared at her reflection in the wall of mirrors above the makeup counter, at Flora Campbell's puzzled expression.

"I was passing by and remembered something I'd forgotten that I meant to take home and finish." Even to Lydia, the explanation sounded weak and patently unbelievable.

"In Barrett's dressing room?"

"I thought that's where he might have left it. He was called away from a fitting and left the costume shop wearing the dress coat from act four."

"Did you find it? Do you need help?" Flora took a few steps farther into the room, looking around for a dress coat with pins in it hastily flung over a chair. "Did you check the armoire?" she asked, opening its doors. "No, I don't see it here."

"I suppose he could have had someone bring it back to the fitting room when I wasn't there," Lydia said.

"That would have been the first place I would have looked," Flora chided. "You know how persnickety he is about his private space."

"I don't really know him well at all," Lydia said. "Only through what Septimus told me and the little I've observed in the past few days."

"I forgot how new you are to the company," Flora said. "You're Septimus's cousin, aren't you?"

"Our mothers were sisters," Lydia said. She pulled a stool out from under the counter and sat down, hoping Flora Campbell would do the same. "My side of the family left the theatre years ago, but Septimus often came to visit whenever he was in town." She smiled and blinked her eyes as though the mention of his name had brought tears. "He often spoke of you."

"Did he?" Flora asked. She gathered a handful of skirt and perched herself on another of the makeup stools. She was nearly as small as a child, very fragile looking. "Septimus was as dear to me as anyone could be. I miss him terribly." Her eyes shone brightly wet.

It looked to Lydia as though the girl were about to cry, but when Flora's face didn't turn red and remained exquisitely unpuckered, she reminded herself that she'd seen the actress pretend to weep onstage. And do a very convincing job of it.

"I think he was in love with you," she ventured, hoping she wasn't moving too fast, counting on every woman's fascination with declarations of affection.

"He never spoke of love." Flora's tears dried up in seconds. "We were in the same company on a western tour, so we saw each other every day, but he never said anything too personal or inappropriate. I would have remembered if he had."

"I was surprised when he told me the two of you had joined Tony Pastor's show down by Tammany Hall on Fourteenth Street." Sometimes, when you wanted to rattle a suspect you were questioning, you dropped more information into the conversation than they thought you knew about. Suspect? Flora

Campbell? So tiny that her feet barely touched the floor as she balanced herself on the makeup stool. "I hadn't realized he could sing that well."

"Tony needed a soprano and a tenor. We came as a duo and we didn't need much rehearsal time because we'd sung together on the road," Flora said.

"Septimus wrote sketches for the road company, didn't he? I wish now I'd asked him to tell me about them," Lydia said. "He was always scribbling and making up stories when we were kids and his parents sent him to stay with us for a while. Usually in the summer. We were supposed to keep each other out of trouble when I wasn't in school."

"I didn't meet him until much later than that," Flora said, sliding down from her stool. "Shall we look for Barrett's jacket in the costume room?"

"I remember he told me how much he wanted to write a real play. He said the sketches were teaching him things like timing and how to create dialogue, but they were short and meant to make the audience laugh. Slapstick. He had ambitions to be a serious playwright someday."

Flora reached for the kerosene lamp she'd carried into the dressing room and handed Lydia the bull's-eye lantern. "Shall we?"

"Not yet. A few more minutes, please," Lydia said. "You were closer to him than anyone else these last few years. Especially in recent months. Did he seem unhappy to you? Was he drinking more than he should have?" She forced a quaver into her voice and crossed her fingers that it didn't sound as phony to the actress as it did to her. "Please, Flora, there's no one else I can talk to about him." She stayed seated and put the bull's-eye lantern on the makeup table where it cast a soft glow over what Barrett Hughes hadn't bothered to put away.

Flora seemed to hesitate. She swayed a bit, as if something were tugging at her. Then she put down the lantern she had picked up and seated herself again on the stool that made her look like a child relegated to the dunce's corner. "He did have ambitions," she said. "Big ones. That's one of the reasons he came with me to Tony Pastor's."

"So you were the one Tony wanted to hire?"

"I auditioned right away when I heard he needed a soprano, and I dragged Septimus along with me. Like I said, we'd sung together on the road, so we were already a duet. I knew it could be a break for me, and I convinced Septimus that it would be good for him, too."

"How was that?"

"New York is the heart of theatre in this country. If you're going to be famous, you have to earn a name for yourself here. Nowhere else counts nearly as much as New York City."

"Was Septimus hoping to write and sell a play? Is that why he agreed to the gig at Tony Pastor's?" Lydia asked.

"When I said he had ambitions, I meant as an actor."

"Are you sure about that?"

"As sure as anyone can be about anything."

"I thought I remembered him telling me that he was writing a play with a part in it guaranteed to make you a star. That he read you scenes and rewrote some of them to give your character more lines."

"I don't know anything about that."

"Are you sure? The storyline he was working on was identical to the one you're rehearsing. *Waif of the Highlands* is Septimus's play, isn't it, Flora?"

Flora Campbell turned up the fuel on the kerosene lantern, making the light brighter, casting a wider illumination. She left Barrett Hughes's dressing room without saying another word.

# CHAPTER 16

"That's Flora Campbell." Prudence leaned forward in Danny Dennis's carriage to get a better look at the young woman who'd come out of the Argosy Theatre's stage door and slammed it shut behind her. "She plays the female romantic lead in *Highlands*. She's also the one Septimus wrote the play for in the first place."

"What was she doing in an empty theatre on a Sunday morning?" Geoffrey asked. He watched as the actress flounced past the cab without glancing up at its passengers, half-hidden behind the lowered leather shade. She was visibly furious about something and even more obviously in a mortal hurry.

"Not empty," Prudence corrected. "According to Little Eddie, Lydia is in there somewhere."

As if he'd heard his name, Little Eddie leaped down from his perch beside Danny, Flower following close behind. "I bet she left the door unlocked," he said, jumping up and down with excitement. "Flower and me'll find Miss Lydia. Don't you worry about that."

"You're not going in, Eddie," Geoffrey said. "You and Flower can wait out here with Danny and Mr. Washington."

"I gotta go in, Mr. Hunter. Please, Miss Prudence, tell him I gotta go in. What if Miss Lydia's hurt or tied up or hid in a closet and Flower needs to sniff her out?" Flower's tail wagged so fast, it was a red-gold blur in the shade of the alleyway.

"He could be right, Geoffrey," Prudence said, though she didn't think Lydia was in need of rescue. Not from someone the size of Flora Campbell. "I'll keep an eye on them," she added in a whisper not meant for the boy and the dog to overhear.

"All right," Geoffrey agreed. "But the two of you stay in sight. No going off on your own."

"We won't, will we, Flower?" Little Eddie promised, barreling through the door and into the backstage darkness. His footsteps and Flower's joyful bark echoed in the flies.

"A better question would be to ask what Lydia's doing here," Geoffrey said. He hadn't liked the feel of this case from the beginning, and he especially wasn't comfortable with Prudence and Lydia both joining the company. Ambrose Deslar hadn't been able to tell when the arsenic had been added to the bottle of whiskey from which Septimus had been drinking, which made it next to impossible to confirm that the actor was the intended victim. Deaths from whiskey, arsenic, or a combination of the two were so common in the city as to be unremarkable. The police didn't pay them much attention and neither did the newspapers.

"I'm guessing something made her decide to search Barrett Hughes's dressing room and office," Prudence said. "There wouldn't be any possibility of getting away with it during a rehearsal, so this was the best—maybe the only—time she could be sure of not getting caught."

"She may have been wrong about that," Geoffrey said. "But what I really don't like is that she didn't check in with us before she acted. That's not how a team operates."

"She wasn't Pinkerton-trained," Prudence said.

"You know exactly what I mean."

They'd made their way carefully through the dark backstage area and into the slightly brighter dimness of the stage itself. Little Eddie stood in the weak spotlight glow of the ghost light, staring reverently at it while Flower sat beside him, head cocked in concentration.

"This is it, Mr. Hunter. This is what I was telling Danny about. They leave the ghost light on all the time so when dead actors walk onstage, they know they're welcome to come back."

"Where did you hear that, Eddie?" Prudence remembered Lydia telling her about the superstition, but she wondered where an urchin of the streets could have learned about it.

"Theatres are good places to sleep, like churches, but you have to sneak in and hide before they lock up for the night. One of the boys who beds down at Danny's once in a while told us about it. He claims he spent every night for a couple of weeks sleeping on a pile of canvas until somebody caught on and he got found. They didn't call the cops or anything. Actors wouldn't do that. But he knew better than to try it again."

"What happens if the light goes out?" Geoffrey asked. Little Eddie never failed to amuse him.

"The ghosts'll get real mad. You don't want a ghost gettin' mad at you."

"I thought I recognized your voices and Flower's bark," Lydia said from the opposite wings. "What are all of you doing here?"

"Following you," Prudence said.

"I saw you come across the bridge and get into a cab, Miss Lydia," Little Eddie said. "So I hitched a ride. I figured Danny needed to know where you'd gone."

"Is Danny keeping an eye on me?" she asked. "He knows I don't like it when he does that."

"Can't help it, Miss Lydia. Danny says you and Miss Prudence are like flies drawn to honey when it comes to getting in trouble."

"Barrett's dressing room and office?" Prudence asked. It was better not to comment on Danny Dennis's surveillance. Whether she and Lydia liked it or not, the Irishman, encouraged by Geoffrey Hunter, was set on knowing their whereabouts whenever they ventured into the city streets.

"The dressing room is clean," Lydia said. "Nothing there that links him to Septimus. I haven't checked his office yet."

"We saw Flora Campbell storm out," Prudence volunteered.

"She caught me going through Barrett's makeup drawers," Lydia said. "I drew her out about Septimus as much as I could, but I think I said too much, too fast."

"What do you mean?" Geoffrey asked.

"She denied there was any romantic attachment between them, and claimed she didn't know anything about his wanting to write serious plays. When I told her I knew he'd written *Waif of the Highlands* expressly for her, she left. I never got a chance to ask why she was here this morning."

"She was angry and in a hurry," Prudence said. "She'll go straight to Barrett Hughes."

"Then we don't have much time," Lydia said.

"Eddie, you and Flower go back outside," Geoffrey directed. "Tell Danny to turn the cab around until it's blocking the alley, then you and Flower get out on Broadway and watch for Barrett Hughes. Warn us if you see him coming."

"I don't know what he looks like, Mr. Hunter."

"He looks like a famous actor. And he'll be in a godawful hurry."

Eddie scampered away, Flower leading him through the dark to the backstage door.

"I've got my picks," Lydia said, holding her bull's-eye lantern up as Prudence and Geoffrey followed her to Hughes's office. She had the lock breached in less than a minute. "Prudence, you take the desk," she directed. "I'll look through the cabinets."

"I've got everything else," Geoffrey said, hands already in

the pockets of a coat hanging on a corner rack. "Out of the way, ladies, I'm pulling up this piece of carpet."

Prudence slid out the desk drawers, searched them thoroughly, and then got down on her hands and knees to look for anything that might have been attached to an underside. Nothing. "He keeps good financial records." She thumbed the pale green pages of an accountant's notebook. "Salaries, production costs. But there's nothing here about other investors. I'll keep looking because I don't think he could back a play like this all on his own."

Lydia nodded. She was deep into folders of newspaper clippings. Reviews of plays Hughes had produced or in which he'd acted. Professional biographies of actors and actresses he'd hired. Stage crews. Costume and makeup people. Everything was alphabetized, organized as well as a skilled secretary could have managed. Whatever you needed to know about *Waif of the Highlands* except proof of who had really written it.

"This may be what we want," Geoffrey said, rising from his knees beside a hidden compartment in the floor beneath the carpet he'd shoved aside. "It's a printed copy of the script, with notations in the margins. At first glance, they look like Septimus's handwriting. Like what we saw when we read *The Hereditary Prince*." He laid it on the desk, where light from the bull's-eye lantern lit up the pages as he turned them. "I haven't found anything else."

"Nothing in the desk drawers," Prudence reported.

"Nothing in the files," Lydia said. "The script may be it."

"We have to take it," Geoffrey said. "But once Flora tells Hughes you were here this morning, he'll know who has it, Lydia."

"I'll deny it. He won't be able to prove I took it. I told Flora I'd come back to pick up a jacket I was working on."

"Did you tell her you'd picked the lock to get into the theatre?"

"I'll say the stage door was open when I got here, that I'd

just taken a chance and come by hoping somebody on the crew might have had to work on sets. If she came before I did, Hughes might buy it. Even if she swore she'd locked the door behind her, she could have been mistaken."

"The least he'll do is fire you," Prudence said.

"But not you. He doesn't know there's any connection between us. Gertrude Marrow is on our side and Bobby the doorman won't say a word."

"This copy of the script doesn't prove anything," Geoffrey said. "Hughes will say he hired Septimus to work on beefing up the dialogue because he had experience writing vaudeville sketches on the road. Very believable because Hughes himself started out in vaudeville." He'd been hoping for the original, handwritten script, but if Septimus had had to surrender it to Hughes, the actor had probably burned it once the printer finished the typesetting.

"Here's something else," Prudence said. She'd pulled another accountant's notebook from the back of one of the desk drawers. It was small enough to fit into the pocket of a gentleman's coat, and at first glance she'd thought it was a record of Hughes's personal expenses. But halfway through the neatly inscribed pages she began to read notations of substantial sums of money, organized by initials. No names. Dates and initials only. "I think I may have found some of the backers we were talking about."

"Take it," Geoffrey said. "We need to get out of here." He closed the hole in the floor and pulled the carpet over it.

Lydia made sure the file cabinet drawers were shut while Prudence reorganized the pens, inkstand, and blotter on the desk.

"If I didn't know better, I'd say no one had been in here since Hughes himself left," Lydia said, picking up the bull's-eye lantern. She stood for a moment in the doorway, taking a last look around, then closed the door and used her picks to lock it again.

No one was in the alley when they came out, pausing only long enough for Lydia to make sure the stage door was secured. They were inside Danny's cab and away toward lower Broadway before Barrett Hughes had finished listening to what Flora Campbell had woken him up to tell him.

"I'll take the notebook with the initials in it to Gertrude Marrow," Lydia said as Danny made the turn onto Broadway. "She's bound to know the name of every backer who's ever invested in a stage show or road company. By the time I leave her house, we ought to have a list of names that match up to the initials Hughes has recorded."

"By now your father knows you've gone off somewhere without telling him why. And on a Sunday morning, too. He'll be worried, Lydia," Prudence said. "Why not let Geoffrey and me take over from here? Danny can drop us at Gertrude's and then drive you home. We're not going to be able to do anything with the information we get until tomorrow, anyway. None of these men will be in their offices."

"Daddy and Clyde have been on tenterhooks lately," Lydia said, taking the small accountant's notebook from her reticule and handing it to Prudence. "Whenever I ask them what's wrong, they clam up worse than usual. They're waiting for something to happen or someone to appear, but I have no idea what or who. You're right, Prudence. It doesn't do my father any good to fret about me. I'll tell him where I went and what we found, bring him into the investigation so he can feel like he's working the puzzle with us. It'll do him good. We're between clients for the moment. That always gives him and Clyde both too much time to think. And remember."

"Benjamin Truitt has one of the most brilliant minds it's ever been my privilege to get to know," Geoffrey said. "But it's housed in a fragile body, Lydia. You can't ever let yourself forget that."

Danny remained parked in front of Gertrude Marrow's

house until the actress opened her front door and ushered Prudence and Geoffrey inside. Just before he pulled away to take Lydia across the Brooklyn Bridge, he leaned down and whispered something to Little Eddie. Moments later the street urchin and the dog named Flower climbed into the cab, one on either side of its passenger. She rested a hand on Flower's soft, red-gold coat and smiled when Eddie slid his grimy, chapped fingers into her palm.

"How'd you get hold of this?" Gertrude asked, eyes scanning the notations in Hughes's hard-to-read handwriting.

"Maybe it's better you don't know," Geoffrey said.

"That was Lydia I saw in the carriage the two of you arrived in. So I'm going to make an educated guess that one or all three of you broke into the Argosy Theatre and searched Barrett Hughes's dressing room and office. Am I right?"

Prudence looked at Geoffrey, eyebrows raised in a question.

"Flora Campbell was there. She caught Lydia in Hughes's dressing room."

"Barrett will know all about it as soon as Flora can get to him. I think we need something stronger than tea or coffee, even if it is a Sunday morning." Gertrude pushed aside the tray the maid had set on the table, replacing it with a bottle of imported Scotch whiskey and three crystal tumblers. "I hope you like it neat, because that's the only way I drink it."

"We think Hughes has kept a record of the men who've invested in *Waif of the Highlands*," Prudence explained. Working with Geoffrey had gotten her used to the taste of whiskey. It still burned her throat, but the immediate effect on her self-confidence more than made up for the momentary discomfort of swallowing.

"Let me take a look." Gertrude emptied her glass in a single swallow and gestured Geoffrey to pour her a refill. "Nothing to it," she said, running a polished fingernail along one of the pages. "Anybody in the theatre could tell you who these men are. They may not be the big names like Carnegie, Rockefeller, Vanderbilt, Morgan, Astor—but they're just as well known in the theatre world. Even before I started reading the initials, they're some of the ones I expected to find. What you've got to remember is that our most respectable families have just as much to hide as the scoundrels. There's always a son or a cousin or a nephew who sets up an actress in a discreetly purchased house and then makes sure the play she's in doesn't close before she's ready to move on to something else. They may be making their fortunes in steel or railroads or oil or real estate, but every man who wears pants wonders what it's like to bed an actress. And every single one of them does his best to find out."

"I had no idea," Prudence said.

"No lady admits to knowing what it's considered ill-bred to acknowledge." Gertrude scribbled full names next to the initials she'd copied onto a piece of stationery. "I assume that when Hughes wrote *No* beside a notation, it meant the individual had turned him down. What do you plan to do with this information?"

"If we can convince some of them that Hughes has stolen the script of *Highlands* and is passing it off as his own, we're hoping that at least a few of his backers will demand their money be returned," Prudence said. "All we have to do is hint that Septimus's cousin and closest relative is contemplating taking the issue of authorship to court."

"You'll put a lot of us out of work if you close down the show," Gertrude said. "Including me."

"Septimus was murdered over this script," Geoffrey reminded her. "Hazel Nugent, too, though we don't know yet how she was involved. Hughes is the most likely suspect, so that's where we'll apply the pressure. You said yourself that David Belasco wanted to see more of *The Hereditary Prince*. If Hughes is out of the *Highlands* picture, wouldn't Belasco want to take over production? We all know it's going to be a hit."

"Lydia wants justice for Septimus," Prudence said. "For Septimus and for Hazel both. I don't think it far-fetched to believe we can trap their murderer without destroying the play he wrote."

"There's nothing like a little scandal to sell tickets," Gertrude said. "And this one could count among the biggest the theatre's ever seen." She put one finger to her lips and thought for a moment. "You'll have to be careful how you approach these men. Nobody likes to admit he's been made a fool of or fallen for sucker bait. You'll have to prove to them that Hughes didn't write a single scene of *Highlands* and that he knew what he was doing when he stole it from Septimus. Can you do that?"

"Not yet," Prudence admitted. "But we will."

"How?" Gertrude asked.

Neither Prudence nor Geoffrey had an answer.

# CHAPTER 17

Midway across the Brooklyn Bridge, Lydia realized she hadn't told Prudence and Geoffrey about Barrett Hughes's violation of Nurse Vivian Knowles during the last days of the war. It wasn't something she'd deliberately not revealed, she reasoned with herself; more that it had slipped her mind after the confrontation with Flora and then the discovery of the annotated script and the accountant's notebook with the backers' initials written in it. But even as she sorted through the sequence of events that could justify her momentarily forgetting to share something so central to Hughes's character, she knew she was making excuses. Feeble ones, at that.

Clyde had kept silent about Vivian's secret humiliation for more than twenty-five years. What was it he'd said? He'd kept quiet and hadn't acted to avenge the indecency because Vivian herself had chosen that path. To do anything else would have destroyed her reputation. A woman's good reputation was all that stood between her and a social rejection that was like a slow death. Clyde had only spoken of the incident to Benjamin Truitt because he believed Lydia's contact with Hughes put her in a danger against which she had to be warned. Together, the two old soldiers had taken it upon themselves to risk bringing the sordid episode to light. For all they knew, Vivian Knowles might have died years ago. Women, especially women who married and bore children, often didn't live long lives.

Everyone in the world of the theatre already knew that Barrett Hughes had more than a casual eye for the ladies. Gertrude Marrow had confirmed what most young actresses had to come to grips with at some point in their careers. The prettier you were, the more likely it became that you'd have to pay for the part that could bring you fame. Even a walk-on role without a single line of dialogue often had to be bought at the price of whatever virtue the performer had managed to cling to in the long, impecunious slog toward recognition. Somewhere deep inside her most private self, Lydia knew she'd made the decision to keep Vivian Knowles's name out of the investigation into Septimus's death. Everyone already knew what type of man Hughes was. Why risk ruining another life just to confirm it?

She'd tell Clyde and her father where she'd gone, what she'd done and why. But she'd also tell them that she was keeping Vivian's past out of the present. For now, at least. For as long as she could.

"All I ever knew about her was that Vivian Knowles came from Vermont." Small chips from the figure Clyde was whittling flew through the air onto the fresh sheet of newspaper he'd spread on the floor. "She mentioned a town once. Had a French-sounding name and the railroad went through it. Might have been the state capital."

"Montpelier?" Benjamin asked. He never forgot anything he'd read or been told, and he carried in his head a map of the United States that was as accurate as anything drawn up by a cartographer.

"That sounds about right. I couldn't swear to it, though."

"Did anyone ever find out how she'd come to be working in a hospital?"

"I'd forgotten until you asked the question. The fellow in the bed next to me for a while talked a blue streak. Said it helped with the pain. He asked how she'd come to be there, being too young and too pretty to be one of Miss Dorothea Dix's nurses, and she obviously wasn't one of the Roman Catholic nuns we'd all gotten used to. She told us her father was a doctor and she'd grown up knowing how to take care of people. When she said she'd wanted to study in New York City to be a doctor herself, it was in a kind of whisper, like she knew none of us would believe a woman could or should do something like that."

"Times have changed since **the war**," Benjamin said. "What else do you remember?"

Clyde set aside his knife and the figure that was gradually resembling a beardless man. He sat quietly for a few minutes, rubbing one side of his head gently, as if to stir up the brain hidden beneath the scarring that stretched from that side of his face into the hair that had grown back in irregular tufts. "That's it, Ben."

"She shouldn't be too hard to find if she went back to Montpelier. Doctors are thin on the ground in most places. Her father's probably gone by now, but she might still be alive. Maybe not a doctor herself, but taken up where he left off. Midwife?"

"I can't leave you alone here. You know very well why." Clyde picked up the knife again, ran a calloused thumb along its blade. "The less said about it the better."

"Lydia will be with me. She's as good a shot as you could want."

"She'll be at that theatre during the day. All the way across the damn bridge." Clyde knew that Lydia was crackerjack with a gun, but it didn't sit well with him to see a woman given a man's job to do.

"Suppose I get Geoffrey Hunter to find me one of his ex-Pinks?"

Clyde thought about it. "Might work. Depends on whether he can hire someone who's gonna stay sober." He was stalling. The trip by train up to Vermont would probably take most of a day, then he'd have to make inquiries about a doctor and his daughter named Knowles. If he was lucky, Miss Vivian was still alive and would agree to talk to him. Another day to get back to Brooklyn. He'd have to carve out a few hours to rest and eat. At least three days total, more likely four.

"All I need is a bodyguard with eyes," Benjamin said. "I can hear better than most dogs, and you know I don't need a lot of sleep. We're not even sure they'll send somebody after me."

"You know too much," Clyde said.

"That's what I get paid for."

"And why somebody thinks you need to be silenced. I don't like that the rumor we heard is still floating around out there."

They'd argued about this many times. Reluctant though he was to concede, Benjamin's innate sense of logic told him that Clyde's reasoning was flawless. Business and wealth in America ran on competition so intense that no tactic was considered beyond the pale. Murder was as incidental and commonplace among the very powerful as it was in the crime-ridden streets of Five Points. The only difference was that in business, the guilty rarely if ever paid for their misdeeds.

"We'll have to tell Lydia where you've gone," Benjamin said.

"It wouldn't be fair to Nurse Vivian not to warn her that when Barrett Hughes falls, her name might surface as a proof of past misdeeds."

"Are you sure you're not doing this to make up for having done nothing to save her in the past?" Not having good eyes to see the face of the person to whom he was speaking, Benjamin could be brutal when a difficult question had to be asked.

"Of course I am," Clyde said. He laid the half-carved wooden figure on the mantelpiece alongside his whittling knife. He'd be back for them. "I'd better go now. I'll catch the next train out of Grand Central to Vermont, but I'll make sure Mr. Hunter sends an ex-Pink here before nightfall."

"You should see Lydia before you go."

"She's lying down. I don't want to wake her if she's asleep."

So it was left to Benjamin Truitt to tell his daughter that a stranger would be taking Clyde's place in the house for a few days. He wouldn't explain exactly why a bodyguard was necessary. A client was proving troublesome. No name. Best to be on one's toes, though the likelihood of anything serious happening was very slight. He doubted she'd believe him, but she had too much respect for her father to argue. She'd be on the alert, and that was really the point.

The rest of Sunday afternoon was as quiet and uneventful as Sunday afternoons were supposed to be.

Barrett Hughes decided to wait until Monday morning's rehearsal before verifying what he suspected had been so important to Lydia Truitt that she'd risked breaking into the Argosy Theatre when no one was supposed to be there. He went for a walk in Central Park to clear his head and plan what to do next. Lydia would have to go, of course. There was no doubt about that. She'd expect to be fired, which could make the moment less fraught with emotion than firings usually were. What he didn't know, what was hanging over him like the Sword of Damocles, was whether Septimus had confided in his cousin before drowning himself in a whiskey bottle and a swallow of arsenic. What were the odds? Barrett's entire life had consisted of playing the odds. Sometimes he lost; more often than not, he won.

He stayed away from the Argosy Theatre for as long as he

could, weighing taking a chance on being seen there on a Sunday against the need to know for sure what Lydia had searched for and discovered.

Central Park was jam-packed with families out to enjoy the unexpected spell of warm afternoon weather. Older couples walked their equally elderly dogs, while groups of three or four female office workers strolled arm in arm, safely scouting the paths for unattached gentlemen. Children laughed and shouted, ran and jumped, reluctantly obeying their parents' commands to behave themselves. It was the best of New York City, Barrett thought, realizing that no one was paying much attention to whatever anyone else was doing. Privacy in a crowd. Monday seemed too long to wait.

No one noticed when he left the park and walked down Broadway to the Argosy. He stood on the corner for a few moments before turning down the alley to the stage door. It was locked. Which made him wonder again where Lydia had gotten a key. Had she stolen one? Had she found one among Septimus's effects? It wasn't Barrett's job to keep track of things like that. That's what stage managers were for.

He'd always resented being burdened with the everyday worries of running a troupe. They interfered with the glory of being one of America's most famous actors, especially now that Edwin Booth had botched his final performance of *Hamlet*. Barrett was about to embark on a new direction in a career that had lasted more than forty years already. Much as he owed his fame to Dickens's Scrooge, he was eager to replace the character with that of a much handsomer, even wealthier man. A leading man of a certain age, irresistibly attractive to women young and mature alike, a role every other seasoned actor would envy.

The only thing worth taking from his office would be the manuscript of *Waif of the Highlands* on which Septimus had scribbled changes he wanted to make in the dialogue and business for the actors that he thought would bring the characters alive onstage. Barrett had seen to the burning of the original, handwritten copy of the play as soon as the first printed version had been delivered to the theatre. Septimus had assured him that no other handwritten copy existed, and he'd never had the funds for a private printing. So, with a handshake and the promise of acting the young co-lead, Septimus Ward had agreed never to reveal that he, not Barrett Hughes, had written what the older actor believed was going to be Broadway's next huge success. What was it P.T. Barnum was supposed to have said? *There's a sucker born every minute?* The only sucker who counted in Hughes's new life was dead. Out of the way. No longer a threat.

He didn't waste time checking files and desk drawers to try to determine if they'd been tampered with. He went straight to the rug behind the desk and pulled it off the barely visible trapdoor. Barrett had had one of the theatre's carpenters create the space, paid him off, and then had seen to it he got a better paying job at another theatre. The hiding place was empty. As Barrett had expected, despite hoping it might not be true. No one else could have taken that copy of the play. No one else would know its value.

He refastened the trapdoor, made sure there were no wrinkles in the square of carpet that concealed it, and sat down at his desk to think. Even if Lydia claimed that the notations in the margins were in Septimus's handwriting, that proved nothing. Actors marked up their scripts from the first moment they received them, and it was no secret in the troupe that Septimus had a flair for dialogue. Still, losing that script hadn't been in Barrett's plan. He'd kept it because the changes were good ones, better than any he himself had come up with, and it wasn't unknown for a play to have revisions made that reflected audience reaction. Even well after opening night. On a long run, the changes could be substantial, especially if a sizable portion of the bankroll had come from the lead actor. The challenge would be to figure out what, if anything, Lydia intended to do with what she'd stolen. He didn't see her as a threat, but she might definitely become a nuisance.

The most important thing, the first item on his new agenda, was to get back the script. So perhaps he wouldn't fire the girl right away, after all. She had to be aware he knew what she'd done, so why not let the uncertainty drag on? He liked the idea that she'd lose sleep over the theft, that her nerves would twitch every time she heard his name. The more Barrett thought about it, the more he relished the idea of slowly torturing Septimus's annoying cousin.

He didn't know where Lydia lived, probably in some dingy boardinghouse like most of the other women who worked in the theatre.

But turnabout was fair play. She had searched his office; he'd hire someone to poke around in the miserable room he was certain was all she could afford. Perhaps she and that friend of hers she'd brought along to the costume shop lived in the same boardinghouse?

What was the girl's name? Started with a P. His actor's memory pulled it out of nowhere. Prudence. MacKenzie. Something about it sounded familiar, but Barrett seldom had time to read the society columns. He knew what was playing in every theatre in Manhattan, what troupes were going out on tour, which leading ladies were rumored to be having affairs with their leading men, but relatively little about Mrs. Astor's Four Hundred. The big names, of course—Vanderbilt, Rockefeller, Astor—and the men he had persuaded to back his latest endeavor with hard cash, but not much about their wives. Society and the theatre were two different worlds. Their paths seldom crossed.

He decided to allow Lydia and Prudence to keep their jobs. For the moment. At least until Lydia made up her mind what she'd do with the script she'd stolen.

Then he'd pounce.

He'd make her sorry she ever dared take him on.

# CHAPTER 18

"We've got firm dates for the final tech and costume rehearsals, ladies," Cynthia Pierce told Lydia and Prudence on Monday morning as they took off their light spring coats and unpinned their hats. The wardrobe mistress stood with arms akimbo over a pile of unfinished costumes heaped on one of the measuring tables. "We have exactly eight days to get everything approved and finished."

"Weren't all the costumes approved already?" Prudence had paged through the folder of detailed sketches with swatches of material attached to each drawing and the physical measurements of the actor or actress who would wear it pinned below the illustration.

"Preliminary approval, yes." Cynthia picked up a pair of scissors and slipped a pincushion onto her wrist. Eyeglasses dangled from a silver chain around her neck and a pencil protruded from her tightly coiled hair. "It's what they look like all together in the gaslight on stage that counts. Thank goodness the Argosy doesn't have electricity yet. Lord knows what that kind of light will do to colors like red or yellow. Steal attention from everything else is what I predict. It'll mean rethinking the whole palette of a scene."

"Well, like you said, we don't have to take electricity into account, so that's one less thing to worry about." Lydia followed the costume mistress's lead, stuffing the pockets of her apron with scissors, measuring tape, magnifying glass, paper and pencil, then fastening a thick pincushion around one wrist.

"You can carry an armload of costumes, Prudence," Cynthia directed. "We'll be able to get to some of the actors in the crowd scenes while Mr. Hughes is giving notes to the speaking parts. He may want to see what the overall effect is from the back of the house, but for right now it's individual quick checks of the final fittings before we start sewing again."

She swept out of the costume shop, Lydia close behind, while Prudence picked up a stack of ragged dresses and patched trousers. Thank goodness all she'd have to do was stand on stage loaded down with what Lydia and the costume mistress would be measuring and sticking pins into. Her sewing skills were still very rudimentary—largely confined to ripping out and stitching new hems—and Prudence knew that any call to make a complicated change could be her downfall.

Mainly she was concentrating on making herself as invisible as possible, which meant staying out of everyone's way and not making eye contact.

Prudence and Lydia had both expected the stage doorman to hand Lydia a note directing her to report immediately to Barrett Hughes's office when they'd arrived that morning, but nothing had happened. They'd looked at each other, waiting for the ax to fall, but he'd waved them on, not a word said about anyone being in the theatre on Sunday.

"Maybe Flora didn't tell him," Lydia whispered as they'd scurried along the dark, narrow backstage corridors to the costume shop.

There hadn't been time for more speculation. Rehearsals

began as scheduled, or all holy hell broke loose. Especially when it was some of Barrett Hughes's own money the actors were wasting if anybody was late or unprepared. That included makeup, costume, prop, stage, and tech crews.

Years of working on all kinds of theatrical productions had made Cynthia Pierce one of the fastest and most efficient costume mistresses in the business. Mouth bristling with pins, she rarely lost time and never missed a deadline, seemingly unfazed by whatever was going on around her. She had three of the crowd scene workingmen in and out of their shirts before Hughes had finished giving notes to the understudy who had taken over the role Septimus Ward was supposed to have played.

Lydia sat on the floor, motioning first one then another of the women to step into a skirt, walk in her direction, turn, walk away, come back, and get pinned. All of this had already been done in the costume shop weeks ago, but there was always the chance that what worked in one setting would seem out of place in another.

From time to time Barrett Hughes glanced in their direction, nodding at the costume mistress as he assessed the crowd scene actors. Did they blend in together? Did any of them stand out and risk stealing the audience's attention from one of the principals? Did they look enough like the real working poor to convince ticket holders that this was the background Flora Campbell's character was trying to escape? Gray and brown, soiled with rubbed-in ash and shoe polish, their clothing had to look in the gaslight like what the audience might have seen a street sweeper, bricklayer, or stevedore wearing. Prudence wasn't sure that theatregoers ever cared or noticed how the lower classes covered themselves.

Every time Prudence saw Barrett Hughes's eyes sweep over Lydia, she tensed, waiting for him to order her friend to her feet and out the door. Why hadn't he fired her? Could Flora have decided not to tell him that she'd discovered Lydia where she had no business being on a Sunday morning? It made no sense and the tension of not knowing was giving her a headache.

An hour dragged on. The smell of the gaslights, the occasional screech from the musicians' pit, and the pins pricking her arms made Prudence's headache worse. Her eyes burned and her stomach roiled. She tried to remember what she'd eaten for breakfast, the taste of half-digested coffee rising in her throat.

"Here you go, honey," Gertrude Marrow said, slipping a sugary lozenge between Prudence's lips. "You look like you're about to pass out. Hand me some of those costumes. I'm done being measured and I look as much like a tenement woman as the real thing."

"It's the smell of the gas," Prudence said. "And the heat the flames give off."

"Coal gas." Gertrude nodded. "You get used to it after a while." She removed half the costumes from Prudence's arms. "We can take these back to the costume shop. Cynthia looks like she's almost finished. She and Lydia can manage the rest. You'll feel better in a few minutes."

Almost as soon as they stepped off the stage and began winding their way along the backstage hallways, Prudence's head began to feel lighter. She was steadier on her feet, and she managed to rearrange the costumes she was carrying so the pins weren't digging into her flesh anymore.

"I had an interesting conversation with someone after you and Mr. Hunter left yesterday," Gertrude said as they closed the door of the shop behind them and laid the pinned costumes carefully on the cutting tables.

"What about?" Prudence asked. She sank down into one of the chairs and gratefully accepted the glass of water Gertrude handed her.

"I've got to get back on stage before Hughes misses me. I'll have to tell you later. Will you be all right if I leave you alone? Cynthia and Lydia should be here soon."

"I'll be fine, Gertrude. Thank you," Prudence said. She'd started to wonder why the smell of the gas should have affected her so strangely. She and everyone else she knew heated and lit their homes with gas and coal. They all complained about the smuts of coal and the lingering heaviness of gas, but electricity was still so new that few were willing to trust it. Even fewer could afford it.

Almost absentmindedly she picked up a pair of trousers Gertrude's skirt had swept to the floor. The smell of something rank wafted up from its folds. Like old sweat and soured whiskey. She held the material to her nose for a few seconds, then threw it as far from her as she could, waving her hands in front of her face to dissipate the odor. Did all of the costumes smell that bad? She picked up a shirt, held it briefly to her nose, then put it down on the table again. Nothing. A faint whiff of body odor from the actor who had tried it on.

One by one Prudence went through the costumes she and Gertrude had carried from the stage. She found another pair of pants that seemed to smell of whiskey, though so faintly she couldn't be sure, and a woman's blouse that had about it something floral but ultimately unidentifiable. The incident puzzled her, not least because she couldn't make sense of the dizziness that had now passed. Any sequence of events—no matter how small or seemingly unimportant—that wasn't logical would bedevil her until she'd unraveled whatever mystery it contained. Sometimes she thought her father had trained her too well.

Lydia and Cynthia hadn't returned to the costume shop yet. Prudence stuffed the three garments she thought smelled odd into one of the linen bags used to cover hanging costumes and spread the rest of them out on the table, trying not to let the pins from one snag the fabric of another. Then she made her way through the cramped backstage area.

Barrett Hughes spotted her in the wings and called to her to come on stage. "Yes, you," he repeated when Prudence stayed where she was. "We need a few more bodies in this street scene, and someone forgot to tell the walk-ons they were needed today. I want to see what it looks like when we have a full complement onstage." He turned and snapped an order at his assistant director, a pale and perpetually trembling young man whose chief responsibility seemed to be to write down whatever Hughes shouted at him.

Lydia raised a hand and beckoned Prudence in her direction while Hughes's back was turned. "This is ridiculous," she muttered as Prudence squeezed behind her. They were huddled together on the steps of the tenement building where Flora's character lived and where her impoverished family was supposedly dying of starvation and disease.

"Haven't you always wanted to be an actress?" Gertrude Marrow teased. "Stand around and do nothing for hours while a foul-mouthed director can't make up his mind what he wants?"

"This is such a waste of our time," the wardrobe mistress complained. She'd stacked the pinned costumes neatly on a bench in the wings but hadn't managed to make her escape to the costume shop before Hughes decided he needed to see more bodies in the street scene.

"Quiet! Places, everyone!" Hughes stepped to the front of the stage, waiting until silence fell before continuing. "We're outside the building where Flora's character lives. Three women on the stoop, a group of men in the street, two pushcarts downstage left, a pair of women with shopping baskets standing by the pushcarts. Kill the lights, then bring them up slowly so the audience has time to discover the scene. A little conversation. Nothing loud. I want the *impression* of speech. When Flora walks onstage, start dimming the lights. Slowly, and not all the way to black. Leave the three lights downstage center on full, so the audience is drawn to her. She stops center stage, makes a half turn toward the house. Music up. She starts to sing, turns back to face the audience. I don't want to be concentrating on anyone else but Flora. Got it, everyone? Let's see what it looks like."

Hughes stepped down to the house and walked halfway up the aisle.

Two lighting men carrying long rods with what looked like candle snuffers on the ends positioned themselves along the rank of gaslights.

"Places!" Hughes repeated. "Kill the lights. Get ready to bring them up and hold until Flora makes her entrance. Then dim down as she starts to sing."

"Let's get this over with," Lydia whispered.

"It's what's called the *sell scene,*" Gertrude murmured. "Worth the price of the ticket. Make or break for our little Flora."

They stood motionless as the gaslights were dimmed and the stage disappeared into blackness. Then the lights came up, street and tenement dwellers gradually responsive to an ordinary New York spring day.

"Hold it, Flora," Hughes shouted. "Lydia, cross over to the pushcart as though you need to buy something."

She picked up an empty basket from the stoop and made her way downstage left.

"Not bad, but slower next time, like you know you haven't got enough money to buy anything but a sprouting potato or half-rotten cabbage. Back to the stoop, please. We'll try this again. Kill the lights, count to ten, then bring them up."

Lydia said something under her breath that Prudence decided she was probably glad she couldn't make out.

The gaslights along the apron of the stage dimmed, near-blackness descended again, and as the lights gradually flickered up, Lydia retrieved her basket and took the first tentative steps toward the pushcart.

Nobody saw exactly what it was that came flying through the air, but the sleeve of Lydia's dress was cut cleanly. Blood began to run down her arm before the knife thudded into a piece of scenery stored in one of the wings.

Lydia collapsed. The stagehands working the gaslights stood as if transfixed. Nobody else moved. No one spoke. Then Prudence picked up her skirts and ran to where her friend lay unconscious in a pool of red.

Moments later Flora Campbell stepped out from where she had waited to make her entrance.

"What happened?" she asked. "What's going on?"

# CHAPTER 19

Finding Nurse Vivian Knowles in Montpelier, Vermont, was easier than Clyde Allen had expected. He'd always known New Englanders had a reputation for being closemouthed and suspicious of strangers, but he'd reckoned without the manpower losses of the war. Vermonters had been forced to welcome foreigners and out-of-staters to the mills that were the region's lifeblood.

The stationmaster looked him over top to bottom before tugging at the brim of his cap and hitching his thumbs into his belt. "What do you need a doctor for?" he asked, stepping back from the danger of foul and miasmic breath. Only a few passengers had gotten off the train, most met by family members who drove them away in buggies and farm wagons. The platform was empty except for a stray cat scenting out early-spring mice and grasshoppers.

Clyde handed him a calling card that had been printed with his name and a fictitious address in Manhattan.

"Inquiry agent?"

"Discreet inquiries." Clyde pocketed the card the stationmaster handed back to him. "Inheritances, mainly." Everyone was interested in money and property left behind by estranged or distant relatives.

"Doc Knowles has a clinic in her house on the corner of Main and State Streets." The stationmaster led Clyde through the waiting room. "It's about a ten-minute walk, but she don't open to see patients for another couple of hours." He kept his eyes looking straight ahead or at the floor, determinedly ignoring what he presumed to be hideously deformed scar tissue under the black mask the stranger wore over half his face. Even in as small a city as Montpelier, there were veterans whose wounds had severely disfigured and maimed them. People got used to pretending to ignore them.

"That gives me time for breakfast."

"Try the station hotel just opposite. Good food at a decent price. Rooms, too, if you're staying a while." He raised a questioning eyebrow.

"I don't know that I'll need a room, but I thank you kindly for the recommendation," Clyde said. He touched a finger to the brim of his hat and stepped out into the street, feeling the stationmaster's eyes on his back as he walked away. There wasn't a doubt in his mind that word of a stranger's arrival in town would precede his visit to the clinic.

The station hotel was like every other establishment of its kind—plain, inexpensive, and catering to the traveling salesmen who made up the majority of its clients. The dining room boasted white tablecloths and smelled of overheated coffee. Early as it was, nearly every table was occupied by commercial travelers tucking into plates of fried steak, fried eggs, fried potatoes, and fried bread. They'd haul sample cases around town until they returned at the end of the day for another heavy meal and a well-earned night's sleep before moving on to their next stop.

Clyde ordered the standard full breakfast, then snapped open a copy of the local paper he'd picked up at the front desk, skimming the ads that were at least as important to the weekly

*Argus and Patriot* as the news it reported. He found the announcement of Dr. V. Harper Knowles's spring office hours in a discreet notice tucked beneath a column announcing the comings and goings of Montpelier's citizens. The stationmaster hadn't been wrong. He'd have more than enough time to enjoy his meal and stroll leisurely up Main Street to State. If the map he'd bought for an additional nickel could be trusted, State Street paralleled the Winooski River and boasted the state's capital building and rows of private homes.

There was something about New England's villages, towns, and small cities that was so unlike the bustling atmosphere of New York City that Clyde felt as though he'd journeyed to another country in a quieter age. If this was where Vivian Knowles had grown up and where she fled for sanctuary and healing after the incident that ended her nursing career during the war, he could well understand why she had remained. The air was cooler; he was glad he'd brought a warm coat as he walked up Main Street. Shops were opening and the clop of horses' hooves drowned out the rush of the river. He saw immigrant faces and heard languages other than English. Not nearly as many as in the city he'd left, but enough to indicate that new Americans could be found wherever you went.

The doctor's office occupied the front three rooms of a substantial family home, complete with wraparound front porch and steeply roofed gables. A bellpull hung beneath the brass plaque announcing the doctor's name. Too late, after he'd already rung, he realized he was at least half an hour early. The posted hours didn't match the newspaper ad.

He heard footsteps echoing along a wooden floor and then a hand pulled aside the lace curtain covering the glass insert of the front door. A key turned in the lock, the door opened, and there she stood. Nurse Vivian Knowles, more than twenty-five years later, but still to Clyde's eyes as beautiful as the last time he'd seen her.

She didn't recognize him. That was obvious from the puzzled frown on her face.

"Unless this is an emergency, the clinic isn't open for another thirty minutes." She held a breakfast napkin crumpled in her left hand. There was a speck of egg at one of the corners of her mouth. "You can wait on the porch, if you like. My nurse will be arriving soon. She'll take your information."

"I'm not here for a medical reason," Clyde began. He didn't want to have this conversation standing in a doorway with someone whose breakfast he'd interrupted. But he thought he'd have to proceed slowly, cautiously, or risk having that door slammed in his face. "I wonder if you remember the Weatherly Military Hospital in Maryland," he asked.

Her face blanched and her fingers tightened on the napkin they held.

"I was a patient there back in sixty-four, when an acting troupe came through. Clyde Allen's my name. The medics didn't think I'd live."

"There were so many badly wounded and dying soldiers," Vivian said. "It didn't matter that we all knew the war couldn't go on much longer. The killing was like a fever that wouldn't break. I try not to remember those days, Mr. Allen. And I'm sorry, but I don't have any memory of treating you."

"I didn't expect you would, Miss Knowles. It was a long time ago."

"Dr. Knowles now," she corrected him.

"I wonder if I could come in for a few minutes. Something's come up that you need to know about."

She hesitated, then stepped back, allowing him to enter the hallway, closing the door behind him and turning the key in its lock. "There's hot coffee in the kitchen," she offered.

"I could use a cup."

Her half-eaten breakfast had cooled on the plate. Vivian scraped the remains of congealed egg yolk and ham into the cat's bowl, topped it with fragments of buttered toast, and poured fresh coffee for both of them.

"You'd better take a seat at the table and tell me what this is about, Mr. Allen." Her eyes took in the black mask that no longer quite hid the scarred half of his face with its empty eye socket, dropping to examine the gnarled fingers studded with cuts from Clyde's whittling knife. It was as if with that one sweeping diagnostic examination she knew what kind of life he'd lived since being discharged from the military hospital where a war-weary staff had refused to let him die.

"I'm not sure how to go about this," Clyde began.

"One sentence at a time."

"Well, ma'am, the night the acting troupe came to the hospital in March of sixty-four was a bad one for me. I'd had enough laudanum to put an ordinary man out for the night, but it wasn't working anymore as well as when Johnny Reb first tried to blow me into kingdom come. I was lying there on my cot trying to will the pain away, so I was awake when Barrett Hughes pushed open the tent flap."

Vivian stiffened on her wooden chair. Her eyes left Clyde's face and fastened on the coffee she hadn't drunk. The napkin dropped to the floor.

"I didn't think much of it at first, because we'd had actors come visit us before after their shows were over, especially if some of us hadn't been able to be carried out to where the stage had been set up. I didn't realize how late it was until I figured out that everybody around me was sound asleep. Hughes was drunk. It didn't take but a good long look at him to figure that out. He was carrying a bottle and rolling from side to side like a sailor with a bad case of sea legs. I saw you go up to him and say something. Then I thought he grabbed you and dragged you into that cubicle behind the nurses' desk. I wasn't sure, because it happened so fast, but then I tried to get out of bed in case you were in trouble. But I couldn't. I don't know whether it was the laudanum I'd already swallowed or the sheer weakness of being half-killed, but I was as stuck to that mattress as a bedbug."

Vivian didn't raise her eyes from the coffee cup, but silent tears began to roll down her cheeks.

"I wish to God and Heaven I'd been able to get my legs under me and my feet moving. But it didn't happen. I wasn't the man I should have been that night, Miss Vivian, and I've cursed myself for it ever since. I know what happened in that cubicle because I'd seen it happen dozens of times when we raided a farm or plantation house in one of the rebel states. I've never doubted what he did to you."

"He violated me," she said in the flat voice of a doctor giving the worst news ever to a patient's grieving relative. "The word for what he did isn't usually spoken aloud—we employ euphemisms to make the act seem less horrific than it is. But that's what Barrett Hughes did, and that's why I was gone the next morning as soon as the first wagon left for the station."

"I knew it that night. I've never forgotten the sound of it."

"You listened?"

"I bore witness. That's what we'd call it when something real bad was happening that we couldn't make go away. Like prisoners being shot dead or bayonetted after they'd thrown down their weapons and surrendered. Worse things than that. Nobody's all the way innocent in a war."

"You said there was something I needed to know."

He told her about Septimus Ward, the play the actor had written and the death someone had engineered for him. "If it's Hughes who killed him so Septimus couldn't try to take back what he wrote, his past is likely to rear its ugly head when he's accused and brought to trial. I don't know if you've got the kind of newspaper reporters up here that we have in New York City, but ours keep digging at a story until there's nothing left to find. Hughes already has a reputation as a ladies' man and it's pretty common knowledge among theatre folk that he makes young actresses pay for the parts he gives them. If you know what I mean?"

"I know exactly what you're trying to say."

"It may come out that an army volunteer nurse resigned and left her hospital in a hurry the day after Hughes and his troupe played there. I saw bruises on your neck when you came out from the cubicle that night. No matter how much you tried to hide them, somebody else probably saw them, too."

"Before I left, I wound a scarf around my throat and explained to the hospital staff that I'd tripped and injured myself on the wooden sidewalk. After I got home, I told anyone who asked that it was for the catarrh."

"I'm sorry to have to be the bearer of this kind of news, but you needed to be able to prepare yourself. In case the worst happens."

"How likely is it?"

"Nobody knows right now."

"The police?"

"Septimus's cousin is working with private inquiry agents to find out who murdered him. The police decided he'd accidentally swallowed arsenic—rat poison—when he was drunk. It happens all the time in the tenements."

"And you're one of these inquiry agents?"

"No, ma'am. Not exactly. The man I'm looking out for has a daughter. She's the one who wouldn't let it lie. She's got the inquiry agents on the case, but she wouldn't stay out of it herself."

"I don't understand."

"She and a friend of hers got themselves jobs in the costume shop at the theatre where Hughes is rehearsing Septimus Ward's play. They figure he'll make a mistake of some kind, show his hand, so to speak."

"Doesn't she realize how dangerous that could be?"

"She knows, but she wouldn't let it stop her."

"What does this have to do with me?"

"Like I said, if Miss Lydia or the inquiry agents find enough evidence that Hughes was responsible for her cousin's death, the police will have to arrest him. There'll be a trial. The lawyers and the newspapers will be on him like fleas on a dog. I reckon a jury will believe that a man who violated women is a man who could commit murder. One evil act leads to another. Could be you'll have to testify against him when they tear into his character and his past."

Vivian's right hand crept to her neck, the fingers lightly stroking where there had once been bruised flesh. "I can't believe they'll go back that far. You said Hughes has a reputation for taking advantage of young actresses. Surely the prosecution will think it's enough to call a few of them to the stand."

"I can't promise you that, ma'am. Nobody can predict what a lawyer will do in court."

"If you're right, how soon will this happen?"

"Could be not too long, could be never."

"I can see a man getting away with abusing women—his victims won't disgrace themselves by testifying against him. But murder?"

"I thought you ought to know."

The front door opened. Footsteps crossed the hall and faded into the consulting rooms. The nurse had arrived. Patients would soon follow.

Vivian stood to lead Clyde to the front door. "I do remember you now, Mr. Allen," she said. "The chief surgeon refused to work on your face, said it wasn't worth his time because you weren't going to survive, so he'd best see to those who had more of a chance to live."

"I didn't know that."

"There were a lot of wounded we had to set aside to die. You were lucky. One of the younger doctors lost his last patient of the day on the table. When he turned away, he saw your stretcher lying on the floor. I remember him saying that maybe it wasn't too late to save just one more. The orderlies picked you up and he set to work. I don't remember his name, but he performed a miracle on you that afternoon."

"Not one I care to look at in a shaving mirror," Clyde said.

"You're alive. That ought to be enough."

"Yes, ma'am."

He caught the midday train out of Montpelier back to New York City.

# CHAPTER 2O

Barrett Hughes lunged forward, grabbed Flora by the arm, and dragged her off into the stage left wings, shoving her into the arms of one of the burly set carpenters.

"Take her to her dressing room," he shouted over his shoulder as he turned to rush back onto the stage. "Don't let her out. Lock her in if you have to. Make sure no one goes near her door." Seamstresses were expendable, not so an ingenue on the cusp of stardom.

Lydia lay pale and motionless in a stream of blood that was slowly spreading across the stage. Prudence tore frantically at the damaged sleeve, ripping through the material to get at the wound. Cynthia Pierce had taken white makeup towels from a costume basket and was scissoring them into strips that could be used to wrap the arm.

"This needs to be stitched," Prudence said, using forefinger and thumb to hold together the edges of the wound. "Has anyone sent for a doctor?"

"I've got needle and thread right here." Cynthia pulled a thin embroidery needle from the pincushion on her wrist. "The main thing is to stop the bleeding." She made a knot at the end of the thread and bit off the excess with her teeth.

"Here we go. This is what she needs," said one of the stage-hands who had doubled as part of the street crowd. He pulled a bottle of whiskey from his trousers pocket, thumbed out the cork, and poured it over Lydia's arm, gesturing to the ward-robe mistress to hold the needle under the stream of brown liquid.

Lydia bucked and screamed as the whiskey flowed over raw flesh. Pain had rendered her unconscious and pain brought her back. Prudence held her as tightly as she could, whispering com-forting words to calm and soothe her friend. Just as quickly as she'd regained awareness of her surroundings, Lydia fainted again.

"It's for the best," the stagehand said, upending the bottle to gulp down the last of the whiskey. "It hurts like hell, but it keeps the wound from festering. We learned that out west when we were on tour. Whiskey did us for everything from snakebite to broken bones."

"This won't take long. Let's hope she stays out until I'm done." Cynthia's embroidery needle flashed in and out of Lydia's flesh as gleams of silver lit by gaslight. She was quick and expert, the stitches small and even.

As Prudence gently wiped away the blood, less and less of it oozed from the cleaned gash. When Cynthia nodded that she'd finished, Prudence wound strips of makeup towel around her friend's upper arm.

"Tight, but not too tight," Cynthia instructed.

The stagehand with the whiskey bottle wandered into the backstage area where he'd hidden another pocket-sized bottle of cheap rye.

Lydia's lids trembled and she moaned softly. Someone handed water to Prudence, who lifted Lydia's head and held the glass to her lips. Someone else brought blankets from a dressing room and spread one of them over Lydia's body. The theatre was always cold and damp.

"Prudence," Lydia whispered.

"What is it?" Prudence bent closer. She could barely hear what her friend was trying to say. "Don't try to talk."

"The knife. Get the knife. Wherever it is, get the knife before someone else does." Lydia's eyes closed again. One hand clutched at Prudence, then fell slackly by her side.

Barrett Hughes shouted for two of the stagehands to improvise a stretcher. They unscrewed a door from the tenement set, folded the other blankets atop the raw wood, made sure Lydia was securely situated in her woolen cocoon, then carried her off stage toward the costume shop.

"She'll be all right. It was a near miss, but accidents happen," Hughes said as Lydia's cortege disappeared into the darkness. "Back to work. Places, everyone. This rehearsal isn't going to run itself. Opening night will be here before you know it. Places," he shouted as cast members began to move slowly across the stage, muttering to one another and shaking their heads. "Someone tell Flora she can leave her dressing room."

He waved an arm at the musicians in the pit. They immediately began to play the opening bars of the song Flora would sing. Hughes herded his actors into position.

If he'd bothered to look toward where Lydia had passed from sight, he would have seen Prudence MacKenzie reach out, grab something from a set piece just beyond the wings, wrestle it from the wood, and thrust it into one of the deep pockets of her apron.

But he didn't. Barrett Hughes had already forgotten about Lydia. She wasn't dead, wasn't likely to die, so the police wouldn't come to the theatre and interrupt things the way they had when that seamstress whose name he couldn't remember had accidentally fallen into a trunk and locked herself in. That incident had cost valuable rehearsal time. He wouldn't allow it to be repeated.

"Places, everyone!"

"Both of you are going home for the rest of the day," Cynthia Pierce instructed. "Don't worry about what Hughes will say. You work for me. I set your hours. As long as the costumes are ready for the final dress rehearsal, he can't complain."

"I sent a boy who was hanging around the alley to fetch Danny Dennis." Gertrude Marrow lowered her voice so only Prudence could hear. "I've got to rejoin the company. We'll speak later. Tonight or tomorrow. It's not urgent."

For a moment, Prudence couldn't think what Gertrude was talking about. Then she remembered that the actress had mentioned a conversation she'd had that she wanted to tell Prudence about. Everything but concern for Lydia had been driven out of Prudence's head at the sight of her friend's blood and the realization that had the knife been a few scant inches to the right, it would have pierced Lydia's heart. And she'd be dead.

While she waited to be told that Danny and his hansom cab had arrived at the theatre, Prudence tried to organize her thoughts, tried to catch hold of the threads of this odd investigation that seemed to have gotten away from her, from Geoffrey, and even from Lydia. Septimus Ward had died before he could officially become their client. Murdered where he lived. A seamstress had been the victim of one of the most bizarre incidents Prudence had ever heard of. Smothered inside a trunk where costumes and material were stored. Despite what the police wanted to believe, it hadn't been an accident. Someone had pushed the young woman into the suffocating piles of silk, cotton, and wool where Prudence imagined she'd pounded frantically on the lid of the trunk until she mercifully lost consciousness. And died.

Two deaths staged to look like mischance. One attempted murder. In a week's time.

"Prudence." Lydia's voice, weak but steady. "I'm not going

home to Brooklyn. Not right away. When Danny gets here, tell him to take us to your office."

"What office?" the wardrobe mistress asked, staring at her two assistants. One who could barely hold her own with needle and thread and the other closely tied to the dead Septimus Ward. "What office is she talking about?"

"It's nothing," Prudence said. "She's confused. I told her I'd take her to a doctor's office to get the wound looked at."

"I have to get back to rehearsal." Cynthia picked up her basket of sewing supplies and costume sketches. "Your hansom cab should be here soon. I'll tell the stage doorman to send someone for you." Impulsively, she bent down and brushed Lydia's hair from her forehead. "Be careful," she whispered.

"Cynthia wanted to say something else, but she didn't dare." Prudence had enfolded Lydia in blankets and wrapped one comforting arm around her friend's waist.

Danny, whom Prudence had never known to be anything but unflappable, sent one of his street boys to warn Geoffrey they were coming. Then he maneuvered the city traffic with his usual skill, making good time to the corner of Wall Street and Broadway, where the offices of Hunter and MacKenzie were located. Mr. Washington tossed his mane and stamped one hoof as Danny hitched him to a ringed post. Then the Irishman carried Lydia into the building, navigating the stairs as though she weighed no more than a child.

"She's stopped bleeding," he said, depositing her on a couch in Geoffrey's private office. "I'm thinking she's better off without a doctor, from what Miss Prudence told me. Whiskey and a clean needle and thread. That's about all you can do for a knife wound." He nodded at Josiah Gregory, who was staring open-mouthed at the torn, bloodstained sleeve Prudence had begun to peel back from Lydia's upper arm. "I'll be on my way, if you don't think you'll need me."

Geoffrey shook his head. "We know how to find you."

"I'll leave one of the boys downstairs. I won't be far away," Danny said. And he was gone.

"Sugary tea," Prudence commanded. "Strong and sweet." She didn't know why sugared or honeyed tea was always given to patients who'd suffered a shock, only that it seemed to be a universally recommended remedy that actually worked.

Josiah scurried from Geoffrey's office to fill the kettle, his organized secretary's mind running over the list of supplies he kept in one of the cabinets. If sugary tea would help Miss Lydia regain her strength, sweet German pastries would also be in order. Fortunately, as he did almost every morning, he'd stopped by his favorite bakery.

"Stop fussing, Prudence," Lydia said, struggling to sit up and throw off at least one of the blankets. "I don't need to be swaddled like an infant. Did you get the knife that did the damage?"

"I did," Prudence said, pulling it from her pocket where she'd also stuffed one of the torn makeup towels around the blade. She handed the stained towel and bloodied knife to Geoffrey, who laid them out on his desk.

"Looks like a Bowie knife, except for the size," he said, running a finger along the flat side of the cutting edge. "Recently sharpened. You can see where someone used a whetstone on it. Not very skillfully. He left scratches."

"That's a throwing knife," Lydia said, leaning as far toward the desk as she could. "Vaudeville acts use them because the balance is good. Most of the time they have the hilts brightly painted or gilded so the audience can see how close they come to their targets. Sometimes the team engraves their name or a symbol that identifies them."

"How do you know that?" Prudence was frequently amazed at what Lydia could explain.

"Haven't you ever been to a vaudeville show?" Lydia asked.

"No, I haven't." Neither had most other society debutantes, Prudence thought. Vaudeville was considered crude, sensational, and utterly below their notice. She made a mental note to read the theatrical section of the newspaper and find out where one was playing in New York City. She'd go by herself if she couldn't convince Geoffrey to take her.

"Knife throwing is one of vaudeville's most popular acts," Lydia continued. "Septimus took me to shows whenever he came to visit, and he told me about watching them rehearse when he was on tour. It's almost always a family act because who else can you really trust that much? He said that if you look close, you'll see that just about everybody in the act has small scars on their arms and legs, covered with costume or makeup, of course. They start the young ones working as soon as they can hold a knife and throw it hard enough to stick in a target."

"I'm betting the knives are never given away," Geoffrey said.

"Never," Lydia agreed. "From what Septimus told me, they're prized possessions handed down from one generation to the next."

"Then how did one of them come to be in the Argosy Theatre?" Prudence asked. "More to the point, who threw it?"

"I was crossing from center stage to downstage right," Lydia said. "To the pushcart. So whoever it was had to be hiding in one of the downstage left wings. Hidden between the legs. Curtains," she explained. "Legs are the curtains that hang down on either side of the stage."

"Somebody had to have seen him. One of the stagehands or the prop crew." Prudence sketched out the stage on a sheet of paper Josiah tore from his stenographer's notebook. "You were here, facing the pushcart. The knife hit your left arm, so the trajectory had to be from center or downstage left. As you said."

"This is backward," Josiah said, examining the drawing.

"Stage directions are given from the actor's perspective," Lydia explained. "As he's looking out into the audience."

"So, if I'm in the audience, left is right and right is left?" Josiah asked.

Lydia nodded. "Simple, once you get the idea."

Geoffrey picked up the knife and dipped the corner of the makeup towel in the pitcher of hot water that had been intended to brew a second pot of tea. He wiped the blood off the blade, hefted the weapon in his right hand, then with a flick of the wrist, hurled it through his open office doorway into the reception area. It thudded into the thick oak paneling behind Josiah's desk and remained there, quivering, while his open-mouthed audience stared.

"Very true aim," he said, crossing into the outer office to tug it from the wall. "Lighter weight than it first appears and easy to handle."

"The better acts throw a dozen or more knives, one after the other," Lydia said. "All around the outline of whoever is standing against the backdrop. No one worth his salt cuts corners when it comes to supplying the throwers with the best blades money can buy."

"Have you ever seen or heard of an accident?" Prudence asked. "Someone in the act wounded or killed?"

"No one talks about stunts that turn fatal. It's considered bad luck. Like the tightrope walkers who've fallen or the trapeze artists who miss a catch."

"I had no idea." Prudence shuddered.

"Vaudeville has always been dangerous. Not as risky as Barnum's circus, but almost as bad."

"Flame eaters?" Josiah asked.

"And magicians," Lydia confirmed. "There's always the chance of something going wrong when you're trying to give an audience a thrill."

"Could we get back to this knife?" Geoffrey asked. He held it out toward Lydia, balancing it on the palm of one hand.

"The odd thing is that it doesn't have any of the distinguishing markings Septimus told me about, nothing to identify the act who used it. There's a small nick in the wood just below the blade, but that might be from use." Lydia reached with the uninjured arm, curling her fingers around the handle, as if to summon up the last person to throw it. "Gertrude Marrow would know who's in town. Vaudeville acts have to stay on the move. Audiences don't want to see the same show over and over again. But Gertrude would know who we could take the knife to, who might recognize it."

"I don't see how, if it doesn't have anything distinctive about it," Prudence said.

"Knife throwers can heft a blade and tell you right away just about everything you want to ask about it. I don't understand how, but Septimus swore they were never wrong."

"I'll take it to her at the theatre tomorrow," Prudence said.

"Danny can drive us to Gertrude's house this evening," Geoffrey said. "After the rehearsal is over. We'll let Hughes and the rest of the company think the knife got lost somewhere in the wings or that someone picked it up and decided to keep it. It might make the thrower nervous if he believes it could come back to haunt him. A distracted killer is easier to catch; he's more likely to make a mistake."

"We tried that ploy with the Lady in Black," Prudence said. "It didn't seem to do any good."

Geoffrey shrugged. "If one trick doesn't work, you try another. In the meantime, if you're sure you don't want a doctor to look at that arm, Lydia, I think you'd be better off lying in your own bed than on a couch in my office."

"What I don't understand is why someone would try to kill me," Lydia said. She sank back into the cushions propping her up, the blood draining from her already-pale face.

"If the knife thrower wanted you dead, you'd be in the Bellevue morgue," Geoffrey said. "Make no mistake about it. This wasn't an amateur."

"Then why?" Prudence asked.

"It was a warning. Back off."

"I think I will have Danny drive me home," Lydia said. "I've had enough excitement for one day."

# CHAPTER 21

Geoffrey and Prudence waited until dusk before ordering her carriage to take them to Gertrude Marrow's house. Danny Dennis had decided to stay in Brooklyn for the early part of the evening with Lydia, her father, and the ex-Pink replacing Clyde Allen.

"Ben Truitt plays a mean game of chess for a blind man," Danny had told Prudence earlier, moments after he'd seen Lydia comfortably ensconced in his hansom cab. "I say the move I've made out loud, he pictures the board in his head, and then tells me what piece he wants to play and where to position it."

"The ex-Pink I sent to the Truitts is dependable," Geoffrey had assured him. "You don't need to be concerned about that."

"I'm sure he is," Danny had agreed. "But I'm also leaving Flower there for a day or two after I come back to Manhattan. It won't hurt to have a dog with a loud bark in the house, and she needs the practice." He wouldn't leave the urchins who bedded down in his stable alone for the entire night, but neither would he neglect to provide the Truitt family with what safety he could.

"Three men and a dog," Prudence commented as the MacKenzie carriage pulled to the curb. "I'd say Lydia is well and truly guarded. She needs sleep more than anything else."

"It wasn't that serious a wound." Geoffrey helped her descend onto the pavement. "As I said, it was a warning."

"I think it's best if you wait, Kincaid," Prudence instructed her coachman. "I'm not sure how long we'll be."

They could see the new electric streetlights along Broadway in the distance, but this block of attached brownstones was still dimly lit by widely spaced gaslights.

"I'll be parked here whenever you need me, Miss Prudence. There's hardly any traffic on a residential street at this time of the evening, so I doubt I'll have to move along. But if I do, I'll circle the block until you come out." Kincaid had driven Prudence in all types of circumstances. The one thing he would never do is leave her or Mr. Hunter to navigate a city neighborhood without the safety of her own carriage nearby.

"I sent a telegram to let her know we were coming," Geoffrey said as they mounted the front stoop. He'd rewrapped the throwing knife in the bloodied but dry makeup towel and stowed it in a specially designed pocket sewn into all of his coats. "She'll know why."

The front door opened while the peal of the doorbell still echoed in the hallway. Gertrude had changed from the dark worsted gown she wore to rehearsals into a lighter weight at-home dress that could be worn without having to be tightly corseted. She looked plumper than she appeared onstage, and much more comfortable.

"Come in, come in," she urged, thrusting her head out the door to glance both ways along the block. "No one's out walking a dog this evening. That's good."

"I doubt it matters," Prudence said, as she and Geoffrey followed their hostess along the dark hallway that led to the parlor.

"It doesn't hurt to keep your head down, though it's not a

good way to learn what's going on," Gertrude said. "I don't take my own advice, of course." She ushered them into the well-appointed parlor where a small fire burned and the drapes had been pulled across the lace curtains, effectively shielding anyone in the room from the curious glances of a passerby.

A slender man of indeterminate but not young age stood in front of the fireplace, hands clasped behind his back. He had the look of a foreigner about him, though his speech, when Gertrude introduced him, was fluent and without accent.

Dark hair and eyes, Prudence noted. A decidedly olive complexion. Italian? Sicilian?

"Angelo Dimundo," Gertrude smiled affectionately as Geoffrey shook his hand and Prudence nodded politely "We've known each other since vaudeville days when we were both considerably less wrinkled than either of us is now. If anyone can identify that knife you've brought with you, it's Angelo."

"It's a good thing Gertie sent word when she did." Angelo rocked slightly forward and back on his heels. "We leave Tony Pastor's to go on tour in a couple of days."

Geoffrey took the towel-wrapped knife from his pocket.

"This is what came sailing through the air and wounded our friend while she was onstage at the Argosy Theatre," Prudence said.

"I've told Angelo everything we know so far," Gertrude added, gesturing toward the velvet tufted armchairs that crowded the room. "Do sit down, everyone."

"She's recovering, your friend?" Angelo asked, unfolding the stained towel.

"The wardrobe mistress sewed up the wound with very small stitches," Prudence said. "There'll be a scar, but the cut wasn't deep."

"Tell her to rub in goose grease, three times a day," Angelo instructed. "Don't waste your money on anything else. Just pure goose grease." He held the knife to his nose for a moment.

"Did you smell the rust?" he asked. "Someone used a whet-stone to remove it, but there are traces between the blade and the handle. This knife wasn't used for years until whoever threw it decided it was time to take it out of its hiding place."

"How long?" Geoffrey asked.

"I'd estimate at least five or six years. Could have been longer. It was probably stored in a piece of canvas to protect it from the wet, but damp has a way of seeping past most wrap-pings. It's well crafted. Good heft and balance, but sadly, not given the care such an object deserves."

"Angelo's family has been knife throwers going back gener-ations," Gertrude said.

"In Sicily, before my grandfather came to this country, we were known for skills that we no longer practice as often as we once did. In America, we make our name and our living on the vaudeville circuit."

Geoffrey smiled. Nodded understanding that Angelo had revealed something much more interesting than a lifetime of knife tricks intended to amuse and thrill audiences without inflicting any real damage to life or limb. "Do you recognize this knife? Is there anything about it that could tell us who owned it?"

"Whoever used the whetstone to do away with the rust also used it on the handle. Whetstones aren't meant for that."

"There's what looks like a nick just below where the blade joins the handle," Geoffrey said.

Angelo rubbed his forefinger over the spot. "It's not a nick. Never was. What you felt is what remains of a very small in-signia, a tower that the Torre family carved into all of its knives. Any Sicilian knife thrower would recognize it. Gertie, do you have a piece of paper and a pencil?"

When she'd fetched them from her writing desk, Angelo sketched the figure of a six-sided tower topped by a curved balustrade. "This is the original, a bell tower in the churchyard of the town where the Torre clan originated. I don't know when the first Torre knife thrower etched it on the handle of his blade, but all the family followed suit."

"Were they in vaudeville?"

"Only one of them immigrated, and that was years ago. He married, played the circuit for a while, and then disappeared. So did his wife and three sons. No one knows what happened to them or where they went, but the family has been cursed for generations. A long-ago son murdered his father over a woman. Patricide can never be forgiven. Or forgotten."

"I'm even more confused than I was before," Prudence said. "How could a knife with a curse on it have made its way to the Argosy Theatre?"

"It's never the knife that's cursed. Always the man." Angelo shrugged. "In Sicily, we don't always try to unravel the secrets of the past. There are too many of them, and it can be dangerous."

"But this is America," Prudence reminded him.

"Then I would say that your knife thrower was given this blade by the last Torre to own it. Or he stole it from him. But it would have happened while both of them were touring in the same vaudeville troupe. The only time Aldo Torre took his knives out of their locked case was to sharpen them or use them onstage in his act."

"Aldo Torre?" Geoffrey asked.

"He was already an old man when I knew him," Angelo said. "Still working, still capable of throwing faster and more accurately than men years younger than he." He paused for a moment. "I saw the case once. Stood beside Aldo when he opened it. There were no knives missing. Each was cushioned in its own velvet slot."

"Do you remember seeing this knife?" Prudence asked.

Angelo shook his head. "He had two rows of six identical knives each for throwing. This knife looks like one of them, but I couldn't swear to it. It was too long ago."

The knife left Angelo's hand without anyone noticing that

he'd aimed and thrown it. Across the room, through the open parlor door, into the dark hallway. It made hardly a sound as it embedded itself into the paneled wall above the stairway leading to the second floor. "A precisely thrown instrument remains silent even when it reaches its target," Angelo said, retrieving the Torre knife and returning to the parlor. "We exaggerate the throws onstage and make sure the wood behind our mark is hollow. The louder the thud, the more the audience reacts."

He laid the knife on the mantelpiece and bowed over Gertrude's outstretched hand. "I thank you for a most interesting rendezvous. But I must get back to the theatre. We have a show to do tonight."

"Give my best to Elena," Gertrude said. "And the children."

"Six young Dimundos at last count," Angelo said. "Enough to ensure that both family businesses will continue to flourish."

"Don't ask," Geoffrey said as Gertrude saw Angelo out.

"I can't even imagine what he meant by *both family businesses*," Prudence said, stubbornly not dropping the subject. Did every man who picked up a knife feel obliged to throw it?

"That's where we need to leave it." Geoffrey tossed the stained makeup towel into the crackling fire. A hint of singed iron drifted into the room as the flames caught the bloody linen.

"I could use a stiff drink," Gertrude said as she bustled back into the room. "Angelo is a lovely man, but a very dangerous one when the money's right." She poured Old Overholt rye whiskey into three crystal glasses. "I had another conversation with David Belasco. That's what I wanted to tell you about, Prudence, before Lydia stepped in front of that blade." She stacked a few sticks of wood onto the fire as they settled into the velvet armchairs again. "He'd already heard about Septimus and Hazel, of course."

"What else did you talk about?" Geoffrey asked.

"Barrett Hughes. There's speculation he was carrying on

with Hazel as well as Flora and that Hazel's death wasn't the accident the police want to believe it was."

"Wait. Are people saying Hughes pushed her into that trunk to get rid of her?" asked Prudence.

"That, and every variation on jealousy you can think of. What Belasco was really interested in was the script Septimus wrote. *The Hereditary Prince*. I let him think Hughes might be connected to it, but that I could deliver if the price was right."

"Did he believe you?" Geoffrey sipped the well-aged rye whiskey.

"Enough so he told me everything about Hughes I wanted to know. I insinuated that if he came up with enough dirt, I might be persuaded to hand him his next big hit."

Geoffrey and Prudence waited. Gertrude smiled, emptied her glass, sighed in satisfaction, stretched out her legs toward the fire, and folded her hands in her lap.

"Barrett Hughes may be popular with audiences—there's no denying that—but the only reason he's tolerated by the rest of us is because he has what Belasco calls *a golden touch*. The man has never been in a flop. Not once. I wish I could say the same. Hughes has never had an enormous success, except for the Dickens play, but he didn't originally produce or direct that one. He's brought the Scrooge character to life hundreds of times, and no one's ever done it better, but he hasn't made as much money off it as people would like to believe."

"What about his backers?" Prudence asked. *Follow the money* was an axiom to which every lawyer worth his briefcase subscribed.

"They take in a tidy, reliable profit, but again, not the enormous amount of money they might have originally hoped for. But they're not stupid investors. They understand that it's safer in the long run to bet on a sure thing, the horse that runs consistently good races, not the long shot that wins on a fluke and trails the pack in every subsequent event. So Hughes can just about count on the same sources of funds for every show he mounts. Nobody turns his back on a proven winner."

"What about his affairs with women? Other than what we think is going on with Flora?" Prudence asked.

"I kept pressing Belasco for gossip I didn't already know about, but there's nothing specific. Hughes is known for keeping company with his leading ladies and for demanding sexual favors from ingenues, but nobody's complained. They take it as part of the business. Everybody knows about it. Everybody does it. It's always been that way and it's never going to change."

"So the only bait Belasco rises to is *The Hereditary Prince*," Geoffrey said. "He doesn't care about Hughes's backers or about his women."

"I dangled the *Prince* in front of him like a fat worm on a fishhook," Gertrude confirmed. "I might be able to use it a couple more times, but eventually he'll realize what I'm doing."

"What went on at rehearsal after Lydia and I left?" Prudence asked.

"We continued as though nothing had happened," Gertrude said. "Barrett sent a stagehand to escort Flora back from her dressing room, and when she balked, he tried to convince her and everyone else that the knife throwing had been a prank that went wrong. It got confusing, but the gist of what he ended up saying was that a couple of the younger stagehands or prop boys had been playing mumblety-peg in the wings. One of them got overexcited, lost control of his throw, and that's when the knife streaked across the stage. I don't know if anyone believed him, but Hughes pays our salaries, so that's the story we all agreed to."

"What's mumblety-peg?" Prudence asked.

"Just about anything dangerous you can think of doing with a pocketknife," Geoffrey said. "Boys play it all the time. When

I was in boarding school, we liked the version where two boys stand opposite each other, feet apart, and take turns throwing a knife as close to a foot as you can manage without actually wounding yourself. The one who comes the closest wins. There's also a game where each boy aims at the other boy's feet."

"That's the most ridiculous thing I've ever heard of," Prudence said.

"Not even by half," Gertrude said. "It's a wonder boys ever manage to grow up. I'm not sure adult men have much more common sense."

"When you're playing mumblety-peg, you throw the knife downward." Geoffrey demonstrated with a flick of the wrist, ignoring Gertrude's condemnation of the male half of the population. "I wouldn't take odds on someone accidentally releasing it at the top of the throwing arc."

"We should have asked Angelo about that," Prudence said. "Whether there was any way it could have been an accident."

"I did ask him," Gertrude confirmed. "Before you got here. He said nothing that involved a knife was unintentional."

"So, knife throwing is a skill that demands practice and patience to master," Prudence said. "But it doesn't require brute strength."

"Meaning?" Gertrude asked.

"A man has been poisoned, a woman suffocated in a trunk, and now another woman wounded by a knife that missed its mark. What does that tell you about the killer?" Prudence elaborated.

It didn't need to be put into words.

Each of them understood that the murderer could be a woman.

# CHAPTER 22

Clyde Allen walked the pedestrian footpath of the Brooklyn Bridge in the bright light of a waxing gibbous moon. Only the occasional clop of a tired horse broke the night silence. It was an hour past midnight, still too early for the morning milk wagons to rumble through the city's streets. Houses and tenement rooms were dark, only the occasional lamp or candle marking a sickbed vigil. The workforce that drove New York slept. Dawn would awaken them, but for now, aching bones and sore muscles rested and healed as much as they ever would.

The lengthy train ride from Montpelier had given Clyde more than enough time to think his way through the dilemma he'd gone to Vermont to address. Vivian Knowles, a lady doctor now, had to be protected. As did Lydia, Ben's only child and as dear to her father's bodyguard as if she were his own.

That's what he'd become, Clyde reflected, a bodyguard. Friendship born of mutual suffering in a military hospital ward had survived years of separation and hardship, resurfacing when Ben finally admitted that he'd outstretched himself. And sent for Clyde. Blind as he was, Ben Truitt had no defense except his daughter against clients who decided he had crossed the line from necessary to a liability. His cryptographic skills, unmatched even among government men, had made at least one powerful industrialist nervous. Put simply, Ben knew too much about stolen ideas and inventions, shady financial dealings, disappearances among bitter rivals. His coding of secret documents had made the deceptions possible.

Clyde expected his ex-Pink replacement to be an alert but invisible presence, so he stood at the front gate of the Truitt house long enough to be identifiable in the moonlight. He'd left for Montpelier before the man arrived, but he had no doubt Hunter had provided a description that would identify him. The leather mask Clyde wore over the ruined half of his face was distinctive and not as common now as it had once been. So many of the war's scarred veterans had died.

A shadow detached itself from the shrubbery, the glint of a Colt revolver warning him not to move yet. From inside the house came loud barking, followed by the glow of lamplight.

"Name's Pritchard," said the shadow. "You'd be Allen. Hunter told me to expect you." He holstered his gun, nodded permission to enter the yard and mount the porch steps, then faded back into the darkness.

"Hush now, Flower," Clyde said, opening the front door with his key. Nobody had mentioned adding a dog to sentry duty, but he'd heard that bark so many times he knew it had to be the nearly grown pup Danny Dennis was training. Forty-five pounds of red-gold fur, gleaming teeth, and wet tongue greeted him enthusiastically. Behind Flower stood Lydia, holding the lantern whose glimmer he'd seen through the window.

"We didn't expect you yet." Lydia reached out to guide her father along the hallway. "I'll put water on for coffee."

"I caught an early afternoon train coming down to the city," Clyde explained. "Didn't mean to wake everybody up." He used one of the hand gestures Danny had invented to quiet the excited dog. She sat and then walked dutifully beside him as Clyde moved toward the kitchen.

"I assume you found her." Benjamin Truitt allowed his friend to guide him by the elbow. He didn't really need assistance inside his own house, but he knew it reassured his daughter and Clyde when he accepted their aid. In the early days of his blindness, he'd rejected offers of help, but he'd learned to be kind toward those who cared for him.

"I did find her." Clyde settled Ben into a chair at the table and directed Flower toward the cushioned wicker basket that served as her bed.

Lydia measured out coffee grounds and water, stirring the coals in the old stove that was still good enough not to be replaced by one of the modern gas ranges.

"She trained at the New England Hospital for Women and Children," Clyde said. "*Dr.* Vivian Knowles now. Her father took her into his practice, and she continued on alone after he died."

"Did she deny what happened?" Lydia asked. It had been her experience that many women were reluctant to admit to having been violated.

Clyde shook his head, then remembered that Ben couldn't have seen the gesture. "No, she didn't deny it. But she did want to know if she'd have to testify to his character if he went to trial. I had to tell her it was a possibility." During the long hours of the train ride, he'd worked out a nearly foolproof way to dispose of Barrett Hughes, should it be necessary. For Lydia's sake he kept the unscarred portion of his face expressionless.

Ben would guess, if it came to that, but he thought the blind man might be the only one to agree that the actor had earned the death Clyde planned for him.

"Flora's coming in this morning to have a fitting for the white dress Mr. Hughes has ordered." Cynthia Pierce spoke around a mouthful of pins, her skilled fingers moving so quickly through billows of fine lawn that nobody but she could follow them. "It's going to be only the two of us until Lydia is well enough to come back."

"I'm not sure I'm up to it," Prudence said. There was no point trying to hide her ineptitude from the experienced costume mistress. "But I'll do the best I can."

"There are ten yards of ruffles to hem." Cynthia glanced at the bulky and unreliable sewing machine crouching in one corner of the costume shop. "I don't think you can be trusted with the beast," she said, "so I'm going to put you to work with needle and thread." She pushed a pincushion and spool in Prudence's direction. "You'll have to hand roll all along the edge of the ruffle."

It was on the tip of Prudence's tongue to ask what hand rolling was, but the wardrobe mistress anticipated her. Fifteen minutes later Prudence had successfully rolled and stitched slightly more than an inch of fabric.

"That's not the best I've ever seen, but it'll have to do," Cynthia said. "You'll get better, but don't try to go too fast or you'll end up having to pull out the seam and start again. And don't hunch over like that or you won't be able to straighten up at the end of the day."

"Can't Mr. Hughes hire another seamstress until Lydia gets back?" Prudence made a mighty effort not to clench her teeth and bend forward in tense concentration.

"I've already asked. The answer was no."

"When is Flora supposed to be here?"

Cynthia glanced at the wall clock hanging over the door. "She's fifteen minutes late."

"Sorry," chirped a voice from the hallway. "We're running behind schedule for act two. But I'm here now."

Flora Campbell danced into the costume shop as though on a ballerina's toe shoes. Except for a cloud of blond curls encircling her face, her silvery gold hair had been gathered into a loose braid that hung down her back to her waist. She wore a thin layer of theatrical makeup that barely hid pale brown freckles and had cracked around her eyes and lips, revealing an unexpected web of faint spidery lines.

*She's older than I thought.* Prudence choked back a cough as she almost spoke the observation aloud. At a nod from Cynthia, she set aside the yards of unhemmed ruffle and gathered bits and pieces of the white dress, some of which had been loosely basted together. This was likely to take some time.

Flora slipped out of her rehearsal clothes and climbed up onto a stool. Clad only in a lace-trimmed cotton combination, corset, and stockings, she held out her arms as Cynthia rechecked the measurements recorded in the costume book. Actresses who put on inches before a play opened or during its run caused no end of problems for the wardrobe mistress.

"I haven't had a piece of pie or a slice of cake since we started rehearsals," Flora volunteered. "No sugar in my tea, either."

"You're exactly the same as you were when I measured you the first time." Cynthia clucked in satisfaction. "Mr. Hughes was very definite about the look he wants for this character and this dress in particular."

"I know. Young, virginal, delicate, on the verge of starvation if she doesn't agree to her suitor's advances." Flora sighed, then laughed delightedly as Cynthia's measuring tape cinched her waist at the same measurement it had registered weeks ago.

"Hold still now. We've got a lot of pinning to do."

One by one, Prudence handed the pieces of the white dress to Cynthia, who continued talking through her mouthful of pins as though the sharp little objects weren't there at all. It was a talent Prudence supposed you mastered after years of sewing, but which she'd decided she wasn't going to try to cultivate.

"Your name is Prudence, isn't it?" Flora asked, moving only her head a fraction of an inch. "Weren't you working with Lydia when she was injured? Aren't you the one who found poor Hazel?"

Prudence made a muffled sound that she hoped sounded like an inexperienced seamstress mumbling around pins she was still afraid of swallowing.

"I'm going to need a new dresser," Flora continued. "I suppose Prudence will have to step in."

"Talk to Mr. Hughes." Cynthia's needle flashed along a seam being left deliberately loose. "I don't make those decisions."

"You know he'll accept whatever you tell him," Flora insisted. "He may browbeat his actors, but he won't rile up the crew." She ran an appraising finger over the bodice line that was beginning to emerge beneath pins and basting stitches. "Are you another one of Lydia's cousins, like Septimus?" This time she stared right at Prudence, willing her to reply.

"Just a friend," Prudence answered. "She knew I was out of work. I appreciated the recommendation."

"I expect a dresser to keep my costumes clean and pressed at all times. You have to be ready to help me make the changes as soon as I come offstage. And there might be other things I'll ask you to do. Do you think you can manage?" Flora ignored Cynthia's half-hearted protest. "Prudence?"

"I'd love to be your dresser, if Miss Pierce agrees."

"That's settled then." Flora's eyes shone with the satisfaction of getting what she wanted. Leads always had their own dressers. It was as much a mark of their importance as a private dressing room with a star on the door. "You might as well tell me about yourself while I'm standing here like a Central Park statue."

"There's not much to say." Prudence tried to remember the details of the cover story she and Lydia had concocted. Basically, she'd borrowed from her maid Colleen's life. It was better not to tell too many lies that could trip you up later. "My mother wanted me to train as a lady's maid, but I always loved going to the vaudeville. If I couldn't be on the stage, I wanted to be behind it." That sounded convincing and remotely truthful for a young woman hoping to escape the tenements.

"Ouch!" Flora swatted at Cynthia's hand. "Be careful with those pins!"

"Lydia said you and Septimus were on the vaudeville circuit together," Prudence phrased it as a compliment. "I wish I could have seen your act."

"Acts, you mean. We did song and dance numbers, and we had to keep coming up with new material all the time. Comedy sketches, too. That was Septimus's strong point. He could write scenes the audience loved as fast as you threw the ideas at him."

"I went to a show at Tony Pastor's once," Prudence said. "At the theatre on Fourteenth Street." She waited for Flora to say that was where Barrett Hughes had first heard her sing, but Flora lapsed into silence. Did she dare suggest she knew more about Flora than the ingenue had revealed? "Lydia said you and Septimus were on the bill there not too long ago. Before *Highlands* started rehearsals."

"Mr. Hughes wants a broad blue ribbon around the waist," Cynthia remarked into the lengthening quiet.

"To match my eyes," Flora confirmed. She was studying Prudence as though she'd discovered something odd or disturbing about the young seamstress who was so obviously inexperienced with a needle.

Prudence stared at the hand Flora had placed at the point on her slender waist where she judged the blue ribbon should lie. It wasn't the hand of a woman who scrubbed for a living, but neither was it unblemished skin. Prudence remembered how fiercely the older sisters of her society acquaintances rubbed creams and lotions into their fingers. Flora Campbell, who was passing herself off as a twenty-year-old, was probably closer to thirty. And suddenly Prudence understood how much was at stake here.

*Waif of the Highlands* was Flora's last chance to grab that elusive ingenue star. If *Highlands* didn't open, she'd likely end up back in vaudeville, where she'd sing and dance and cavort to raucous crowds until the hardness of the life and the cheap whiskey that made it bearable raddled her face and put pounds on that no amount of corseting could disguise.

Prudence did some quick calculating. Lydia had said that Septimus was thirty-four years old. No telling how many vaudeville tours he and Flora had worked together as an act. Gertrude Marrow maintained that gossip flowed through theatres like swollen rivers during a heavy rain. Maybe someone remembered the birth of a baby girl so beautiful she'd been named after the Roman goddess of spring and flowering plants. She'd ask Gertrude to make inquiries.

"I need to get back onstage." Flora plucked at the pins holding the white dress together.

"Don't move, don't move," Cynthia ordered. "Stand still until I can get it off. If you mess up the measurements, we'll just have to do it all over again."

*I've spooked her,* Prudence thought. *I wonder what I said that did it.*

"I've changed my mind." Flora let both her hands fall to her sides, turning them palms out so the delicate skin that wrinkled so easily with the passage of years was hidden. "I won't need Prudence to be my dresser, after all. I do my own makeup, so I can just as well see to getting my costumes on. There aren't that many changes. All I'll need is someone to lace me up the back." She read the look of surprise and disbelief on the wardrobe mistress's face. "If that won't work, I'll get Mr. Hughes to hire me someone. He won't object. Especially after opening night." She grabbed her rehearsal clothes from the chair where she'd flung them and disappeared behind one of the dressing screens. Moments later she was gone, swallowed up in the backstage darkness.

"That was odd," Cynthia remarked, draping the white gown

over a dress dummy. "You'd have made a good dresser, Prudence. I don't think you'll ever win any prizes as a seamstress." She shook her head over the unsewn ruffle. "Best get back to work. I don't have time to do that for you."

*Motive*, Prudence decided as she stabbed the needle into the fabric that slipped away under her fingers. Hughes has motive, and now so does Flora. She can't afford to let anything delay the play's opening night. For both of them, *Waif of the Highlands* was a last chance.

Nothing and nobody could be allowed to stand in their way.

The ruffle needed ironing. It looked as though a purely amateur seamstress had done serious battle with the hem before wrestling it into submission. Which, of course, was exactly the case.

Prudence had been careful to work only with clean hands and not to prick her skin with the needle she still handled awkwardly, but there was no ignoring the wrinkles. Cynthia would insist that they be smoothed out before the trim could be stitched to the all-important white dress. It had taken Prudence hours to do the yards and yards of hemming. No telling how long it would take her to iron it.

The cast-iron stove wasn't hot enough to heat the three irons she'd have to use in rotation to get the job done, and the coal scuttle was empty. So was the wood box. Was it her job to keep them full? Prudence couldn't remember. It seemed that every time she turned around, she was given a new task to perform. With Lydia out, the work was never-ending.

She picked up the metal coal scuttle and the woven basket used to carry small amounts of wood. Somewhere in the depths of the theatre's basement were the coal bin and the woodpile. She supposed she could ask one of the stagehands to get her what she needed, but after hours of bending over the blasted ruffle, every muscle in her back ached. She could use the exercise.

Prudence did have to ask one of the stagehands to direct her toward the entrance to the basement, and as he pointed the way, she thought she caught a glimpse of Flora Campbell watching them from the wings where she'd just come offstage after finishing a scene. *Probably thinks I'm flirting with him*, Prudence thought, giving the stagehand a coquettish smile and rapid bat of the eyelashes. She really did not like Flora Campbell at all.

It took longer than Prudence anticipated to find the coal and wood bins. Then she had to locate a shovel for the coal and a pair of gloves for the splintery wood. Both lay almost out of reach atop the piles where the last user had tossed them. It took a bit of maneuvering, but she managed to get what she needed without more than a thin film of coal dust on her shoes.

She'd left the door to the costume shop off the latch, so with both hands full, Prudence nudged it open with her hip. Something about the smell of the room seemed off, not quite as she'd left it. The scent of the perfume Flora Campbell had been wearing during the morning's fitting seemed stronger than when she'd left, and there was a definite smell of burning coal, as though the fire in the stove grate had sparked back into life.

She circled one hand a few inches above the top of the stove, surprised to feel how hot it was. So, too, were the three sad irons she'd arranged there. Could Cynthia have borrowed some fuel from one of the other shops to speed along the ironing process, then gone about the business of chasing down actors who needed fittings? It wouldn't be unlike the costume mistress to do whatever needed seeing to, even if it wasn't strictly speaking her responsibility. She was generous that way.

The new sad irons Cynthia had requested for her seamstresses were safer but heavier to use than the ones they'd replaced. The most important innovation was a wooden cylinder that fit over the sad iron's metal handle, shielding the palm of the hand from the danger of a disfiguring and disabling injury. Just in case, there was a pile of thick pads on a nearby cutting table. Awkward to use, but better to fumble a bit than suffer a bad burn.

Prudence picked up one of the pads, dropped it, picked it up again. Despite Colleen's tutelage, she hadn't mastered the art of ironing. Having to wield the sad iron barehanded was bad enough. Guiding it along a ruffle and not letting go of the thick protective pad would be more annoying than it was worth.

She tapped the wooden handle of the closest iron with one finger. Definitely not too hot to manage. In fact, it seemed much less warm than the last time she'd pressed something. Good. She'd have the ruffle wrinkle-free in no time. Cynthia would be pleased.

When the wooden cylinder cracked open, the red-hot iron handle burned through the tender skin of Prudence's right hand. Down to the bone.

She didn't remember the blackness that engulfed her, nor the fall to the floor of the costume shop.

But no one backstage who heard Prudence's agonized scream would ever forget it.

# CHAPTER 23

"I don't think Lydia should come back." Flora walked her fingertips through the chest hair that always made her think of someone who'd been a far better lover. Barrett Hughes was old and gray. He obviously didn't dye *all* the hair on his body. She wondered if his other women also secretly laughed at him for the vanity of it. "She makes me nervous. The way she looks at me. I never liked the idea of her being my dresser."

"You're the female lead. You have to have a dresser."

"Then hire one. Just not Lydia."

"What about her friend, the one with those odd gray eyes who's also working in the costume shop?"

"Prudence? I don't know why you allowed Lydia to persuade you to give her a job in the first place. She doesn't know a thing about sewing, and she's got no family in the business. It's not like you to be so generous, Barrett."

"Lydia's a Fancham, Septimus's cousin. She looked a little shabby when she came to tell us about the viewing and the burial, so I figured she could use the work. I'm not paying her that much. The friend came cheap, and I couldn't afford to have

Cynthia quit on me because she doesn't have enough help. Costume mistresses can be as temperamental as actresses." He cupped one of Flora's small breasts, kneading the nipple until it hardened, wondering how old she really was. Definitely well past twenty. He'd seen enough women's bodies to be certain of that.

"I don't want Prudence, either. She asks too many questions and butts in where she's not wanted. Put the word out on the street that we need two new seamstresses. I guarantee you'll have a line halfway down the alley by tomorrow morning."

"Get up," he said, slapping her on the derrière that was skinnier than he liked them. He had a late dinner at Delmonico's with a nervous backer who needed to be reassured that losing a young actor to drink was no great disaster. Every part had its understudy.

"Did she tell you what she was doing in the theatre Sunday morning? Lydia, I mean," Flora asked. She very deliberately hadn't given Hughes all the details of the conversation that had temporarily rattled her. Especially the last question Lydia had asked: Waif of the Highlands *is Septimus's play, isn't it, Flora?* "I never did believe that story about needing to find a jacket of yours she meant to take home to work on."

"If I don't allow her to come back, it won't be because you can't get along with her," Hughes said, walking naked to the armoire where his evening clothes hung.

"Why, then?"

"She may know too much. We don't have any idea how close she and Septimus were before he got careless with the whiskey. So don't play coy with me, Flora. *Waif of the Highlands* will be the making of both of us. After opening night you'll be Broadway's newest star. I wouldn't replace you in that part even if I could. You'll be like Sarah Bernhardt to *La Dame aux Camélias*. Nobody will be able to think about *Waif of the Highlands* without remembering Flora Campbell's performance. We'll play to sold-out houses for as long as we want. As soon as I can swing it, I'm buying the Argosy and renaming it. The Barrett Hughes Theatre. It has a ring. I like it."

She'd wondered what lay behind Hughes's drive to claim *Highlands* as his own. Why he'd pushed Septimus so hard into handing over the play Flora had seen him working on night after night for more than a year while they played the circuit. She'd never written so much as a line of it herself, but she'd sat opposite him in the light of a single candle, drinking coffee to stay awake, dreaming up scenes that would show off her ability to cry on demand and faint gracefully. Septimus had made the deal without consulting her, an act of generosity so stunning it had taken her breath away when he'd told her.

Septimus had been in love with her, of course. Most men were. They fell hard and fast, but they didn't stay in love. Flora's demands eventually turned them off like water from a spigot. The majority of them left her with only a few cheap trinkets to remember them by. Barrett was the most important man she'd gone after, discovering to her delight that the pursuit was mutual. He recognized in her that special gift very few actresses possessed, the ability to reach across the proscenium arch and dig her fingers into an audience's heart. In him, Flora sensed a rock-hard ambition that would not be denied. Second in America by a hairbreadth to the aged and failing Edwin Booth, Barrett Hughes needed only to own a theatre bearing his name to surpass the legendary actor whose brother's reputation would forever resonate louder than his own.

The true authorship of *Waif of the Highlands* was a subject both Flora and Barrett avoided discussing. It was better not to put into words a theft the entire theatre world would condemn, despite the fact that *borrowing* happened far more often than anyone wanted to admit. Life was short; an actor's time upon the stage could be more severely limited than most careers. Actresses lasted only as long as their looks held out. And Flora was uncomfortably aware that hers would soon begin to fade.

"If you do hire me another dresser, make sure it's not one of your incompetent would-be ingenues," Flora directed. "I need an older woman who knows what she's doing and who's prepared to stay for the run of the show." She caught his grimace and knew what it meant. "Save your strength, Barrett. You're going to need it."

"What do you mean?"

"Morgan Sandling may be nearly as handsome as Septimus. But even as an understudy, he was weak. He'll have to do, because it's too late for someone else to learn the part, but I think that after opening night, you should gradually reduce his lines. We need to rely on the two of us, you and me, to carry the show."

"I can't write him out entirely."

"I wasn't suggesting that. The whole tension of the plot rests in the conflict between his character and yours. Just shorten his speeches and lengthen your scenes with me. The audience will eat it up." Months ago, before Septimus had handed his work over to Hughes, Flora had made the same suggestion. She'd never seen the end result of what she'd proposed, which was too bad because inflating Hughes's part automatically meant increasing her own. Somewhere, she thought, there had to be a copy of the play with Septimus's notes on proposed changes in the margin. Too bad her dead lover had been so secretive with the discarded pages he routinely fed into his parlor fire after he'd rewritten them.

"I'm going to be late." Hughes tied and retied his silk cravat until it lay in a knot that concealed the sagging skin beneath his chin. He never allowed Flora to stay in his apartment after he'd left it.

"I'm ready." She picked up her reticule and the bills Hughes had left lying beside it. Hansom cab fare, he always said, because she consistently claimed never to have ready cash with her. She knew he considered her a nobody he'd been able to hire initially for far less than she would demand if *Highlands* proved to be a resounding success.

Women in the theatre got used to accepting casual gifts to make ends meet.

"No morphine," Prudence pleaded. The pain was excruciating, and she was drifting in and out of consciousness from the agony of it, but the fear of awakening her addiction was greater.

Dr. Charity Sloan ignored her patient's protests. She slid a needle into Prudence's arm and moments later smiled to see her drift into insensibility.

"That should do it for the moment. Now let me take a look at the burn." She very gently eased back the curled fingers of Prudence's right hand, then opened the heavy black leather bag she kept packed for emergencies, reaching inside for rolls of clean gauze bandages and jars of soothing ointments. Prudence's maid, Colleen, had already brought basins of hot and cold water from the basement kitchen, and laid a white sheet over a table that would hold whatever else the lady doctor needed.

Danny Dennis had rushed Dr. Sloan from the Friends Refuge for the Sick Poor in the Five Points neighborhood, pulling the hansom cab to a halt in front of the MacKenzie mansion on the corner of Fifth Avenue and Twelfth Street in record time. Butler and housekeeper had escorted her up to Prudence's bedroom, their faces grim with worry.

Now Cameron and Mrs. Neil had retreated to the hallway, leaving their employer's door cracked in case she should cry out or need them. The rest of the staff—maids, cook, footmen, hall boy, and coachman—sat in the servants' hall over untouched cups of tea. Cameron would have said the house was as silent as the grave had the comparison not been too grim to contemplate.

"I begged her to take a few drops of laudanum when they

brought her here." Colleen's face was streaked with dried tears. "But she wouldn't."

"Who's the family doctor?"

"Dr. Peter Worthington, but he's not in the city right now. Mr. Cameron used the telephone, but there wasn't any answer, so he sent one of the stableboys to the office. There was a note on the door that he wouldn't be back until Friday. That's when Danny Dennis thought to fetch you."

"I'm acquainted with Dr. Worthington," Dr. Sloan said. "He's a good man. His wife is one of our volunteers. She's been worried for the past few weeks about their daughter. First baby, you know. They're often late. I imagine the proud grandparents-to-be have gone to Pennsylvania in the mistaken belief that their arrival will hurry things along."

The palm of Prudence's right hand was so bright red it might have been dipped in henna. An enormous blister had formed, puffed up to the size of a teacup. The tips of her fingers had gone white, as though the blood had stopped flowing to them, while elsewhere more blisters were taking shape.

"I can't hear her breathing," Colleen said. "Dr. Sloan, is Miss Prudence going to die?"

"It's too soon to worry about that," soothed Charity Sloan. "She's strong and I've known many patients to survive burns that were far worse and more extensive than this one." She motioned to Colleen to dip one of the clean cloths into the cool water. "Wring it out a bit. We don't need water running all over her dress."

Colleen's features smoothed themselves out as she concentrated fiercely on following the doctor's orders. She dipped and wrung, dipped and wrung again.

"That's good, Colleen. Now lay it on Miss Prudence's palm."

"Me?"

"I need to hold her hand still and feel for any reaction when the cool water touches the burn," Dr. Sloan explained. "You washed your hands the way I told you, so you're as good as one of my nurses."

"The water smells funny."

"It's the carbolic. You saw how much I put in. Not enough to harm the skin, but we don't want anything dirty touching the burns."

"The water's clean, Dr. Sloan. I saw Cook put it into the pitcher herself. And the hot water came right from the teakettle. We've running water in the house, you know, even upstairs in the servants' quarters. The MacKenzies have always had the best."

"The carbolic takes care of invisible dirt." It was a grossly oversimplified explanation of Dr. Joseph Lister's great discovery, but one that Colleen could easily understand. "You can't always see the things that hurt you."

"They're in the air," Colleen said, repeating a popular belief. She picked up a second cloth, dipping and wringing it out, holding it ready to replace the one Dr. Sloan was lifting from Miss Prudence's hand. "Will you lance the blister?" she asked, proud of herself for thinking of the right medical word, remembering that Cook had used it when she'd cut open a nasty wound from boning a fish. It meant you sharpened a knife and sliced right through the puffiness. When Cook did it, yellow pus had come out, but Colleen didn't think pus formed inside burns.

"We'll wait a while before making that decision," Dr. Sloan said. "Right now, we're going to continue cleaning the hand, then we'll apply a poultice of honey, linseed oil, limewater liniment, and ground slippery elm bark. Then we'll wrap the hand in soft bandages and change them every few hours."

A frenzied pounding on the front door echoed up to the second floor. Cameron swayed to his feet and made his way down the stairs as quickly as his elderly body could manage. It wouldn't help to fall and supply Dr. Sloan with another patient.

"Where is she? How is she?" Geoffrey Hunter tore through

the entryway, slinging hat and coat at Cameron as he took the stairs in great leaps. If the leg that still carried a bullet in it hurt him, he paid no attention. Danny Dennis had only been able to tell him that Miss Prudence had been badly burned in an accident at the Argosy Theatre and that Dr. Charity Sloan had been sent for. That was enough.

On the sidewalk outside, Josiah Gregory watched the ex-Pink sprint into the house as if the demons of hell were chasing him.

"I don't think it's that bad," Danny said, fastening a water bag around Mr. Washington's muzzle. The big white horse was shiny with sweat. Puffs of heavy breath steamed in the cool spring air. "Painful, but not fatal."

"You never can tell with burns," Josiah replied gloomily. "How did it happen?"

"Nobody could tell me. Some sort of accident with an iron in the costume shop."

Gertrude Marrow arrived while Prudence lay unconscious under the first dose of morphine. She carried a heavy bag with her and brushed off Cameron's protests that Dr. Sloan wouldn't allow visitors into the sick room.

"Tell Mr. Hunter I'm here," Gertrude ordered, pushing her way past the butler. "I'll wait in the parlor." She'd known without having to be told that Geoffrey Hunter would be nowhere but at Prudence's side. They were business partners, but Gertrude's finely tuned instincts for human emotion told her they were something much more.

She composed her face and set the heavy bag on a table as soon as she heard footsteps descending the stairs.

"Prudence is asleep," Geoffrey said, running a hand through dark, disordered hair. "Dr. Sloan says she won't heal without rest, and she can't rest if she's in pain. So she's giving her morphine, like they did to the badly wounded in the field hospitals."

"For as long as it lasted." Gertrude and everyone else who

lived through the war had heard the horror stories. Medical supplies that never reached those who needed them most, resold for enormous profit by unscrupulous speculators. Amputations done without anything except whiskey to dull the patient's senses, a piece of wood clamped between the teeth. Worse. Twenty-six years and no one had forgotten the horror.

"You need to keep up your strength." The housekeeper bustled into the room, three steps ahead of a maid carrying a tray of coffee and sandwiches. "I'll send something to Dr. Sloan, too. She says Miss Prudence is to have warm beef broth and milk when she wakes up. If you don't need me, I'll see that gets done."

"Thank you, Mrs. Neil," Geoffrey said. "Tell the staff we'll keep them informed."

"I will, sir. They'll be grateful. Some of them have known Miss Prudence since she was a little girl."

"I've something to show you," Gertrude said when she and Geoffrey were alone. "It's the iron Prudence was using in the costume shop." She opened the carpetbag and took out a heavy Potts iron, both ends tapered to reach into a garment's corners where adjacent seams were joined.

"When the accident happened?" He poured coffee into two cups, the heavy fragrance filling the air.

"It was no accident," Gertrude said grimly. She held out the iron by its metal handle. "You know three of them are always used at the same time. One to do the pressing, the other two heating up on the coal stove."

Like most men of his social standing and era, Geoffrey had never ventured into a laundry or kitchen. Someone else saw to his clothing and his meals. "Maybe you'd better explain that," he said, handing coffee to Gertrude.

"Imagine an ironing board."

"What does it look like?"

"It's a narrow board on legs with a white cloth pinned to the top. Sometimes it's stretched between the backs of two chairs.

The irons have to be very hot to press out wrinkles, so you start by putting two or three of them on a stovetop over a good fire. They cool off quickly, so the person who's ironing is moving constantly between the stove and the board. Can you picture that?"

"I think so."

"This is a Potts sad iron with a removable wooden handle."

"Why is it sad?"

"Sad means heavy," Gertrude said. "A sad iron can weigh anywhere from four or five pounds to as much as nine or ten. They're solid metal, including the handle. So, when the person ironing reaches for a hot iron from the stove, she has to grip it with a folded cloth. Even with a thick pad, the heat could easily burn a hand. About twenty years ago someone came up with the idea of encasing the metal handle in wood. Some of the handles are removable so they don't heat up enough to catch fire."

"Where is this going?" Geoffrey asked.

"This iron has one of the removable handles. You clamp it tightly around the metal when you remove the hot iron from the stove. The wood is cool, and there's less chance of burning yourself. But when Prudence picked up this iron, the wood split open, so the palm of her hand was tightly wrapped around the metal handle before she realized what was happening. It was red hot."

Geoffrey put down his coffee cup. Gertrude handed him the heavy sad iron with its distinctive oval-shaped body. He wrapped his fingers around the metal handle, picturing Prudence doing the same, hearing in his mind her screams of pain as tender flesh burned and the smell of singed meat filled the costume shop.

"She dropped it, of course," Gertrude finished. "And luckily it missed her feet. No telling what kind of damage might have been done. Broken toes, smashed bones across the top of each foot."

"It was rigged," Geoffrey said, setting the iron down as

gingerly as though it had just come off a hot stove. "Someone cracked the handle just enough so make it break apart when she picked it up."

Gertrude nodded. "I asked the wardrobe mistress, Cynthia Pierce, if she'd ever heard of an accident like that. She hadn't. Which isn't to say mishaps with irons and their wooden handles couldn't have happened, but they aren't common anymore. Before the wooden handles came along, it used to be that a presser would get distracted talking to another presser and reach for a hot iron without remembering to grab it with a pad. Maybe touch the metal handle for a second, but not pick it up."

"Men handling hot shell casings on the cannons during the war sometimes suffered terrible burns," Geoffrey said.

"That's where we learned what to do and what not to do." Charity Sloan had come downstairs so quietly that neither Geoffrey nor Gertrude heard her even though the housekeeper had left the parlor door open. "Is that coffee I smell?"

"How is she?" Geoffrey asked while Gertrude poured.

"Asleep. And that's how I want to keep her for at least twelve hours. We don't want to risk losing the hand." Dr. Sloan drank deeply from the cup Gertrude gave her. "Is that the guilty party?" She nodded toward the sad iron.

"It is," Geoffrey said. "Gertrude's just given me a lesson in how to use it."

"If I had my way, we'd all go around in wrinkled clothing and call it the latest fashion. I can't tell you how many women come to the clinic with burns that need more treatment than they can give themselves at home. Prudence's case is one of the worst I've seen."

"But she will recover?" Geoffrey heard himself ask.

"No promises," Dr. Sloan said. "Except to do the best I can."

# CHAPTER 24

Amos Lang crossed the Brooklyn Bridge on the pedestrian walkway with crowds of New Yorkers making their way homeward after a long day's work. There was little conversation, even between people who had glimpsed each other daily for months or years. When you lived in a city, you kept yourself to yourself.

As he walked, he turned his face upward to catch droplets of the cool, early-evening drizzle. He'd had a few too many drops of laudanum the night before. No special reason for the indulgence, nothing more urgent than the daily need to forget the past. Mostly some of the things he'd done as a Pinkerton. He wondered if Geoffrey Hunter had the nightmares, the phantom dreams that stole sleep and left him wringing wet with the stink of guilty sweat.

He stepped off the bridge into Brooklyn and turned toward the Truitt house. Disciplined his mind to organize the questions he planned to ask.

Amos had only met Clyde Allen once, but he never forgot the features of anyone's face. The man who answered his knock was slight, armed with a wickedly sharp knife and a piece of whittled wood. The scarred skin and missing eye that had cost him a fiancée and very nearly his life lay concealed beneath a black leather covering out of whose edges spread a spider's web of ridged skin. He hadn't changed since that initial introduction, when Geoffrey Hunter had identified Amos as one of the ex-Pinks he called on for jobs no one else could or would take on. Clyde had nodded, shaken Amos's hand, and asked no questions.

"I need to speak with Miss Lydia," Amos said. There was no need to explain why he'd asked for Miss Lydia. Whatever the reason, it had to be urgent.

"Miss Lydia and Mr. Truitt are drinking tea."

"I'll have whiskey." Amos couldn't stand tea and only sipped at it when a job required. With or without milk and sugar, it was a drink for old ladies and sick people.

"They're in the parlor. I'll take you there. I don't suppose you'd care to show me the weapon you're carrying?"

"Don't mind at all." Amos pulled up one trouser leg to show the knife strapped between his knee and ankle, the other trouser leg to reveal a Webley .450 British Bull Dog. A larger Colt like the one Geoffrey Hunter carried nestled in a shoulder holster. He'd tucked a pair of brass knuckles into a jacket pocket. "Just in case. You never know."

"We're pretty sure someone's coming after Ben," Clyde said, closing and locking the front door. "Just not who or when."

"I heard Pritchard was out here for a couple of days. While you were up in Vermont."

Clyde shot him a quick, admiring look. He liked a man who had good sources.

The parlor door was open, like every other door they'd passed on their way down the house's main hall. Sound carried. Made it harder to break into a place if every room wasn't shut up tight as a drum. Amos nodded approval.

"Amos Lang has come calling, Miss Lydia."

The woman who smiled a greeting lay stretched out on a chaise longue, one arm heavily bandaged and protected from elbow to shoulder by a basketweave of wicker to protect the wound from bumps and scrapes. "I'm glad to see you again, Mr. Lang. It's been a while. I don't think you've met my father."

"I haven't had that pleasure, ma'am."

Amos crossed the room to the wide armchair where an older man wearing smoked glasses sat close to the fire, one shawl wrapped tightly around his shoulders, another covering his legs. The grip of his hand was surprisingly strong for a blind invalid. "Welcome to our home, Amos Lang. I hope Clyde has offered you something decent to drink."

"Whiskey, sir."

"I didn't think you were the kind who indulged in tea."

"I try not to touch the stuff."

"I wish I could say the same. But I've grown to appreciate it over the years. Good days and bad days, like all of us have."

Clyde handed Amos a heavy-bottomed glass with a good measure of whiskey in it. "Kentucky," he said.

Amos wouldn't have cared if had been Five Points rotgut. Whiskey was whiskey. It burned your throat, settled your stomach, and stayed with you for a while.

"I'm sorry to barge in on you like this while you're convalescing, Miss Lydia," he began.

Lydia waved her good arm in airy dismissal of his apology. "It's not as bad as everyone is making it out to be."

"You've heard about what happened to Miss Prudence?"

Clyde stilled his whittling knife, Ben touched one finger to the bridge of his dark glasses, and Lydia went white and still. "We haven't. You'd best tell us."

Amos hadn't seen Prudence since the burning, nor had he talked to Geoffrey Hunter. But both Danny Dennis and Josiah Gregory were as good sources of information as though they'd witnessed what had happened. The account Amos recited was brief, but he left out none of the important details. "Dr. Charity Sloan has her under morphine. From what I understand, she thinks the hand can be saved. She'll be badly scarred, but Miss Prudence should have the use of it once it's healed up." He didn't turn in Clyde's direction, but he caught a glimpse of a finger making sure his face mask was in place.

"I take it you're going after whoever fiddled with the sad iron?" Lydia asked.

"Yes, ma'am. Mr. Hunter is sitting at Miss Prudence's bedside, and he won't leave it until he's sure she's on the mend. Not to put too fine a point on things, that could be too late. Good evidence has a way of getting lost or destroyed."

"Let us think on this for a few minutes, Amos. May I call you Amos? I believe that if we're going to be working together, we ought to be on handshake terms, at least." Lydia edged her feet off the chaise longue, turning her body toward where her father had sat up straighter in his chair and kicked off the shawl covering his legs.

"The only way this puzzle fits together is if one person is designing the pieces," Benjamin Truitt began.

"I agree. Septimus, Hazel Nugent, me, and now Prudence. Each of us targeted for a different reason, but linked by cause and effect," Lydia said. "Drink your whiskey, Amos. We tend to think out loud, and sometimes it takes a while."

"A series of murders isn't unlike the solving of a code," Ben explained. "Each segment means something, by itself and in the context of the whole. You just have to figure out the hidden significance and then juggle things around until the bits make sense. I was a cryptographer during the war. Now I earn my living by decoding the secrets of companies that want to seize control of the marketplace and destroy their competitors. Not unlike a military campaign, but a lot quieter. And the pay is better."

"Septimus was killed because he'd written a play that was

bound to be a commercial success. He was foolish or desperate enough to give authorship to someone with boundless ambition and no scruples." Lydia paused. "When I said foolish, I meant Septimus fell in love. We all know that love makes dolts out of the wisest men."

The three males in the room didn't say a thing. If each of them had known a love that turned them temporarily into chowderheads, not a one of them was about to admit it.

"Why was Hazel Nugent pushed into a trunk and locked inside to suffocate?" Ben asked.

"She knew or saw something," Lydia said. "Either she was blackmailing whoever killed Septimus or she was about to. Our killer is cautious. He doesn't take chances. If Hazel revealed herself or if he only suspected her of being a danger to him, the end result was going to be the same."

"Get rid of her. Permanently." The whiskey had loosened Amos's reserve. "Suffocating her inside a trunk in the theatre's prop room isn't how I would have done it."

"Too obvious a link to the theatre, the play, and Septimus's death," Ben agreed. "It was a crime of opportunity. A moment of spontaneous action."

"A mistake," Clyde said, so quietly that no one was quite sure he'd spoken.

"Our killer panicked when Lydia and Miss Prudence came on the scene," Ben said.

"Was his aim off or did he intend it to be a warning?" Lydia asked. "I've run those moments onstage over and over in my head until I'm sick and tired of examining them. I can't decide."

"Looking at it from an outside perspective, I'd say you were being warned," Amos said. "Anyone who could throw a knife accurately enough to slice through the sleeve of your dress and make a wound that was painful but not fatal could have killed you if he'd wanted to. Your back was to him."

Clyde raised an empty hand and motioned flicking a knife

through the air. "A human back is a big target. Hard to miss if you know what you're doing. That knife wasn't owned by an amateur, Miss Lydia."

"Maybe he figured one more death connected to the Argosy would finally interest the police enough to shut down the show or conduct a decent investigation." Lydia tried and failed to scratch her arm through the wicker cage. "It's itching. That means it's starting to heal."

"Closing the play was the opposite of what he wanted to happen," Amos said.

"We can't know that." Ben reached for his teacup, finding and raising it to his lips without spilling a drop. "It's too soon in our reasoning to make that assumption."

"Septimus told Prudence and me that he was determined to make Hughes give him back author credit for *Waif of the Highlands*. He was adamant about it. Someone thought that killing him was the only way to stop whatever he was planning to do."

"I'll give you that as a logical deduction," Ben conceded. "But your cousin's death didn't cause a ripple in the world he inhabited. Buried without fanfare, not even a notice in the *Times*, replaced as an actor by an understudy. His name won't appear anywhere on the program. It's as if he never existed."

"The only thing that remains of Septimus is the play that will open in a week's time." Lydia wasn't ready to reveal that he'd written a far different piece, a serious drama that might have launched him on the career of his dreams. After Amos had left and Clyde returned to solitary whittling in the kitchen, she might tell her father about *The Hereditary Prince*.

"Hazel Nugent is the key to this code," Ben decided. "She knew who Septimus's murderer was. Discover her killer and the whole thing will unravel."

"Each attack has been a little less successful than the one that preceded it," Clyde said. "Have you noticed that?"

"Explain." Lydia nodded encouragement.

"The police decided that Septimus's death was an accident. So no investigation. Hazel attracted some interest, but then a detective opined that she'd fallen into the trunk on her own and the lid slammed shut before she could reach out a hand to prop it open. Again, no investigation. But a closer call for the murderer."

"It was a little harder to convince the company that she'd leaned so far into the trunk that she lost her balance than that a drunken Septimus had mistaken the rat poison for the whiskey bottle," Lydia said. "There was a lot more whispering, more speculation. But rehearsals had to go on and Hazel was a nobody. So another murder was swept under the rug."

"We have to ask ourselves if that will be the last one." Ben adjusted his dark glasses. "Always leave open the door to speculation."

"I won't be able to go back to the costume shop before opening night." Lydia grimaced as she tried to lift the injured arm. "And Prudence will take even longer to heal."

"Hazel Nugent?" Amos asked. "Can we be sure she knew the killer?"

"I'd wager a decent cigar on it," Ben said.

"What can you tell me about her, Miss Lydia?" Amos twirled his empty whiskey glass.

"I can give you the address of her boardinghouse. With any luck, the room won't have been rented out yet. Prudence and I searched it. Empty, curiously empty for a seamstress. Especially someone working in the theatre. You'd expect the kind of touches that a woman handy with a needle would create. Nothing. There wasn't even a family photograph. It was as though she was deliberately hiding herself out in plain sight."

"That doesn't make sense." Clyde stirred the wood shavings on the piece of newspaper at his feet.

"That kind of behavior reminds me of myself when I'm undercover," Amos said. "Everything that could be linked to who I really am gets left behind. A change of clothes is all I bring with me, and most of the time it's newly bought. Off a secondhand barrow."

"It's a place to start," Lydia said. "She had a garnet ring in her reticule. Good quality stones set in solid gold. But the costume mistress didn't remember ever having seen her wear it."

"Do you still have the ring?"

"I do. Prudence and I showed it to Geoffrey, but then I slipped it into my pocket when I left. Look in my sewing kit, on the table over there."

The garnet ring shone in the firelight when Amos laid in on the palm of one hand for everyone to see. The circlet of five large garnets interspersed with smaller stones was a deep red burgundy, the gold at least eighteen carats.

"Slip it on your finger, Miss Lydia," he said, holding it out to her.

"My fingers are too big. It doesn't fit. I've already tried that."

"Did Miss Prudence?"

"It fit her right ring finger. But it was tight. She had to tug to get it off again."

"Would Hazel Nugent have been able to wear it?"

"Let me think a moment." Lydia closed her eyes. "The only time I ever saw Hazel was when she was already dead. Her nails were cracked and bloody, like she'd scratched and pounded at the trunk lid trying to get out. I remember seeing that and thinking how frightened and desperate she must have been." She opened her eyes and shook her head. "Even alive, she could never have worn that ring. She wasn't a big person, but she had a working woman's hands. A seamstress's fingers. Slightly flat and a little bit swollen with pinpricks."

"Are you sure?"

"I'd bet another one of my father's cigars on it, Amos. I hadn't thought of it until you started asking questions, but that ring never belonged to Hazel Nugent. She never wore it a day in her life."

"But she kept it in her reticule to remind her of someone," Amos said, getting slowly to his feet. He tucked the ring into his vest pocket. Lydia nodded consent. "I thank you for the whiskey and the information. Best be on my way. I'd appreciate it if you didn't mention this visit to Mr. Hunter. He's got a lot on his mind, and I don't want to add to the load he's carrying."

"Josiah will want a time sheet. You know how he is."

"I don't intend to submit a bill for all of my services this time around." Amos picked up his hat and handed the empty whiskey glass to Clyde. "You take care of yourself, Miss Lydia. It was an honor to meet you, Mr. Truitt."

"Let me know if you need another pair of hands," Clyde said as he unlocked the front door. "I don't blend in the way you do, but I can get a job done. Any kind of job." He stropped his whittling knife against his trouser leg, then slipped it into its sheath. "A man shouldn't get away with what was done to that lady doctor I visited in Vermont."

Amos looked both ways along the street before stepping off the porch. "Especially if he makes a habit of it."

Then he was gone.

No one on Prudence's staff was scandalized when Geoffrey Hunter insisted on sitting beside her bed the night they were afraid she might die.

They all had hoped since the first moment he walked through the door that their mistress would give up her independent ways and dangerous adventures for what could clearly be matrimonial bliss with one of the handsomest men any of the women had ever seen.

Cameron, who'd been the MacKenzie butler since before she was born, was too reticent and dignified to voice the wish aloud, but he'd noticed that Mr. Hunter had lately started carrying around in his vest pocket what could only be a Tiffany-sized ring case.

Colleen was making novenas and saying the rosary every night for a special intention.

Even Cook, who'd only glimpsed the ex-Pink through her basement kitchen window, thought he'd make an excellent match. Tall, wealthy, a gentleman to the marrow of his bones—what else could a sensible woman want? But Miss Prudence wasn't always as levelheaded as her name suggested.

"The crisis, if there's to be one, will happen around midnight." Charity Sloan approved Colleen's most recent bandaging, then sent the maid off to bed. The girl could hardly keep her eyes open. She'd be no use if she didn't get some sleep. "They always do. It's a great medical mystery I doubt we'll ever solve."

"What does that mean?" Geoffrey asked. He felt awkward and too big for the delicate chairs in Prudence's bedroom, out of place surrounded by pale blue curtains and bed hangings.

"Prudence has a high fever. That's to be expected. I don't see signs of infection yet, but it can come on very fast. Red streaks up the arm, toward the heart. The skin cracks open where the burn is the deepest. The wound looks yellow, starts to weep. Her heart will begin to race, and she'll have trouble breathing. If she goes into shock, which is what I'm most worried about now, we might not be able to bring her back. Chills, sweating, uncontrollable shivering—that's in addition to everything else I've already described." Charity spooned a few drops of laudanum between her patient's lips. "It's not as strong as the morphine, but we have to be careful. Overdosing is as bad as not giving enough."

"I'll watch her," Geoffrey said. "You can doze off for a while. I'll wake you if there's any change." Charity Sloan's descriptions of what Prudence might suffer had been too graphic to misinterpret. "There's probably a bed for her lady's maid in the dressing room."

"I won't go that far. But I will close my eyes for a few minutes. *Physician, heal thyself.*" She smiled, settled herself in a chair as uncomfortably small as the one on which Geoffrey had perched himself, and was immediately asleep. It was a trick doctors learned, or they didn't survive their training.

The house grew increasingly still as the minutes and hours ticked by. Banked fires ceased to crackle, the gas in lowered hallway lights didn't hiss, no one walked the rooms and hallways. The carriage traffic on Fifth Avenue became sparse. The occasional trot of a horse or a drunken song echoed off in the distance. Muffled bells rang out as even Trinity Church settled into its night vigil.

Eyes fixed on Prudence's face, Geoffrey watched and waited. He held her left hand in his, gently rubbing his fingers against hers. Letting her know, even in her morphine- and laudanum-induced unconsciousness, that he was there.

Every now and then he leaned across the bed and slid the lace-edged sleeve of her nightgown up over Colleen's neat compress and bandage. No streaks of red crept up Prudence's arm. Nothing yellow and noxious oozed from beneath the wrapped cotton. He felt her pulse, thanking Allan Pinkerton that he'd insisted his agents have rudimentary medical training before setting off into the field. Prudence's heart beat steady and strong.

He laid his gold pocket watch on the bedside table, hinged lid opened to hands that moved far too slowly for his liking. By midnight, his nerves were so taut he couldn't make out Prudence's pulse anymore. His own was racing too fast. What was it Charity Sloan had said? The medical crises always happen around midnight but nobody knows why.

He fumbled for the square, velvet-lined box in his vest pocket. It held the purest diamond Tiffany had been able to find. Not ostentatiously large, but not small either. Free of flaws. Like Prudence herself. Geoffrey flipped open the lid and eased out the ring. If she did slide into a crisis, she would do so with the proof of his love on her finger.

Charity Sloan stirred. Her cool hand came to rest on Prudence's forehead. "The fever is breaking," she whispered, catching the diamond's sparkle as Geoffrey moved his hand to cover it. "Congratulations. And may I say that it's about time. Does she know?"

"Not yet. But I couldn't take the chance of losing what I didn't even have yet. That doesn't make sense."

"Of course it does." Charity had sat at too many bedsides not to understand what he meant.

Geoffrey raised Prudence's left hand to his lips, the lightest, most fleeting touch he could manage. He whispered something Charity could not hear.

And Prudence opened her eyes.

She looked into Geoffrey's nearly black pupils and saw her own reflected there.

"Yes," she said. "I will."

# CHAPTER 25

"I couldn't help her," Kingston Sally told Amos Lang. "She came to me too late."

"What does that mean?"

"She was nearly five months gone. I'm careful with the girls and women I help. Nobody dies on my table. That's because if she's too far along I tell her right away nothing can be done that won't risk killing her. And I won't take that chance."

"Do you remember if she went to someone else?" Amos knew there were almost as many abortionists in New York City as there were houses of ill repute. Some of them catered to society women, others to ladies of the night. Every tenement neighborhood had a midwife who could advise a married woman on how not to increase the size of her family and mix her a potion if she slipped up. Or offer another, more dangerous solution. All of it illegal under the Comstock Act.

"She wanted me to suggest where else she could go. Cried when I refused. Like I told you, she said her name was Letitia. She was a sweet little thing. Frightened, of course. When she first came in and I'd examined her, I asked if she'd told the boy. Sometimes the father will do what's right and marry the girl."

"Had she?"

"She looked at me with the saddest eyes I've ever seen. Said he wasn't a boy. So then I inquired if he was a married man. She said he wasn't the marrying type." Kingston Sally handed back the garnet ring Amos had shown to a dozen women of her profession before finding the one who recognized it. "She offered to pay me with that. Her fingers were so slender I couldn't even get it to slip down over the first joint of my pinkie."

"You could have pawned it."

"Cash coin only. A ring like that is easy to trace."

"What else can you tell me about her?" Amos signaled the barmaid for another round of drinks. Kingston Sally, like most successful abortionists, only revealed where a procedure would take place after she'd assured herself the client wasn't a police informer and the full fee had been paid. A saloon like the one in which she'd agreed to meet Amos was so noisy that nothing either of them said could be heard at the next table. She was cautious and suspicious. It was why she'd lasted as long in the business as she had.

"I wouldn't send any baby to one of the city orphanages," Kingston Sally said. "I told her that. But I also let her know that sometimes I can pair a girl with a couple who can't have a child of their own. They'll take the girl in or pay to have her boarded out somewhere, then if the baby is born healthy, the mother can start a new life for herself with some money in her pocket. It doesn't happen often, but nothing's impossible."

"Is that what she ended up doing?"

"She could have. I'd a couple in mind, but Letitia refused to allow me to contact them. She knew the man who'd taken advantage wouldn't marry her. She'd told me so herself. But she was so desperate and so blinded by love or whatever you want to call it, that she approached him one last time."

"And he turned her down."

"Flat. Fired her, too."

"He was her employer?"

"It's not as uncommon as you might think." Kingston Sally folded her hands as if to steel herself for what came next.

"Then what?" Amos prompted.

"About a week later she came to see me again. She didn't look good. Tired, like she hadn't gotten much sleep. But determined about something. I didn't know what, and she didn't tell me. But she handed me a package wrapped in brown paper and asked me to mail it for her in two days' time. I said she could mail it herself at the big post office on Broadway opposite City Hall Park. She said she was going on a trip and wouldn't be around to do that, but it was important the package get off on a certain date. I asked her what was in it. She said she wanted her sister to have her garnet ring, and that she'd written a letter explaining why she was sending it."

"So you agreed."

"I did. I mailed the ring on the day she told me to. I never thought I'd see it again."

"Did you ever find out where Letitia went?"

"Into the East River, Mr. Lang. She jumped off that beautiful new Brooklyn Bridge. Nobody claimed the body. She's out on Hart Island now, in one of those trenches they dig that can hold more than a hundred dead people. At least she and the baby she was carrying aren't alone."

"Did she tell you who the father was?"

"I'd say that however you got the ring, you could trace the purchaser through the jeweler who sold it. Or ask Letitia's sister what was in the letter. I remember her name from the package. Hazel Nugent."

Four days after Prudence suffered the nearly bone-deep burn to her right hand, Dr. Charity Sloan judged her strong enough to endure a treatment she'd read about but not yet tried on a patient.

"We don't know why blisters form as a reaction to injury, but we're starting to think there's something in the fluid that promotes healing," Dr. Sloan explained. "Soldiers during the war whose powder burn blisters were not drained seemed to recover better than those who had the swelling lanced. Nobody knew anything about carbolic acid in those days, so wounds were seldom properly cleaned and instruments never. Most burn victims died, many of them screaming for exactly that release."

"Tell us what you want to do," Geoffrey said. Although he still spent many hours beside Prudence's bed every day, he'd allowed the housekeeper to prepare a suite of rooms in which to sleep and bathe. Josiah had packed a gentleman's wardrobe trunk with everything his employer could possibly need and had Danny Dennis deliver it to the MacKenzie mansion.

Even after Prudence regained consciousness, there had been some frightening moments when her fever returned, spiking so high that she babbled incomprehensibly in hallucinatory ramblings. Each time, Charity had ordered cool cloths to be laid on her forehead and limbs, changed as soon as they became warm. Once, when the fever would not come down, Geoffrey had carried Prudence into the room where a bathtub had been installed when running water was piped throughout the house. He'd stood on the other side of the doorway but within earshot as Charity and Colleen sponged Prudence's burning body.

That was the day Cameron ordered fifty-pound blocks of ice and painstakingly chipped away at what wasn't packed in straw and stored in the cellar's cold room. A procession of maids carried bowls of splintered ice up two flights of stairs to where Colleen, under Dr. Sloan's careful direction, slowly added it to Prudence's bathwater. It was exhausting labor, but it broke the worst of the recurrent fevers and saved her life.

"She's been sipping beef broth for forty-eight hours now and keeping down bits of bread soaked in warm milk," Charity told Geoffrey. He needed reassurance.

A needle and a forceps lay in a shallow basin of hot water

fortified with carbolic. Colleen had draped a napkin over the bowl to contain the acrid smell.

"I'm ready," came a quiet voice from the heap of pillows that raised Prudence's head and made it easier for her to breathe and sip at the nourishing broth. "The treatment sounds very logical." She reached toward Geoffrey with her uninjured left hand, the exquisite Tiffany diamond sparkling despite the drapes being drawn and the dimness of the room.

"This will only take a few moments," Charity said. She removed the napkin from atop the basin, rinsed her hands in the carbolic water, then used the forceps to remove the long surgical needle. "I don't think you'll feel anything, Prudence. I'm going to make a very tiny needle prick at the edge of the blister so some, but not all, of the fluid inside it can slowly drain out. That should prevent the blister from rupturing. When I think enough has been released, I'll put a piece of sticking plaster over the hole. Colleen will clean the area, apply more ointment, and wind a new bandage around your hand. That's it."

"Don't look at what she's doing," Geoffrey urged. "Close your eyes and imagine the most beautiful wedding dress that's ever been created by Worth or any other Parisian designer." When Prudence laughed, he ran one finger lightly over her eyelids. "I'll tell you when to open."

The moment Dr. Sloan's needle pierced the enormous blister, a clear, yellowish fluid began to flow into the small china bowl Colleen held beneath Prudence's hand. It seemed to leak out for a very long time.

"Two minutes," Charity said, fixing a small bit of sticking plaster over the tiny wound. "I timed it."

"It seemed much longer," Geoffrey said. He'd been surreptitiously glancing at his own pocket watch.

"I think we could all use a cup of tea," Charity said as Colleen cleared away the medical debris.

"Bourbon," Geoffrey requested.

"You've earned it," Prudence whispered. She'd been apprehensive but determined to project confidence. She wasn't going to mention the laudanum craving she could feel in every fiber of her body. Charity had reduced the dosage to just enough to control the worst of the pain, but Prudence knew the drug hunger would continue to plague her long after she was no longer consuming it. She'd won the addiction battle once and would fight to win again.

It had taken persuasion and three ten-dollar gold pieces, but Amos left Kingston Sally and the public house with a second name.

"Orla Clancy," Kingston Sally said, hefting the small leather pouch in which she could hear the lovely clink of more money than she'd ever dreamed of being paid just for information. "She's the one told Letitia what she needed to do. Brought her to see me herself. I'd helped Orla out once, so she knew I could be counted on to get a girl through the worst of it."

"How did this Orla meet Letitia?"

"That I don't know. Only that they seemed to be more than acquaintances. Friends, I'd say, from the way they acted."

"Do you know where either of them worked?"

"Orla was a seamstress. She didn't say so, but I could tell by her dress. The cloth wasn't the best, but the workmanship was good. Small, even stitches, none of them raveling out."

"Did she do piecework?"

"I think she had a proper job somewhere. She didn't look like a girl who was half-starved."

"Can you describe her?"

"Orla? Not pretty and delicate, like Letitia. Orla was big boned and clumsy, except that you could tell by the way she handled things that her fingers were sure and steady. She had dark hair, dark eyes, a big bosom for the size of the rest of her. Skin that always seemed chapped. She had a bit of a brogue, if

I'm not mistaken, like she might have come over from Ireland as a child."

"Anything else?"

Kingston Sally shook her head, then almost immediately corrected herself. "It might not mean anything, but she had one of those theatre handbills in her pocket the day she brought Letitia to me. I saw it when she pulled out her handkerchief."

"Could you tell which theatre was being advertised? The name of the play?"

"The only theatre I go to is Tony Pastor's place. I love the vaudeville. It makes me laugh so hard my corset creaks. The world seems a better place when you can smile at something."

Danny Dennis sent his street Arabs out to scour the neighborhood around the theatre district for a seamstress named Orla Clancy. "They're faster than the telegraph," he told Amos. "Everybody knows they work for me, and that I always repay a favor."

Little Eddie was the first one back to the stable. He couldn't read or write, but he never forgot whatever he overheard or was told. "She's always got work, they say. Sews like an angel, though she doesn't look like one."

"Who told you that?"

Little Eddie shrugged.

"You're sure it's the right Orla Clancy?"

"There's only the one, Danny." Little Eddie wasn't shy about standing up for himself.

"Where do we find her then?"

Little Eddie held out his hand. Amos laid a dime in the boy's palm. Another. A third.

"That's enough," Danny said. "We don't want the man thinking we're highway robbers now, do we?" He scribbled the address Little Eddie recited and gave the scrap of paper to Amos. "Not far from here, but I'd watch the alleyways."

Amos patted Mr. Washington's neck and rubbed Flower's feathery ears. Tossed another coin to Little Eddie and tipped his hat to Danny.

"He's the one they call the Ferret?" Little Eddie asked when Amos had stepped out onto the street.

"That's him."

"What's a ferret?"

Amos Lang waited until Orla Clancy's last customer of the day had left her dressmaker's shop before gliding into the reception space and locking the door behind him.

He held out Letitia's garnet ring by way of introduction. "The woman who supplied your name will vouch for me, if necessary." He waited in silence while Orla Clancy made up her mind about him. She seemed to be weighing agonizing memories against the attractive possibility of doing something hurtful to the individual who had caused them.

When Orla Clancy nodded her head, Amos knew he had found an ally.

"I'd know that ring anywhere. May I?" Amos nodded and handed it to her. Orla clenched the ring in her fist for a moment, a surge of anger mottling her cheeks. "I warned Letitia about him, but she thought he'd be different with her. She said they were in love. I didn't believe for a minute it was anything but a ploy to take advantage of her. In the end, he lived up to his reputation."

"Who was it?" Amos asked.

"Letitia's been dead for almost a year now. There's no proof he ever fathered a child on her. She never revealed his name to anyone but me."

"Not even to her sister?"

"Especially not to Hazel."

"You seem very sure of that."

"I have a copy of the letter Letitia wrote." Orla stepped behind the counter where rolls of fabric were displayed and unlocked the small cash drawer in which she kept change for hansom cabs and messenger boys. She handed an ink-splotched and many-times-folded piece of wrinkled paper to her visitor. "Read it for yourself."

"How did you come by this?" Amos asked, scanning the nearly illegible text.

"We shared a room in a boardinghouse back then, so we didn't have any secrets from one another. And we were friends, too. I knew what was going on with her. She didn't try to hide it from me. She said she was planning to go home, and that she'd send a letter to her sister to warn her she was coming. Letitia could read and write, but she hadn't had much practice at it. You can see all the crossings out. She made a clean copy, and I don't think she remembered that she'd crumpled this up and thrown it away instead of burning it. I took it out of the bin when she wasn't looking. I've always hoped someone would come along someday to punish him for what he did to her."

"She writes that he's the handsomest, most talented man she's ever met, and that she'll never love anyone else," Amos said. "He gave her the ring as a token of his love, and she wants Hazel to have it to remember her by. No mention of her condition."

"I thought that was a bit odd, but we were so busy at the theatre that I didn't have time to stew over it. Dress rehearsal was right around the corner. That's always a nightmare for the wardrobe mistress." Orla stroked one of the bolts of expensive fabric. "I don't advertise it, but I'll not deny that I started learning my craft in costume shops. It takes imagination to create something that looks good onstage, and the stitching has to be strong enough to survive quick changes every night."

"You and Letitia worked in the same theatre?"

"I was in the costume shop, and she was part of the acting troupe. Not an ingenue yet, but she had hopes. Hughes put her in crowd scenes and gave her a few lines."

"Barrett Hughes was the director?"

"And the leading man. He likes to run the whole show himself."

"Did you know that Hazel Nugent had come to New York?"

"I didn't write that her sister had taken her own life. I hoped she'd never find out."

"How is that possible?"

"Letitia says in her letter that she's going away. I thought Hazel might assume she'd married the man she was in love with. Moved west like so many are doing." Orla shrugged. "None of us at the theatre realized Letitia was the unidentified drowning victim we read about in the *Sun*. I was the only one who knew she was in the family way. Me and one other. Who didn't care. I guess I was hoping she was telling the truth about going home. I should have known better."

"When did you learn what she'd done?"

"Weeks later. I know an attendant who works at the Bellevue Morgue. He told me about a young woman who'd drowned and was still so beautiful that they put her body in the viewing window. I recognized Letitia from his description. That's when I knew the truth. It was ugly."

"Hazel Nugent suffocated in a trunk in the prop room of the Argosy Theatre," Amos said. "Where Barrett Hughes is directing and starring in a new play. The police decided it was an accident. The story was in all the papers."

"I run a business that's always one commission away from failure," Orla said. "I won't tell you what I had to do to find the money to rent this place, but I'm not going to let it collapse under me. So I don't sleep much, I work harder than I ever did in the theatre, and I don't have any spare time to read the newspapers." She held out the garnet ring. She'd gripped it so hard that the palm of her hand was pocked bright red with impressions of its stones.

"Two dead sisters," Amos said.

"Make him pay for it." Orla unlocked the front door and ushered the Ferret out into the early-evening darkness. "Whatever you have to do, make him pay."

# CHAPTER 26

"Hazel Nugent's parents are dead," Amos Lang told Gertrude Marrow.

He'd talked his way into her parlor because he wouldn't take no for an answer when she'd opened her door to him and then nearly slammed it in his face. He snaked a foot between the door and the jamb, mentioned Lydia's and Prudence's names, referred to his and Geoffrey's Pinkerton experiences. What did the trick was a promise that Danny Dennis would vouch for his character and occupation. Amos was inside the house and seated on one of her velvet tufted chairs before Gertrude quite realized how he'd done it.

"What does that have to do with the way Hazel's life ended?" she asked.

"It's why she didn't leave Pennsylvania and come to New York when the letter and garnet ring arrived from her sister Letitia. And when she later learned Letitia had died. The parents were already ill, both of them. Hazel remained at home until they no longer needed her care. Then she sold the house and set out to learn the truth about what happened."

"Letitia?" Gertrude asked.

Amos told the whole miserable story the way he'd heard it from Kingston Sally and Orla Clancy. "The last thing Orla said to me was to make him pay for it. Make him pay."

"Barrett Hughes fathered a child on Hazel's sister and then left her to fend for herself? Fired her when she tried to get him to take responsibility?" It wasn't the first time Gertrude had heard a similar tale, but the hearing never got easier.

Amos nodded. "That's how I see it. There's no proof, but it makes sense if we're to believe Kingston Sally and Orla Clancy's stories."

"What do you want from me?" Gertrude asked.

"A likeness of Hazel. Did she perhaps bring a family photograph into the costume shop? Lydia told me that when she and Prudence searched Hazel's room, they found nothing personal."

"I've spent hours in the Argosy costume shop. Cynthia Pierce is good to the seamstresses she employs, but she believes in keeping work and private lives separate. If Hazel had had a family picture, it would have been in her reticule. And it wasn't. Lydia found the garnet ring there and a key to her boarding-house room, but nothing else."

"Then a sketch of Hazel will have to do," Amos said. "I brought someone with me. He's outside. Can I ask him to come in?"

"Who is he? I can't have every Tom, Dick, and Harry in off the street."

"You have a reputation as being someone who looks out for struggling young actors and actresses. Even to letting them camp out on your sofas when they can't afford a bed any-where."

"That's different. They're theatre people."

"The fellow I want you to meet is a sketch artist," Amos ex-plained. "Freelance now. Selling court and crime scenes to the newspapers. He's got a knack for producing a lifelike image from a good description. His sketches are almost as accurate as if a camera had taken a photograph."

"What am I supposed to describe for him to draw?"

"Hazel Nugent. You saw her every day for weeks during rehearsals."

"And what good would a sketch of a dead woman do?" Gertrude asked. She was becoming intrigued despite herself.

"I have an idea she might have been lingering around Septimus Ward's boardinghouse. Might have seen his killer go in or come out. Maybe tried a little blackmail. That's why she died locked in a costume trunk."

"You've got quite an imagination, Mr. Lang."

"Humor me."

Gertrude walked to a parlor window that looked out onto the street. She twitched aside the curtain. "Is that him?" she asked.

A shabby, underfed-looking fellow carrying an artist's sketch box leaned against the iron fencing that protected her handkerchief-size garden from dogs and boys.

"His name is Noah Watson," Amos said, joining her at the window. "He might become famous someday, if he lives long enough." Not waiting for her assent, he tapped on the window, made a beckoning gesture when Noah turned around.

"I hope I don't regret this," Gertrude said, brushing past him to unlock the front door.

"You won't," Amos promised. "Miss Lydia's been knifed, and Miss Prudence could have lost a hand. It's up to us to finish what they started."


Clyde Allen had stirred up a past that Vivian Knowles had over time persuaded herself she'd buried beyond fear of resurrection.

She stopped sleeping without the aid of the laudanum she'd once dispensed to grievously wounded soldiers. The liquid opium made her tired and listless. Her skin itched, she lost her appetite, couldn't move her bowels, and was unutterably, profoundly sad. She knew she'd nearly reached the breaking point the night she found herself pacing back and forth across her bedroom floor, tears pouring down her cheeks as she relived every agonizing moment of her violation. She was alone in the house, but she was carrying on a conversation with herself that was loud enough to echo off the walls.

The idea came to her gradually, sneaking past the mental defenses she raised against it. She'd neither seen nor spoken to Barrett Hughes after he'd used and abused her. Not one glimpse, not a single word. Over the years she'd pushed him farther and farther back in her memory, trying to convince herself that she could neither recall what he looked like nor recreate the sound of his voice. That she didn't hear in her nightmares the hoglike grunting noise he'd made as he pumped her against the foot of a metal bedstead.

It had all been a lie. She knew that now.

Barrett Hughes was as alive and present in Vivian's thoughts as though no time at all had passed. She stared at herself in the cheval mirror that had once belonged to her mother, noting with professional medical dispassion the lines in her face, the downward pull of age on once supple muscles and taut skin. She imagined the changes time would have wrought on him, thinking about men she'd known in Montpelier all her life, picturing them as boys, young married fathers, middle-aged husbands, grandfathers bending as they walked. What would he look like now? Would he recognize her if she stood in front of him in plain sight?

What would she say? What would she do?

Days passed. Sleepless nights exhausted her. Impossible that she would confront him. Accuse him. So then what did she want? What would drive the ghost of him from what remained of her life?

She couldn't bear the idea that Clyde Allen, thinking to warn and protect her, had instead set loose a demon that would destroy her. What would come next? A deliberate overdose of laudanum? A bullet fired through the roof of her mouth from the gun she'd inherited from her father? Who had used it on himself, though she never knew why. Perhaps a walk along the railroad tracks and a quick sidestep into the path of an oncoming train? Thoughts of suicide—how to commit the act, the moment of blackness, the nothingness—consumed every waking moment that was not absorbed by patients.

Finally, on the day she walked out of the examining room without touching or speaking to the woman with the tubercular cough, and stared at but did not extract the splinter from the Moore boy's finger, she knew she had to act. She spoke to the town's other doctor about tending her most serious cases, drafted a notice to post on the clinic door, and brought a carpetbag down from the attic. As soon as she read in the *Times* that *Waif of the Highlands* was expected to open, she would buy a round-trip ticket to New York City.

She would see Barrett Hughes, at a safe distance, from a seat in the Argosy Theatre. Then she would come home. It was like getting inoculated against the smallpox. One painful moment for the preservation of the rest of her life.

Noah Watson would have studied at the National Academy of Design or the much newer and more daring Art Students League if he could have afforded either one of them. He'd been able to capture astounding likenesses with charcoal and pencil for as far back as he could remember, but he'd also been hungry all his life, parentless before he'd outgrown short pants, and usually without two spare nickels to rub together. Jacob Riis had found him in an alley, sketching with a piece of coal on dirty concrete. The tenement photographer bought him a meal and wangled him his first newspaper commission.

It was a miracle he'd survived, and an even greater wonder that his talent grew without guidance or much encouragement. He sketched what he saw, every drawing better than the previous one. He was saving every spare penny for a boat ticket to Paris, where art was treasured and artists from all over the world gathered to learn from one another. He'd read about the City of Light in a newspaper; it sounded like the place he'd been dreaming of all his life.

So when a forgettable-looking man named Amos Lang offered him five dollars to sketch a woman from a description someone who had known her would provide, Noah had jumped at the chance to earn more in a single afternoon than he sometimes did in several days. He didn't ask why Lang wanted the woman's portrait; he didn't care. Five dollars would bring him closer to that magical boat ride across the Atlantic.

The woman who provided the description would have made a good subject herself, but there wasn't any money in it, so he concentrated on visualizing and drawing the face she remembered in great detail. From something Lang said, Noah got the idea that the woman in whose parlor he sat was an actress, which made sense, because theatre people were always observing, always imitating real life. He covered a blank page in his sketch pad with swooping lines and sweeping smudges, quickly resolving them into an image that caused the actress to clap her hands delightedly.

"That's her! That's Hazel!" she said, rising from her chair to lean over his work. "Her eyes were a little farther apart, and her chin was slightly sharper."

Was she dead, the woman he was drawing?

Detail by detail, the portrait came alive until finally the actress declared herself satisfied.

"I've never seen anything like it. That's Hazel in the flesh," she said.

Amos Lang handed Noah a five-dollar coin in return for the drawing carefully ripped from the sketchbook the artist brought into courtrooms and jealously guarded beneath his threadbare coat.

"Don't fold it," Noah warned. "You'll smudge the shading." He showed him how to roll the thick paper and secure it with a piece of string. Unrolled it to show them how to guarantee no damage was done. "Make sure it doesn't get wet. I could have made a watercolor wash for you if you'd given me more time."

"This will do nicely," Gertrude said, marveling at the reborn Hazel smiling at her from the portrait. She fumbled in her reticule and gave Noah another coin. He looked so down at heel and was so talented that he reminded her of the hundreds of young actors and actresses she'd seen crushed by the destruction of their dreams. It was a hard, cruel world.

Noah bounded out onto the street, hopes buoyed by the coins in his pocket and the heavy packet of sandwiches and cakes that the old actress handed him as he brushed past her in the doorway.

Gertrude ordered tea for herself, coffee for Amos. "Now what?" she asked.

"Did you ever meet Letitia?"

"We never worked the same show." Gertrude tapped her front teeth to stir up the memories she occasionally felt drifting away. Age did things to the brain that were worse than what the passage of years wreaked on a woman's body. "From what Kingston Sally and Orla Clancy told you, my guess is that the sisters resembled one another. Small, slender, fine-boned, the same eye and hair color."

"Does Hughes favor one type of woman above any other?" Amos asked. He'd known men who married three or four times, each wife younger than her predecessor, but so alike in looks that even people who knew them sometimes became confused.

"Female, that's his type," Gertrude said. She poured a slug of whiskey into her tea, offered the bottle to Amos, who liberally doctored his coffee. "Though if I had to characterize his conquests with one trait, it would be that each of them was terribly gullible. You see young actresses like that all the time. They believe that if they trade their bodies for the promise of a decent speaking part in a play, the bargain will be kept. It hardly ever is. They wear a hurt, wounded look for the rest of their lives, never understanding what they did wrong. The answer, of course, is that they trusted. You can't put your faith in anyone in this business."

"That's a very cynical thing to say."

"Women especially need to face reality. The worst thing they can do is deny it."

Tessa Carey put on spectacles to study the sketch Amos Lang handed her. "Pretty little thing," the landlady said. "I gave her a cup of tea not too long ago. It was raining outside, and from my parlor window I'd seen her standing across the street for more than an hour. She was soaked through. Septimus Ward was such a handsome fellow. It never surprised me when a young lady claiming to be his sister or his cousin asked me to let her into his room."

"I assume you didn't honor any of those requests," Amos Lang said, letting the tea cool.

"I was tempted once in a while. Just to see what would happen." Tessa Carey's bulk shook with laughter. "But I didn't. Septimus was a serious young man. Always scribbling at his table and muttering to himself as he came and went. You say Miss Truitt and the lady inquiry agent looking into his death were both injured?"

"Attempts were made on their lives." Not quite, but it made for a better story than intimidation tactics.

"He didn't seem like the type to confuse arsenic with whiskey," Tessa said. "But I went along with what the police decided happened. The patrolman who wrote up the incident may not be the brightest of boyos, but he's a good man at heart, and he comes on the run when you need him. Jimmy Kilaren's his name."

"What I'm trying to find out is whether this young lady might have had a romantic attraction to Septimus Ward. And if the interest was reciprocated."

"I can't say one way or the other, never having seen them together. You can tell a lot about a man and a woman when you watch them walk along the street side by side or stand under a gaslight having an argument." Tessa looked off into the distance, as if setting up the scenes she'd just described.

"When you gave the young lady a cup of tea," Amos urged, "did she tell you why she was watching the house?"

"Come to think of it, she did. I didn't believe her, because girls always invent a friend when they try to pretend they're not spying on some young man they fancy. You can see right through them. I don't know why they bother."

"What was the story she told you?"

"Said she'd gotten a letter from her sister saying she was in love with the handsomest, most wonderful man she'd ever met. That she wouldn't be coming home again and enclosing a ring she showed me. That's the part I thought didn't make much sense. If the sister was going to run off with this fellow, maybe even get married, why would she give away her engagement ring?"

"Hazel said it was an engagement ring? And that Septimus was the one who gave it to her?"

Tessa shook her head. "No, that's not what she said. It's what I inferred. She clammed up when I told her I'd never set eyes on her sister."

"Was that the only time you saw Hazel Nugent?"

"Is that who she was? The seamstress who got herself locked into the wardrobe trunk at the Argosy? Backstage can be dangerous, and there are always accidents, but I'd never heard of anything like that happening."

"How did you come to know about it?" Amos asked. The tea had a scum on it now.

"Word of mouth. The way everything gets passed around. There were some who were saying that two deaths in one theatre was a curse." Tessa made the sign of the cross on forehead, chest, and shoulders. "You're thinking Septimus was murdered, and maybe this girl, too." She set the sketch down beside her teacup. "I'll get us something stronger."

Two whiskeys later, Tessa had trotted out every theory she could think of, but nothing fit. "I suppose he could have up-ended the bottle of rat poison and swallowed some before he realized what he was doing," she said, coming back to what Jimmy Kilaren had reported to his precinct. "Seems a little odd, though. I use Fowler's Solution to control vermin around the house all the time, and I'd never confuse it with whiskey carried in from the saloon on the corner. The bottle is a lot smaller than the ones they fill from the rotgut barrels, for one thing. But I guess it could have happened that way. Jimmy said he sees it all the time."

"Makes it easier for the police if it was an accident," Amos said.

"But this girl? I can't see her diving headlong into a costume trunk."

"Could she have come back after that day you took her in out of the rain and gave her a cup of tea?" Amos asked.

"She could have. I don't have much time to stand at my parlor window staring out into the street. The only thing that made sense out of everything she told me was what the sister said about the man she was in love with. Septimus was heart-breakingly handsome, and he was also one of the sweetest young fellows who's ever rented one of my rooms. Lovely manners, too." Tessa started to say something else, stopped, emptied her whiskey glass again.

"I know about the box he asked you to keep for him," Amos said. "The one you gave to Miss MacKenzie and Mr. Hunter."

"What was in it? They never said."

"A play he'd written."

"That's what all the mumbling and scribbling was about, then. The theatre's like a disease, you know. Once you're infected, you've got it for life."

Amos rerolled the sketch of Hazel Nugent, promising a

slightly tipsy Tessa Carey that he'd come back when he had answers for her instead of questions. He never would.

The Ferret stood for a while under the tree across the street, trying to read the minds of the two dead sisters.

Letitia's letter had been misleading. Deliberately so? Had she wanted Hazel to believe the best of her, that she'd fallen in love and been loved in return by every woman's dream suitor? The truth she couldn't face was that the man was at least thirty years her senior and known throughout the theatrical world to be a long-standing cad—a scoundrel, charlatan, blackguard, despoiler of susceptible women.

Hazel, when she found employment with the company, had done so not because she suspected Barrett Hughes of taking advantage of her sister—he was, after all, nearly as old as Edwin Booth—but to observe and perhaps eventually confront Septimus Ward. As Tessa Carey had reminded him, Septimus was a handsome devil, and as far from being a whoreson as it was possible to get. Hazel wasn't sure; she had her doubts. And so, one unlucky evening, she spied Septimus's killer enter his boardinghouse. Where he had no logical reason to be. And she was still under the tree a short while later. When he left.

When the killer spotted her. Recognized her. Knew she could be the death of him.

So Hazel, too, had to die.

# CHAPTER 27

"That's the end of act two," Lydia Truitt said, returning the pages she'd been reading aloud to the box that contained Septimus's handwritten manuscript of *The Hereditary Prince*.

"That's enough for today." Benjamin took off the smoked glasses that concealed his blindness and rubbed his eyes. They always ached and sometimes, as now, itched so badly that it was all he could do not to scratch hard enough to draw blood. "It's not a bad play, but the plot is too melodramatic for my taste."

"Mark Twain did something similar in that book he wrote. *The Prince and the Pauper*." Lydia placed a cool, damp cloth in her father's hand, lifting it to press against the reddened eyelids. "And Dumas hypothesized that the prisoner in the iron mask was King Louis XIV's twin brother. So Septimus's idea that a changeling could be substituted for a weak baby prince at the moment of birth isn't that far-fetched."

"What will you do with it, Miss Lydia?" Clyde Allen asked, pointing his whittling knife at the box whose lid she was refastening with a length of strong cord.

"The play? I'm not sure. I haven't made up my mind. I was

planning to ask Gertrude Marrow's advice. She's already talked to David Belasco and believes he might be interested in producing it. Up and coming, she calls him. Says he'll make a name for himself as a theatrical producer, probably also a director."

"But does it belong to you?" Benjamin asked. "You might have to prove that in a court of law."

"Geoffrey and Prudence think there's a good chance a judge would rule in our favor. I'm Septimus's closest living relative and he also wrote a holographic will in my favor. He signed the sealed envelope in the presence of his landlady and had her sign it also. We found it in the bottom of the box."

"Soldiers wrote those things before a battle," Clyde remarked. "I did it myself, though I didn't have much to leave behind. The chaplain and the captain used to come around and urge us to set our affairs in order, as they called it. Sometimes the volunteer ladies in the field hospitals wrote them out for the boys who didn't know their letters. Witnessed them when a man made his mark." Clyde sketched an X in the air.

Lydia stretched out her injured arm. She'd taken off the awkward wicker cage that was meant to protect the wound and was doing her best not to bump against furniture or doorways. She thought she just might take her father's suggestion and slip a couple of drops of laudanum into her tea. The throbbing gave her a headache, and now there was a sharp pain every time she flexed her elbow.

"Time to change that bandage, Miss Lydia," Clyde said. "I'll fetch some warm water from the kitchen kettle. You stay right where you are."

"You never did tell me how deep the cut is," Benjamin said. "Or how many stitches the wardrobe lady made to close it."

"It's not deep at all, Papa. Never even cut through muscle. And I don't think Cynthia took more than ten or a dozen passes with the needle and thread. I don't know why it bled so much."

"Clyde does a good job looking after all sorts of things. He's been a gift to me from that God I don't believe in. I'm glad he's decided to stay."

"Was he planning to leave?"

"He seems to think the threat we were worried about has blown over. Could be that the client who was ready to get rid of me decided I was more valuable to him alive than dead after all. For the moment. Clyde and I talked. He's of the opinion that I don't need a bodyguard. I told him I was of the opinion that I needed a friend. So he won't be going anywhere. Not in the near future."

"I've gotten used to him. He's grown on me."

"That's good to hear. I wouldn't have encouraged him if I thought he made you uneasy. Not every lady can tolerate a whittling knife and chewing tobacco can in her parlor."

"I'll ask him to bring that bottle of plum wine I put up last summer," Lydia said. "It'll make a nice change from tea."

"Just as long as you tell him to bring the store-bought lemon cake, too." Benjamin smiled. He could feel his daughter's warmth in her voice. Once again he thanked the God he didn't believe in that whoever threw the knife had decided not to take Lydia's life. He didn't for one second accept Barrett Hughes's assertion that the incident had been nothing more serious than a careless mumblety-peg accident. Any idiot could have figured out that the knife Lydia had described was far too big for a game played by nimble-fingered boys.

"Here's the warm water and more clean bandages." Clyde put down the basin in the space Lydia had cleared of *The Hereditary Prince* box. "I'll take it slow and easy, but you let me know if I'm hurting you." The whittling knife sliced through Lydia's bandages.

When Clyde lifted off the stained linen, he sat for a moment without speaking. He and Lydia both stared at a wound that had gotten red and puffy. A thin line of yellow pus oozed between the wardrobe mistress's even stitches.

"That doesn't look good," Lydia said to save him the effort

of pretending the healing was progressing the way they'd hoped it would. "But there aren't any red streaks. That's something to be grateful for."

"Describe it to me," Benjamin said.

"We'll just clean it up and put a new bandage on, Papa. It'll be all right," Lydia said.

"Describe it to me," Benjamin repeated.

"The stitches are holding," Clyde began. He dipped a clean cloth into the warm water and wiped gently at the line of pus. "I remember the docs in the hospital used to say that festering was a sign of healing—as long as it didn't cause a fever."

"If there's red streaks, the arm will have to be amputated," Benjamin said. "We can't take a chance that the poison will reach her heart." He mumbled something from the volumes of medical lore he'd memorized over the years, pages from which Lydia had learned to read as a child. He only had to hear something once and it was his forever. "Guide my hand, Clyde. I want to feel my daughter's forehead."

"Warm, but not hot," Clyde pronounced as he touched Lydia's skin with the back of the hand that held Benjamin's sensitive fingers.

"We might ought to get Prudence's Quaker doctor friend out here," Benjamin said. "I like the idea of a gentle lady taking care of you, Lydia."

"Before you wrap me up again, Clyde, get some of my father's whiskey out of the cabinet and pour it over the stitches," Lydia ordered.

"It'll sting like the devil, miss. I opened up the wound again when I cleaned off the pus."

"Whiskey, honey, and goose grease," Lydia said. *And laudanum in my tea.*

Amos's first instinct was to say nothing to Geoffrey Hunter about what he'd learned and what he now suspected Hazel Nugent believed that led her to stand outside Septimus Ward's boardinghouse in the rain.

Miss Prudence was recovering from a burn that could still cost her the use of a hand, Miss Lydia had been warned off the case with a knife to the arm, and they had no solid proof that murder had in fact been done twice. It was the kind of case your Pinkerton boss would think hard about, then order you to walk away from. Not solvable and expensive in terms of manpower. *You can't win them all.* It was a phrase Amos had heard dozens of times and never once believed.

He had his own way of settling a case that was threatening to fall apart. Consultation could get in the way.

Danny Dennis was of the opinion that whatever direction Amos decided to take, he needed to let Mr. Hunter know the facts he'd uncovered. "You'll regret it later if you don't," he warned. "Hunter will find out. He always does. He may be watching over Miss Prudence now, but once she gets well enough for Dr. Charity to declare her out of danger, he'll be tracking down this murderer just as though he'd never stepped aside for a while. You don't want to lose that man's trust, Amos."

"I don't intend to." He didn't realize he'd made up his mind until he heard the words come out of his mouth. But Danny was right. Hunter had to be told. Sooner rather than later.

"I'll take you over to Miss Prudence's house," Danny said, putting on the top hat with the emerald green feather that he wore when driving—rain or shine. "Mr. Washington could use a little more exercise today, and I'd like to hear firsthand how she's doing."

The cobblestones in front of the mansion had been covered over with a thick layer of straw, the way they did when someone was dying. The hay muffled the noise of horse-drawn carriages and warned neighbors and passers-by that another soul was losing the battle to stay alive. Sometimes black crape wreaths were hung on doors and windows even while the straw was being laid down. It gave an eerie quiet to a normally noisy city street.

"You don't suppose . . . ?" Amos said as he climbed down from the hansom cab.

"Mr. Hunter ordered it," Cameron said as he stepped out onto the stoop, then walked down the steps to place a hand on Mr. Washington's neck and reassure Danny and Amos that Miss Prudence was holding her own. "He got so mad the other night when some idiot raced his carriage down Fifth Avenue well after dark that he would have torn the wheels off if he could have caught him. Next morning, we had a crew of street cleaners out here raking up the manure and pitching hay. The foreman checks in twice a day. You'd think it was the Queen of England who couldn't be disturbed."

"I need to talk to him," Amos said. "Privately."

"I'll set you up with some coffee in the parlor," Cameron said. "You might have to wait a while. He won't leave Miss Prudence unless someone else can sit with her. Colleen's been sleeping in the dressing room."

The coffee was hot and rich, served with slices of raisin cake. Amos never had much of an appetite, but he found himself pouring a second cup and eating cake when Geoffrey Hunter opened the parlor door. He'd decided what needed to be done, but he hadn't made up his mind exactly how the plan could be carried out. Or who would finish it.

"Miss Prudence?" he asked as soon as he could swallow the mouthful of crumbs that was all that was left of Cook's generosity.

"Dr. Sloan says it's something of a miracle. The burn is healing and there's no sign of festering. It will take a while and she'll have scarring, but she won't lose much dexterity in that hand." Geoffrey walked to the window, nodded to Danny Dennis waiting patiently at the curb, then turned back to Amos. "I assume you're here because you've got a report for me."

"I do. Hazel Nugent, the seamstress who was found in the property room trunk, had a sister. Letitia was her name. I haven't been able to find out when she came to New York from their home in Pennsylvania, but about a year ago she found herself pregnant. Waited too long to be able to do anything about it. Appealed to the man who'd seduced her and was rebuffed. She wrote a letter to Hazel and sent her a garnet ring that she said her soon-to-be husband had given her. Those weren't the words she used, but she implied that she was getting married and moving away from the city. She wanted Hazel to have the ring to remember her by. Then Letitia climbed onto the railing of the Brooklyn Bridge and jumped."

"Hart Island?" Geoffrey asked.

"No one claimed the body, so she and the unborn child ended up in one of the trenches out there. Hazel looked after their parents until they died, then she decided she'd find out the truth of where her sister had gone. It was a while, apparently, before she learned about the pregnancy and the suicide. And she made one huge mistake."

"What was that?"

"She believed the lie Letitia wrote in her letter. That the man she was in love with was handsome, charming, kind. So when Hazel learned that her sister had gotten herself a small acting job in Barrett Hughes's troupe, she assumed Septimus was the baby's father. She also thought Septimus was a longtime member of the company, which we know he wasn't. Tessa Carey told me she'd seen Hazel standing outside the boardinghouse in the rain. She said she felt sorry for the girl and invited her in for a cup of tea. My theory is that Hazel came back more than once, and it was her bad luck to be there when Septimus's killer arrived. She was recognized, which means it had to be a member of the acting company or somebody working backstage at the Argosy."

"Whoever it was wouldn't be able to explain being at Septimus's boardinghouse the night or day he drank the arsenic-laced whiskey. Which meant that Hazel had to die. She was the only witness." Geoffrey paced to the window again, ticking off in his mind the steps that had brought Amos to his conclusion. Testing their logic. "She didn't think it was Barrett Hughes who took advantage of Letitia because in her mind Hughes was too old to be handsome. She knew he was neither charming nor kind because she'd seen him lose his temper and treat actors badly during rehearsals. So it had to be Septimus."

"The only thing I don't know and won't be able to find out is whether she confronted Septimus with her suspicions."

"I doubt it," Geoffrey said. "I don't think there was time. And remember, no one had a harsh or critical word to say about him. It's possible Hazel had begun to doubt whether he was her sister's lover. She might have begun considering Hughes, once she'd heard the gossip about the way he treated the ingenues and other young women he employed."

"I'd like to stay on the case," Amos said.

"What are the odds you'll be able to prove anything?"

"Slim to non-existent." Amos shrugged. "But I don't see how it could hurt to hang on a while longer. I'm not contracted anywhere else."

"And I've told Josiah that the agency won't accept new clients until after we see how Miss Prudence does. We're all due some time to ourselves. It's been a busy three years."

"I'll make another trip out to Brooklyn to talk to Miss Lydia. Let her know what you've decided."

"You can tell her that as far as she and Miss Prudence are concerned, they're no longer working undercover," Geoffrey said. "I don't care if the whole city finds out their story. I don't want either of them attacked again. It's not worth it."

"I'll tell her."

"Let Benjamin Truitt know that if he wants another ex-Pink to keep an eye on things for a while, Hunter and MacKenzie will be happy to provide one."

"He's got Clyde Allen living with them. Clyde's as good as they come."

"And I don't really believe we'll hear anything else from our killer. He's won. Why strike again when he doesn't need to? Why put himself in danger of discovery? We've got a good idea who poisoned Septimus and locked Hazel Nugent in the trunk. That's going to have to be enough."

*Maybe for you*, Amos thought. *But I'm not finished yet.*

# CHAPTER 28

"That play Miss Lydia's cousin said was stolen from him has to open," Clyde Allen told Amos Lang. The two men were sitting on the Truitts' front porch, eyes swiveling up and down the street, a pile of wood shavings growing at Clyde's feet.

"I didn't predict it wouldn't." Amos hardly ever said exactly what he meant.

"You didn't opine it would, either."

"And if it doesn't? Septimus Ward is dead. The man who likely killed him shouldn't be allowed to get away with reading his name in rave reviews of a play he didn't write. He'll have more cash in his pocket than you and I will see in our lifetimes."

"Miss Lydia has a mind to find out if she can interest a producer in that other play Septimus wrote, *The Hereditary Prince*. She's been reading it out loud every night. Ben's not crazy about it, but I kinda like the story."

Amos grunted.

"It's about this queen whose babies have all died. She worries that the next one won't survive either, so she and the midwife cook up a scheme. They'll switch the little prince for a peasant's child born the same day. Well, the years pass, and the phony prince turns out to be a weakling. And morally depraved into the bargain. While the real prince gets educated in a monastery and grows up strong and educated and honest."

"That's ridiculous," Amos said. "It would never happen like that in real life."

"This is a play. And the rest of it is how the actual prince proves his true identity, becomes king, and marries a beautiful princess. It's the kind of thing Miss Lydia says audiences love, and it's a better written play than the one they're rehearsing now. The way she reads the lines out loud to us, you can't help but think she's right."

"What does that have to do with *Highlands*?"

"Miss Marrow came out the other day. She's got Miss Lydia convinced they'd be more likely to sell the play to somebody with money to produce it if they could tell him that the author of *The Hereditary Prince* wrote *Waif of the Highlands,* too. She says everybody's saying *Highlands* is going to be bigger than anything else on Broadway this year."

"All right. I don't like it, but I'll wait," Amos said. "If it'll benefit Miss Lydia, I'll keep my hands in my pockets and my nose out of the newspapers. I don't think I could hold myself in if I had to read about what a genius actor and author Mr. Barrett Hughes is."

"Don't forget Flora Campbell. Miss Marrow doesn't seem to like her, and neither does Miss Lydia, from what I could hear of their conversation, but Septimus Ward gave up everything so Flora could star in his play. The two of them seem to think he bought her future with his death. I'm pretty sure I heard something like that."

"This is the damndest case I've ever worked." Amos cracked his knuckles and wished he'd slipped a bottle of laudanum into his pocket. He'd made a rule for himself that he'd never take a dose except just before he crawled into bed at night, but he thought today was a good time to allow an exception. "I don't like it when things get complicated."

"Nothing stays simple once you throw a woman in the mix." Clyde put down his knife and flexed his fingers. "Have you ever seen this Flora Campbell?"

Amos shook his head.

"Miss Lydia says she looks and sings like an angel."

"Here you go, Flora. I used this concoction all the time when I was younger. Still do, even though I don't have much of a singing voice left." Gertrude Marrow closed the door to Flora Campbell's dressing room and handed the actress a cup wrapped in a napkin. "It's warm, not hot. Make it last, don't gulp it down."

"What's in it?" Flora sniffed at the pale liquid and frowned.

"Honey, lemon juice, and water from the teakettle. The honey soothes your vocal cords, and the lemon juice cuts through whatever phlegm you're trying to cough up. Your throat sounded a little scratchy to me."

"I've sung that song a hundred times if I've sung it once," Flora complained, sipping at the drink. "This tastes wonderful, Gertrude. I do remember vocalists brewing up all kinds of mixtures before they went onstage. They all swore by something different. I've been using Thayer's lozenges." She took another sip and sighed. "Barrett keeps adding new business to the number. I'd just as soon stand still in the middle of the stage and sing it straight out into the audience."

"That's probably what he'll end up having you do. But he won't be content until he's tried every trick in the book to tug at the heartstrings."

Gertrude had added a dollop of whiskey to the drink and stirred it vigorously to release the liquor fumes, hoping the ingenue wouldn't notice. She'd watched Flora take one bite of her lunch and throw the rest away. Actresses did that for a week or more before opening night. God forbid their costumes should be too tight to lace up. Whiskey on an empty stomach, even just a small amount, did a lot to relax the body and loosen the lips.

"I imagine you're thinking about Septimus right now. We all are. It's a shame he didn't live to see his name on the program," Gertrude said, touching a handkerchief delicately to her eyes.

"Morgan's doing a good job with the part." Flora took a larger mouthful of the honey and lemon juice tonic. "He'll grow into it. Right now, he's worried about forgetting lines on opening night."

"I was thinking more about something else," Gertrude said. "Septimus was a wonderful actor and so handsome, but we all know he was more than that. Everybody in the cast heard that argument he had with Mr. Hughes." It wasn't what actually happened in the theatre that day, but Gertrude was a past master at adapting the truth to suit the scene she was constructing.

"I believe I'd already left," Flora said.

"He was so angry. Septimus, I mean. Well, both of them," Gertrude said. "I don't know that Mr. Hughes would ever have agreed to put Septimus's name on the play as author, but we'll never know now. Coauthor, maybe?"

"You've been listening to gossip." Flora drained the cup and handed it back to Gertrude. "I'd advise you not to poke your nose in where it's not wanted."

"Where someone might snip it off, you mean?"

"We don't want any more accidents around here before opening night." Flora wiped a trace of honey and spittle from her lips.

"Now don't get angry with me," Gertrude said. "I'm just repeating what people are talking about."

"Who? Who's saying that?"

"That would be telling."

"They'd better not give interviews to any reporters." Flora's lips were stretched tight across her teeth. Tiny bubbles of foamy saliva gleamed at the corners.

"Well, you knew Septimus much better than I did," Gertrude said, prodding ever so carefully.

"We were in the same vaudeville company, and then we played Tony Pastor's Theatre together. We never tried to hide any of that."

"It's hard to break those ties. I know from my own vaudeville days. You get close when you're on tour. Not necessarily romantically close, but near enough."

"There was nothing like that between Septimus and me."

"You don't have to pretend with me, Flora. A beautiful girl like you and a good-looking young man like him? He can't tell tales on you now, but that's no reason to pretend nothing ever happened. I'll bet the two of you found ways to slip past his landlady plenty of times."

"I was never in Septimus's room." Flora's denial was so fast and flat that it had to be a lie.

"Whatever you say."

The orchestra started tuning up again in the pit. Barrett Hughes walked onstage with a sheaf of notes in his hand.

Gertrude's time with Flora was over.

"Five more minutes," Geoffrey said, tucking his watch back into his waistcoat pocket. He held Prudence by her uninjured arm, guiding her back and forth across the sitting room that adjoined her bedroom. "Dr. Charity said a little moderate exercise every day would help restore your strength."

"There's nothing wrong with me except a burned hand that's healing nicely, thank you very much." Prudence was close to refusing any more laudanum and putting on a brave if grouchy front for Geoffrey, Charity Sloan, and Colleen. But every time the bandages had to be changed, the pain came back nearly as bad as the day she'd gripped the iron and fainted from the ex-cruciating torture of seared skin. The warm water laced with carbolic stung like sea nettles, and even though the salve Colleen layered on her palm was soothing, there was a constant itch that nearly drove her crazy. Dr. Charity said it was a sign of healing. *Whatever you do, don't scratch.*

"Amos stopped by. He told me a very interesting story. And he's come up with a credible hypothesis." Geoffrey knew that Prudence's laudanum hunger was building. She was due for an-other dose in half an hour. He'd make the next thirty minutes easier by distracting her. She could never resist discussing whatever case they were working.

"I know what you're trying to do, Geoffrey Hunter." Pru-dence leaned against him for a moment, luxuriating in the scent of his cologne and the lingering aroma of the cigars he smoked. "And I don't mind it a bit. Now tell me what Amos had to say. He's such a strange fellow."

He stretched out the story of Letitia Nugent—her ill-fated love, doomed pregnancy, suicide, and wretched burial in a trench on Hart Island. What details Amos hadn't supplied, Geoffrey made up, spinning a tale as elaborate and heart-wrenching as any to be found in the penny dreadfuls or the ro-mance novels pitched at women's sensibilities. He heard the longcase clock in the upper hallway strike the hour and knew he'd successfully carried Prudence through the difficult min-utes before Colleen would mix laudanum in a glass of sherry and hold it out for her mistress to swallow.

"That's terrible," Prudence said, eyes sparkling with unshed tears. "Barrett Hughes deserves to be horsewhipped." She held out her left hand, admiring the perfect Tiffany diamond Geof-frey had chosen for her, imagining another, dead hand and a garnet ring. "To think that Hazel stood outside Septimus's boardinghouse who knows how many times and for how many hours because she believed he'd fathered her sister's baby, and she was trying to get up the courage to face him. And then to be murdered in that dreadful way by Septimus's killer because he thought she could identify him. And you said Amos thinks he'll get away with it?"

"Amos wants to stay on the case, but he's not very sanguine about finding proof that could bring Barrett Hughes to trial. I think you'd be astounded at how many crimes are never punished, how many murderers and thieves go scot-free. Hughes isn't the first and he won't be the last."

"It seems strange not to be closing a case. Lydia and I are sidelined for the moment, and you've stepped away."

"I'm where I want to be. Where I need to be." He would have bent down to kiss her if Colleen hadn't been in the room. Not exactly a chaperone, but close enough.

Prudence held out her left hand again. "It's the most beautiful ring I've ever seen, Geoffrey. How long have you been walking around with it in your pocket?"

He shook his head. "Too long."

"When did you know?"

"When did *you* know?"

"When you were shot on the train, and you lay in my arms bleeding your life out. I realized then that the world would never be the same if you weren't in it. If I didn't have you beside me every morning, day, and night."

"We've both witnessed unhappy marriages, Prudence. Ours isn't going to be anything like the hell your father's second wife created or the armed truce that existed for years between my parents. We're better than that, and you've fought too hard for your independence to ever have an iota of it taken away from you."

"The law doesn't agree."

Now he did bend down to kiss the soft lips raised trustingly to his. Colleen be damned. "We'll live as though the laws restricting women's rights don't exist. And they won't. Not for us. I promise you that, Prudence. With all my heart and soul."

She'd never known him to break his word. Once given, a promise was a sacred trust.

"Is it too late to say how much I love you?" Prudence asked.

Careful not to hurt the poor wounded hand, Geoffrey held Prudence in his arms with all the tenderness of his heart and all the passion held so long in check.

Colleen slipped from the sitting room.

Neither of them noticed she was gone.

# CHAPTER 29

Five days before opening night one of the stagehands caught his leg in a line and fell headlong down from the fly loft toward the stage. Thanks to a sandbag, he stopped short of a landing that would have fractured his skull and broken most of the bones in his body.

"He'll be bedridden for a couple of weeks. Maybe more," the head of the stage crew told Barrett Hughes. "He may not ever be able to work the flies again if the torn muscles and tendons don't heal right."

"Replace him," Hughes ordered. "Pay him what he's owed but not a penny more."

"I already have. I've put one of our experienced scenery people up in the loft and got the new man working down below."

"He's worked backstage before? We can't take a chance on having to teach someone the ropes. Not this close to opening night."

"Not to worry, Mr. Hughes. He's been around a long time. Just got back into town from a tour and reckons he'd like to stay put for a while."

Barrett Hughes didn't bother asking the new hire's name.

He seldom spoke to individual members of the stage crew except to berate them for being too slow, too clumsy, or too often underfoot. As long as they all wore black from head to toe, stayed offstage when the actors were in their places, and wore soft-soled shoes whose footsteps couldn't be heard by the audience, he didn't care who they were.

The new stagehand was Amos Lang.

He figured he'd go crazy if he had to sit around watching wood chips fall from Clyde's whittling knife or, worse yet, listen to Miss Lydia read aloud from *The Hereditary Prince*. There wasn't much he hadn't learned about Barrett Hughes, both from what Gertrude Marrow told him and buying drinks for theatre folk who never remembered who he was or what he'd wanted to know. Amos wasn't one for spending time in bars once he decided he'd milked the drinkers dry. Most of the saloons had a narrow back door the bartender kept locked, and a front door that could be dangerous to try to get out of in a hurry. He didn't like the feeling of being trapped.

So when he looked around for a place to light until after *Waif of the Highlands* opened and he could get on with things, the logical spot to land was the Argosy Theatre. What better niche to occupy than amidst the cast and crew where Septimus and Hazel Nugent had spent their final days? Barrett Hughes was where he could keep an eye on him. And Amos was curious about the ephemeral Miss Flora Campbell. Love of Septimus's life. Unknown vaudeville performer about to become a Broadway star. Said to be so delicately beautiful, she captured every man's heart without half trying.

He paid a stagehand to invent an accident and handed over another tidy sum to the stage crew's boss. No one saw the mishap happen, but everybody heard about it. In excruciating detail. Amos reported for work, was introduced to his fellow crew members, and immediately forgotten. No one could have described him. He faded into the dim recesses behind stage, where he could see and hear everything, watch people coming and going, and remain as hidden as the ferret after which he was nicknamed. He was armed, of course, but more out of habit than because he expected to use either of the knives he carried or the revolver whose barrel he'd had a blacksmith cut down until it fit snugly into a hidden holster.

He liked the darkness of the theatre, the warm stuffiness and air of bustling but controlled activity. The actors were too self-absorbed to pay him any attention, far too preoccupied to realize that he was watching their every move, listening to their every word. He'd played roles all his life, so Amos was entranced by this group of people who got paid for performances that everyone knew were make-believe. They all wore makeup, men and women alike. The older an actor, the thicker his hairpiece. The actresses complained nonstop about the weight of their wigs, the lacing of their corsets, and the pinch of their shoes, but they wouldn't have changed their situation for the life of a married woman in the tenements for love or money. The thing about the theatre was that for a few hours every night you could pretend to be someone else. And who wouldn't want that?

"What are you doing here?" Gertrude Marrow asked. Big and bulky as she was, she could almost match the Ferret for stealth. And she had the advantage of knowing every inch of the Argosy Theatre: dressing rooms, prop rooms, costume shop, scene shop, halls, staircases, the house, stage, and backstage.

"How did you spot me?" Amos wasn't used to being found unless he intended to be unearthed.

"You're very good at what you do, but you're not one of us," Gertrude said.

"What does that mean?"

"Nothing you'd understand. Now, once more. What are you doing here?"

"Watching out for Barrett Hughes." No point lying to her.

Gertrude was as deep into this case as any of the Hunter and MacKenzie team.

"He'll be directing from the house when he's not onstage. We open in less than a week."

"I also want to take a look at Flora Campbell. Will you point her out to me?"

"Flora? You can't miss her. She carries every scene she's in and she's the only one who sings."

"I just started this morning, so I haven't worked a rehearsal yet."

"That's about to be remedied."

"Places, everyone!" The stage manager's voice carried to every corner of the stage and backstage area.

"Don't let Barrett Hughes spot you," Gertrude warned. "The crew wears black so they're invisible to the audience. Hughes doesn't want to know you're there, either. You'll recognize Flora the minute she walks onstage."

He did. Amos had followed many female suspects and protected dozens of women clients during his Pinkerton years. Some of them had been famous beauties, darlings of the society and gossip columns. But he'd never come close to anyone like Flora Campbell.

She shone. There was no other word to describe her presence. The bank of gaslights running across the proscenium had been enhanced by extra pots that were designed to create a halo around Flora when she stood center stage, but Amos thought they were hardly needed. Flora's pale blond hair radiated light, her blue eyes pooled brightness, and her flawless porcelain skin seemed to shine from within.

She was simply the most beautiful, most ethereal creature he had ever seen. Tiny, so slender, a man longed to clasp his two hands around her waist until his fingers touched. Yearned to claim her as his own and keep her from all others.

Amos was an ex-Pink, tough as nails, hardened against emotion by the life he'd lived until he had to quit or upend the laudanum bottle. For the first time in years, he felt something shift in the center of his chest where his heart was supposed to be.

When she sang, even Barrett Hughes appeared to hold his breath in awe.

Amos thought he finally understood why everyone was calling her a star in the making. He wondered if the Divine Sarah and the incomparable Jersey Lily had had the same effect on their crews and audiences in the days before they became household names. He didn't think that could be possible. Flora Campbell was one of a kind.

The rehearsal continued until nearly midnight. Some scenes were played so many times, the actors were near tears and Hughes's voice grew hoarse from shouting at them. This was only their third week in the Argosy. Before that, the company had been working in an unheated rehearsal hall that had once been a saloon. Cheap digs, far more affordable than the rental on the Argosy. Even with a decent slate of backers, finances were a crapshoot.

"It's always like this," one of the stage crew told Amos during a break. "At the beginning, when they make the switch from rehearsal rooms to a theatre, and then again just before opening night. The actors' nerves are so tight, they're bursting through their skin and the director turns into a monster. I've been in this business since I was a kid, and it's never any different." He took a swig from the whiskey bottle Amos held out. "Much obliged."

"How do they stand it?" Amos asked.

"They love it. They feed on it," the stagehand said. "I've never known an actor yet who wasn't wrung dry and then came back for more. The actresses cry like babies, wipe their faces, and go at it as many times as the director orders. Gertrude Marrow's been around longer than just about anyone else. She'll tell you."

"I didn't think the cast talked much to the crew."

"Gertrude's a good egg. She survived the vaudeville circuit in better shape than a lot of them. Could be because she had a gentleman admirer who remembered her in his will."

"What about Flora Campbell? From what I've heard, she's coming out of this a big name."

"Flora is a survivor. She doesn't snub anybody, but neither does she let you get close. Most of the actresses who cut their teeth in vaudeville are easygoing, but Flora's different."

"Word is she and that actor who drank the rat poison by mistake were involved."

"You know a lot for someone who just walked in off the street."

"I've been around. Everybody in the business was talking about Septimus Ward right after it happened."

"There might have been something between them when they were playing Tony Pastor's Theatre. But that ended the minute Hughes laid eyes on her. That man doesn't tolerate competition, not when it comes to women."

Amos proffered the whiskey bottle again, but this time the stagehand shook his head and waved it off. He was through drinking for the night. Through talking, too.

Amos watched from the wings as Flora's character made the heartbreaking decision to leave the poor but handsome love of her life for the older, wealthier man who promised to raise her from poverty to wealth.

He thought the lines were sometimes too syrupy to be believed. Nobody talked like that. *Mushy, sloppy, cloying* were the words that echoed in his head as he carried props on and off stage, swung scenery into the loft on thick hemp ropes, positioned the flats that descended from the blackness above or had to be lugged from backstage storage. Despite the tear-jerking unbelievability of the play, he found himself enjoying being a part of it, something that rarely happened on a job. There were moments when he forgot that he was supposed to be observing and cataloging Barrett Hughes's every word and action. He got lost in the dubious magic of the production. The theatre bug had bitten Amos Lang.

He came out of it when the clean-up crew arrived onstage carrying brooms, dustpans, and mops. The footlights were extinguished one by one until only the ghost light remained. Haggard-faced actors and actresses wearing street clothes fumbled their way toward the stage door, so tired they complained they could hardly drag one foot after another.

Amos retrieved a page he'd torn from Flora's understudy's script and hidden beneath the cushion of an armchair. Walking quietly in the soft-soled crew shoes he hadn't changed for outdoor boots, he made his way along the backstage corridor to the only dressing rooms on stage level. Everyone else had to climb a spiral staircase from the communal dressing rooms one floor below, but the leads—Barrett Hughes, Flora Campbell, the former understudy Morgan Sandling, and Gertrude Marrow— enjoyed private, though small, dressing spaces they didn't have to exert themselves to reach. Amos had planned the subterfuge carefully, calculating when and how to approach Miss Flora Campbell while she was most likely to be alone.

He wasn't satisfied with studying her from afar. He wanted to be close enough to read the expression in her eyes, hear the honesty or lack thereof in her voice, calculate her age by the dryness of her skin. He'd felt as mesmerized by her as most men, but that only made him distrust her and himself all the more. For a few moments, Amos had languished in a half-conscious daze that reminded him of the warm illusions of laudanum. He used the liquid morphine to make life bearable and sleep possible, but he didn't trust the drug, just as he didn't trust the magic Flora Campbell had worked on him.

He knocked softly on the door, then turned the knob without waiting for an answer.

"Sorry to bother you, Miss Campbell," he said as soon as

he'd stepped inside the cluttered room that smelled of powder, face cream, sweat, and greasepaint. He held up the page of the script. "I think this may belong to you. I didn't find it until just a few minutes ago."

She'd turned from the mirrored dressing table, smudged makeup towel blotting a thick layer of cold cream from her face. Her eyes did a quick assessment of him, head to toe, then dismissed Amos Lang as unimportant and not a threat. "Leave it on that chair over there." She pointed with the towel and turned back to the mirror.

He didn't move.

"All right, hand it to me," Flora said, snapping the towel down on the dressing table. "I've been off book for weeks now, so I don't see how that could have gotten onstage." She rummaged through a forest of bottles and tins, brushes and hairpieces, empty coffee cups, and plates of shriveled salad greens. Actors were superstitious about their scripts, lugging them around even after they'd memorized their lines and business, scribbling notes to themselves on pages already crowded with penciled directions. The worst piece of bad luck that could happen was to lose that precious heap of paper.

"Here it is." She pulled her script from beneath a piece of intimate clothing carelessly tossed atop the dressing table and paged through it. "Here, see, I told you." She laid the loose page beside its twin and looked from one to the other. "I don't know whose this is, but it's not mine." She threw the script back onto the dressing table and held the single page out to him. "Put it in the stage manager's mailbox. Let him take care of it."

Amos stood where he was, doing his best to appear so starstruck that he couldn't or dare not move. He smiled what he hoped was the foolish grin of a gibbering idiot or a man rendered senseless by feminine beauty.

And she bit.

Flora stood up, walked over to Amos, and stuffed the script

page into his jacket pocket. She met his eyes, for all the world as if there was a bond of intimacy between them, and stroked his arm lightly. She couldn't help herself. Flora had to charm every man who got close enough to touch. It was as automatic as breathing, as satisfying to her ego as the fulsome praise she expected as her due. It didn't matter that this stagehand was a nobody. She played the game with anyone wearing pants.

"I'll do that, Miss Campbell," Amos said into the silence that had begun to feel warm and inviting. "I'll put it in the stage manager's box. He'll find out who it belongs to."

He stepped back, pivoted like a soldier on parade, and was out the door and into the hallway a moment later, thanking his lucky stars the spell had been so quickly broken.

He knew her now. He knew what Flora Campbell was.

# CHAPTER 30

Amos waited in the alley until the last of the crew left the Argosy. He'd signed out, as required, then hid in the smelly darkness behind a pile of broken crates.

Barrett Hughes and Flora Campbell emerged from the stage door together, Barrett calling out to the doorkeeper whose job it was to check that the theatre was empty before locking up for the night.

He couldn't make out the conversation between Barrett and Flora as they ambled slowly toward Broadway, but laughter floated back to his hiding place. When Amos dared a quick look at their departing backs, their figures had melted together, and he heard no footsteps until they broke apart.

The stage doorman came out a quarter of an hour later, humming to himself as he pocketed his key and gave the doorknob a quick, reassuring pull. This close to opening night, Hughes wouldn't tolerate mistakes, wouldn't overlook a bum sleeping off his drunk in the glow of the ghost light. He suspected the local precinct had been paid to send patrolmen by during the night. Morning would be here in a few more hours. Time to go home. Crawl into bed. Finish off the whiskey bottle he'd picked up backstage a few days ago.

He sauntered out onto Broadway.

The lock on the Argosy's stage door was laughably easy to pick. Amos remembered Lydia saying that it had taken her only a few minutes to gain entrance on the Sunday morning she'd unexpectedly encountered Flora Campbell there. Flora and Barrett Hughes were both gone for the night; Amos didn't think either of them would return.

The ghost light cast a pale glow over downstage center. A kerosene lantern, it sat atop a piece of slate that had once been part of someone's garden pathway. Amos supposed it was the stage manager's idea of how to protect the building from fire — that and turning the flame down so low, the wick was barely burning.

He lit one of the bull's-eye lanterns the crew kept in a locker backstage, and made his way through coiled ropes and scenery flats to Flora Campbell's unlocked dressing room. It didn't look as though she'd bothered tidying up before leaving. Greasepaint tubes, cold cream jars, brushes, combs, hairpieces, towels, and undergarments lay strewn across the surface of the mirrored makeup table. Other clothing had been heaped on chairs and thrown over the screen behind which a scantily clad Flora could carry on conversations while shrugging into a robe to make herself decent. If she cared.

Amos thought it likely she didn't.

He'd come back for something he'd spied in the final few moments before he'd managed to break the spell Flora had cast on him, while her small hand still stroked his arm.

It lay beneath the upholstered fainting couch, half-hidden in a pile of colorful discarded clothing a dresser should have scooped up to launder and press. But Flora didn't have a dresser. Lydia had been warned off with a throwing knife and Prudence was suffering from a burn as bad as anything Amos had encountered in one of the war's field hospitals. Hughes hadn't gotten around to hiring someone new.

Amos focused the light of the bull's-eye on what he'd caught a glimpse of. It took a moment, but gradually the leather distinguished itself from the fabrics in which it had nested. When he pulled the sheath out from beneath the couch, he knew immediately what it was. He'd seen something similar hanging from Clyde Allen's belt every time he'd met up with the man.

Wide and deep enough to hold a Bowie knife. Thick enough so the blade wouldn't cut its way through the leather. But cracked and worn. No one had used neatsfoot oil on this knife sheath in years.

What was it doing in Flora Campbell's dressing room?

The question running around in Amos's head as he continued searching her dressing room was whether the delicate Miss Flora Campbell had ever been on the same vaudeville bill as the Torre family act. Had she passed idle moments watching them practice, then perhaps persuaded one of them to teach her the skill of outlining a human body without harming it? Amos and other Pinkertons had competed against each other for hours on end, arms sore and fingers calloused from hefting, aiming, and pitching their knives at targets pinned to bales of straw. Guns jammed. Knives didn't.

Wrestling or punching an opponent into submission was a man's fight. Guns and knives could be picked up by anyone— male or female. Even children had been known to point, fire, and kill.

He wondered where in the wings Flora Campbell would have stood to get an accurate bead on Miss Lydia. He pictured the actress's slender white arm upraised in a knife thrower's arc. Imagined the downward snap and release. Visualized the blade sailing fast and true past other actors to find its mark. Not impossible. But was it plausible? Or had someone else planted the sheath where it was sure to be found eventually?

Did someone want Flora Campbell tangled in the Gordian knot they had begun twisting with Septimus Ward's death?

Amos slipped his belt through the leather sheath, settling it comfortably over one hip. He saluted the ghost lamp as he passed across the stage, locked the Argosy's alley door behind him, and set out for where he knew Geoffrey Hunter was most likely to be.

Miss Prudence's house.

He didn't remember how late it was until he stood outside the mansion on the corner of Fifth Avenue and Twelfth Street. Every window was dark except one on the second floor where a light had been turned down low. The street was silent, deserted except for the occasional private carriage passing along Fifth Avenue.

Ordinary people went to bed at night and slept until morning. Pinks and ex-Pinks worked around the clock. The people they shadowed or guarded and the crimes they investigated weren't bound by minutes or hours. You interpreted a clue when you found it, consulted with another operative as soon as you could locate him, and never let the grass grow under your feet. Not even in a city where you stood on concrete or cobblestones all day.

Amos hesitated before picking the lock on Miss Prudence's front door, but only long enough to appreciate that the lock was a very good one. Mr. Hunter had obviously had a voice in its choosing. It took Amos longer than it should have to slip silently into the entryway.

"You're out of practice, Amos," a voice said out of the darkness.

He heard the snick of Geoffrey's revolver being uncocked, the slip against leather as he reholstered it.

"When did you spot me?"

A dim light suddenly illuminated the entry hall enough to see the staircase leading to the second floor and the open door to the parlor that overlooked Fifth Avenue. Miss Prudence had been among the first householders to set aside gas jets and kerosene lanterns in favor of the exciting innovation called electricity.

"I came down for a nightcap." Geoffrey ushered Amos into the parlor, closed the door behind them, and poured whiskey into two crystal tumblers. "Looked out the window before turning on a light, and there you were. Standing on the sidewalk, trying to decide what to do. It was serendipity. You hadn't done anything yet to give yourself away. I decided not to chance that it was someone else who resembled you in the dark. Hence the gun."

"People do look out their windows. Even in the middle of the night." Amos allowed himself a rueful smile at his carelessness, then raised his glass. "To Miss Prudence's good health."

Geoffrey lifted his glass, downed the whiskey in one swallow, but said nothing.

"I've brought something I thought you should see right away." Amos unfastened the empty knife sheath from his belt. "Where I found it makes all the difference." He handed the sheath to Geoffrey, then picked up the glass he'd set down.

"It's old," Geoffrey said, running his hands over the stiff, cracked leather. "Hasn't been taken care of by anyone who knows how to oil decent hide. Where did you come across it?"

"Under a fainting couch in Flora Campbell's dressing room at the Argosy. It looked like someone had kicked it into a pile of discarded clothing."

"Then forgotten it?"

Amos shrugged. "Hard to say. That would depend on when the knife it contained was last used. And who handled it."

"Miss Lydia was injured a week ago."

"The same day Clyde Allen went up to Montpelier."

"What are the odds the sheath's been lying there all this time?" Geoffrey opened the drawer of a small antique desk.

"You think someone planted it?"

"Could be." Geoffrey held up a Bowie knife, then slipped it into the sheath he was still holding. "Fits like a glove."

"Anybody who works with knives knows to wet down a sheath so it molds itself to the blade," Amos said.

"Which somebody did. A long time ago. A while back, at least." Geoffrey handed the knife in its sheath to Amos. Poured another round of whiskey.

"Flora was part of a traveling vaudeville troupe."

"We knew that. She and Septimus did a song and dance routine together."

"What I need to find out is whether a knife act was on the bill with them."

"I think we should assume that. Until we learn differently. Gertrude Marrow said knife throwing has always been one of the most popular stunts in any vaudeville show."

"She's right about that. As usual. Just about every time I've paid my two bits, there's been a knife thrower."

"Two bits?" Geoffrey asked.

"I sit with the hoi polloi," Amos confessed. A ticket in the good seats at Tony Pastor's Theatre could cost a dollar and a half.

"So, if we assume Flora Campbell persuaded someone to teach her how to throw a knife and not kill her target, she also had the skill to engineer a deliberate near miss."

"She'd have to be in the downstage left wings to pull it off," Amos said, recreating the knife's trajectory in his mind.

"Find out if anyone saw her there at the right time," Geoffrey ordered. "Tell Gertrude we need to know the other acts that were on the bill when Septimus and Flora were touring together."

Footsteps sounded in the hallway above them.

"That'll be Colleen coming to change Miss Prudence's bandage," Geoffrey said. "I'm not leaving here until Dr. Sloan assures me there's no more danger of infection. You'll have to wind up this case on your own, Amos."

"Clyde Allen and me."

"That's up to you."

"He's dependable. Ben Truitt and Miss Lydia vouch for him."

"All right, then. The decision is yours."

*Best man with a knife I've ever seen. And with a good reason to see that Barrett Hughes gets what's coming to him.*

But Amos didn't tell Geoffrey that.

Vivian Knowles tried to order an opening night ticket for *Waif of the Highlands* by mail but was informed by return post that the show was already sold out for the first month of its run at the Argosy Theatre.

At first she was relieved, knowing her plan to see Barrett Hughes from afar was no longer workable. It was as though the Fates had stepped in to spare her. Safe in far-off Vermont, she could read the *Times'* review of the show, then banish him from her mind forevermore. No need to see him in the flesh or hear his voice. The turmoil Clyde Allen had stirred up within her would eventually subside. All she needed was time.

But the nightmares grew worse, and her clothes hung loosely on a frame that had never boasted excess flesh. The nurse who kept patient records took to bringing pastries to the clinic, urging Dr. Knowles to indulge at midmorning and midafternoon. Vivian could seldom manage more than a small bite and a sip of milky coffee.

"Did you change your mind about going to New York, Doctor?" the nurse finally asked. She thought a trip somewhere would get the doctor's mind off whatever was bothering her, but it wasn't her place to be too inquisitive.

Vivian didn't answer. She treated the rest of that day's patients with her customary warmth and thoroughness, but when she'd locked the clinic door that evening, she slid the carpetbag out from under her bed and began to pack. At the last moment, she added her father's pistol to the neat pile of clothing she folded into the bag.

She knew no one in New York City with whom she could stay while she went to the Argosy box office every day hoping for a cancellation. Respectable women of her social class did not reside in hotel rooms without the protection of a male relative. None of that mattered.

New York was far more crowded than any place Vivian had visited in Vermont. It should be easy to pass unnoticed in its crowds. She would locate a hotel near the Argosy, pay whatever she had to for a room, and ignore the desk clerk's frown.

There was always a way to get around a seemingly insurmountable obstacle. She'd learned that in the war. If she couldn't buy a canceled ticket at the theatre's box office, she'd stand on the sidewalk before showtime and offer to purchase one from a theatregoer more interested in making a profit than seeing the play.

There was one more possibility, but it was an alternative about which she wasn't at all sure. Clyde Allen had scribbled an address on the card he'd given her, explaining that it wasn't in the city proper, but across the East River in a place called Brooklyn. If she needed him, that's where he could be reached.

Sometimes a man could easily get what a woman would expend all her energies on and never succeed in obtaining. Frustrated females agitating for the vote called it *the way of the world*, and yearned for a time when equality would no longer be denied them. For Vivian, Clyde represented a means to an end. Could he buy the ticket she hadn't been able to acquire? He seemed to know a great deal about Barrett Hughes, the Argosy Theatre, and *Waif of the Highlands*. Was it possible he also knew someone in the company who could get him a ticket? One of the actors or actresses? Someone who worked backstage?

She sat down at the desk where she'd spent so many hours studying her father's heavy medical tomes and wrote a short note to the ex-soldier she'd once nursed. He might not be able to find her in a city where there were hotels without number, but she could find him. At the last moment she added an invitation to accompany her to the Argosy if he managed to fulfill her original request. Two tickets instead of one? Naturally, he would come as her guest.

She sealed the note, affixed a stamp. Touched a finger to her lips and then to the envelope. For good luck.

# CHAPTER 31

"Of course Dr. Knowles will stay with us," Lydia said when Clyde asked if she could use her influence with Barrett Hughes to get another ticket to *Waif of the Highlands'* opening night performance. "And she'll join us in the box seats Geoffrey's bought. There's to be no discussion and no argument. I won't have it any other way."

"Best to go along with her." Ben Truitt smiled in the direction of his headstrong daughter whose arm was healing very nicely, thank you. According to her. He lowered his voice. "Your doctor friend can have a look at that wound while she's here."

"I heard that, Papa."

"I wouldn't dream of trying to hide anything from you," Ben said. "Does she mention what train she's taking, Clyde?"

"There's only one train a day that runs all the way from Vermont to New York City. I'll be on the platform when it pulls in."

"Have Danny Dennis bring you back to Brooklyn," Ben suggested. He waited until he heard the swish of Lydia's skirts leaving the room. She was more restless now than he'd ever known her to be. "Not that you're expecting any trouble, but Danny should know what Vivian Knowles looks like. In case Hughes gets a notion to make sure she doesn't shake things up for him."

"When I talked to her in Montpelier, she seemed anxious to leave the past in the past." Clyde paused his whittling knife.

"Women change their minds," Lydia said from the doorway. "I've made tea, but I can't manage the tray yet."

"You don't think she's planning to confront him?" Ben asked as Clyde returned from the kitchen, tray in hand. "I'll have a piece of whatever it is you brought home from the bakery this morning."

"I can't imagine she'd want to put herself through that pain." Clyde picked up his knife and ignored the tea Lydia poured.

"Have you ever witnessed an exorcism?" Lydia glanced at each man in turn. They shook their heads. "I didn't think so. I've only read about them myself, but what the priest does is call up the demon who's taken over his victim. Then he casts him out. The point is that you can't get rid of what you can't see. That's an oversimplification, but it'll do for the moment."

"Where are you going with this?" Ben maneuvered his teacup with the skill of long practice.

"I think Vivian Knowles is going to perform the equivalent of an exorcism on herself. She wants to see Barrett Hughes in the flesh and hear his voice. Both have haunted her ever since that night in the field hospital you told us about, Clyde. Once she's done that, she can cast him out of her memory. Like a devil who can't be gotten rid of any other way."

"Suppose he sees her?"

"She'll be in the audience in a dark theatre," Lydia said. "He was drunk that night and after only one thing. There's a good possibility he didn't remember her face afterward."

"That makes what he did even worse."

"I remember from when I went to the theatre with your mother, Lydia, that the stage lights reflected up into the boxes.

People down below used to stare at the big shots and try to figure out who they were." Ben didn't add that it had been before the war, before the shell exploded that took his sight.

"Barrett Hughes isn't the kind of man who remembers his conquests, let alone a nurse he forcibly violated more than twenty-five years ago. But I agree that having Danny know what she looks like adds another layer of protection."

"I didn't think you'd heard me," Ben said.

"You're not the only one in this house with the ears of a cat." Lydia put a second piece of bakery cherry pie on his plate.

"She won't stay with us more than a day or two," Clyde said.

"You might think about escorting her back to Montpelier," Lydia suggested, not looking directly at him. "She's bound to be a very strong woman, but even someone as determined and resolute as a lady doctor can use a helping hand every now and then."

She'd planted the seed. Whether it grew and he acted upon it was up to Clyde.

Opening night was never easy. Backstage smelled like sweat, greasepaint, and vomit. Stagehands deposited pails and damp towels in the wings for last-minute emergencies. Nerves were taut, tempers barely held in check. Costumes proved difficult to put on. Sticks of greasepaint got misplaced. Entrance and exit lines couldn't be remembered. Damp hands clutched scripts that had been memorized weeks ago. Bowels loosened.

Every actor and actress longed for an opening night on Broadway. It was the most wonderful of all theatrical experiences.

"I brought you some warm water, lemon juice, and honey." Gertrude Marrow used an elbow to push open Flora's dressing room door. She'd put soda crackers on the tray with the drink. They calmed the stomach better than anything else and they weren't hard to throw up if the settling didn't work.

"You can put it at the end of the table. There's no room any-where else."

Flora's skin shone translucently pale even though she hadn't applied any greasepaint yet. Her eyes sparkled as though lit from within. An open box of Dr. Lloyd's Safe French Arsenic Complexion Wafers stood at her elbow, next to a small brown bottle stoppered with an eyedropper. Belladonna.

"I hope you're not eating too many of those," Gertrude said. She picked up the box of Complexion Wafers and make a *tsk-*ing sound. "I don't care what the advertisements promise. Nib-bling on something that's used to kill vermin can't be safe." It was on the tip of her tongue to remind the girl that Septimus Ward had died from arsenic poisoning, but Flora's lips tight-ened and her hands trembled. The girl's skin might be whiter than snow, Gertrude thought, but it was dry and cobwebbed with tiny wrinkles. The greasepaint could hide them, but Gertrude would keep a vivid mental picture of what the unen-hanced Flora looked like. She was more sure than ever that the actress was older that she'd led others to believe.

"The lemon juice and honey loosened up your throat the last time I made it for you," Gertrude said. "We all need whatever help we can give ourselves on opening night."

Flora reached for the thick stick of greasepaint lying beside the box of complexion wafers. It was labeled No. 1, the lightest paint an actress could apply. While Gertrude watched, she ran the stick over her cheeks, then rubbed the greasepaint into her skin, repeating the procedure on her forehead and chin. There was hardly any difference between the pallor achieved by in-gesting the arsenic wafers and the thick layer of makeup de-manded by the gaslights.

Almost absentmindedly, Flora reached for the glass Ger-trude had set out for her, drinking at least half of it at one gulp. Opening-night jitters made you thirsty as well as sick to your stomach. She didn't order Gertrude out of the dressing room, but neither did she chatter the way some of the other cast members did. Flora seemed comfortable in silence. It revealed nothing she needed to keep secret.

Gertrude balanced herself on the foot of the fainting couch. Waiting. In her years of backstage and onstage experience, no actor or actress could remain quiet for long. She wasn't sure what she hoped Flora would blurt out during these final minutes before the curtain went up, but it was probably her last moment of real vulnerability. Once the reviews came out in the morning, Flora would be the talk of Broadway. A star. Untouchable.

Her script lay open on the dressing table, a pencil stub beside it. But the handwriting in the page margins wasn't Flora's. Gertrude had seen notes she'd written, always in a girlish, curlicued penmanship that was also the scrawl of an uneducated young woman. The penciled scribble on these pages—the scene in which Flora sang her showstopping lament—was unmistakably masculine. Gertrude picked it up to take a better look.

"What are you doing with my script? Put it down." Flora would have grabbed for it, but her fingers were slippery with greasepaint.

"It's lovely that you have something of Septimus with you on opening night." Gertrude was operating on instinct, but she was close to being certain she was right. "He's written you additional stage directions for this scene. And a personal note," she added, bringing the script closer to her nearsighted eyes. "You must be missing him terribly right now."

Flora applied more of the greasepaint, rubbing fiercely at her skin. She picked up a jar of rouge, put it down again. Hesitated over a row of eyebrow brushes and tiny pots of dark colors to ring her eyes and blacken the lids.

"Am I making you nervous, dear?" Gertrude asked. She thought she knew the answer to her question. "Septimus was so handsome, so talented. Everyone in the cast adored him. It's such a shame that he isn't here to read his name in the papers tomorrow. It would have been the ultimate triumph for a former vaudevillian. The legitimate stage. You must be carrying him in your heart tonight." *Better stop. No need to overdo it.*

She waited, but Flora was made of sterner stuff than she'd given her credit for. The eyebrows were penciled on above darkened eyes, the cheeks rouged just enough to suggest a cheekbone. When Flora reached for the fall of golden locks that would fill out her own abundant curls, Gertrude stood behind her, tweaking the fit here and there, smiling as motherly an expression as she could muster.

"Did Septimus write you those notes when the two of you were going over the scene at his boardinghouse?" she murmured, as though it had been settled long ago that Flora was a frequent visitor there. Would she remember that she'd once said she'd never been to Septimus's rooms?

"He had a different perspective on the scene than Barrett wanted," Flora said. Her eyes darted here and there over her face and hair, searching for anything that needed improvement, another touch-up. It was as if she wasn't thinking at all of what she was saying.

"But Barrett won out in the end." Gertrude sighed. "He always does, doesn't he?"

"Not entirely. I kept some of the business Septimus wanted. He saw the character as far stronger and less uncertain than Barrett wanted her played."

"So you compromised." It wasn't a question. "Did you also manage to talk Septimus into compromising with Barrett on the authorship question?"

Silence. Flora took the brush from Gertrude's hand. She placed the glass of lemon honey water and the dish of crackers back onto the tray. Picked it up and held it out. "Now leave my dressing room," she said. "I need some time to myself before they call *Places.*"

\* \* \*

"I'm sure she was in Septimus's room at the boardinghouse," Gertrude told Amos, pulling him deeper into one of the wings where she'd tracked him down. "I thought you should know."

"Did she admit it? Did she say she'd been there?"

"Not in so many words, but I can read faces and the way a liar's body tries to deny what's been said. Flora was in Septimus's room more than once. I'd stake what's left of my career on it. At least half a dozen times. Maybe more than that. He wrote personal notes for her in the margins of her script, and they didn't look like he'd done it balancing the paper on his knee. These notes were written with the script laid out on a tabletop, using an artist's pencil to make the writing dark enough to be easily read by gaslight. I'm not wrong about this, Amos. If Flora's been deceiving everyone about spending time alone with Septimus, what else is she trying to hide?"

"Not here," Amos whispered. "Later."

"One more thing. Before I forget. Flora uses arsenic complexion wafers to whiten her skin."

"Arsenic wafers? Is she crazy?"

"A lot of women eat them. They can be bought anywhere." Gertrude faded deeper into the wing, disappeared into the darkness of backstage.

*Arsenic?* He wondered what else Flora Campbell did with it in addition to bleaching her complexion.

Dr. Vivian Knowles pronounced Lydia's arm on the mend. "Whoever told you to pour whiskey over the wound did you a favor." She rewrapped the area with clean white linen. "Sometimes that's all we had during the war. Surgeons weren't using anything but their own dirty hands and instruments then. Lister had only begun to experiment with carbolic acid to ward off infections."

She and Lydia had quickly discovered a warm kinship that had as much to do with their personal strengths as their professions. Medicine, Vivian maintained, was as much an investiga-

DEATH TAKES THE LEAD 293

tory endeavor as Lydia's forays into the world of private inquiry agent. Clyde had stayed close by Vivian's side from the moment he'd met her at Grand Central Depot and introduced her to Danny Dennis and Mr. Washington.

Vivian wasn't fooled. "I'm grateful that Danny and his huge horse know who I am should the unlikely happen and I need them, but I don't believe I'm in any danger from Barrett Hughes," she told Clyde on the long ride to Brooklyn. "I'm not here to make trouble for him. The time for that is long past. I only want to see with my own eyes the man whose bestiality has haunted my dreams for far too many years. I want to rid myself of the memory. Bury it. Bury him."

"Lydia said you were performing a self-exorcism."

"She's right. And very perceptive."

They'd talked easily together after that, Vivian drinking in the broad expanse of the East River as they crossed the Brooklyn Bridge. By the time the carriage arrived at the Truitts' home, the stiffness of being strangers except for one excruciating experience during a long-ago war had melted away. They'd shifted from nurse and patient to a dawning of mutual trust and burgeoning friendship.

Vivian had brought with her a gown suitable for an opening night gala on Broadway, one she had had a dressmaker create expressly for the occasion. "I decided I wouldn't look like anyone's poor relation," she told Lydia.

"I can't imagine you ever appearing to be someone's poor relation." Lydia thought Vivian had an inborn dignity about her that would never falter, no matter the circumstance in which she found herself.

"I tend to dress with practicality in mind when I'm working."

"My goal is usually to blend into a crowd so no one will notice me." Lydia smiled, remembering the many times she'd managed exactly that. She'd once told Prudence that if her father hadn't needed her, she might have become a female Pinkerton.

Clyde caught his breath when the two ladies walked into the parlor, imagining for a moment a first glimpse from the orchestra seats below as they entered the reserved box at the Argosy. Miss Prudence would probably be wearing a fortune in jewels inherited from her mother, but Vivian and Lydia's grave simplicity and pronounced dignity would provide a perfect accompaniment. Older women tended to be eclipsed by the pale colors worn by debutantes, but Clyde decided that Vivian's dark blue gown and Lydia's russet ball dress would more than hold their own. He whispered a description to Ben, who bowed his head to listen and breathed in their perfume as though it brought back memories of when he could see a woman's beauty.

Danny handed them into one of his finest carriages, drawn by the meticulously brushed Mr. Washington, whose coat had turned silvery white under the eager hands of the street urchins who shared his stable and sometimes his stall. The April evening was clear, scented with the promise of a glorious spring.

Septimus, although he remained *Waif of the Highlands'* anonymous author, was about to be vindicated.

Manhattan and Broadway beckoned.

# CHAPTER 32

"I'm not staying home." Prudence cradled her bandaged hand in the crook of her good arm and stared stubbornly at Dr. Charity Sloan. "I had no fever today and only a single small dose of laudanum."

"I know you don't like to change your mind once it's made up, but I do have to make the effort." Charity smiled persuasively.

"You said once the fever passed, I could begin to resume something resembling normal life."

"I did. But that didn't include a late night at the theatre."

"Why don't you join us, Charity? You'll enjoy yourself and you can keep your doctor's eye on me," Prudence wheedled.

"I'm going back to the Refuge as soon as I've taken a last look at your burn. One of our women who was badly beaten is about to give birth."

It took only a few minutes to remove the most recent bandage Colleen had neatly wrapped around Prudence's hand. The doctor checked for signs of infection, bathed the palm in a solution of boiled water and weak carbolic, smoothed on honey and a soothing herbal paste, then rebandaged it with clean strips of white linen. The blistered area was much less angry looking. Charity thought she detected signs of new skin creeping toward the worst of the burn. It was so much better than she'd dared hope for that she couldn't help smiling.

"Evening gloves could be a problem," she said. "They'll be too tight, and we don't want anything to chafe against the bad spots. What you could do is have Colleen slit open the palm of a glove, then stitch in a panel that won't be seen as long as you don't raise your hand."

"That's a brilliant idea," Prudence said.

"The women who come to the Refuge have discovered all sorts of ways to hide what their husbands and lovers have done to them. Have you decided what you'll wear?"

"I think Colleen's already made that choice for me." Prudence gestured toward a rose-colored silk Worth gown hanging from the mirrored door of her armoire.

"I've ironed your stockings and given the shoes a good brushing. Satin collects so much dust," Colleen fussed, bustling into the bedroom. She busied herself at Prudence's dressing table, laying out rose-colored ostrich feather plumes for her mistress's hair, and a fall of Tiffany pearls and matching earrings that two generations of MacKenzie women had worn.

"I'll be on my way then," Dr. Sloan announced. "See that Miss Prudence has a cup of beef broth before she leaves," she said quietly to Colleen. "You've done a wonderful job of looking after the burn. I couldn't have done better myself."

"Thank you, Doctor." Colleen's cheeks burned red with embarrassed pride.

"When will Mr. Hunter arrive?"

For the sake of Prudence's reputation, Geoffrey had moved back to his suite in the Fifth Avenue Hotel.

"He's downstairs now." The look in Colleen's eyes told her that Geoffrey Hunter in full evening dress was not a sight she should miss.

"I'll stop by the parlor on my way out." Charity leaned forward and kissed Prudence lightly on the cheek. "I don't entirely approve, but I wish you a lovely evening, just the same. I suppose I'll have to read the reviews in tomorrow morning's papers. And the society column in the *Times*. Your name is bound to be listed in the same paragraph as Caroline Astor's."

Prudence shrugged. She was used to seeing her name mentioned in the press. Sometimes with a sly innuendo about a young lady stepping close to scandal. "I'm going to see how the play differs from what I saw in rehearsal, but really to help Lydia get through it. She's bound to start thinking of Septimus as soon as the curtain rises."

"Remember, if your hand starts throbbing, you're to leave the theatre immediately," Charity said sternly. "Is that clear? Do you promise?"

Prudence smiled but didn't answer.

It was all the reassurance Dr. Charity Sloan was likely to get. She decided she'd give the same caution to Geoffrey. He was much more likely to pay attention to it.

"I'm so glad you thought of getting us a box for tonight, Geoffrey." Prudence rested her bandaged hand on the pillow Colleen had handed into the carriage at the last minute. She'd swallowed half the cup of beef broth Dr. Sloan had insisted on, but it wasn't sitting well in her stomach. Or maybe it was just the excitement of an opening night. She was starting to feel slightly dizzy and much too warm for a cool spring evening, but she didn't dare touch a hand to her forehead.

"Are you sure you're up to this, Prudence?" Geoffrey asked. "You look a little flushed. When was the last time Colleen took your temperature?"

"I'm fine. Charity checked me over when she changed my bandage. You know how thorough she is."

He also knew that the Quaker doctor was of two minds about Prudence's insistence on attending the opening of *Waif of the Highlands*. She'd said as much during their brief conversation in the parlor. An outing could be tiring for a patient, but it also sometimes did them a world of good. He'd promised to bring her home if Prudence showed any sign of having over-exerted herself.

He held her left hand in his, one finger touching the Tiffany diamond he could feel through the evening glove. At some point during the performance, perhaps during the intermission, he hoped she'd draw off the glove and reveal the ring to every-one else in the box. He had an engagement announcement ready for her to read over before he sent it to the *Times*, but close friends deserved to be told the news before the rest of the world found out.

"We'll be seven in the box," Prudence continued. "I wonder what Clyde's doctor friend from Vermont is like."

"Vivian Knowles was a nurse during the war," Geoffrey said, eyes on Prudence's face as the new electric streetlights along Broadway illuminated the interior of the carriage like a flickering magic lantern. "Union, of course. It wasn't until after she'd gone back to Vermont that she trained to become a doctor and joined her father in his practice." He paused, then decided not to tell Prudence yet all that Amos had reported to him.

"Don't you think it odd that Clyde got in touch with her again after all these years? And that she's come to New York expressly to see the opening of Septimus's play?"

The story of Barrett Hughes's rape of Vivian Knowles dur-ing the last days of the war was on the tip of Geoffrey's tongue, but again he remained quiet. Any hope Prudence would enjoy her evening at the theatre rested on her not knowing the whole truth about the play's director and leading man.

"I wonder if Lydia knows why," Prudence speculated.

"I can't imagine anything going on in that house of which she's unaware. Her father is blind, and his caretaker only has half a face. Both of those old men adore Lydia. They count on her to bring a little joy into their lives. The price of that pleasure is the surrender of confidences. Old soldiers reveal themselves when they talk. More than any of them realize."

*So do former Pinkertons,* Prudence thought.

Barrett Hughes spent the final hour before curtain time trying to remember how many opening nights he'd experienced in his career. When he gave up mentally listing the plays in which he'd been cast, he turned his attention to the problem of Flora Campbell.

There was no doubt in his mind that she'd receive slavishly favorable reviews, and that her name would be on every producer's and director's lips. A star couldn't always guarantee that a vehicle would be a box office success, but it was the next best thing. He had her under contract for the run of the show, but he thought it inevitable that she'd demand a substantial raise in salary. Which he was prepared to give her.

The slightly more ticklish dilemma was whether to keep Flora in his bed, and if so, for how long. He didn't relish rehashing every performance as a nightly prelude to exploring her body and teaching her new ways to pleasure him, but women tended to want to talk instead of perform at those moments when they should keep silent and concentrate on the matter at hand. Past experience had taught him that they all seemed inclined that way. He found it greatly diminished an initial attraction and damped down excitement faster than a bucket of cold water.

But it was important to keep Flora happy. A contented costar made for an easier time on the boards and good box office. It kept the company chugging along reliably if the other actors and actresses didn't have to witness a headliner's temper tantrums.

He'd already bought her an opening night gift from Tiffany and decided on the size of her new salary. What he hadn't figured out was how to disentangle himself from her physical charms so he could move on to someone younger and more likely to capitulate to his every whim. He sensed that Flora would probably tire of him as quickly as he would have a surfeit of her, but it was important to choose the moment carefully. A man could never allow the slightest hint of dissatisfaction to enter into the negotiation of leave-taking. Women had to be constantly reassured of their beauty and desirability if one was to avoid tears, recriminations, and the threat of an accusation of unlawful seduction or an actual trip to court.

At first, he'd thought he might steer her in Morgan Sandling's direction. It was a long-standing tradition in the theatre that costars have an affair during at least part of the run of the play. It spiced up the atmosphere during rehearsals and guaranteed speculation among audience members. Are they or aren't they? Was that sign of affection onstage real or the product of the thespian's art? Morgan, however, did not share Barrett's intense preoccupation with the pursuit of females.

There were financial backers, of course, and in time Flora would undoubtedly find her way into many of their beds, but for the moment she and they were keeping their mutual distances. Evaluating the lay of the land. Sizing up the possibility of suspicious wives who might have gotten used to a former mistress but would object to a new one. Barrett wouldn't push them or his female lead.

His best hope was that Flora herself would drift away from him and into the arms of a rich stage-door Johnny. The only obstacle he could foresee was that he was certain Flora was a woman of more experience than anyone but he suspected. Which meant that she would take her time assessing the senders of extravagant floral bouquets and Tiffany trinkets. She was in it for the big prize, not for a quick and short-lived dalliance.

"Ladies and gentlemen, this is your thirty-minute call," came a voice from the hallway, followed by a brisk but courteous knock on Hughes's dressing room door.

Time for a last-minute costume and makeup check. He'd sent his dresser into the hall to give himself a few moments of privacy before walking onstage under the gaze of several hundred playgoers. He called it pulling everything together.

Barrett liked what he saw in the dressing table mirror, admired the mostly dark but slightly gray hair he'd decided on, the clean-shaven face, thick brows, and accented jawline. He wasn't exactly denying his age, but he was definitely hinting that a wealthy, older man could be just as attractive as a poor, younger one. And not just because of the money.

Poor Septimus. He'd turned out to be more of a stumbling block than Barrett had originally thought he would be. Undoubtedly with a strong writing career ahead of him, as well as a real presence on the stage. But he hadn't had the common sense to know when to step back, when to bargain. *Waif of the Highlands* was Barrett Hughes's vehicle, and in the best tradition of a company whose primary actor was also its director and manager, he had to be the author of many of its plays. He'd explained that to Septimus, and then used extortion when reason didn't work. Flora Campbell would only be cast if Septimus agreed to give up—forever—his writer's credit.

Strange that Barrett should be thinking of him on opening night, this close to the curtain going up. But perhaps not. After all, if there were a figure hanging around the ghost light on the Argosy stage, it was more than likely to be Septimus. A shame he had had to die, but it worked out for the best. Just as Barrett had known it would. Still, it was a good idea to keep that pesky specter happy. "Break a leg," he whispered to the departed Septimus, tapping on the wooden dressing table for good measure.

Barrett wasn't afraid of ghosts. He'd never seen one. He really didn't mind that Septimus might be haunting the Argosy, or that his spirit could be lurking in the wings on opening night. In the real world, Septimus was dead, and Barrett was about to embark on what could be the most glorious moments of a long and storied career.

"Break a leg." This time he whispered it to himself.

\* \* \*

The box Geoffrey had bought for opening night was a red velvet jewel case, luxuriously appointed to show off the exquisite gowns and glittering precious stones of the ladies who occupied it. The gentlemen in their crisp black and white stood out against the crimson, too, of course. But they were no more than backdrops to the women they escorted.

"Do you think anyone knows we're the walking wounded?" Lydia asked. She was only half-serious, so the comment brought a smile to Prudence's lips. "I don't know about you, but I would have insisted on coming even if we hadn't figured out a way to hide the bandaging."

Under cover of the satin cape she hadn't yet slipped from her shoulders, Prudence undid the buttons at the wrist of her long evening glove and freed her left hand. The Tiffany diamond shone like a brilliant new star in the gaslight.

"Oh, my dear! Congratulations!" Tears sprang into Lydia's eyes. She'd been a widow for far longer than she'd been a wife, but the memory of that passionate wartime young love was as alive as on the day her new husband had put on his blue uniform and marched away from her forever.

Geoffrey caught the glint in Lydia's eyes and smiled. He nodded permission to whisper the good news into Ben Truitt's ear, which meant that Clyde heard it, too. Dr. Vivian understood that something wonderful was being communicated.

Josiah was beside himself, as extravagantly delirious with joy as his embroidered evening vest was outrageously bright with all the colors of the rainbow. He'd been waiting almost three years for this moment, ever since he'd caught Geoffrey Hunter looking at Prudence MacKenzie in a way no student of romance could misinterpret.

Smiles replaced the words that seemed to fail all of them. As the orchestra began to play, Prudence slipped her fingers back into the glove, and rebuttoned it. It was as though she'd revealed a secret, then gathered up its bits and pieces and hidden them deep in her heart again.

\* \* \*

The magic began the moment Flora Campbell stepped onto the stage. When Septimus had been alive, the enchantment had unfolded with him—his good looks, compelling presence, impassioned voice, and a rare ability to bond immediately with the audience. His replacement was good, but Flora easily outshone him. When she sang, there wasn't a dry eye in the house.

Barrett Hughes finally stepped into a role that made everyone watching him forget that they'd always before tonight associated him with the character of Ebenezer Scrooge. He was no longer that famous and infamous elderly miser. He'd transformed himself by word and appearance into an elegant, dignified gentleman of great wealth and personable disposition, exactly the sort of husband every father hoped to find for his daughter.

Prudence and Lydia sat transfixed by the transformations that had been wrought since the last time they'd attended a rehearsal. The theatre was expert sorcery that took hold of the heart and mind and would let neither of them go for as long as the performers remained onstage. When the gaslights brightened at intermission, Lydia finally stole a glance at Vivian Knowles.

"It's all right, Lydia," Vivian whispered. Her face was pale but composed, and although she held a crumpled handkerchief in her gloved hand, her eyes were dry. "I'm free." The pain she'd borne deep within her for so many years had broken loose and lost itself in the Argosy's world of magic and make-believe. The fear was also gone. She was empty and at peace, a strangely comforting combination of emotions.

Geoffrey had ordered champagne brought to the box. They drank to the engaged couple, to Prudence and Lydia's return to health, and to Septimus.

"I don't mind any more that we'll never know the truth of his death." Lydia spoke so quietly that Prudence had to lean toward her friend to hear what she was saying. "I think perhaps it may be best that way."

Geoffrey said nothing. Ben Truitt adjusted the smoked glasses that hid his eyes. Vivian Knowles seemed lost in her own thoughts. Josiah tried to interpret Prudence's blank expression.

Clyde Allen knew it would not be long before things changed. The resolution might not please everyone, but it would close the case.

Tidy up the loose ends.

Mete out justice.

# CHAPTER 33

Barrett Hughes and Flora Campbell arrived at Delmonico's shortly before midnight, escorted to their reserved table by the restaurant's headwaiter. The applause that greeted their entrance was enthusiastic but politely brief, as suited the restaurant's genteel clientele. Many of the diners had been at the Argosy for opening night and knew they were in the company of Broadway's newest stars.

Barrett maintained the persona of dignified, elegant gentleman of a certain age, while Flora floated in a cloud of innocence and purity. Barrett had made her change the evening gown she'd chosen for the after-opening-night appearance at New York's most famous restaurant. Too low-cut, he'd insisted, but not until he said it made her look older than she really was did Flora listen and choose something a debutante might have worn.

"Don't drink too much," he whispered when the waiter had poured their champagne and left the table. "We'll leave right after the early edition of the *Times* is delivered. I spotted their reviewer in the audience. He was smiling and jotting notes on the program. What he writes can make or break a show."

Flora sipped delicately at the bubbly French wine, trying not to stare too hard at the society mavens seated all around her. Left to her own devices she would have laughed, tossed her head, and poured champagne into her glass until the bottle was empty. Then demanded another. But Barrett was right. For the time being, at least, they both had parts to play offstage that were as important as the characters they created at the Argosy. Theatregoers didn't mind a little scandal from their favorite actors and actresses, but not at the start of their careers. Barrett would be all right no matter what he did, but Flora was another story. She had to step carefully. For a while.

Russian caviar on toast points. Tiny tidbits of salmon crowned with more caviar. Miniature pastries stuffed with shrimp, cheese custard, and black truffles. Finger foods for which one removed one's gloves. Slices of rare roast beef, bowls of olives, delicate mounds of liver mousse topped with crumbled egg yolk. Flora wasn't always sure what she was consuming, only that everything was more delicious than anything she'd eaten before.

"That's enough," Barrett snapped in a smiling whisper. "Ladies have a care for their waistlines."

"Lillian Russell doesn't," Flora said. The famous diva was known for her exuberant embrace of excess in everything from her choice of men to the shows in which she appeared.

"You're not Lillian Russell. Do what I tell you or we won't wait for the papers to come out."

"Too late!"

The Delmonico's headwaiter was threading his way across the dining room, holding aloft in one hand a copy of the early-morning edition of the *New York Times*. Fresh off the press. Rushed from the *Times* building to the restaurant by messenger.

Even the clink of cutlery against china faded into silence as Barrett Hughes opened the newspaper with a flourish and paged through to the review he knew would be there. Breaths were held all over the restaurant as diners watched his face. When he folded the paper and handed it to Flora, the smile on his lips told the story.

Another hit! Another triumph for the actor who had created the theatrical Ebenezer Scrooge. Applause broke out again. Hughes rose to his feet, bowed in several directions, and then applauded his audience. Everyone breathed a sigh of relief. The conversation level returned to normal.

"I can't believe what he's written about me," Flora breathed. "He compares me to the Divine Sarah." She pushed away the glass of champagne she'd been about to raise to her lips. The actress in her rose to the occasion. She had a part to play, one in which Barrett, with all his years of experience, had coached her well.

"Enjoy the moment, but don't let it go to your head," Barrett cautioned. He'd been a little worried that he wouldn't be able to control Flora as much as he felt she needed. But she hadn't let herself be overwhelmed by Delmonico's. She'd followed his instructions almost to the letter once it became clear he knew what he was talking about. Looking at her flushed face and glittering eyes, he figured she'd have to let loose sometime tonight or burst from the effort of holding things in.

The director in Barrett Hughes began to relax. His star pupil was following the script he'd laid out for her, and it was already reaping benefits. Some of Delmonico's wealthy patrons had nodded in his direction in that special way that moguls telegraphed their financial interest. *Highlands* was already—on its opening night—forecast to break box office records. He'd have no dearth of investors for whatever play he chose to present next. And for the theatre he would purchase and rename the Hughes Theatre. He could see the marquee in his mind's eye. Perhaps instead of just the Hughes Theatre, he would christen it the Barrett Hughes Theatre. So no one could doubt for a moment that it commemorated and housed America's greatest living actor. As soon as Edwin Booth got on with the business of dying.

Flora began to feel her champagne and caviar as Barrett's carriage drove the rough, cobblestoned streets of the theatre district. She'd drunk and eaten more than either of them realized, not curbing her appetites until he'd barked at her shortly before the *Times* arrived.

She'd been deeper into her cups than this before, but she'd also never curbed her eating as stringently as she had in the weeks prior to the opening. Consuming prodigious amounts of liquor was as much a part of the vaudeville circuit as the constant packing and unpacking, the long train rides, and the cheap hotels. For some of the performers, it was the only way they held on to impossible dreams and broken promises. You learned early on to drink, throw up, and drink some more.

Maybe it was the caviar. Flora wasn't used to rich foods. She lived on boardinghouse meals except when a stage-door Johnny took her out to a fancy restaurant. And recently, because Barrett insisted on it, she'd played the shy, reluctant virgin with the men who sent flowers and telegrams imploring her to honor them with her presence.

The caviar was threatening to come up. Flora pressed her handkerchief to her mouth and motioned to Barrett to roll down the carriage window next to her. She leaned her head out into the crisp night air and gradually the nausea subsided.

The carriage stopped beside a newsstand where Barrett regularly picked up the newspapers that carried columns about the New York theatre world.

"Congratulations! Not a bad review in the lot." The stand's newsagent wore a green canvas apron and a black fedora. He knew Hughes by sight and often boasted about the famous actor who made a point of buying the day's papers from him and no one else. "I made up a bundle for you."

The smell of fresh ink and newsprint filled the carriage as Barrett placed the tightly wrapped stack of newspapers on the seat beside him.

Flora waved her handkerchief in the fresh air of the open window.

"We're almost there." Barrett moved away from her. He handed over the folded blanket that was intended to shield cold feet. "Use this, if you have to."

"I'll make it," Flora whispered through clenched teeth. Her face was deathly pale.

It was a close call, but Flora did make it, at least as far as the luxurious bathroom Barrett Hughes had recently added to his apartment.

"Better?" he asked when she finally rejoined him in the bedroom. He'd opened another bottle of champagne and was stretched out on the bed enjoying it. He wore a pair of black Chinese silk pajama bottoms. Newspapers lay strewn around him.

"I shouldn't have come here tonight. I feel miserable." Flora presented him her back so he could unhook the cream-colored gown she'd worn to Delmonico's. Remarkably, there wasn't a stain on it. "Unlace me," she commanded as the gown pooled around her feet. The corset that molded her figure into the wasp-waisted silhouette demanded by fashion left red stripes across her back and stomach, as though someone had taken a light whip to the pale skin.

"Put this on." Barrett tossed her the top to his pajamas. Frogged and embroidered with gold thread, it turned Flora into an imp from a Chinese brothel. "I'm not in the mood, so cover yourself." Barrett ached in every muscle of his body, especially the facial muscles he'd stretched for hours into unending smiles. He'd chased, caught, and tamed Flora, refashioned her into his own creature. The allure had faded. It was time to renegotiate their relationship. "We'll find you an apartment. Starting tomorrow. You can't continue living in a boardinghouse. And you certainly can't move in here."

Sharing space with Barrett was the last thing Flora wanted. She'd lived much of her life without a shred of privacy or comfort. Now that it looked as though she'd be working in the same theatre for a while, she yearned for the luxury of rooms belonging to her alone, perhaps with a maid to keep them clean and pick up the clothes she'd toss on the floor. It was an existence she'd dreamed of in every flea-bitten flophouse that was all she could afford on the road.

"I'll need more money." Might as well get right to the point.

"We're renegotiating your future, Flora. I don't mind paying for success, as long as it's a reasonable increase."

"What's your idea of reasonable?"

"I'll talk to my backers and look at the books." Barrett already knew to the penny what he planned to pay his new star, but he judged it best to make her wait for a specific figure. Make her sweat a bit. She had something on him that he had to make sure she was never tempted to use, so he wouldn't push her too far. Just enough so she had no doubt who was in charge.

"I saw Prudence MacKenzie and Lydia Truitt tonight, in the most expensive box in the house." Flora had almost flubbed a line when she glanced out into the audience and spotted the two seamstresses dressed in society finery and escorted by a handsome man wearing formal white tie. There were others in the box, but she had eyes only for those three.

"Forget them." Barrett Hughes gathered up the scattered newspapers, flinging them across the room. His valet would see to them in the morning.

"The MacKenzie woman is an inquiry agent and a lawyer to boot. I asked around about her," Flora said. "Lydia was apparently her client."

"I told you to forget about them."

"Lydia is Septimus's cousin. Which I think also makes her

his heir." Flora was pushing it, but if the negotiations Barrett had talked about were to be anywhere near fair, he had to know how vulnerable he was. She could bring him down with very little effort. Rumor spread like wildfire in the theatre. And it was just as destructive.

"She can't prove anything." It was as close to admitting what Flora already knew as Barrett was willing to come.

Flora didn't contradict him. She undid the mass of golden hair pinned in the latest Parisian style, gave her head a shake, and sat there. In Barrett's bed. Dressed in Barrett's black silk pajama top.

Prudence MacKenzie and her client might not be able to prove that Septimus Ward was the real author of *Waif of the Highlands*, but there was someone else who could. Flora waited patiently for the unspoken threat to register fully. She wasn't afraid of Barrett Hughes. But this was the first time she'd let him know that he wasn't now and would never be the master he imagined himself to be.

"You shouldn't have used arsenic, Flora," he said. "It leaves a scent trace on your fingers if you're not careful. A very distinctive smell of almonds. We were together not long after you left his room. You should have washed your hands or used gloves."

"I don't know what you mean."

"And shoving poor Hazel into a costume trunk? I doubt our very inventive Septimus himself could have come up with a more ridiculous way to kill someone. You were very lucky, you know. New York City policemen are easily persuaded that accidents happen."

"You're talking nonsense."

"I didn't kill either your precious Septimus or the seamstress. So you must have taken care of both of them. Not that I blame you. Getting rid of Septimus was in the nature of a necessary evil. He'd become a threat to both of us. Hazel's accident had me puzzled for a while. Then I realized that she must have seen you entering or leaving Septimus's boardinghouse. I imagine you waited outside until the landlady left with a market basket on her arm. And for some reason of which I'm ignorant, Hazel had also concealed herself where she could watch when he came and went. I wonder if you saw someone who looked familiar as you hurried away, or perhaps Hazel was foolish enough to attempt a bit of blackmail."

"My cousin drank too much. The seamstress was clumsy and careless." As long as Flora stuck to her story and wasn't goaded into contradicting herself, she was safe.

"I don't doubt for a moment that both assertions are accurate. But they needed help getting out of your way, didn't they?"

"I'm going home."

"It's late. You'll never be able to flag down a hansom, and I decline to make my carriage available. So, unless you want to walk—a very unwise choice—you're stuck here until the morning. I suggest you make the most of it."

She tried to shrug off the arm holding her onto the bed, but Hughes was too strong for her. She remembered his boasting once that no woman had ever left his presence until he was ready to be rid of her. She fell back against the pillows and forced her muscles to unclench. The actor looming over her might be physically more powerful, but was he smarter? Could he think on the fly?

"I sent one of the stagehands to look for the knife you threw at Lydia. That was nicely done, by the way. But careless. A fellow vaudevillian would be bound to wonder. The stagehand never found the blade, though he did locate the notch where it struck one of the flies. My guess is that our amateur sleuth retrieved it. You made a mistake that could have gotten you caught when you tampered with the sad iron; it's something only a woman would have thought of doing. Don't ever forget that luck has been with you so far, but it won't last forever. I would have fired Lydia and her friend, but you grew impatient,

Flora. That's a character trait you need to restrain. If you stand aside and wait long enough, most issues that seem initially threatening resolve themselves."

She untied the drawstring of his pajama bottoms and with the other hand caressed the nest of gray hair on Barrett's chest.

"I told you I wasn't in the mood."

Under her expert fingers she felt his body respond. Flora had never failed to arouse any man she set out to entice, drunk or sober, young or old, initially interested or not. She needed time, and the best way to gain it was to distract him, to lull Hughes into thinking she was as stupid as he believed her—and all women—to be.

Tomorrow's performance had to be even better than tonight's. Theatregoers who read the reviews would expect nothing less. She needed sleep. Rest. Quiet in which to regroup her forces. But first, she had to sidetrack the man who knew too much. He could never prove any of his allegations, but his guesswork was too close to the truth. If Barrett Hughes had figured out what lay behind the Argosy Theatre murders, someone else was likely to do the same.

He was safe for a while because Flora needed him. But as he covered her body with his own and dragged her with him into the rough sex he favored, she decided that someday soon—when her reputation no longer needed his support—Hughes's heart would fail.

As it did many men of his age.

Her only regret was that it would probably be a relatively painless ending of his life.

# CHAPTER 34

Backstage buzzed with the euphoria of better-than-hoped-for reviews and the promise of a long run on the second night of *Waif of the Highlands*. Cast members smiled and hugged one another, hummed as they applied makeup and got into their costumes. Every mirror above every makeup table had a review attached to it. Most of the praise had gone to Barrett Hughes and Flora Campbell, but Morgan Sandling as the spurned young lover and Gertrude Marrow as the heroine's long-suffering mother were both mentioned by name. The crowd scenes were deemed authentic, the costumes and staging so realistic as to transport the audience to another world, and the song that Flora Campbell sang was forecast to be on everyone's lips in the coming months.

*Highlands* was a hit. Cast and crew had only to settle in to enjoy the fruits of their labors. Backers could look forward to substantial returns on their investment.

The stage manager knocked on dressing room doors, announcing as he strode the dark backstage hallways, "Ladies and gentlemen, this is your thirty-minute call."

From behind the curtain, stagehands could hear the audience

filling the house, chatting and laughing as they located their seats. They knew they were in for an entertaining evening, well worth what they'd paid for their tickets. The orchestra tuned up; the gaslights began a slow dim. With this latest success, no one doubted that the Argosy would be fitted with electricity in the near future. So much was changing on Broadway. What would actors look like when the stage on which they played was flooded with bright white light?

"Places, everyone, places."

The stage manager knocked a second, then a third time on Flora Campbell's dressing room door. Odd that she didn't answer. His hand drifted down to the doorknob. Locked. He'd never known her not to leave her door open in those final moments before she appeared onstage. There might be a last-second costume adjustment. A change in business. He started to panic.

Barrett Hughes's dressing room was only a few steps away, but there was no answer there either. The stage manager knocked, rattled the doorknob, raised his fist and pounded. No response. He could hear the orchestra launching into the opening bars of the song Flora would sing, the show's signature musical theme.

"Something's wrong," he whispered to a passing stagehand. You didn't speak in anything but a whisper this close to curtain going up. "Get the keys hanging on my board." In the second-night excitement of a guaranteed hit show, he'd forgotten to attach them to his belt. "Get word to the orchestra that curtain will be delayed for a few minutes."

The stagehand stared at him, then sprinted off.

Word spread backstage like water leaking from a dam. The play's two stars were locked in their dressing rooms and not answering the places call. Faces turned toward the hallway where the stage manager paced, clipboard clutched to his chest. What could possibly have gone wrong? Were they napping? Drunk? There was one other possibility, but if that's what was going on, they'd step out of one of the dressing rooms, readjusting their clothing as soon as they realized how close they'd cut it. A few of the actors sniggered, then quickly assumed serious faces.

The stagehand with the ring of keys hurried back across the stage, bull's-eye lantern in hand so he wouldn't trip over something and fall. The orchestra started playing Flora's song again.

The stage manager knocked one more time on the door to Flora's dressing room—just in case—then inserted a key into the lock.

Fully dressed in her opening scene costume, Flora sat bent over and facedown at her dressing table, arms hanging loosely at her sides. Bright red blood bloomed flowerlike across the back of her dress. Her eyes were open, her lips spread in surprise. The end had come unexpectedly, quickly, and expertly. The knife that had been angled to pierce her heart had been withdrawn and carried away. Nothing in the room had been disturbed; there was no sign that anything had been taken.

Barrett Hughes was also dead. Also seated in front of his makeup table, lying facedown atop the tubes and jars and towels he'd used to transform himself. There was more blood across his back, but he was a big man. His arms also hung at his sides, no indication that he'd tried to fend off his attacker. His mouth was open as if to bellow an order, and his lifeless eyes stared straight ahead as the stage manager bent over him. But Barrett Hughes would never again direct or star in a play. He would never name a theatre after himself.

"Ten-minute delay to curtain." The stage manager locked both dressing room doors and checked his fingers to make sure he hadn't bloodied them.

"Notify the understudies they're on tonight."

The murders at the Argosy made headlines in the *Times* and every other New York City newspaper. There was speculation that *Waif of the Highlands* would go dark. Shut down. Be relegated to that small set of bad luck plays said to be cursed. Like the Scottish play whose name was never spoken aloud in a theatre. A play that bankrupted its backers, caused actors to be injured or killed, or burned down theatres that presented it was purely to be avoided. *Highlands* had seen its two stars stabbed to death in their dressing rooms, but who knew what might happen next?

The news hadn't broken until the morning after the second night's performance, when an initially angry and disappointed audience had been charmed by the pathos of the heroine's predicament and the undeniable talent of the understudies who went on in place of Flora Campbell and Barrett Hughes. By an extraordinary stroke of good luck, a few of the reviewers who had attended opening night opted to use the extra second night tickets supplied them. You never knew. A reviewer could fall ill, his mother could die, or he could just be too deep in his whiskey to remember to attend. Hence the extra night's tickets. And the glowing reviews that appeared in the same editions as the murder headlines.

Despite the good reviews garnered by the understudies, the Argosy box office expected to be inundated by cancellations and furious ticket holders demanding their money back. But that didn't happen. As the hours passed before curtain time the third night, it appeared that violent death had lent a certain cachet to *Waif of the Highlands*. Everybody wanted to see this play before it was forced to close. So it didn't.

Lydia accompanied Vivian Knowles to Grand Central Depot when she caught the train back to Vermont on the second morning after opening night. Newsboys had been shouting descriptions of a horrible double murder somewhere in the city, but Clyde hurried them out of Danny's cab into the station and onto the platform before the women could make out who had been killed and where. The newsboy who delivered the *Times* to the Truitt household had missed them that morning. Clyde said the paper wasn't on the porch when he went out to pick it up.

He knew Lydia and Vivian had stayed up late talking on opening night. He'd heard the sound of agonized sobbing once, and the cooing noise women made when they comforted one another. He guessed Vivian had broken her years of silence and confided her humiliation to Lydia.

Clyde had studied Vivian's face whenever Barrett Hughes had been onstage. He'd read pain, fear, and something unfathomable in her eyes. Her hands had writhed in her lap like a nest of newly hatched snakes. He guessed that she was reliving that long-ago night in the medical tent when the world as she had known it collapsed around her. Reliving and reburying it, this time forever. Gradually, with each of Hughes's successive appearances throughout the play, Vivian had relaxed a tiny bit more, until he saw her smile at one of Flora Campbell's lines. By this time, her hands lay loosely curled in her lap, fingers at rest. When he heard her tell Lydia that she was cured, he half believed her. He thought that perhaps the hours spent in the parlor with Ben Truitt's compassionate daughter had finally broken the last barrier to heart's ease.

Vivian Knowles might be whole again, but Barrett Hughes could not be absolved of the damage he'd done her. It was past time for the debt to be called. And so it was.

Amos had gone about his business with the silent efficiency of long practice. He'd made keys for both dressing rooms, handing one to Clyde before they entered the backstage area together. No one noticed the additional stagehand.

It made no difference to Amos that Flora Campbell was a woman. All that mattered was that she'd used arsenic on a decent man who loved her and suffocated a young woman in search of the truth about her sister's death. He believed, too, that she'd thrown a knife at Miss Lydia and nearly cost Miss

Prudence her hand. Flora Campbell would kill again—as soon as anyone else stepped between her and her ambition. What had to be done didn't merit discussion.

Clyde agreed. Barrett Hughes was a foul-smelling stain on humanity. He'd consigned Vivian Knowles to years of lonely shame and driven another young woman to suicide. That they knew of. Clyde suspected that Vivian had been neither Hughes's first nor his last victim. Permanent removal was the surest way to deal with men of his type, No one missed them when they were gone.

Together, Clyde and Amos had left the Argosy Theatre through the stage door while the stage manager was calling the thirty-minute warning in the hallway outside Flora Campbell's dressing room door. The carriages of late arrivals were pulling back into the Broadway traffic when they emerged from the alleyway. Danny Dennis's hansom cab picked them up and drove them to the stable where the Irishman's crew of street urchins was already bedded down in heaps of hay. While Danny unharnessed and brushed down Mr. Washington, Amos filled a bucket with clean water, then emptied it into the gutter when he was done with it. Filled and emptied it two more times, until the water stopped running anything but clear.

By the time Clyde eased his way into the Truitt house in Brooklyn on that second night that *Highlands* played in Manhattan, the rooms were dark and silent. Miss Lydia was used to his comings and goings. She never asked about his business or his destination, knowing he would only smile and shake his head. And this evening, he had heard her tell Vivian that she would make an early night of it. The next morning's train to Vermont left early from Grand Central Depot, and both of them were exhausted from opening night and the hours of talking after they'd gotten home. He'd done what he had to do with no one the wiser. Except for Amos. Who'd had his own charge to fulfill.

Clyde slept the slumber of the just that night.

\*    \*    \*

In his tiny apartment across the bridge, Amos measured out a smaller than usual dose of laudanum before climbing into bed and blowing out the candle. His eyes closed and his breathing grew relaxed and steady within minutes. It was always that way when he finished a job as planned and without a hitch.

He smiled as he drifted into sleep.

# EPILOGUE

Geoffrey Hunter didn't believe for a moment that the murders of Flora Campbell and Barrett Hughes were the work of a random, deranged killer, but he kept his opinion to himself.

The newspapers hypothesized that an actor rejected by Hughes had lost the balance of his mind and taken bloody vengeance. Perhaps because he'd been denied a role destined to make him a star? In retaliation for some slight committed years ago, in a theatre on the vaudeville circuit? Everyone knew that actors drank far more than was good for them. And indulged in laudanum, needles that injected morphine, and drugs hardly known by name to decent people. The theatre might not be part of the criminal underworld, but it was close enough to the fringes so as not to make much difference. No one reading the press accounts expected the police to solve the crime.

More important than what Geoffrey thought was probably a long overdue reckoning was the announcement of his and Prudence's engagement and the wedding plans that declaration entailed. Now that she was seated in his office, just a few feet away across the desk, he'd gently bully her into some serious planning.

"I wouldn't mind a very simple ceremony in front of a justice of the peace," Prudence declared to Josiah's horror.

Injured hand still bandaged and unusable, she'd taken to dropping by the office for a few hours a day after the Argosy Theatre murders had played out in the press. Not so much to work as to sit and marvel at the decision she'd made and didn't regret. Especially not with Geoffrey so close, she could smell his sandalwood shaving lotion.

"No new developments," she informed Josiah as she watched him tidy up and close the agency file on Septimus Ward.

She handed over that morning's *Times*. In the last story in which their names would appear, the *Times* reporter revealed that Flora Campbell and Barrett Hughes had been buried beside one another in Green-Wood Cemetery in Brooklyn. Unusual, but fitting because neither of them had any known relatives. Or at least none who chose to come forward. Surprisingly, because he lived high, Hughes at his death was found to be broke and in debt. Flora had only the few dollars in her reticule and coins stashed in an otherwise empty sugar bowl in her boardinghouse room. A collection was being raised to provide headstones at some future date. Talking about the two dead stars made people uneasy. Gossip was dying away faster than anyone could have predicted.

"You'll regret to your dying day not being married in Trinity Church." Josiah's belief that Miss Prudence should have a splendid society wedding was firm and unshakeable. He'd already made a list of florists and caterers. Her gown would come from Paris, he'd decided, where the House of Worth, which had made much of what she wore, could be depended upon to create a flattering and unforgettable gem that would be the talk of the town.

"On this, I actually agree with Josiah," Geoffrey said, handing scissors and the copy of the *Times* with the final Campbell-Hughes story in it to the secretary. "It doesn't have to be elaborate, but Lina Astor will never forgive either of us if we don't do what's proper and expected."

"Lina Astor and her Four Hundred don't tell me what to do." Prudence was in the enviable position of being able to get away with ignoring the queen of New York society's dictates. Both her parents had been members of blue-blooded Knickerbocker families whose fortunes were nearly as grand as the Vanderbilts and much more respectable.

"It's good for business." Geoffrey picked up the hand that wore the Tiffany diamond and brought it to his lips.

"You are both impossible!" Prudence would have slammed her other hand down on Geoffrey's desk except that it was still so wrapped in bandages that it resembled a polar bear paw. And it hurt. She'd sworn off laudanum and was battling a terrible craving again. That was probably why she was so restless and short-tempered.

"I can reserve the church once you decide on a date." Josiah pulled a file folder from the stack in his desk drawer and labeled it *Wedding*.

"I don't believe what I'm seeing," Prudence fumed.

"It never hurts to be organized," Josiah insisted. "The guest list will take some time to put together. Three hundred if you insist on keeping it very small, Miss Prudence. Four or five hundred would be better. Less chance of leaving out someone important. Delmonico's will have to be contacted." He hummed as he began his lists, heading each one with elaborately scrolled curlicues.

"Is anyone here?" called a voice from the outer office.

"Back here, Lydia," Prudence answered.

"I'm a free woman again. Dr. Charity has taken out my stitches." Lydia raised her arm to shoulder height. "Not all the way healed yet, but close enough. What on earth are you doing, Josiah?" She'd caught a glimpse of the wedding folder and its lists.

"Planning Miss Prudence's nuptials."

"An elopement ought to do it." Lydia smiled mischievously at her friend. "Unless Geoffrey insists on something more elaborate."

"Trinity Church, Delmonico's, wedding trip to Europe." Josiah shuffled his papers, stacking them neatly in their folder.

"I surrender," Prudence said. She wasn't going to admit it, but she'd suddenly fallen under the spell of a mental image of herself processing down the center aisle of Trinity Church dressed in a Worth masterpiece. She could hear the organ playing and the choir singing, see and smell white flowers everywhere, recognize familiar faces in the pews filled with the cream of New York society. Delmonico's afterward. First-class passage across the Atlantic. Europe with Geoffrey would be heaven on earth. "There's no point fighting the two of you. Tell me when to show up." As long as she didn't have to organize any of it.

"That's my girl," Geoffrey said. "All you have to do is decide on a dress. Josiah will take care of everything else, won't you?" He winked at their secretary.

"I do need a date."

"How long does it take to make a wedding gown?" Geoffrey asked.

"Months and months," Lydia contributed. "And if it's to be a Worth creation, it could be much longer than that."

"Let me think about it," Prudence said. She'd heard of a new French designer, formerly of the House of Worth, who'd opened a house of haute couture in New York City. "I'm sure you didn't stop by just to tell us your stitches were out," she said to Lydia.

"Tea?" Josiah asked. He sensed an important discussion about to begin.

"We'll have it in here," Prudence said. She reached for the wedding folder, but Josiah was faster. He had it in his hand and out the office door to his own desk before she could protest.

Geoffrey settled the two ladies in his client chairs but left the office door open. Josiah would be back with a tea tray and his stenographer's notebook.

"Do you remember Gertrude Marrow telling us that she'd talked to David Belasco about *The Hereditary Prince*?" Lydia asked. The pearl earrings Septimus had beggared himself to buy for Flora Campbell hung from his cousin's ears. Letitia Nugent's garnet ring had become a small brooch.

"David Belasco, the producer?" Prudence cradled her bad hand in the palm of her good one.

"Exactly. She gave him the first act to read, and then when he showed an interest in seeing the rest of it, she made up some story about having to get the author's permission. She said she was just dipping a toe in the water."

"And now something's come up?" Geoffrey asked.

"I took the manuscript to a printer friend of mine who does rush jobs for my father sometimes."

"When was this?" Prudence asked.

Lydia shrugged. "While everything else was going on. I didn't want to say anything in case Belasco didn't like the rest of what he read. But that didn't happen."

"He wants to produce it," Geoffrey said, certain that was what Lydia was leading up to.

"To open on Broadway next season."

"The fall, then."

"Mid November," Lydia clarified. "When everyone is back in town from Newport and Europe. Right after opening night at the Academy of Music. He thinks the plot of *The Hereditary Prince* is one that will appeal to our royalty-obsessed society matrons."

"He's right," Prudence said. "The Prince of Wales makes headlines if he just wakes up in the morning."

"Not quite." Josiah poured the tea and readied his notebook and pencil. "But close." He was as rabid an Anglophile as any society mother hoping to marry her daughter into impoverished British aristocracy.

"You'll need a contract," Geoffrey said.

"That's why I'm here," Lydia answered. She sipped her tea. "I know that between the two of you, I'll have a contract so iron-clad that Belasco won't know what hit him."

"Are you up to it, Prudence?" Geoffrey asked, turning to his wife-to-be, knowing the answer before he finished asking the question.

Her first contract. First real case. What had happened in Niagara Falls last October didn't count.

Prudence's eyes shone as bright as the diamond on her finger.

"We have a wedding to plan, Miss Prudence," Josiah reminded her.

"That's your concern, Josiah. I'm turning everything except the dress over to you. I have lawyer's work to do."

# ACKNOWLEDGMENTS

It often feels to writers as if they are doing this alone. Writing the book. Wrestling with plot and characters. But they aren't, of course.

Thanks to the critique partners whose suggestions helped to keep the narrative moving.

Thanks to John Scognamiglio, my wonderful editor, who always makes me feel that I've created a masterpiece.

Thanks to Jessica Faust and Bookends Literary Agency who truly work as a team to support their clients.

Thanks to copy editor Pearl Saban and her painstaking search for whatever I've missed.

Thanks to the readers who make it all worthwhile.